T.M. SMITH

EVERNIGHT PUBLISHING ®

www.evernightpublishing.com

T.M. SMITH

DEDICATION

Family and friends are essential in this writer's life. While there are many of both, I will single out a few. Thanks to Michael, Kelly, Zoe, and Kate for being you, though sometimes I was too busy writing to notice. Thanks to Glenda for actually thinking my books make great gifts. Thanks to Vicki and Cindee who know the importance of reviews.

T.M. SMITH

Terms and Places for the Blood Coven Series

Aerilon
The ylve region of Scath.

Aeternals
A species made up of various breeds who pre-date *Homo sapiens* on Earth. Their creator is the Genitrix Gahya, an immortal who resides in The Vast. After centuries, they grew more cruel and violent, feeding from humans, threatening the continued existence of mankind.

The Alliance Security Agency
A human agency where employees have a distant Aeternal ancestor in their family trees. Once travel between the realms of Scath and Earth became possible, these descendants created an organization to assist Aeternals. Their organization provides Aeternals with access to trade on Earth and assistance in policing Aeternals who enter Earth illegally. They operate a successful cover business, hiring out as bodyguards, private security, and soldiers of fortune. The internal structure includes the Legal Division, Human Resources, Information Services Division, Security Division, and Finance. A board of directors oversees the company.

Amanita Muscaria
A drug used by berserkers before battle. It whips them into a frenzy.

Amori
The incubus and succubus region of Scath.

Angor

A dimension of dark storms and unpredictable weather where immortals are tortured and punished. It is also the final destination of unworthy Aeternals after they die.

Arisen Dawn
A rebel group led by Cerberus. Their beliefs include purity of the breeds and the domination of mankind.

The Assembly
The local government elected by mages.

The Awakening
A ceremony marking an Aeternal's attainment of full power, usually in their early to mid-twenties. The event is different for each breed.

BCA Variant Test
A test developed by Eliphias, Alarik's science lead, to determine if the subject is a Blood Coven descendant.

Blood Coven
Led by the Cambion from Wales, these powerful mages created the realms of Darque, Earth, and Scath in AD 452 where only one world had been before. Aeternals went to Scath, mystical creatures to Darque, and humans remained on Earth. It was the only way the two sentient species would survive.

Bludclan
Vampires are identified by their Bludclan, a social/family group.

Blud Den
A place which specializes in feeding all Aeternal breeds, not just vampires. An Aeternal feeds on the host's blood,

soul, fear, energy for magic, lifeforce, orgasm, power, or arousal. O blud dens are more specialized. Here a host takes a drug (most notably opium). The feeding from the host provides a high but is not as addictive as taking the drug itself.

Bludfrenzy
When a vampire is controlled by the need for blood. It becomes the sole reason for living, an addiction.

Bludhaven
The vampire region of Scath.

The Bludhunt
A violent ceremony marking the mating of two vampires.

Breeds
Amazons, berserkers, demons (seven tribes within their breed), djinn, incubi and succubi, mages (or witches and warlocks), satyrs and nymphs, vampires, and ylves. Though each breed has distinct gifts, or powers, all are stronger than *Homo sapiens* and possess better sight, hearing, and smell. Like humans, breeds eat food, but they must supplement it with other nourishment—blood, soul, lifeforce, flesh, fear, arousal, orgasm, or energy for magic.

Camp Follower
An Aeternal who makes himself or herself available as food or sex for Jarek's Firebrands.

The Cede
The Aeternals' funeral ceremony.

The Coalition

The alliance of Firebrands, loyal Scath citizens, loyal members of Scath's government, and humans to defeat Cerberus.

Covenkirk
The seat of Scath's government, the mage region, and the location of the Eastern Stronghold.

The Cubes
Run by gaffers, holding cells for Scath prisoners awaiting trial or interrogation.

Custodes Templii
Formed on Earth by the Cambion before he died. Through the centuries, the group keeps track of Blood Coven descendants, the offspring of the mages who stayed on Earth after the Karmic Schism.

Darque
The realm of mystical creatures, home to harpies, questing beasts, Kalli, Spriggans, Yeti, gagans, polar rats, hellhounds, and more.

D-chip
Digital Implant Communication Chronometer. It is an amazing device embedded into the wrist of each Firebrand warrior and wired to their brains. Its functions are many–telepathic communicator, shadowflasher, GPS locator, emergency portal creator as long as the Firebrand is out-of-doors, a more efficient version of a portal jumper to allow travel through established gateways, temporary cell for captured offenders, and more.

Dionysia
Local government of nymphs and satyrs.

Directorate of Seven
The local ruling body of demons. Each member represents a tribe—animus, avarice, carnal, envy, hedon, pride, sloth. They are chosen by combat.

Elysian Isle
The nymph and satyr region of Scath.

The Encampment
The Amazon, berserker, and djinn region and location of the Southern Stronghold on Scath.

Evermore
A dimension of serenity where worthy Aeternals go when they meet true death.

Freron
A term used by Firebrands to denote another brother- or sister-in-arms.

Gaffers
Like police, the managers of the day-to-day minor crimes on Scath.

Genesis Rite
An ancient ritual where demons fought in combat. The winner spent the night with the ceremony's guest of honor.

Gold Dust
An addictive drug, making users fanatic followers of Arisen Dawn.

Humans First

A paramilitary unit organized by Dante to gather intel on and expose Aeternals.

Isolationists
A group originally organized by Simonis, an ylve, to protest Scath's involvement in affairs outside the realm. He was shoved out as the group became more radical, espousing breed purity and displaying a rising nationalism set on conquering humans. It became the foundation for Cerberus's Arisen Dawn.

Karmic Schism
The splitting of the world into three realms. In AD 452, the Blood Coven cast spells to create Scath and send Aeternals there. At that time, they also created the realm of Darque for magical creatures and Earth for humans.

Knife's Edge
The demon region of Scath.

Lawgivers
Elected drafters of the laws for Scath. A member is chosen from each breed.

Outcast Keep
An area on Darque where Aeternal prisoners are kept.

Ministry of Compliance
Governmental office which regulates travel. Boden is the current director.

Ministry of Coin
Governmental office which regulates finance and drafts the realm's budget.

Ministry of Culture
Governmental office which regulates education, schools of magic, and Awakening ceremonies.

Ministry of Death
Governmental office which operates prisons, the Cubes, and Outcast Keep on Darque, controls day-to-day crime and gaffers, and regulates the use of explosive weapons.

Ministry of Labor
Governmental office which regulates worker welfare.

Ministry of Prosperity
Governmental office which regulates trade with wildings and humans.

Ministry of the Shield
The only governmental ministry which reports to the Temple of Justice rather than the Lawgivers. The Scion Firebrands are under its auspices. Cadmon is both high commander of the Scion Firebrands and director of this ministry.

Ministry of Well Being
The governmental office responsible for medical facilities, research, science, technology, and history. Alarik is the current director.

Ministry of Wildings and Realm
The governmental office which regulates the wildings and both realms' natural resources, parks, and environments.

Mitakon
A bi-annual Olympics. Winter events are in North

Shelters and summer events in the Encampment region.

Monarchy
The king and queen who lead the incubi and succubi.

North Shelters
The shifter region and location of the Northern Stronghold on Scath.

The Path
The words of the warrior Ohngel as recorded by the Cambion from Wales and contained in five-volumes. These books relate tales of the salvation, the betrayal, the creation, the fall and rise, and the destiny of Aeternals.

Pitchblende
A substance which weakens djinn.

Portals
Gateways to and from the realms, created by the Blood Coven at the time of the Karmic Schism but not accessible by all. In the beginning only powerful and approved mages could cast spells for travel. Later, GPS technology allowed for portal jumpers to be distributed to authorized Aeternals.

The Prophecy of Karma
A scroll found by the fire-winged assassin Ohngel, the mentor/guide to the Cambion from Wales, in a cave in the Vakataka Kingdom. The first stanza, though it presaged a dark future for mankind at the hands of Aeternals, it predicted a coven would save them by separating humans and Aeternals. The second stanza noted the rise of Hades's hound who would lead an army to enslave humans. The last stanza hints at the role of

destiny in the prophecy.

The Rage
When a demon loses control of the beast. Usually, they must be put down.

The River Am
A river which defies explanation and natural laws. The witch Indigo, as the Guardian of Time, reads the river. The middle course is the present. Possible futures flow upstream. The lower course, or downstream, shows the just-past to the long-past. No one but Indigo knows the river's location.

Scath
The realm where Aeternals have lived since the Karmic Schism.

Schools of Magic
There are seven schools of magic–Elemental, Conveyance, Forging, Influence, Investigation, Manipulation, Protection. Each mage's powers fall primarily into one category where they are trained in those gifts at the Thaumaturgy Institute. Extremely powerful witches or warlocks may excel in more than one school of magic.

Scion Firebrands
The elite warriors of Scath who follow in the footsteps of an ancestor. Founded soon after the Karmic Schism, they protect Scath and Darque from the most violent Aeternals or creatures. As a side-gig, they also protect humans from the threat of Aeternals who escape to Earth. When Aeternals are called to join, the initiation begins with the Phoenix brand which burns itself onto the

candidates' upper left arms. They experience intense pain until they reach a decision. Join or reject the offer.

The Settling
The demon mating ceremony.

Shadowflash
Old, powerful vampires can trace from shadow to shadow as long as the spot is within sight. It makes travel faster. D-chips give Firebrands this ability also.

Strange But True
The Seattle paranormal tabloid owned by George James, Braelyn's father.

Strigodierna Ceremony
A vampire spiritual ceremony. It is led by the Cruor and his fifty Carnemia.

Supreme Pack Alpha
Chosen through combat to lead the shifters.

Temple of Justice
The body of elected justices who try offenders on Scath. A member is elected from each breed.

Thaumaturgy Institute
Where witches and warlocks are trained in the different schools of magic.

Tribes
The sub-breeds of demons. The inspiration for Christianity's Seven Deadly Sins--animus, avarice, carnal, envy, hedon, pride, and sloth.

Triumvirate of the Wise
Chosen every fifty years to govern ylves. A chancellor, an imperial secretary, and a grand commandant.

Vampire Conclave
The local rulers of vampires, led by the bludcrown.

The Vast
A dimension of clear skies and pleasant weather where immortals, such as Gahya, Gabriel, and the OneCreator reside.

Walkabout
The requirement for influential Aeternals to live on Earth for periods of time to keep current with human activity.

War Council
The governing body for Amazons, berserkers, and djinn, chosen by combat to govern locally.

Watchers
The mages who keep an eye on and maintain the portals and the whorl for Alarik's ministry.

The Whorl
What separates the three realms from each other. Travelers to another realm access it from a portal, travel through it, and reach a portal in the other realm.

Winged Assassins of the OneCreator
Aka The Feard. They or Michael are the only beings who can bring true death to an immortal. Ohngel, the Cambion's mentor and guide, is the fire-winged assassin of the OneCreator.

T.M. SMITH

LIST OF CHARACTERS IN *THE SATYR'S GUILT*

Abrahm   Murdered Kole's parents, an ancestor of Skyler Maxwell, demon

Aedon   Kole's father, Firebrand, animus demon

Aisen   Silas's half-brother, operated stockades for Cerberus, vampire

Alarik   Director of the Ministry of Well Being, Rein's father, Indigo's half-brother, warlock-incubus

Alden Maxwell   Skyler Maxwell's father, once the CLO of the Alliance

Allias   Alarik's employee in Echo's history division who finds evidence of *Custodes Templii*

Amelia   Dante's daughter

Amylyn   Flirts with Ram in the Blood Shed, witch

Anarai   Original Blood Coven, warlock

Anna   Skyler Maxwell's administrative assistant at the Alliance

Anthive   Jarek's grandfather, djinn

Aras   High Justice of the Temple of

Justice, eagle shifter

Bade	A Firebrand recruit, vampire
Ben First	One of Mars's men in Humans
Boden Compliance, sloth demon	Director of the Ministry of
Bounty	Kole's executive assistant, vampire
Braelyn James *True*	Rein's mate, writer for *Strange But*
Brak	A carnal demon, Firebrand
Cage	Takes Gold Dust, coyote shifter
Cal Alliance	The assistant legal officer at the
Carl	Leslie's husband and abuser
Celene Bailey daredevil, adrenalin junkie	Held captive by Cerberus, heiress,
Cerberus foretells will destroy the portals and enslave mankind	The hound of Hades who prophecy
Chay ylve	Full name Chayton, Firebrand,
Cleatra witch	A scryer who works for Alarik,

Clese   A tracker for Jarek, grizzly shifter

D Monz   A demon rapper

Daire   Lawgiver, incubus

Dania   Viktor's mate, vampire

Dante   Upper class Englishman who conspires with Cerberus; aka, Lord Ellington

Darius   Jarek's second, Firebrand, djinn

Dax   Full name Daxton, Firebrand, vampire

Denim Quinn   Alliance agent, ex-military, ex-police officer

Dolph   Temple of Justice, warlock

Draven   Temple of Justice, vampire

Dr. Messenger   Dante's scientist/medical doctor

Echo   Chief historian at the Ministry of Well Being, a pride demon

Eirene   Original Blood Coven, witch

Eliphias   Chief scientist at the Ministry of Well Being, warlock

Engel   Original Blood Coven, warlock

Eron   Temple of Justice, female demon

Eydris   Original Blood Coven, witch

Faelan   Original Blood Coven, warlock

Fera   Supreme Lawgiver, shifter

Gabriel   The creator of *Homo sapiens*, an
immortal in Vast

Gahya   The Genitrix, creator of Aeternals,
an immortal in Vast

Galena   Firebrand, Amazon

George James   Braelyn's father, owner of *Strange
But True*, Alliance board of directors

Gilda   Temple of Justice, Amazon

Golarg   Berserker who comes to Spear's
door

Hannya   Young female who was injured in
New Orleans, demon

Harry   Miller Nash's second, tracker for
Custodes Templii

Hassem   Responsible for Jarek's
enslavement, djinn

Farahmand

Hestia Kole's mother, Firebrand, animus demon

Horach Kole's uncle, Directorate of Seven, animus demon

Isaac Lipton General, US Army

Indigo Guardian of Time, Alarik's half-sister, Rein's aunt, witch

Jace de Vries Held captive by Cerberus, worked as vintner in New Paltz, NY

Jeffrey Jeffie, Leslie's child she brings with her to Safe Haven

Jarek Rostamian Firebrand commander of the Southern Stronghold, djinn

Jezzi Proper name is Jez, Firebrand, panther shifter

Jonquil Ram's daughter, nymph

Kara One of Jarek's Firebrands, Amazon

Karth Sells Gold Dust, shifter

Kat Full name is Katrina, Firebrand, witch

Katya Child Ram finds on Darque, Spriggan

Kilem   One of Jarek's Firebrands, warlock

Kole   Firebrand commander of the Eastern Stronghold, animus demon

Leslie   Abused woman who comes to Safe Haven with her child Jeffrey

Licia   Norah's mother, vampire

Lizette Lee   Radio talk show psychologist at WMR radio production studio in New York, Spear's sex slave

Locasta   She is the medical examiner at Alarik's ministry, witch

Lort   Cerberus's general, vampire

Luka   Thorn's brother and pack alpha, wolf shifter

Manny   One of Mars's men in Humans First

Margo Hunter   Sculptor from Cleveland, OH

Mars   Dante's general of Humans First paramilitary

Mateo Garcia   Colonel, US Army, sometimes called Matty

Marta   Operator of Safe Haven, a home in

THE SATYR'S GUILT

New Orleans for abused women

Masoud   Original Blood Coven, warlock

Miller Nash   Head of *Custodes Templii*, Blood Coven descendant, ex British intelligence

Morgana   Original Blood Coven, witch

Nace   Full name Nacon, commander of the Northern Stronghold, Firebrand, jaguar shifter

Nico Abello   Lead agent with the Alliance until he becomes a Firebrand

Niviane   Original Blood Coven, mother of Seraphine, witch

Noor   Original Blood Coven, warlock

Norah   Captured with Varik, vampire

Ohngel   The fire-winged assassin of the OneCreator and mentor to the Cambion, an immortal

OneCreator   Ruler of Vast and Evermore

Ossar   Norah's father, vampire

Philomena   High priestess, nymph

Ram   Firebrand, Satyr

Rein   Vampire-Warlock-Incubus mix, Firebrand, Braelyn's mate

Rode One of the young Aeternals Denim and Galena find in New Orleans, vampire

Rolf Young Aeternal who went to New Orleans with girlfriend, demon

Roshan Temple of Justice, djinn

Sabine Celestial nymph, Firebrand

Seraphine The daughter of Niviane and the Cambion

Sig Firebrand recruit, demon

Silas Ran stockades for Cerberus, disgraced Firebrand, vampire

Simonis Founder of the Isolationists, ylve

Skyler Maxwell Chief legal officer of the Alliance

Solemnia Original Blood Coven, witch

Sparce Spriggan chief

Spear Keeps Lizette Lee as a sex slave, berserker

Steven Denim's abusive ex-husband

Stian Original Blood Coven, warlock

The Cambion The Cambion from Wales is the

warlock who gathered the Blood Coven and created three realms of Earth, Scath, and Darque from one world in AD 452

Thorn   Firebrand, wolf shifter

Tyr   Firebrand, warlock

Uwrick   His spell isolated Kole and Skyler
on Darque, warlock

Varik   Son of Viktor and Dania, vampire

Viktor   Lawgiver, father of Varik, vampire

Warner   Dead body in New Orleans,
incubus

Wynnfrith   A respected Firebrand killed by a
harpy

Xanthe   Original Blood Coven, witch

Zora   Alarik's executive assistant,
succubus

T.M. SMITH

THE SATYR'S GUILT

The Blood Coven Series, 3

T.M. Smith

Copyright © 2023

Prologue

The ragged claws of the past are buried in the flesh of the present and future.

—Ohngel, an eagle perched on his forearm

Wales, Seven Years After the Karmic Schism of AD 452

The cave waited. Moisture dripped in fingers down its calcite-draped walls. Bats hugged the dark ceiling. The crisp smell of fresh, cool water arising from an underground river wove through the still air. Yet, the cave waited.

Finally, the Cambion walked through the entrance of the place he called home, his robe whispering as it shifted through the dirt. The black-cowled figure set his basket of supplies on the ground. He removed and stacked dried leaves, spicy cedar needles, twigs, and branches. Bending, he rubbed his fingers together to cast a simple spell. Once he created a spark, it jumped onto the pile, one leaf catching fire, then a twig, and another. Hissing flames danced, igniting the tinder, breaking the eerie silence, creating a play of shadow and light in the cave.

He brushed debris from his palms, placing them on his knees, pushing upright, his joints not yet suffering the ravages of time. The flames snaked higher, swirling, slithering upward. The powerful warlock, the Cambion from Wales, reached out with steady hands and drew the smoke toward himself while awaiting visions.

A farmhouse appeared in the haze. Then a barn. The Cambion tilted his neck, his head rolling back, his eyes following the white ash as it trailed upward in the dank cavern lit only by the fire's light. Flames licked the hem of his robe, but he paid them no attention. In his vision, cackling chickens roamed a yard, pecking the ground. A milk cow grazed behind a fence. The smoke twisted, rising, fanning out along the mountain's womb, caressing it, revealing secrets to the black-cloaked warlock.

A small girl materialized, her simple linen dress soiled at the hem. As she kicked a ball along in front of her, a misty fog wove through the plentiful rows of corn which lined the road where she played.

From a porch, an older female called out her name. "Seraphine."

The child struck the ball with her foot one last time before answering the farm wife's call. She turned.

Gasping, the Cambion beheld the child's eyes, the sharpness of her chin, the cut of her cheeks.

The powerful warlock regularly searched Scath for a glimpse of the child, his and Niviane's offspring whose existence could alter destiny. Never had he found her until today, seven years after the Karmic Schism when the Blood Coven created three realms from one world. They did it to avert the disaster predicted in the Prophecy of Karma. They did it to save mankind. Aeternals went to Scath while mystical creatures made their homes on Darque. In this way, the thirteen mages guaranteed humans, who remained on Earth, would multiply, grow strong, and build defenses. They would survive as a species, separated from the savage Aeternals who pre-dated their existence.

At the time of the Karmic Schism of AD 452, the Cambion ordered the Blood Coven to remain behind on Earth, hidden with their offspring, scattered and cut off from their own kind because they or their children could be used to re-open the portals. If done, Aeternals would once again threaten humans with extinction. Niviane compromised the tenuous plan for salvation. Indeed, she had betrayed him. She had betrayed humanity. She had betrayed her own kind. Aeternals.

Anger exploded from the warlock, waves of it reaching every nook and cranny, sending bats flying and spiders scurrying to escape its deadly path. Like shattered glass, it cut through the cave. Spewing from the entrance, it formed black storm clouds, erupting in claps of thunder as streaks of lightning raced across the valley. The earth shook while simple peasants in a nearby village grabbed their children, holding them close to await God's fury.

With a deep breath, the Cambion gathered his wrath, reeling it in like a big fish on a line. A menacing yet weary scowl crossed his face. His eyes grew as dark as the smoke into which he stared. Indeed, Niviane had borne his child, named her Seraphine, and sent her to Scath despite his directive.

Though the warlock longed for a rest, the solace was ripped from him. Chaos could sprout from his own seed.

He glanced toward a high ledge where Ohngel waited, his fiery, razor-edged feathers glinting in the flickering light. His mentor, the enigmatic immortal male, had warned him of the betrayal, encouraging him to seek proof.

When the warlock threw a log onto the fire, Ohngel faded but reformed in the blaze as spiraling, undulating, brilliant hues of light. Blue. Gold. Green. Crimson. Exploding, the colors rose and coalesced into a shape. The shape took the form of the Phoenix, whose mournful screech as it swooped out of the flames beckoned the Cambion to follow.

The warlock's eyes widened when the giant avian morphed into a Chimera near the cave exit. As he glanced at the creature, it flicked its neck from side to side, fire spitting from its mouth. When it trudged onward, he trailed behind. He would wander the world seeking to understand the betrayal, seeking answers, seeking a means to control the fallout.

Chapter One

New Orleans, Present Day

Denim Quinn peeked through the wide-angle peephole.

Outside, a young woman clenched a toddler against her chest. The boy hugged her neck, thumb in mouth. The visitor pivoted her head to glance behind her, maybe expecting Jason Voorhees to pop out to trim the hedges. When she spun back to the door, rapping on the wood, her nervous eyes twitched left and right.

Denim drew back three deadbolts, fisting the brass knob to open the door a crack. She left the chain in place. While she checked out the surroundings, she bit into a fresh-baked oatmeal raisin cookie grasped in her other hand. Sliding the chain off and flinging the door wide, she joined the visitor on the porch.

The woman carrying the child scrunched a Safe Haven flyer in trembling fingers.

"Welcome. I'm Denim. What's your name?" As she asked, she combed through a strand of her long, loose hair to be certain it covered the scar on her cheek. No need to frighten the woman.

"Leslie."

With a reassuring palm on the young mother's shoulder to usher her through the door, Denim glanced up the street. Down the street. *Old habit.* "Let's take you and…"

"Jeffrey."

"Jeffrey inside."

Leslie didn't look as if she'd broken twenty. Her mousy brown hair was swept away from her face, exposing a fresh shiner. The bruise was big, as if she'd gone wild with purple eyeshadow. Then there was the limp. She winced with each step across the large area rug while keeping a firm grip on the boy. Her bare upper arm revealed massive contusions in the shape of fingers. Large fingers.

Denim pushed the door shut, throwing each latch along with the chain. *Be prepared. The Scout motto. Girls or Boys?* "Here. Let me take the kid … er … Jeffrey." Denim hefted the boy into her right arm.

The shelter owner exploded from the kitchen like a firecracker. The bundle of energy on two legs was all heart, though. "Who do we have here?"

"Marta, meet Leslie. Leslie, this is the caretaker-in-chief," explained Denim.

Part Creole, part Cajun but all NOLA, Marta rubbed a palm across Leslie's back. Through squinted lids, she examined the arrivals as if she were an emergency room doctor. Her scan took in the young mother from ratty Keds to ponytail, zeroing in on every bruise, every scrape. "Come into the kitchen. We're gonna get you fixed up. Then you'll both have oatmeal cookies and milk."

There was the great thing about Marta. Cookies and milk solved everything. Along with a hug and *beaucoup* conversation.

Denim, on the other hand, subscribed to eye-for-an-eye biblical justice. It soothed her soul more than words. If she were Leslie, she'd rest better if her fist plowed into the orbital socket of the guy who'd doled out the shiner. Payback was a bitch, but she was Denim's bitch.

On the way to the kitchen, the young mother's chest heaved until she finally broke down, shaking and crying. "He'll find us. I know he will. Then he'll kill me." Her accent was rural Louisiana, making her sound fresh from a dirt-poor farm.

When the little guy squirmed in Denim's arms, she bounced him on her hip. "Were you followed?"

Leslie's shoulders bobbed with each gulping sob. "I d-d-don't think so."

Marta patted the frightened mother's arm. "Now there, child, you let us worry about that man. You and this baby boy are safe here."

The shelter owner shooed two young mothers along with their children out of the kitchen. Marta liked to cook while she did her intakes. But she didn't need extra eyes scaring the new arrivals. "Denim, you do the honors with Leslie while I finish making dinner."

It was the first time Denim flew solo on an intake interview, but she had assisted Marta other times. She set Jeffrey in a highchair, giving him an oatmeal cookie. With a second thought, she snatched a stuffed bunny, its fur patchy from small hands along with too many washings. She wiggled it in front of Jeffrey, handing it over when his dimpled fingers reached out. Next, she fetched the first aid kit from a cabinet. As she slapped antiseptic and Band-Aids on Leslie's cuts, she spoke softly to the mother who took a seat at the table.

"Did Jeffrey's father do this?"

"Shur nuff." Leslie's pupils stayed glued to a spot on the floor.

Typical behavior. The mother was too ashamed to talk eye-to-eye. "Has he hit you before?" asked Denim.

Leslie nodded. "I landed in the hospital a couple times. Carl made me say I fell down the steps. I don't think they believed me."

"Has he hit the baby?"

"Not yet, but he will. That's one reason I left. If he'll do this to me, no tellin' what he'll do to my Jeffie."

Denim walked over to snag a bag of peas from the freezer. "Here, *cher*. Keep this on your eye. How's the leg and arm?"

"Just sore. Nothin' too bad."

"Ribs?"

"Nah. They're okay."

"How old is Jeffrey?" asked Denim.

"He's three. I'm nineteen. Mom and Pa made me marry Carl when they found out I was pregnant."

"How old's Carl?" Marta threw this in from her spot by the stove while her spoon circled the pot faster and faster.

"Twenty-nine."

"Will your mom, dad, or other relatives take in you and the boy?" Denim scooted her chair closer to the table.

"No. We're on our own."

"You came to the right place, *cher*. You can stay here. We have people who'll help you. I see you have our brochure." Denim took the crumpled pamphlet out of Leslie's hand. "You are not alone."

Leslie swiped at her eyes. "Thank you."

"No thanks needed. We're here for you now and for as long as you need us."

Leslie started to cry again when Marta set an oatmeal cookie and milk on the table by her and the child. "I d-d-don't have any money or clothes. For Jeffie or me. None of his toys. I just ran."

When Jeffrey spilled his glass of milk, the mother's gaze pinpointed Denim. She cringed as if she expected a slap down when the trail of white liquid puddled on the floor. "No harm. No foul." Denim chuckled, got a rag, and wiped up the mess. Marta poured the boy another Brown's Dairy.

Leslie's shoulders relaxed.

"You'll love the other women and kids here. Let us handle the other stuff." Denim tossed the cloth on top of the washer.

Marta gave the big pot on the stove one more stir before she joined the table conversation. "There's a boy Jeffie's age takin' his nap now. When he wakes, your son will have a playmate."

"He'll love that. You're both so kind," said Leslie.

Denim patted her hand. "I am sorry this happened to you. You do not deserve it."

"When the house wasn't clean, Carl..." She pointed to her eye. "...did this. Jeffie had been fussy. I just didn't have time."

Denim nodded, staring straight at Leslie. "You do not deserve this treatment. If you remember one thing I say, *cher*, remember this. You do not deserve what happened to you."

"You can never understand what this means to me." The back of Leslie's hand wiped away new tears streaming along her cheeks.

Denim exchanged a look with Marta. "We can. Finish your snack first. Afterward, I'll show you around, take you to your room, and get you clothes and stuff to last a few days. Essentials. One of the women will go shopping with you tomorrow. Do you have a job?"

"No. Carl never let me work."

"We can help you with that later. It's not a worry-about-it-now thing. Also, Marta will review the house rules. Not today. Plenty of time later. Settle in first."

"I'm afraid he'll come for me."

"Let me deal," said Denim. "I was in the army and served as a New Orleans cop. I'm licensed to carry a concealed weapon because of my current job. If I'm not here, there's Marta. She's a great shot. We're not worried, *cher*. This is what we do."

After showing Leslie upstairs, Denim helped

Marta set the table for dinner. "I've got a check for you." She rummaged in her purse after putting out the plates.

Marta turned off the burner under the pot. "Child, don't spend your money on us. We get by fine. Do somethin' nice for yourself. You deserve it. Take a vacation. Be fun again."

"I'm fun."

Of course, I'm fun.

Did her friend and sometimes partner Galena see her as a fuddy-duddy? She'd ask later.

Marta raised her brows.

"Okay. Fun-ish."

"Put a bathing suit on your fine athletic body, slap sunscreen on your pasty white skin, soak in the sun on the beach, and flirt with all the guys who hit on you. Ooh, girl. Especially the ones in tight Speedos with their junk showing."

"I'm giving you this money for me. And for your information, I don't like guys in Speedos." She grinned, though.

"Hmm. You should get out more. A beautiful thing like you. I don't mean to the gym."

Denim patted the hair covering her scar. "I have a week coming to me, Marta. I plan to spend it here."

"Nope. Don't need ya. Don't want ya. Beach it, party it, or dance it but do not show your face here. Too much serious stuff rattles around in your head. Take in the season."

"You mean party like you do?"

Marta shook a finger at Denim but struggled not to grin. "Hey. My guy and me get around."

"Yeah. Right after you take care of everyone else."

"This isn't about me. It's about you puttin' your past to rest. I've made peace with mine. Can you say the same? Now call the crowd to dinner."

Denim rose and stuck the check inside the old cookie jar. "This will help get supplies for unexpected tenants. I insist."

"Stubborn girl."

"I'm learning from you." Denim headed to the base of the stairs, yelling out to the residents.

Marta might be right. Denim had been fun once. She'd worn pretty sundresses, flaunted a lot of skin, busted sexy dance moves, batted lashes at handsome guys, and laughed at unfunny jokes. Where was that girl? Would she ever appear again? She missed her.

In a room connected to the kitchen, three large tables formed a horseshoe. Today several chairs were empty. The missing women and children had traveled into town for the Mardi Gras activities.

"Leslie, it's going to get very noisy in here," Denim warned the new arrival and her toddler when they came downstairs.

Marta made introductions while boisterous kids and women poured in, scooting out chairs, carrying platters and bowls of food from the counter to the tables, and greeting one another.

Marta sandwiched Leslie and Jeffie between herself and a long-time resident who chucked the boy under his chin as her own two kids made faces at him, getting him to giggle.

Denim leaned back in a retro slatted chair, crossing her arms over her chest while she watched. She did that a lot at Marta's table. Mashed potatoes passed from hand to hand. Jeffrey banged a spoon on his highchair tray. Marta shouted above everyone's racket, and all the women jockeyed to involve Leslie in a conversation.

They were a family, something Denim had

experienced only in flashes. Her mother died when she was quite young. No known father. A variety of group homes followed, but none made her feel welcome.

Her military unit ate together in the mess, shared stories, and bound themselves in a common cause, a war. But a roadside bomb stole her closest buddies. Cops were always tight-knit, meeting for breakfast or popping into a bar after work, but she wouldn't call any of them family.

"Denim, wake up. Pass the chicken," shouted Marta.

"Sorry. Spaced it." She snatched the platter and passed left. "Anybody want the gravy?"

A freckle-faced boy mumbled *yes* with his mouth full. His mother threw a gentle elbow at him.

Yep. A real family.

For a short time, she'd had a grandmother. The white-haired woman had pushed into her life and shared an unbelievable story. For a while, the two of them were family, but the older woman died not long after dropping the major info bomb.

The wild tale about Aeternals who once walked among humans led Denim to the Alliance Security Agency for a job. After she joined them, she'd built a couple relationships. *Only one close.* That friend was … unusual. She couldn't exactly hang with Galena whenever or visit, kick back, and watch old movies at her place.

At the agency, Denim had also made the biggest mistake of her life, but it was behind her now. *Or was it?* Marta didn't think so.

"There's the doorbell." Denim was unsure anyone else heard it. "I bet Lois left her key here. She was meeting a friend for lunch."

It rang again. Leslie dropped her fork, her hand shaking. A normal response to stress. The fight-or-flight syndrome.

Gotta love the adrenal medulla.

"Don't worry, everybody, I got this." Denim pushed back her chair and left to get the door.

That's when the Titanic hit the iceberg. A man fixed his ugly puss to the peephole. He was pissed enough to be a psychotic abusive A-hole. And each of the women in the dining room had one. Denim pressed the intercom button. "Yes?"

"You got my wife in there." He pounded on the thick wood, his lips in a snarl and his brows drawn tight.

Thud. Thud. Thud.

Denim knew the drill. She yelled into the kitchen, "Safe room. Now." Chairs scraped across the floor, kids and women cried, feet scurried, and Marta tossed around orders like a master sergeant.

Once Denim heard the clunk of the steel door leading to the basement, she pressed the intercom again. "I don't know who you are, but we've called the police. I won't be letting you in the house. Leave."

"Not without Leslie and my kid."

Leslie's Carl.

Denim did not acknowledge his wife was here. "Like I said, cops on the way. Be warned. I'm on a diet, cranky as hell, and packing a loaded gun."

He snorted. "The police have more than they can handle with Mardi Gras craziness. They won't be here for hours. And don't think I'm afraid of you and your popgun, bitch. Let me in."

Denim thought he might be right about the cops, but she'd handled bigger scumbags than this guy. In the army she'd patrolled roads littered with IEDs and raided houses where armed terrorists popped out of the walls. She never underestimated her enemy.

His fist thundered against the wood. Through the

peephole, she saw him move away, raise his foot, and slam it into the door. It shuddered but held. Kicking down a door wasn't as easy as it looked on TV. He hauled back, striking it again. It sounded as if he shouldered the wood, causing a crack to form.

Denim toppled a large coffee table, dragging it to block the kitchen doorway as added cover. She stood it on end. Her gun drawn, she checked the magazine and patted her pocket for a backup. She examined the chamber.

All's good.

Concealed in the kitchen, she had a good view of the front entry. In her right hand, she gripped her Beretta.

Muscle memory. It felt good.

She steadied the weapon with her left hand, took a firing stance, and prepared for the asshole to break in.

Was it asking too much for him not to be carrying? Was it asking too much for her to stop him with one shot? How about for the cops to arrive and haul him off all bloody and contrite?

Yeah. Probably.

The door splintered, a loud crash following as the guy flew through, dropping to the floor in a crouch.

Damn. He's armed.

She didn't call out a warning because she wasn't a cop anymore. He didn't deserve a tip-off. She fired, but he rolled. He ducked into the bathroom as she let off another two shots.

He answered.

Ping. Ping. Ping. Ping.

Carl could have nine rounds. *Hell.* He could have a lot more.

When he peeked around the corner, she fired again, the bullet biting into the frame near his head.

A hit would be sweet.

His next move was downright stupid. It cost him. He must have seen too many movies. *Dirty Harry. The Matrix. The Terminator.* They probably topped his list. He centered himself in the doorway, spread his legs, and straight-armed his weapon.

While he was setting up, Denim chuffed, took aim, and put a bullet into his shoulder. *Clunk.* His gun tumbled to the ground. The melody was as good as Louis Armstrong marching along Bourbon Street playing his trumpet. She raced forward, kicked his piece aside, and kneed him in the groin.

Carl cradled his crotch, fell to his knees, and moaned, puking onto the floor like the chicken shit he was. A little vomit didn't bother Denim. She locked an arm around his neck and jammed her pistol against his temple. "Please move, dick breath. My finger's twitching for some action. I'm hoping you're in the mood for suicide by bitch."

She lifted her head, listening.

Saved by the siren.

"Fuck you."

"Ew. Not in a million years, you syphilis-ridden degenerate."

She locked the Beretta against his flesh until the cops rolled in.

When Denim turned the scumbag over to them, they perp-walked him out to their car, handcuffed, yelling and screaming about how she'd assaulted him. Fortunately, she knew both guys. *And happy day.* One of them was Marta's boyfriend. Carl couldn't catch a break. Chances were good he'd arrive at the station with two black eyes, busted ribs, and extra bruises.

Yay for New Orleans' finest.

Denim knocked the all-clear on the basement door as her cell rang out with the Dead Kennedys' "I

Fought the Law."

"Galena, hey." She checked her watch. "I'm not late. … Yeah. … Just finishing here. On my way." She disconnected. "Yo, Marta, gotta head to work. See ya when I'm off. Call if you need me before then."

"Stay safe."

Safe may not be possible.

She snagged a scrunchy from her pocket, pulling her hair into a high, tight ponytail. Her scar was visible. Vanity on the job was too dangerous.

Chapter Two

Darque, Present Day

Ramirez yelled over his shoulder at the three Spriggans hauling ass behind him. "Beat feet. Put some air under those wide fuckers." A pack of hellhounds chuffed at their heels, chasing them across the Narobi Flats at the base of the foothills.

Earlier in the morning, the Spriggans' chief had requested assistance from the Scion Firebrands. A five-year-old kid was missing. Since he was one of his commander's best trackers, Ram drew the short straw and was dispatched to find the brat.

He portaled near the Spriggan Enclave on the realm of Darque, picked up the two males and the female racing at his six, and traced the kid's scent to the foothills. When their foursome started to ascend, following the trail, the hounds charged out of a canyon. Bounding, snarling, fur flying, eager to kill. He'd had worse days. He just couldn't remember one at the moment.

"Move your asses or be dinner," he shouted.

The red-eyed bearers of death were as tall as Ram's shoulder and pawing the ground at a speed nearly matching his own. That was saying something since he was a satyr with enhanced Scion Firebrand muscle and power. The Spriggans behind him were slower, making them potential dog meat.

"Those trees." Ram punched a finger in the air toward a cluster of oaks in the distance. With his arms pumping, his knees kicking high, he sprinted ahead. He leaped a gully, veering left, jumping low brambles and side-stepping larger shrubs. Brushing aside scraggly branches, he stumbled but caught himself before he fell.

The terrain was rougher than imagined. Risking a glance over his shoulder, he saw the struggling Spriggans falling farther behind.

Ram considered shadowflashing. A single tap on his D-chip would leave his companions alone to fend off the pack while he darted from shadow to shadow, moving ahead quickly. At the end of a long self-debate, he decided against that route. Now he was reevaluating the choice.

When did I become a damn Boy Scout?

More underbrush. Saplings. Rocks. Thickets. Finally his destination, the stand of trees. Near the exposed roots of an oak, he paused, waited, and motioned for his panting, oxygen-sucking companions to climb three nearby large trunks.

Once they had hand-over-footed it to safety, he selected his own tree, clutched a low branch with both hands, pulled himself onto it, and swung a leg over the sturdy limb. He repeated the action until he was well out of the hellhounds' reach.

The final limb bowed under his six-foot-five solidly muscled frame. Praying it didn't snap and tumble him to the ground into the jaws of his hungry attackers, he wrapped himself in his satyr camouflage, cloaking himself in an invisible fog.

The beasts arrived in a savage fury, growling, leaping, snapping. The pack divided, some picking one tree, some another. Ram was fairly sure the biggest hounds stuck with him.

Lucky.

Their heads butted the thick trunk, drool dripping down their matted fur. Their nostrils worked overtime, sniffing, pinpointing his location. Obviously, they didn't fall for his camouflage.

"Give it a rest," he shouted, dropping his useless

defense in order to avoid wasting energy he might need later.

The tree shook hard when the biggest of the pack, probably the leader, threw his whole body at it. Despite a solid grip, Ram slipped off the bough but snagged a lower limb. He scrambled back up before their pearly whites neutered him.

"And take a bath."

Think. Think.

He patted the dagger handles sticking out of his chest harness. They and the two short tactical swords at his spine were useless unless he wanted to fight the whole pack up close and personal. He didn't. Only one choice left. Natch, he had never tried it on non-sentient beings.

He checked out his companions before he shouted above the yelps and howls of his attackers. "Are the rumors true? If you stare into a hellhound's flaming red eyes, you die?"

The Spriggans shrugged. At least it looked that way from this distance. *Well, hell.* He had to lock onto the mangy critters' peepers to work his satyr hoo-doo. Guess he was about to see if the old canard was truth or myth.

Great! A test case.

If his plan succeeded, he and the Spriggans might escape. As a satyr, his concentrated gaze could neutralize an enemy, rearranging their memories, making them groggy or knocking them out cold. Or if used just right, seduce a female. He'd never used it for that. Of course, sexual side effects usually accompanied his gift. Maybe the hounds would hump each other until they were too tired to give chase. If his powers worked at all with beasts.

Hell. What do I have to lose?

"Hey! Big guy." He bent as low as he dared.

The lead hellpup cast blazing red orbs at Ram. The Firebrand's own translucent irises turned neon green, glowing bright while they held the killer's gaze.

Eyeball to eyeball, they snarled and growled. The savage beast versus the Firebrand. A clock ticked in Ram's head. One second. Two seconds. Five seconds. Ten. Finally, the lead bearer of death staggered. He dropped to the ground, causing what felt like a minor earthquake. His bestial companions snapped their heads up to stare at Ram.

Plop. Plop.

They both hit the dirt.

Three down. Better odds.

Ram swung to the lowest limb to taunt a few animals lunging at the other trees. "Here, doggie, doggie. Come to papa."

Four Darque monsters snapped their yaps shut, went silent, and pivoted their short but thick necks in the direction of his voice. They spied their fallen pack leader. They paused. Then the barks, yips, and howls resumed while they raced toward Ram. He scrambled back up his tree, locking onto the eyes of the charging hellhounds. The first pair crashed, followed by the other two, all within seconds of the stare-down.

Ram called out to the remaining five hounds, their red eyeballs shifting to their fallen comrades. The Firebrand tapped near his pupils with two fingers. "Look here, puppies." Three beasts toppled, followed by the final pair who fell prey to the Firebrand's bright green gaze.

Dropping to the dirt and stepping over the wildings' bodies, Ram called to his Spriggan companions. "Let's get out of here. No idea how long this will last."

The tallest guy clapped a hand to Ram's shoulder. "Well done, satyr." The others nodded their approval while they dashed off.

They raced back to the Narobi Flats where Ram had originally scented the missing kid. When he caught it again, the team searched the foothills while the hellhounds enjoyed their nap.

The trail led halfway up a heavily bouldered rise. Ram raised a hand. He drew a deep breath, brushed aside a shrub, and stepped around a hickory tree. The odor was stronger now. His sharp hearing detected sobs coming from behind nearby rocks. He signaled he was heading up the hill. When the cries grew louder, Ram tripled-timed his pace.

A motion out of the corner of his eye caught his attention. He sighted branch-like things which protruded from every Spriggan's noggin like deer antlers. Pulling himself onto a slab of rock, he spied her. Crouched in the dirt. Her head tucked in tight.

"Hey," he said.

Nobody could claim this species was good looking. Except maybe another Spriggan. Their broad lips, long noses, beady eyes, and skin the color and texture of bark were not his idea of beauty. To make matters worse, they weren't known for being friendly with the Firebrands. *But damn.* The kid was cute as hell.

Her little peepers opened wide when she saw Ram peeking over the top of her hiding place.

Assuming a non-threatening stance and pretending to glance around, he said, "I've been looking for a lost female, about so high." He raised a hand to his waist. "You haven't seen her, have you?"

She jacked off the ground, straightening her shoulders. "I'm a lost girl."

"What luck." He held out a hand, winking at her.

She wiped the snot from under her nose with the sleeve of her shirt. After she blinked, she curled her lips into the brightest smile ever. Scooping her into his arms, Ram lost his heart to the frightened child.

She clasped her thin arms tightly around his neck as if she feared he would leave.

His thumb wiped the tears from her dirt-stained cheeks. "What are you doing this far from home?"

"First I knew where I was. Then I didn't." She suddenly spotted the three Spriggans climbing toward her. "Are all you peoples looking for me?"

"You know it, little one. You're very important." Ram handed the girl over to the female, but not without having to tug the child's hands off his neck.

With the girl asking nonstop questions of Ram, the five headed back to the enclave.

"Are you a Scion Firebrand?"

"Yep."

"My pap says Firebrands are strong. Are you?"

"You bet. I can tackle a questing beast, knock him out, throw him over my shoulder, and climb the mountain over there."

"Really?"

"With a hand tied behind me." He tickled the girl.

She giggled and asked another question. "Can I see your ol' bird?"

"My Phoenix? You bet, beautiful. Watch." He rolled up his sleeve. When he flexed his thick bicep, the wings of the brand on his upper arm spread wide. He relaxed and the image contracted. He tightened his muscle again. The symbol seemed to flutter and take flight. Ram repeated the motion several times.

The girl clapped her hands, squealing. "Are there lots of you?"

"Firebrands?" he asked.

She nodded.

"Lots. Males and females. In fact, most of the females are stronger than I am."

"Do you live on Scath? I've never been there."

"I do. In Wildwynd among my breed, other satyrs, but my stronghold's in Covenkirk."

She pulled her brows down. "Do you kill us Spriggans?"

"Hell … I mean, heck no. Who told you this?"

"Some of my peoples."

"Firebrands keep everybody safe—Darque and Scath. Even humans if we have to. Our job is to go after bad guys. Sometimes we get to rescue pretty girls like you."

She smiled, her cheeks flushed with color.

A hundred questions later, they arrived at the bottom of a windswept, rocky cliff. Ram looked up, scowling at the endless, snaking steps leading to a barely visible plateau in the clouds. At the top was the enclave, protected by a gigantic circular grey stone wall topped off with a thatched roof.

He drew a deep breath, his gaze sweeping up the lengthy trail. "Oh. Hell no." He grabbed the girl out of the Spriggan's arms. "We'll meet you outside the gate." He touched his D-chip to throw a portal while the five-year-old held onto his neck, still jabbering.

Embedded into the Firebrands' wrists, D-chips linked to their brains. With them, they could do almost anything, but creating a gateway, as he had done, gobbled up energy. Better than using his legs after a long chase, though.

Two surprised guards posted at the entrance into the enclave marched forward when Ram and the girl flashed in nearby. Having enjoyed the ride, she was bouncing and squealing.

The satyr Firebrand dwarfed both males who clasped wooden spears bigger than they were. The taller guard with generous lips and skin like the bark on a white elm lifted his weapon, pounding it shaft down into the dirt. He turned sparkling eyes toward the child. "Welcome back, Katya." When he bowed his head, his huge branch-like appendages brushed the ground. "Your parents are inside. I expect you'll get your bottom warmed."

Tall wooden doors opened wide, noise blasting out from the crowded marketplace where tents and booths lined a narrow path.

Rubbing her bottom, Katya frowned at the guard as two Spriggans dashed toward them along the bazaar's winding road. When the girl saw her parents hurrying in her direction, she pushed herself out of Ram's arms, running to meet them. "Mam. Pap."

With tears rolling down her cheeks, Mam swept her daughter off the ground. "We thought mayhap you were eaten, Katya."

"Almost, Mam. But I was more faster than them hellhounds. I rolled in dirt to hide my smell. Just like you told me."

"She's a smart little bugger." Ram clamped a gentle hand onto the child's shoulder.

Mam squeezed her daughter harder. "I hope she didn't talk your arm off. She's inquisitive, this one."

"No. She's a charmer."

The child's mother smiled at Ram, swiping at a tear on Katya's cheek. "That is so."

"We cannot tell you how grateful we are, Firebrand. To you as well as to our fellow villagers who accompanied you." Pap hugged both child and mother in his beefy arms. "Join us. We will celebrate the return of our beloved Katya. Aye?"

"Will there be drinking involved?" asked Ram. He was in a mood to celebrate. *Hell*. He'd saved a five-year-old kid. What could be better?

"Drinking, dancing, and eating. Aye," the father elaborated while he led them along the winding, narrow path deeper into the marketplace where loud hawkers haggled over goods, selling colorful fabrics, bright woven rugs, sparkling jewelry, and hanging meat in the bazaar. They were Darque's traders, drawing shoppers not only from their own realm but from Scath as well.

They pushed their way through the gawkers, who were fingering products, trying on bangle bracelets or quilted vests, and tasting food.

A large central courtyard was already filling with people wanting to see Katya along with her saviors. There, a female Spriggan turned a hunk of meat on a spit over a blazing fire pit. It could have been any animal. He hoped it wasn't a hellhound.

Ram settled cross-legged in front of the welcome evening fire beside Pap. Though it was spring, in the mountains of Spriggan Enclave the air was cool. Someone shoved a hide flask into his hand.

A male dressed in crimson pants and a bright yellow silk shirt, hands on hips, commandingly blocked the Firebrand's view. His spine was straight, authority and a certain amount of mistrust in his eyes. "I'm Chief Sparce. I called your commander to request assistance when Katya went missing. We could not find her. Though Kole and I have our differences, he sent us you. For this, we are grateful. Now drink."

Their differences? That was one way to put it. After Kole had captured Sparce's brother, he turned him over to the Temple of Justice. Ram couldn't remember the crime. But it was serious. The gaffers held the male in the Cubes until the Justices delivered a quick verdict.

With an axe through his neck, they released him to the Evermore.

Simple justice.

"Do I want to know what this is?" Ram waved the flask in the air.

"Helmslag." Katya's father volunteered the info as he rested alongside his daughter's hero, the girl bouncing in his lap. With a hand on her shoulder to still the child, he clasped his own drink. He removed the cap and took a long pull. "Ah-berserker-berserker. Know only this." The Spriggan dropped his lids, giving a swift shake of his head. "It's strong enough to take down a male warcat and still let you hump your female all night long. Aye?"

With the smell of meat cooking, Spriggans high-fiving, and a male playing a bandora as couples danced to its sweet ballad-like sounds, Ram popped the cap, took a swig, and gasped. His hand flew to his throat. He squeezed as the liquid burned all the way into his gut. "Son-of-a-pig-nosed-rat. Bring it on." He tipped the flask again to take a longer pull.

In front of the Firebrand, a female with light-colored antlers swayed in time to the music. She was decked out in a cobalt-blue skirt barely covering her slim thighs and a tight knit top showing off her headlights. Her navel peeked below the cropped shirt. With her hands waving high above, her curvy hips gently undulated. She threw in a few bumps, a few grinds, a wink to boot.

Ram shook his head, sending her away. He gave her an A for effort, though.

Katya's father punched his arm. "Drink a few more swills of helmslag. She will look good to you. Aye?"

Ram watched the female's shapely ass wiggle

when she stopped in front of another male. "Mebbe."

He laughed. He joked with the villagers. He drank some more. Tipping the flask, Ram swallowed another slug of helmslag. Having used heaps of energy today, he was suddenly hungry. A satyr fed on arousal as a vampire lived off blood. The flirtatious dancer reeked of sexual need. Besides, he was fairly sure Spriggan females had the right parts.

Chapter Three

New Orleans, Present Day

Denim Quinn squeezed her lips together, biting back a gag. It wasn't because of the body at her feet. Her cast iron stomach didn't object to guts, gore, and blood. She'd seen plenty of that in Afghanistan. More when she walked a beat in the Lower 9th Ward. Her lunch wanted out because of the overpowering stench of the alley. Discarded food from two restaurants, stale booze from a bar, urine puddles, and what she thought might be a few dead rats.

Yep.

The scene was grisly. The left side of the body's face was blown away. Dirt blended with blood, brains, and unidentifiable fluids which oozed under its head like a halo. As if the bullet hadn't been enough, the killer had jammed a knife into the guy's chest, shimmying it around until the cavity was mincemeat.

Overkill. Even though the dead guy was an Aeternal.

Deep cuts scored the groin. An arm had been cut off and flung to the side near a dumpster like so much trash.

Somebody was pissed enough to use a gun and a big-ass blade.

The soldier-turned-cop-turned-Alliance-agent rose, her knees popping. She dusted off her hands. Pinching her nostrils, she shot a question at her partner. Every year during Mardi Gras season, an Aeternal paired with a human Alliance agent to prowl the streets of New Orleans.

Denim's employer, the Alliance Protection Agency, was a front, hiring out as bodyguards, private security, and soldiers of fortune. But their real mission was to provide access to trade, assistance in returning illegal Aeternals to their realm, and a lid on secrets about Scath's breeds. All employees at the organization bore a smidgeon of Aeternal DNA thanks to those who had remained behind after the Karmic Schism. Though most of the species went to Scath, others with human families on Earth stayed. Once travel between the realms of Scath and Earth became possible, the humans created the Alliance to assist their ancient ancestors, the Aeternals.

Denim's partner was also the "unusual" friend, an Amazon who lived on Scath. Girls' night out wasn't easy to arrange. They lived a realm apart. As a Firebrand, Galena had a nifty device which allowed her to travel through portals whenever. Alliance agents did not. So Denim was Earth-bound. "Do we know who he is, Galena?"

Her partner knelt beside the body but twisted her neck to look at the other team. "Thorn, do you know?"

The wolf shifter answered, absent-mindedly waving the severed arm through the air. Blood splattered on the brick wall, creating an impromptu Jackson Pollock. Thorn was a Scion Firebrand from the same Covenkirk stronghold as Galena. He wiped an errant splash from his cheek. He, along with his human Alliance partner Rod, were first on the scene. "His prints sync with the phone call info we got. He's an incubus. Warner's the name."

Denim followed Thorn's gestures with the arm. "Damn shame. The guy was probably looking for a little fun, not causing much mischief. When did you find him?"

"I got buzzed a half-hour ago. Was told an incubus had called in a panic, being attacked near this portal by humans. Here he is. Doornail dead."

Rod threw his two cents into the conversation. "In Nawlins, especially during Mardi Gras season, we say *laissez les bon temps rouler,* but this is too much *bon temps roulering.* Not only is the Aeternal dead, but he's carved up worse than a Thanksgiving turkey. Your young'uns usually cross over for the parades, wild sex, all-night binges, and hijinks. Now we have a murder to investigate. Not good. Lucky someone else didn't find him?"

The Creole with the thick accent was an Alliance agent like Denim, but he side-jobbed as a Big Easy cop. Hence, he was in a position to plug holes in the levee if a big Aeternal problem cropped up. A dead Aeternal unmasked in a police morgue would count as a big problem.

The two teams stared at what was left of Warner's body. Thorn checked out his cowboy boots, probably looking for bloodstains. "After I got the call, Rod and I hit the road running. He made sure no calls got through to NOPD. A pile of shit would rain down on our heads if we'd been exposed. We'd have Firebrands, lawgivers, the Temple of Justice, the board of directors at the Alliance all imbedding a foot in our collective asses."

"Yeah," added Rod. "No reports reached homicide. In the day of smartphones, Instagram, Facebook, Twitter, Snapchat, YouTube, U-fuck, and Instabitch, that's real lucky. I hope our *gris gris* lasts. An ME would find shit in one of your guys which shouldn't be in a human."

Galena combed her fingers through her straight shoulder-length black hair, rising to her full height of six feet. "Was he coming or going?"

Thorn kicked a pebble with the toe of his boot. "I got the feeling he was heading home."

Nodding while she moved away from the body,

Denim slid her phone out of her back pocket to answer a call. With it pressed to her ear, she walked to the alley entrance where she could see out into the busy street. She glanced one way and then the other. "Got 'em. Thanks."

An Aeternal-Alliance team who had their hands full with a few randy young satyrs called with a heads-up on some partiers they couldn't get to. Disconnecting, she returned to her partner. "Hotshots up the street. Let's book, Galena." She grinned at Rod. "The body, such as it is, is yours, *cher*. You found it. You keep it."

Rod scratched his nose with his middle finger.

The women exited the alley, passed Pat O'Brien's on St. Peter's, and hurried toward Bourbon Street where they spied their targets turning a corner.

Though it was night, streetlights lit up the surroundings like hundreds of tiny suns. Overhead, drunken carousers celebrated the festivities by crowding onto iron-scrolled balconies while they chugged beer or fancy drinks. Beneath the classic New Orleans structures, revelers spilled onto the streets, shouting, gyrating to the rhythms of sidewalk bands or music blasting from raucous bars. Lots of color, masks, feathers, and wigs.

Hustling toward their objective, they elbowed their way through the merrymakers. Out of place in jeans, dark T-shirts, and combat boots, they trailed four young vampires who were migrating toward a famous local nightclub.

"Young guys all looking to score. God spare me." Denim's chestnut-colored ponytail swished back and forth with her hurried steps. Truth be told, she was having a great time. The excitement of Mardi Gras season was infectious. It whisked her away from her own problems. She complained about the job to her partner, but aside from the dead body, she enjoyed the noise, the music, the crowds, the rush of chasing errant juvenile

Aeternals.

No one ever said I was sane.

Galena nodded. "No argument here. Same story every year. A bunch of horny youths steal their parents' jumpers, open a portal, cross through the Whorl to Earth, and play spin the human. In the early morning, they run home with a collection of beads along with great stories." When a drunken partier stumbled into her path, she grabbed his shoulders to clear him out of her way.

"Hey, beautiful. Let's dance." The man slurred his words, trying to latch onto her arm but missing.

Pushing the same Bo Jangles wannabe out of the way, Denim shouted over the noise at Galena. "I'm glad we were such good girls when we were younger."

Galena chuckled. "My Mardi Gras stories would curl these kids' toes."

"You have to share, girl."

When they neared the young males, one was hitting on a long-haired blonde, his gaze raking up her shapely legs on the way to her mini-skirt. His head whipped around as if he sensed their approach. Showing the tips of his fangs, he jabbed his buddy's arm. "Firebrand."

He must have recognized the Phoenix brand on Galena's upper left arm. The young Aeternals did a cut-and-run.

Denim picked up the pace. "Excuse me. Excuse me." She pushed fun-loving dipsomaniacs to the side.

"Hey." A petite chesty brunette, whose strapless top was dangerously close to malfunctioning, flirted with two guys. "Watch it."

Denim ignored her to sprint forward, losing sight of the males briefly in the crowded street. Fortunately, Galena possessed the aura-spidey senses, which worked even from this distance. Not only could she tag a person as an Aeternal, but she could ID their breed. *Handy*. As a human, Denim lacked the skill.

Over the blaring karaoke sounds pouring out of The World Famous Cat's Meow, Denim's partner shouted, "Over there." She pointed at the juveniles while they disappeared into the popular French Quarter booze joint.

As the Alliance agent and the Scion Firebrand entered the bar, a guy in a cobalt-blue wig belted out a song on stage. Denim scanned the room. She signaled Galena when she spotted the four vampires already chatting up two ladies who wobbled on their five-inch spiked heels, liquid splashing over the rims of their glasses. For the moment, the males seemed more concerned with scoring than running.

Hormones on two legs.

"Hey, handsome." Galena sidled up to one of the males, locking her arm through the crook of his elbow.

Denim pushed between the spiky-haired blond and the youth with a nose piercing along with other penetrating slivers of metal. "Wow! We are glad to see you boys. Mom wants you to come home to do your chores."

"Busted." The blond eagle-eyed Denim and Galena's tight jeans and snug T-shirt. "How about we hang with you two hotties?"

"We'd burn you, baby." Galena chuckled, flipping her black hair away from her face. "Are you coming willingly or are we dropping you right here in front of these shit-faced chicks? And just in case you're thinking about doing the 100-meter dash on us, I know your parents, Rode." She spoke to the heavily pierced vampire youth.

The four males bobbed their heads at the drunk chicks, muttered their goodbyes, and walked out of the bar with their embarrassed gazes on the booze-stained floor.

The group proceeded to a quiet side street where Galena led them into a private parking garage. She opened a portal. Before they transported back to Scath, the blond kid spun toward Denim to pass off his phone. "Punch in your number. I'll call you sometime."

She waved it away. "In your dreams, *cher*. Now don't get any ideas about coming back. We're patrolling the Quarter all night."

"You don't know what you're missing, baby." The young vampire Lothario shrugged when he stepped through the gateway behind his friends.

Denim checked her cell while Galena tapped the D-chip embedded in her wrist. "Any more reports of horny crossovers?"

"None at my end. How about you?"

"Nope," said Denim. "Let's indulge in a Hurricane at Pat O'Brien's until the next jackasses pop up. After which, it'll be quitting time anyway."

"Count me in."

They maneuvered through the streets more slowly this time, still pushing and shoving to make progress while they headed for the famous New Orleans attraction, the home of a popular libation.

Inside, they muscled their way alongside a couple seated at the bar. While they waited to order, the woman twisted her head around, smiled, and shouted in Denim's ear. "We're leaving. Heading for the next joint. You want our seats?"

"Do we ever. *Mersi*," Denim yelled above the noise.

Settled into two lucky stools, they waved off a guy who offered to buy their Hurricanes.

"What'll it be, ladies?" The bartender swiped a

rag along the counter.

"Two of your tourist traps, *cher*," replied Denim.

When he returned with the drinks, Galena took a sip of the bright red alcohol-heavy treat in a tall glass. "Yum. No wonder everybody wants one of these."

When a hand brushed against Denim's arm, she swiveled in her stool, prepared to tell some flirt to buzz off. Instead, her face turned ashen. Her mouth dropped open. She popped off her seat to challenge the intruder. "You're supposed to stay five hundred feet away from me, Steven. This is a hell of a lot closer than the order demands."

"You're my wife. Some court order isn't gonna tell me how close I can get."

He latched onto the bar but swayed, nearly stumbling. Steven had been a different guy years ago. Handsome. Fun-loving but sober. Concerned with his appearance. Considerate. The Steven in front of her in Pat O'Brien's was wearing wrinkled dirty cargo pants, a stained button-down, a ragged jacket. Straggly blond hair stuck out under a tattered Houston Astros cap. This guy was on a long bender. Of course, this was Steven's standard MO at the end of their relationship.

"Maybe the court order won't work, but I thought I gave you plenty of incentive to get lost and stay there. Do you want another visit from me?" Denim's eyes narrowed into a glare.

Galena slid off her stool. She reached to her hip, where she kept a holstered knife under her T-shirt.

With her attention never wavering from Steven, Denim spoke to her partner. "This is my wife-beating alcoholic ex-husband. E-X," she shouted over the bar din. "The Alliance fired him, I bitch-slapped him, and the court served him with an order to stay far away from me."

Galena topped Steven's five-eleven as she looked down her nose at him. "It's time you go poof, buddy."

"Yeah? Look, you cu…"

Before he could finish his statement, Galena tapped his crotch with her blade. "You might want to rethink what you're about to say. I get this nervous spasm in my hand. When I do, my knife slips."

Denim's lips curled into a grin. She nodded. "Remember the guy the other night? You almost took off one of his balls. I felt sorry for him."

"Geez, girlfriend. I was real sorry about that. Why'd you have to bring it up again?"

Steven backed away, snarling. "I'm just here to have a good time with my guys." He pointed to the other side of the bar where two muscle-laden losers glared in their direction. "Just wanted to say hey to my wife." His gaze flipped from Galena to Denim before he nodded, spinning on his heel, staggering away.

"E-X. Asshole." Denim plopped down to sip her Hurricane, drumming her fingers on the bar.

The physical wounds had healed. Except for the scar on her face. The psychological ones were fading at a snail's pace. Having burrowed into her brain, they surfaced at inconvenient times. Like when a nice guy asked her to dinner and a movie. That's when she flashed on Steven's fists slamming into her jaw, his steel-toed Danners cracking her ribs. She lost her dream of a family and her confidence to choose the right man.

Marta may have a point. The past is alive, a worm inside my head.

Galena slid onto her stool.

"I've never told you about Steven. And you've never asked. Thanks. I'm still raw. Anyway, I worked with him at the Alliance about a year before we started to date. It was another year before I agreed to marry him.

Bad idea, huh?"

"I'm not in a place to judge."

"As it turns out, it was a terrible idea. Life was great at first. Of course, we both worked long hours, but after each day, we'd eat out, enjoy a few beers, laugh a lot. The trouble started when I moved up the ranks while he stayed in place. He resented my success."

Denim tightened her ponytail. "I don't know, maybe he was always a bastard, and I didn't notice. All I saw was a handsome, popular guy who could have any woman he wanted. He chose me. By the end, he was a mean drunk who tried to make me weak, submissive, the perfect punching bag. And I guess for a time, he succeeded. I don't know why I'm telling you all this. Like you really need to hear my sad story."

"Hey! You're telling me because I'm your sidekick, girlfriend."

"Thanks." Denim pushed her stool back, settling her boots on the floor. "I've lost interest in this place. Let's move on."

"I'm with ya."

When they hit the noisy, bustling street again, Galena checked her D-chip.

Denim grabbed her partner's wrist, turning it over, back, examining it. "That is so cool. It's a smooth black disk. Does it do everything I've heard?"

"Real futuristic shit. A Digital Implant Communication Chronometer. It's a mouthful. Yeah? Easier to say Dick Chip. Kind of scary to think it links to my brain. I can talk to anybody, pop through portals, flash from shadow to shadow. I can even get the time of day. With a tap and a thought, it will do almost anything. Want a selfie?"

"I need one of those."

Galena wagged her finger. "Not for lowly

humans, but I see by my very fashionable, for-Aeternals-only-Flash-Gordon watch that we still have no problems. Let's just wander."

Like salmon swimming upstream, the two worked their way to Bourbon Street. Then onto Toulouse. A guy tossed a set of beads at Denim, who laughed as she caught them. She spun around, waving them at Galena. That was when she spotted Steven and his two buddies crossing the street about a block behind.

"Here comes the asshole with his fidiots-of-the-month. We need to get out of here. He's nine ways of crazy. I don't want you dragged into my problems."

"Don't bother about me. I've got an idea, though. Since we're about off shift, I know where he can't follow. Jump to Scath with me. You said you're off for a few days anyway. You can have a mini-vaca at my place. We'll do the spa thing. You haven't felt anything until wee imps walk all over your back. They're ugly as mini hellhounds but, girl, can they work the kinks out of your muscles. Next, we'll paint our nails Hannibal Lecter red, slip on some sexy rags, and tip back a few at the Blood Shed."

Denim tapped her index finger to her chin. "That actually sounds fun. I've never been to your realm. No suitcase with me, though."

"I'm a great shopper. You try on. I'll sit on a couch drinking wine, oohing, aahing."

"Will my credit card work?" Denim raised her hands while she danced her way through a gyrating couple in the street.

Galena chuffed. "Are you kidding? We're bigger capitalists than you guys. We don't turn down any medium of exchange. Paper. Coin. Plastic. Lamb. A bushel of corn. Pet rock. All's good."

"I'm also supposed to get a blood test. You know,

one of the mandatory ones to see if my drop of witch is because of a Blood Coven ancestor."

"You can get it at the Ministry of Well Being. Let's double time it. We'll lose these bastards."

As they started running, Denim peeked over her shoulder. *Yep.* Steven and his men were definitely giving chase. "They're gaining. I can't wait to see their faces when we take the portal."

They turned a corner, entering a deserted side street. Air whizzed by Galena's ear. A pop sounded. "What the fuck?"

Pop. Pop. Pop.

"They're shooting." Denim picked up the pace.

Pop. Pop.

Galena opened the rolling door into the garage hiding the portal. "I've got you." She looped her arm through Denim's, touching her D-chip. They disappeared.

Chapter Four

Scath, Present Day

Ram was nursing a Black Bush at the Blood Shed, the Firebrands' favorite hangout.

Tyr strutted alongside. As usual, the warlock was all jeweled up and dressed in bike leathers. A key dangled from one ear, a hoop from the other. A silver bar pierced his brow while a metal collar ringed his neck and a crapload of shiny shit circled his wrists. A sickle tat sat under his eye. At well over six feet, he was a seriously disturbed Firebrand.

When the bartender shuffled over, Tyr ordered what Ram was drinking. He fisted his two fingers of Black Bush, gulped the whiskey, slammed the glass on the bar, and signaled for another hit. "Hell of a week."

Ram requested a second. "Yeah? You think? Were you nearly hellhound chum? Because if not, shut the fuck up."

"Hellhounds? On the real?"

"Affirmative."

"Cool. Nothing so exciting for me, but Kole pulled me in to lend an assist to Commander Nace in North Shelters. I'm assigned to work with the elusive but psycho vampire Dax. Seems drugs are running wild in the shifter region. When there's a serious problem, who do they call?" Tyr tapped his chest. "Yep. Me. Super warlock."

"Gotta be more talented mages out there somewhere."

"Kiss my glutes." Slugging back his drink, he pounded it on the counter while he waited for another. Fortunately, most alcohol had little effect on Aeternals.

Brak, an Abrams battle tank, pulled up on the other side, elbow-jabbing Ram's ribs.

The huge carnal demon caught the barkeep's attention.

"What'll it be?" The guy refilled Tyr's glass while asking.

Brak eyed the libations in front of his *frerons*. "Black Bush. Sissy drink. Give me some Macallan. The really old stuff."

"You hit a jackpot?" asked Tyr. "That shit costs."

Brak was silent until the bartender served him. He raised the tumbler, took a pull, and shook his head, licking his lips. "Now there's a drink."

Finally answering the question, he said, "Nope. Just decided to go top shelf. I'm carving out my niche. I mean, look at our guy Ram here." He waved his hand in the Firebrand's direction. "His threads are slick, but I'm sticking with my leathers. It's not like I'm ever gonna be a pretty boy." He leaned around Ram to take in the warlock. "You've got the market covered on perverted Goth. Dax has scary locked down tight. Rein is a strong, silent, wicked powerful iceberg. Kole has the whole fire thing going for him. My trademark is gonna be top-shelf merchandise. Only the softest, most expensive leathers. Weapons made by craftsmen. Pricey Scotch. A fast, sleek car. Got my peeps on a special baby."

Ram pivoted to survey the room, his back to the bar. He listened to Brak's rant while he glanced around for a little in-and-out action. He was acquainted with most of the females giving him come-on winks as they strutted by his spot. *Hell.* He'd been inside most of them. A satyr needed arousal to feed, but tonight the whole sexual stimulation routine seemed stagnant. He needed to get in the game.

A grin tweaked his lips when a female whose name he couldn't remember sidled alongside and squeezed between Tyr and him. She locked arms and grabbed a fistful of his hair. When he was level, she smacked him with a kiss. He let her. She was okay. After all, a nymph was a nymph. His eyes shone green as he fed from her.

An appetizer.

Next thing, Amylyn, a witch he'd screwed a few times, hauled up on the other side. Her fingers strolled across his chest.

What's a hungry satyr to do?

Her lips were kissable. She was available. He bent his head to lock onto her mouth, his tongue working hard.

Maybe Amylyn and What's-her-name would be okay with a threesome. That would really feed his hungry satyr.

****

Denim had been watching the gorgeous man at the bar. He was at least six and a half feet of untamed power with caramel-streaked hair flowing down his back like a waterfall. Her gaze traveled across his broad shoulders, angling to his trim waist. She ogled the tan dress slacks molding to his deliciously taut buttocks.

Two menacing Aeternals had walked in to bookend the gorgeous guy. Any other time, they might have ranked as stars in an erotic dream, but tonight she reserved her fantasies for the sexy dreamsicle.

On one side of the hottie, a man clad in Hell's Angels duds and sporting spiked black hair chatted him up. A behemoth who weighed in at nearly three hundred pounds of pure muscle in a tall package had parked on his left.

After performing a one-eighty with predatory grace, the dreamsicle rested his elbows on the bar, leaned back, and crossed one ankle over the other. He managed easygoing and predatory at the same time. She fixed on the muscular forearms exposed beneath his rolled-up black sleeves. With each breath, his chest expanded, threatening to pop buttons on the silky collared shirt clinging to his solid pecs.

His sexuality was a gravitational field, sucking in the women along with a few men who sauntered past. They swished their hips, wandering by him to get a closer look-see. Some sidled alongside to flirt openly.

His lips curled into the sexy smile of a man who reveled in his effect on the opposite sex. But his eyes. They were translucent pieces of pale beach glass, framed by thick lashes.

They swept the room, probably looking for an easy score. All the handsome ones were searching for a mark, weren't they? An easy woman. A woman they could manipulate.

Unfortunately, Denim was a sucker for a guy who pulled off polished gigolo and dangerous man in one body.

As women walked past the sexy guy, his irises latched onto their asses. No doubt about it. He was a player. A troller. A bullshit artist.

While Denim continued to monitor the action around the sexy guy, a skank in five-inch heels and a barely-there skirt had slithered alongside. With her mitts wrapped around gorgeous guy's enormous biceps, she planted a kiss on dreamsicle's lips, her boobs pressed against his chest. Could she have been more blatant?

As if he had opened for business, a tall curly-haired woman squeezed between him and the behemoth. Her fingers strolled across his pecs, probably leaving greasy smudges on his expensive shirt. This time, he bent forward to drop a kiss on her.

As Denim continued to monitor the situation, Galena poked her arm. "Who's snagged your interest?"

She followed her partner's gaze. "Oh no, girlfriend. Wrong direction. Wrong Firebrand. The slab of steamy beef is Ramirez. Man-whore should be tattooed across his forehead. Of course, he's a satyr. So it comes with the territory."

Pfft went her fantasy, but it wasn't as if she hadn't already guessed.

She sipped her Alabama Slammer. "Don't worry, *cher*. I've learned the hard way to stay away from his type. Obviously, my man-dar is broken or I wouldn't have married the idiot wife-beater." Denim cocked her head in Ram's direction. "Women ogled Steven, too, but he had eyes for me. Sure he did. He thought I was a push-over. And I was. For a time."

Denim was due a little R and R. But while she was hoping for rest and relaxation, gorgeous guy was likely searching for some rock and rut.

Galena pivoted in her chair to check out the Shed. "It's raining males tonight. How about the guy over there?"

"Nice looking, but I'm not in the market."

"He's got a big gun and knows how to use it, if you know what I mean."

"You've screwed him?"

Galena nodded, finishing off her drink. "Of course. How else could I recommend him?"

"Ew. That's just wrong. I'm not taking your seconds like a poor country cousin, *cher*." Her gaze returned to the bar.

"You've got a thing for satyrs, huh? Ram will give you a good time. No complaints from any of the ladies about him."

"Have you messed around with him, too?"

"No. I avoid knocking boots with the warriors stationed in my own stronghold."

Denim sighed, relieved Galena hadn't done her fantasy he-man.

"I can tell you're not gonna let him go." Galena pursed her lips before she shared. "Ram's not a Steven. He's not cruel or abusive. Just stiff as a board all the time. But he's a satyr. Hell, sticking their wicks in females is a biological imperative. It's how they feed. They need the arousal which comes with sex. Can't live without it. Like blood to a vamp. But you can't count on them being in bed to warm your feet the next morning."

"I don't know if I'm good at casual hook-ups."

"If you're interested in the satyr, you better get good at it. It's the only way he flies. He never returns for seconds unless he's sure the female has no designs on him."

Having disengaged his lips from Tall and Curly, the corners of Ram's mouth curved into a self-satisfied smile, but his eyes moved away from the bar slut.

Holy hell.

The dreamsicle's translucent gaze was hooked on Denim, and it was flashing green. She swiped a hand across the back of her neck. "Is it hot in here?"

"No."

"Too bad. I caught a blast from a furnace."

****

Sandwiched between What's-her-name and Amylyn, Ram spotted Galena across the room whispering to a newcomer. A human with chestnut hair hanging seductively over one eye. It caressed her shoulders in big waves and bounced with each animated gesture as she talked. Her brows arched above sparkling irises, the same shade as her hair. Her full lips were tinted pink. A snug blue top exposed the swells of her gorgeous twins. Ample. Just the way he liked them.

Ram's eyes flashed green, and he fed from the

plentiful arousal in the air at the Shed, including the vibes coming from the stranger at Galena's table. Human females were catnip.

Too bad they were breakable.

He straightened, boosting his elbows off the bar. "Ladies, hands off."

Taking the hint, they changed their target. "Hey, big guy, want a threesome in the back?" asked Amylyn as What's-her-name on the other side rushed toward his carnal demon *freron.*

Hmm. They are into doing a group hug.

Brak surveyed the witch and crooked his lips into a grin, his gaze crawling over her friend as well. Apparently liking what he saw, he finished his drink and slammed it on the bar. "Let's go. I have something I think you're gonna love. If you're good, I'll let you use it like an all-day sucker."

As the three walked off arm-in-arm, What's-her-name giggled.

"You sick?" Tyr tossed back another Black Bush.

"Naw. I spotted something interesting."

Turning, Tyr followed Ram's gaze. "She's human."

"Yeah."

"You don't like human females."

"Do you know about the catnip syndrome?"

"Never heard of it."

"Tasty stuff but dangerous. It's best if I keep my Prada brogues planted right here."

Since he'd been scrutinizing the female's merchandise, however, four males had idled by Galena's table, sizing up the human. Two stopped to chat. Though satyrs couldn't read minds like some powerful vamps, he knew what they were thinking. It was enough to make Ram kick into protective mode.

What the hell. A chat can't hurt. No harm. No foul.

Against his better judgment, he ordered three beers. Gripping the necks in one hand, he strolled toward his Amazon *freron's* table, putting swagger into his walk, advertising his goods with a prowling stride.

Tyr signaled the bartender for another, shouting over the noise, "Have at her, satyr. I think I'll stand here getting shit-faced."

****

"Oh, damn. Here he comes." Denim watched raw, coiled energy stalk toward her. She finger-combed a length of hair over her scar. It was only two inches long, running from the outside corner of her right eye onto her cheekbone, but the memories with it were soul deep. If Ram was perfection, she was damaged goods.

The guy had a cocky walk, one which said he knew he was hot. His gait was loose and easy, his thigh muscles flexing with each step. His chest moved in rhythm with his strides.

"What's it gonna be?" Galena tossed an arm over Denim's shoulders.

"I'm done with X-rated man-whores. I deserve a nice man who wants a white picket fence and 1.93 children."

"Sounds boring. Ram's not that kinda guy. But if you weaken, you can do him in a backroom. We're cool here. Everyone comes to the Shed to relax. No shame. No judgment. Aeternals have overactive libidos. It's in our DNA. If we don't find release, all hell breaks loose."

A smiling vampire sauntered over to their table, the tips of his fangs exposed. Before he could chat, Ram arrived to give him a head bob which said *shoo*. The guy obliged, looking happy to get away with his balls intact.

"Galena." Ram dipped his chin. "Who's your

friend?"

He was tall enough Denim had to bend her neck unless she wanted to talk to his groin. When she gazed up at two hundred and forty pounds of pulchritudinous muscled he-man, she nearly gasped. She was pretty sure her dazed expression told him she wanted to jump his bones.

Which I absolutely will not be doing.

He set a beer in front of Galena. Another in front of her. "Hi, doll. I'm Ram." His voice was deep and as mesmerizing as lazy swamp water. He kicked out a chair, lowering himself into it. As he took a long draw on his brew, he brushed a strand of caramel-streaked hair over his shoulder.

Yum.

Her hand shot out to shake his. "Denim. Denim Quinn. Pleased to meet you, *cher*."

He stared at her palm for a long time before he wrapped his big hand around it. Instead of shaking, he held on tight. Heat crawled along her arm to her elbow, onto her neck, and straight south from there. His eyes flashed green.

Galena smirked. "Knock it off, satyr. She's not a snack."

Denim had no idea what her friend meant. When Ram released her, she gave him a silly-ass grin.

"Denim is my Alliance partner in New Orleans this Mardi Gras season." Galena sipped her beer.

"Alliance, huh." Ram's forehead wrinkled. Denim felt he wanted to run, but he stayed seated. He cocked his head to the side, sizing her up. "You're pretty but fragile. You should be in a less dangerous line of work."

Denim prickled. He was another asshole who resented strong women, who thought they shouldn't handle tough or dangerous. "First, I'm not fragile. I'm tall for a human woman. Admittedly, nothing like the Amazon here. I also train to take down large, misogynistic men."

He downed his brew, popping a finger into the air to signal the waitress. "I bet you do. Care to try me?"

"Hmph. Second, I don't want a less dangerous line of work. I'm good at what I do."

"What are some of the things you're good at? Maybe I'd enjoy them." He winked.

Galena set her beer on the table and glanced around the room. "Can't you find some sweet thang to screw?"

Ram said, "I have."

It took Denim a sec before she caught on. "Nuh-uh. Take me off your list."

While they bantered, a short-haired guy who looked like Joe College with red-rimmed eyes waved at Galena from another table. She turned to Denim. "Do you mind if I slip away for a minute? I see a friend." She tapped her chin as if she were thinking. "Make it several minutes. The vamp looks hungry."

"You go ahead. I'll be fine here." She glanced at Ram. "Won't I?"

"You'll be better than fine." A grin tugged at his soft, full lips as he stood to pull out her friend's chair.

Galena rose, spun around, and jabbed a finger into the satyr's chest. "She's my partner. It's been a hard week. So no shit. Huh?"

Ram's brows shot up. "Me? I'm Prince Charming."

"Yeah? Not usually." She faced Denim. "I'll return, honey. He's gonna hit on you 'cause it's what satyrs do. If his eyes flash neon green, he's feeding on your arousal. He can't help it. It's his breed's way. If it's not what you want, kick him in his balls."

"With pleasure."

"Doll, my nads are in your hands. Treat 'em with kindness. And, Galena, thanks for the praise. It touches my heart." He tapped his chest.

Galena shrugged, leaving the table. She marched over to the vamp, bending to whisper in his ear. He rose, his hand moving up and down her ass.

Ram glided closer. "You've got a nice drawl. Everything you say sounds smooth, sexy."

"Uh-huh."

When a man stopped at the table to ask Denim if she'd like to dance, Ram snapped a quick reply. "No. She doesn't."

The guy scurried away.

Ram ignored her glare. "Go on. You were telling me what you're good at." A lazy smile crept onto his face.

Denim leaned back in her chair, her arms crossed. When Ram stared at her breasts, she shifted positions, folding her hands around her beer bottle. "I'm a great shot."

"Guns are illegal on Scath."

"I'm good at Muay Thai."

"The martial art. So, you like mat work? I'm in favor of perfecting my skills on a mat."

"Besides twisting my words, what are you good at?"

"I'm good with my hands." Scooting in closer and brushing her hair aside, Ram stroked her cheek.

Denim flinched when he touched her scar. "Don't."

"Does it bother you?"

"Yes." She covered it again.

"It makes you more beautiful. The scars on the

inside are the ones you have to worry about. What if I touch you here?"

What did he know about scars? He was perfect. She didn't bother to tell him because she was busy responding to his caresses.

He traced Denim's mouth, his knees brushing against hers.

She parted her lips and licked his finger. *Crap.* She'd not meant to do that. At least she stopped before drawing it into her mouth and giving it a workout.

His eyes flashed green.

He continued to vex her by traveling down her chin and along her neck, leaving a trail of fire. He paused above the swell of her breasts, lowering his voice until it was a raspy whisper. "I'd start here."

Denim moaned and arched into his touch. Before he dipped into her shirt, she shook off his effect and grabbed his hand. "Hold on, pretty boy."

His thigh rubbed against hers. "Are you sure? I can make you feel great."

Swallowing the dry lump in her throat, she had no doubt. "Are you doing something to me? Something satyr-like?"

"Nope, doll. Clouding a female's mind is no better than rape in my book. I believe in consent. This is pure seduction. No breed tricks."

Denim was tongue-tied. The thought of getting down and dirty with the satyr made rational words race out of her brain, stumbling all over themselves. She flipped a hand, indicating he should back away. "No more touching."

To his credit, he obliged. The two sat for some time in a painful silence, sipping on their beers.

"If I can't stroke your delicious skin or lick you until you scream my name, it's going to be a long night.

You might as well tell me your story. Why choose a job where you're in danger of being toe-tagged? Another beer?"

"Sure." She could use something cold.

He held up two fingers for the waitress.

"I like to kill assholes." She let her gaze slide up his muscled body. "Mostly men. Mostly men with egos like big balloons full of hot air and gas just waiting to be pricked."

He leaned back in his chair, spreading his knees wide. "I do have a noticeably big ego. For a reason. Want to know what else is big?"

Fast and without a brain in her head, Denim grabbed his crotch, squeezing it until he moaned. She yanked her hand away and swallowed a quick drink. "I've felt bigger."

When she giggled, she smacked her palm over her mouth.

"Gotta tell ya, doll, that's not the reaction my cock usually gets."

"Sorry. I was picturing you in a Speedo. Private joke." Marta would understand it.

"Never wear one. Too snug. Shows my junk. Gotta keep it hidden, but you can take it out of my pants for a spin. You might want to get on your knees first."

"*Cher*, if I sucked your dick … on my knees … you'd blow up like a beach ball and explode." Good lord. Where was this talk coming from? She'd grabbed his frickin' penis. Sure, it was in his expensive wool trousers, but still. Of course, she'd never tell him the truth. His dick was enormous, hard. What's worse, she wanted it, but she wasn't getting on her knees for him. Not now. Not ever.

"Enough foreplay, doll. The Shed has rooms in the rear. How about we finish our convo in one of them?" He took a swig of beer. "Unless things are moving too fast for you."

"They are. And I love things real slow, satyr." She licked her lips, leaned forward onto her elbows, and let Ram look down the front of her shirt. "Slow lane slow. Molasses slow." Her voice dropped to a whisper. "Slow like a Southern drawl on a hot sultry night in the bayou."

He grinned. The nerve.

The satyr unfolded from the chair, all six and a half feet of pure masculine grace. He offered an assist. "A little chat to get to know each other. A little petting before the big show. Then slow in. Slow out, doll. Repeat. Until you weep."

She did not grab his outstretched palm. "Sit your ass down. I'm not going anywhere with you."

Before he could sound off, she held up a hand. "Don't speak. You are a gorgeous man until you fly off at the mouth."

"Make up your mind." He puzzled his brows. "You run hot and cold."

He was right, but she couldn't seem to help it around him. "See? Your talking is ruining the effect. Do your lines usually work?"

After he lowered his ass into the seat again, he took a long pull on his beer. "Always. I'm a satyr."

"What's that mean anyway? Is it an excuse to be a player?"

"Pretty much. It's our breed. It's our role. It can get wearing to have so much responsibility on my shoulders. The females have expectations."

They sat mute, tilting their beer bottles back, swallowing.

Galena returned, looking from Ram to Denim. She chugged what was left of her warm brew, grabbing her friend by the elbow. "Sounds like I arrived in the nick of time. Let's dance. I need to burn energy."

Denim shot Ram her best brush-off smile, heading onto the dance floor, shouting over her shoulder, "Bye-bye. Good luck with someone else, *cher*."

Galena pulled her partner over to yell in her ear. "It won't hurt to hand satyr-boy a little rejection. He so rarely gets it."

When the DJ played TI's "Big Things Poppin'," Denim added bounce and extra hip to her routine.

Ram strode off with barely a peek over his shoulder.

She watched his mountainous shoulders dipping with each stride, the muscles in his tight ass flexing, his powerful legs carrying him away. He was one beautiful man even if he was a misogynistic horndog. The backroom. Really?

Hah!

Galena tapped Denim's arm, arching her brows.

"Just looking," Denim shot back over the heavy beat of the music.

Galena was right. Ram wasn't Steven. He didn't break bones. Worse. He broke hearts. *A broken heart never heals.* So why did he stir her emotions?

Chapter Five

Ram stuck a hand into his pocket while he glanced over his shoulder at the bewildering human. Her scent told him she'd definitely been aroused. In fact, he'd fed. Ingesting her sexual excitement was so overwhelming he almost jerked away.

She'd shut him down, though. Here he thought he'd been charming, hardly a crass comment passing over his lips.

The females he hooked up with were obliging Aeternals who weren't fragile. Satyr snack candy. He sure didn't want a human who thought she was tough because she was an Alliance agent who could handle a man with a few Muay Thai moves. An easily broken, sexy human. A mouthy human who wasn't so obliging.

Hmm. What a mouth.

It could be useful. Especially if it was wide open while he shoved his dick inside, pumping in and out, accompanied by a loud song with a heavy beat and her throaty moans.

Hell. What am I thinking?

No human females. Not even one with perfect lips, a hot body, and a sweet Louisiana drawl whose comebacks set him on his egotistical ass.

He had vowed he would never be with a *Homo sapiens.* He forgot the vow the moment he saw Denim Quinn across the room. Fortunately, he wouldn't see her again. *Ever.*

She was bumping and grinding on the dance floor, swooshing her arms high through the air in time to the music.

He chuckled. The human was wrong about one thing. His lines always worked. Before Denim. Of course, that might say something about the females he chose.

Yep. Obliging.

Wasn't that what he wanted? Easy females. No sass.

Ram slid into his old spot beside Tyr. A mellow Brak had obviously had a good time with What's-her-name and Amylyn. Normally Ram would have given the carnal demon some static over the swack action, but he wasn't interested. His thoughts were elsewhere.

The only horizontal refreshment he was interested in was with the human shaking her jean-clad butt in time to the music. And she was out-of-bounds.

Tyr glanced his way. "What's up, satyr? You look a little off your game."

"Just ran head-first into a brick wall." His D-chip interrupted his thoughts. *Hey, Kole. What's up? ... Where? ... Do we know who? ... Tyr and Brak. ... Only the warlock. ... Gotcha. We'll flash over to load up first.*

He disconnected and nudged Tyr. "Let's kick rocks. The commander wants us to meet and greet two demons who barely escaped from Earth in one piece. The female's injured."

"Where are we headed?"

"The portal outside Beltane Temple here in Covenkirk. They came through after a jaunt in New Orleans. The comm's sent the GPS."

"What about me?" Brak nursed his pricey Macallan.

"Naw. Kole just wants me and super warlock. Have another drink if you can afford it." Ram surveyed the dance floor. Denim was still working the kinks out of her delectable body.

He snatched Tyr's arm.

The warlock tossed back his Black Bush. "Kole

wants me to make you look good, satyr."

"I look so good now it's impossible to make me look better, but you can try. Let's stop by the stronghold. We'll change duds and arm up."

No way he was ruining his Saint Laurent shirt, Zegna pants, and Prada brogues. He had dressed for love, not fighting. Good thing he was ambidextrous when it came to fashion. He could swing any way necessary. BDU's, T-shirts, and shitkickers. Merino wool slacks, silk shirts, and fancy-ass loafers. Whatever got the job done.

"We're outta here, demon. We could be back. You never know. Keep the females hot and the drinks cold."

****

Ram and Tyr portaled near the Beltane Temple in Covenkirk, hoofing it to the entrance.

Two young demons waited for the Firebrands. The female slumped on the ground with her back against a white stone wall. She cradled her leg as blood trickled through her fingers. As if she were sleepy or about to pass out, her chin kept bobbing on her chest.

An equally young male was pacing and scrubbing hands through his dark, shoulder-length hair. Ram thought he might be muttering "Oh, shit" each time he made a turnabout.

Tyr stood over the female. "You okay? Do you need a healer?"

Her eyes popped wide at the warlock's size. His jeweled piercings didn't give off a friendly vibe. "Not right now. Maybe later."

His *freron* nodded while he scrutinized her companion, who stopped with the back and forth. "So, let's do names. I'm Tyr. This ugly guy with me is Ram. Your turn. Then the story from the beginning."

"I'm Roff, and my parents are going to kill me. Kill me. I can kiss my future goodbye. Adios. Sayonara."

Ram shrugged. "Gotta tell you, Roff. I'm not concerned about how your ass is in a sling one way or the other. I want to know what happened Earthside. Get me?"

"Well, Hannya and I … she's Hannya … we jacked my dad's portal jumper. Just to have a good time. Everybody's doing it. No biggie." He ran his fingers through his hair again. "They're just gonna kill me. I'll be on permanent lockdown."

"Once again, Roff. Not concerned one way or the other. Let's just say, I don't give a shit. Leave it at that. Tell us the particulars as to why Hannya's got a bullet in her leg. You worrying about your daddy removing your testicles or grounding you until your Awakening ceremony is making me yawn. I realize you may never have your big I'm-now-a-demon-stud party. Thus, you may never turn into a full-fledged Aeternal with a brain and all."

Roff's shoulders slumped as he let a groan escape from his mouth. "I am so screwed." He held up a hand. "I know. You don't care. Anyway, Hannya and I went to New Orleans, drank a few, danced a little, glad-handed our way along the streets, looking at all the weird humans until we decided it was time to get home. We headed to the portal…"

"Which portal?" asked Tyr.

When the young male demon gave Hannya the head tilt with the scrunched-up forehead, she managed the conversation. "Over by Jackson Square. It's in a garage off an alley."

Ram nodded. "And then?"

Roff picked up the chit-chat again. "We were still in the alley when we noticed three humans coming our way. We stopped what we were doing while we … uh … waited for them to leave."

Hannya gave him an eye roll before she twisted toward Ram. "We were making out. We thought they'd get the hint and leave, but they just kept coming. It's not like there was anywhere to go. The frickin' alley dead-ended where we were."

"Yeah. So, they're moving in on us, and I … uh … reluctantly stop what I'm doing to ask nicely, 'Can you give us a little privacy?' At which time, they draw out these big ass guns and point them at us. Holy shit. I pushed Hannya behind me while I grabbed for the jumper in my pocket."

"When did Hannya get shot?" Ram rested his palm on the hilt of his Scottish dirk.

"I was getting to that part. When I shoved her behind me to open the portal, I think they shot at me but missed. The bullet accidentally caught her. Anyway, we made a quick exit through the gateway and poofed back here."

Hannya shook blood off her hand and returned to cradling her leg. "The first thing we did was call the Firebrands. That was good, right?"

Tyr gave her a thumbs-up. "Abso-effing-lutely. You're certain the guys were human? Can you describe them?"

"Definitely Earthers. Two big guys. One with a tat on his neck. He wore camo topped off with a muscle shirt. That's why I could see the tat. Another had hair about my length but pulled back. He was stylin' with some swank jeans and a dark T-shirt. The shortest male was the leader, though. He had on a baseball cap. That's all I got a look at before we jumped through the portal."

"Why do you think Baseball Cap was the leader?" Ram cocked his head to the side.

"'Cause he was calling orders. The other guys kept looking at him, too. You know, like they were taking his lead. He was about five-ten or eleven. Not very big."

"How long ago did you cross back?" Tyr checked out the female's leg.

"Ew." Hannya slapped her hand back in place. "I hate blood."

"I can stop the flow for a bit, but you might need to see a healer." Tyr flicked his wrist.

Ram felt the air cool as he cast a spell.

Hannya fielded his question when Roff shrugged. "Thanks. Better. We got here about twenty minutes ago. I'm really tired. Is that normal with a bullet wound?"

Ram pulled his brows tight. "Not really. Did you drink a lot?"

"No. But ever since I was shot, I keep falling asleep."

"She does." Roff nodded.

Ram and Tyr locked eyes but shrugged. Being sleepy after a minor wound from a bullet, even a bloody one, was unusual.

"Tell me about the portal. When you exit the garage, is there much cover in that alley? In case I check things out." Ram thought he might have to soldier up.

"This one's all yours, Roff," said Hannya. "My lids were clamped tight."

"A big green dumpster is on the right side of the door coming out of the garage. Oil drums are on the other side. About five. All lined up in a row. No oil in them, though. I have a pretty good sniffer for a demon my age."

"Tyr, you stay here with the lovers. Call their parents. Hannya, check in with a healer even though it's a through-and-through. I'm gonna duck across to New

Orleans. It's highly unlikely their attackers are still there. Probably just bangers making their bones. Call when things are settled here."

Tyr arched a pierced brow. "You think that's a good idea?"

"Dude, I have nothing but good ideas."

What a lie. Hitting on the human female tonight had been a barking mad notion.

Ram hightailed it to the gateway. He tapped his D-chip.

****

The Whorl messed with his brains. What with the free-floating thing along with the stomach flips, he fought the urge to upchuck.

Leaping out of the portal in New Orleans, Ram fell into a crouch. All clear. He thudded across the garage to the door into the alley. Stepping through it, he was in the open. A bullet whizzed by his shoulder. Another.

Pop. Pop.

He dove to the right, sliding on trash as he took cover behind the dumpster.

WTF. The shooters are still here. How lucky can I get?

Having jumped from Scath with his dirks in a chest holder and two short tactical swords strapped to his back, he was underpowered for facing off against guns. But you dance with the female you bring to the party. Well, he didn't. At least not if a better offer came along.

With alley shit on his clothes after his slide behind the dumpster, he was happy he had ditched his silk shirt and Merino wool pants.

A deep-voiced male shouted an order. "Land a solid shot, assholes. Do not lose the mark. If this one dies or escapes, I'll shoot you myself. Orders are, we bring in a live one."

A live one?

Ram hoped they'd venture closer. If they did, he could whammy them as he did the hellhounds … if they didn't plant a bullet into his heart first. Depending on their firepower, they could shred it. Shredding could be bad. A repair to the heart required some material to remain intact. And it was his second favorite organ. His favorite being his dick.

Is that an organ? It should be.

They stayed put, firing at him.

Ping. Ping.

More shots to the dumpster.

He couldn't survive getting his head separated from his body, either. And fire. The last two seemed unlikely in this action.

He peeked around the dumpster.

Ping. Ping. Ping.

He pulled his head back.

He could run faster than the approaching humans could shoot. Maybe. It was possible he'd make it back to the portal without too many holes in his flesh. That move would get him no intel on these assholes, though.

He could speed behind them one by one, taking them out. Again, he might end up with a lot of pits in his skin. Or the whole shredded-heart thing.

Best bet was his satyr camouflage. He would cloak and sneak up behind the attackers. As a Firebrand with an extra boost of power, he was strong enough to hold the illusion for hours, unlike most of his kind who were good for maybe fifteen minutes tops. He could slit a throat before they could react. Trouble was, he wanted to snag one to question. Normally, he could hide another being with his personal body fog if they held still. Chances were good these assholes would put up a bit of fight.

Concealed in his satyr mist, Ram drifted out from behind the dumpster. He inched along the side of the old brick building.

The three males stalked toward the dumpster like gunslingers in an old Western, spread out, guns drawn, blasting bullets. Once they determined he wasn't there, they scratched their heads, exchanging bewildered glances.

"Holy shit," the human male with the deep voice yelled. He pointed toward a door on one side of the alley. "Run. This guy's like the Invisible Man."

The sprinter wore a shabby leather jacket, jeans, and black boots. Messy blond hair stuck out under the baseball cap. Navy blue. Orange brim.

As the male fired off a few wild shots, not knowing where to aim, he beat it toward the door, his buddies hot on his tail.

Ram dropped his illusion when his fucking D-chip signaled a call. *What do ya need, Magic Man? I was a little busy dodging bullets, about to pursue some guys.*

****

Tyr stepped out of the portal with a grin on his face. "What an awesome ride. I love to travel between realms."

"You're seriously screwed up. Through that door." After exiting the garage, Ram pointed. "Three of them. Armed and shooting."

Both warriors' boots thudded on the cobblestone as they pounded their way toward the door their targets had taken. Ram entered first, turning left in the cavernous warehouse with concrete floors and pillars. It was empty. He held up a hand to listen, his satyr hearing acute. "Out that way."

They thundered toward the exit. That door emptied into another alley.

Tyr caught sight of a guy heading into another side door. "There."

"Yep. That's them. I recognize the baseball cap."

Thud. Thud. Thud.

They pulled up short inside the next building. The room was dark. Ram eyed a big screen. Vin Diesel's voice boomed across the movie theater.

Bigger than life, right on the screen was one of Ram's heroes. A ridiculously small crowd slouched in seats while they watched Buster in *Fast and Furious.* This was the best part of the flick. His bald idol spouted a good motto to live by. "It don't matter if you win by an inch or a mile. Winning's winning."

Ram searched the rest of the movie house. Spotting the three miscreants hauling ass along the aisle, the satyr Firebrand jumped onto the closest seat back. He used the next row and the next as steppingstones to the center aisle.

Good thing the place was nearly vacant. In Ram's estimation, too few people went to good movies these days.

Adrenaline pumped through the satyr. He loved a good fight.

Hell, almost as much as he loved a good… Nah. Not quite that much.

He barreled ahead just as the targets sprinted out the lobby door onto the street.

He and the warlock raced after them. The New Orleans boulevard was crowded. Jam packed for the season.

Shouldn't these humans be in bed?

Any other time, Ram would have been happy to join a celebration, preferably with a curvy female on his arm, a nymph with a willing mouth and two big assets.

He searched for the targets since he was itching

for some blade-on-blade, fist-on-fist action. Firing off a gun never excited him. Anyone could do that. So, he'd have to disarm them first. Not much of a challenge.

"There." Tyr pointed to the right, pushing revelers out of his way.

"Hey," shouted some human in the crowd. "Watch it." When he turned around, Tyr growled at him. The guy swallowed his next words before they departed from his lips.

The warlock was an intimidating picture. All decked out in black leathers. At least, the coat hid his weapons. Likely his sickle-sword was stashed there since he didn't go anywhere without the gift from his father. Nothing said loving like an ancient Assyrian sword from Daddy.

Ram unfortunately wore his arms in full view. A couple Scottish dirks stuck in a chest holster and two short swords strapped to his back. With all the other costumed Mardi Gras drunks, maybe he fit in. Of course, his and Tyr's get-ups were less about "let's party" and more about "let's maim and kill."

A baseball cap bobbed in the crowd, the male surrounded by party-goers. "There," shouted the satyr.

"If I can get a steady fix on one of them, I can cast a spell to hold him in place," Tyr yelled over the noise.

They pounded forward, shoving through the crowd, ignoring angry voices, but eventually they lost sight of the three males.

They hunted the streets, popping in and out of music venues, bars, and other joints for a half hour with no success.

Tyr halted. "Let's cut and run."

Ram snarled, his upper lip twisting.

Bummer.

He rested his palm on a dirk's hilt. "I have a bad feeling about these guys. They should have been long gone if their attack on Hannya and Rolf was a random crime. I think they were waiting for somebody to arrive. As if they knew an Aeternal might pop out of the garage."

Chapter Six

His favorite nymph was laid out on a bed with her blonde hair loose, haloing her. Gone were the Heidi braids. No shirt or bra blocked his view of her porn-star breasts. With her nipples pink and swollen, ready for his lips, she locked her long legs around Nico's thighs. He was fucking to a nice rhythm, something like G-Easy's "No Limit." When shit was getting good...

Fingers snapped in front of his face. "Are you listening to me, Abello?" Sabine, his daydream inspiration, pulled her brows tight over her translucent green eyes. Unfortunately, she was clothed. In his revelry she was naked, eager to satisfy his needs. In real life, she wasn't likely to do a striptease for him. She was a thorn in his side.

On a good day.

And not a rose with pretty little thorns. No. She was a honey locust tree with gigantic, dangerous sharp weapons. Sabine was everything he wanted and didn't want in a woman. She had the body and face of his best fantasy fucks. A plus. The woman also had brains and physical strength, but he wanted to be the thinker and protector in a relationship.

Yeah. Call me a throwback. I want my little woman to need me, to meet me at the door in nothing but an apron and after a proper horizontal greeting to put dinner on the table. If a burglar breaks into the house, I want to shove her behind me while I handle the situation.

He doubted Sabine could cook, and she wasn't likely to let him handle the burglar alone.

Nico wrapped a palm around the white mug in front of him at the coffee shop in Covenkirk, the strong-brewed aroma floating to his nose while his partner talked on and on about the mission. Either the caffeine or the fantasy was creating a bulge in his pants.

He'd never heard of caffeine as an aphrodisiac. That left the prickly nymph.

Too bad.

"You haven't listened to a word I've said."

He fixed on her luscious lips, picturing them plump from his kisses. "I hang on your every syllable." He sipped his black coffee. "There's a bunch of ylves along with an assortment of Aeternal breeds meeting regularly to talk about slipping onto Earth to do damage. We need to stop them."

"No."

"I'm pretty sure that's what you said."

"I said we should watch them, find out who their leader is, and discover their plans. When it's time to stop them, we'll call in more Firebrands as backup."

"Whatever. In the meantime, you're my nanny while I marinate in the Scath stew."

A while back, Sabine and Tyr showed up in Nico's office at Alliance headquarters in Chicago. He'd had a respectable job as Agent Abello, a man in charge of a team investigating Skyler Maxwell's dive off an L platform, a blackmailing blogger group, and the death of their lead tech. Natch, he'd balked at being shuffled off to Scath, an order since the powers-that-be discovered he was a mage descendant of the Blood Coven. The blonde nymph, who took orders seriously, had her warlock partner knock Nico out with a spell before they schlepped him to their realm.

Sabine took on the job as his caretaker. So he didn't whack out from boredom, he used a little constructive blackmail. He'd either tag along with the Scion Firebrands or he'd do a disappearing act. His demand was met.

In the meantime, Nico was showing no signs of his mage gifts. He was without friends, away from a job he loved, no longer a hot-shot Alliance agent. Rather, he was a pussy who had to be protected from the big-bad, relegated to being ordered around by Superwoman Barbie who wouldn't give him the time of day. The last part might have been a tad unfair. The nymph hadn't asked for the babysitting duty. But here they were. He was not pissed much.

Yeah. He was.

Nico combed fingers through his hair, brushing back an unruly lock. "Okay. I'll focus. Run the road map by me again."

"Arisen Dawn was once a group called the Isolationists. Mostly ylves. Now, we have reason to believe they have new leadership. They're spouting nationalistic bullshit about taking their rightful place on Earth. The whole domination luggage. Aeternals are stronger, braver. We deserve to lead. Yada. Fucking. Yada. Other breeds are joining them. Incubi, succubi, vamps, shifters, djinn, berserkers, satyrs, nymphs, and demons are rallying to the cause. We need to investigate. But we can't go off half-cocked."

"Speaking of 'half-cocked,' when are we going to fuck?" A little action between the sheets would be a worthy diversion from his current woe-me's.

"Smooth. How could I pass up such an offer?"

"What would get you into a horizontal position?"

"A sniper's rifle and my eye on a target. Focus!"

"Maybe if we hooked up once, sweetness, I could concentrate better."

"Look, cuddles, I don't mix business and pleasure."

Sabine was a huge detour from the job. How long since he'd had sex with someone other than his hand?

Too long, obviously. Still, he didn't want an obsession with the nymph to become a boulder around his neck. He needed his freedom. And he sure didn't need a fucking hashtag babysitter. Even one who rocked a sizzling body, big jugs, and dynamite curves.

Being penned up at the Covenkirk stronghold was bad for his libido. *Hell.* The other Blood Coven descendants lived there on his floor with their mates. Happy as pigs in slop, as his farmer granddad would have said. Braelyn with Rein. Skyler with Kole. Margo with Chay.

Nico was with nobody but his lotioned palm.

He needed to get his head in the game and out of his pants. This woman, regardless of how hot she was, would not squeeze between him and the assignment.

He brushed back the same errant strand of hair which relentlessly dropped across his forehead. "More's the pity. Where are we off to?"

See? I can be all business.

"One of Jarek's Firebrands … Jarek's the commander in the Encampment region … tracked an Isolationist-turned-Arisen-Dawn guy to a set of warehouses. He staked the area out for a while, but it stayed pretty quiet, according to his report. Recently, he noted an uptick in activity. A few trucks arrived. Military types. Unloading stuff. Leaving. A few Arisen Dawn members took up residence. Since Jarek is spread thin, we're in the watch rotation."

He tossed back his coffee, jerking out of the chair. "Let's go. One thing, sweetness. If we run into a problem where you feel compelled to step in front of me like a bullet-proof shield, think twice. You do, I'll paddle your tempting ass until you can't sit. Read me?"

"I read you, cuddles. I'll do my job as ordered. If it means saving your ugly ass, I'll do it."

"You think my ass is ugly?" He chuckled. "I doubt it. I've caught you looking at it. Course, you've never seen it in the flesh. Just stay out of my way. Fair warning."

Sabine ignored his words, set her coffee on the table, and rose. "Come on, hero. We're out of here."

****

"Bounty, where the hell are they?" Kole tamped the sparks shooting from his fingers. He didn't like waiting.

"They're probably dragging their asses because I told them how unpleasant you are today, Commander Bossy. None of the Firebrands are eager to do a face-to-face. Besides, they keep their distance during Mardi Gras since you're pissed all season."

His secretary, or executive assistant as she liked to be called, ambled to his doorway on long shapely legs, leaning against the jamb, hand on hip and one ankle crossed over the other. The generous-breasted, narrow-hipped vampire eyed Kole, locking her lips as if she fought to keep another insult from sliding across them.

Years ago, her looks had gotten her through the door for an interview with the commander, but her brains kept her here. That and the fact she could take out the meanest, scariest, deadliest fighters in the realms. So went the rumor anyway. None of his Firebrands had actually gone toe-to-toe with her. Losing to a secretary, even one who called herself an executive assistant and hadn't trained to be a warrior, would be too embarrassing.

He mumbled under his breath, "Smartass. I'm surrounded by smartasses." She was right, though. The New Orleans celebration drew young Aeternals to Earth. Feeding. Fucking. Frolicking. Never as bad as this season. And it was his job to drag them home before they did too much damage.

"I can hear you." She narrowed her smoky eyes and scrunched her pouty lips. "By the by, I need the payroll authorized for overtime in New Orleans. You have to do it on the funny thing collecting dust. It's called a computer."

"Just do it for me like always. Damn it."

"My name's not 'damn it.'" Bounty flipped her blonde hair over her shoulder as she swung around.

Old joke.

Kole glanced at his drudgery, listening to her high heels tap on the floor while she headed back to her desk.

He shuffled through a stack of shit. "Where the hell is the file on New Orleans?"

"Are you talking to me?"

"Who else would I be yelling at?"

"It's on your desk where I set it this morning. You've probably covered it with a bunch of useless crap by now. I also put a digital copy in your documents folder. I cleverly named it 'New Orleans.' Your documents folder is in your computer, by the way. I dare you to find it."

When a file slipped off the edge of his desk, he leaned over to pick it up, looking at the tab. "Got it. Thanks so much."

"My aim in life is to please you. Now stop bothering me. I've got shit to do. My asshole boss gives me too much work."

Smartass crossed his mind again, but he kept it to himself. Thorn lumbered up to his door.

The shifter stopped. At six-four he was shorter than Kole but fierce in a one-on-one fight. As with all Scion Firebrands, he'd beefed up significantly once he accepted the Phoenix brand's call to duty.

Thorn's shoulder-length brown hair was still wet.

Obviously, he was fresh from a shower. Claw marks marred his jaw, an injury from before his Awakening. His bright golden irises with black pupils were common enough for wolf shifters, but deadly cold on the Firebrand. All in all, the vibe screamed *don't fuck with me.*

"Did I disturb your workout?" Kole asked. Not that he gave a shit. When he wanted a meeting, it happened.

"No. I'd finished. I washed off, though. Figured I'd smell better."

"Thanks. Hope you dried off well. Nothing worse than the odor of wet dog."

Thorn grinned, shaking his hair like a soaked canine, sending water droplets flying. Probably just to irritate Kole. Everything got under his skin today. An irritated animus demon who could call hellfire was not good.

Galena popped in behind Thorn. "Hey, Wolfy. Getchur hunking ass outta the doorway." She shoved him aside.

"I thought you liked my ass."

"Love it." She pinched a glute. "Tight. Perfect."

"Thanks. It's all those cheek crunches." The shifter selected a wall to lean against, his bulky arms crossing over his chest. Well-worn cowboy boots fitted out his feet. No shitkickers for Thorn. Rumor said he owned a Western hat but saved it for when he rode horses at his recently purchased Montana ranch. Kole heard the place was as big as a small country.

Throwing herself into a chair, Galena propped combat boots on her boss's desk. With her endless legs clad in ripped jeans and her belly-revealing muscle shirt, she was a great-looking female. And a fierce fighter. She made big males scream aunt. After which, she broke their arms for grins and giggles.

"Who we waiting for?" she asked.

Kole stacked papers off to the side of his desk. "Ram. Hey, Bounty…"

"The satyr will be stomping into your office in a sec. He just closed the locker room door."

Ram's deep voice filtered in from Bounty's office. "Gorgeous. You look scrumptious as always."

"I know. It makes you hard, doesn't it? You'll have to do me some other day. Commander Cranky awaits."

Ram entered laughing but wiped the cheer off his face when he confronted Kole's frown.

"Fantastic! You have time to flirt with my secretary."

"Executive assistant," yelled Bounty.

Ram shrugged before he aided Thorn in keeping the wall upright.

"We've got problems. If we don't solve them soon, our nuts will be in a grinder." Kole's gaze flipped to Galena. "You know what I mean."

"No balls here, but I feel your pain, Comm."

"Glad to hear it. You and Thorn fill us in on New Orleans. It's looking like a worse shitstorm than usual."

Galena bobbed her head. "Wolfy and his partner Rod were first on the scene the other night. Bloody mess. Thorn's dumbass boots got splattered with the shit." She paused to watch the shifter polish the toe of one on his pant leg. "A dead incubus looked as if two wildings used him for a wishbone." She waved a hand at Thorn to carry on the dialogue.

"Word. The dead male got off a panic call to his home while he was being attacked. He didn't conversate much before his phone died. It was found at the scene, by the way, smashed to perdition. Dad called Firebrand central. Then the action got passed to Rod and me. Galena's right. Somebody did a good slasher routine on him after a bullet to the brain. We took photos. Director Alarik sent his brainiacs to examine the locale. After which, the cleaners got busy. We'll know more when we get the lab report."

"Ram, you're up. Talk." Kole slammed his elbows onto his desk.

"Tyr and I had a fun time. A female demon, Hannya, was injured but not badly. She and her boneheaded breed lover traipsed into New Orleans for a little fun, having stolen the parental jumper. On the return trip, they were pounced on by three human males."

"Humans for sure?" Thorn fiddled with his bolo tie.

"Yeah. After grilling bonehead and date, I rode through the Whorl. On the other end, the Earthers were waiting, guns firing. When I cloaked, they scurried away like rats. Tyr joined me for the after-chase."

"So they're locked in the Cubes?" Galena snorted, probably having heard the story.

Ram smirked. "No, but you see, they ran into a movie theatre. Since my favorite flick was on the big screen, Tyr and I got some buttered popcorn and flopped into seats to watch the ending. What the fuck, Galena. Fire me. We lost them on the crowded streets. The city's crazy during Mardi Gras."

"Any way to ID them?" asked Thorn.

"I'd recognize the male who's their leader. An oddity. They could've been waiting for us. Nutty thought. If they were, we and the young demons were not random vics. BTW, anytime we go Earthside during the Mardi Gras this year, we need to carry. I was caught with my pants around my ankles. Normally, I don't mind being in that situation, but I want more for the effort than a bullet in my ass."

Kole lifted his landline when it rang. He didn't bother with a hello. He just listened while someone else talked. When he disconnected, he leaned forward on his elbows. "You three, check with Lacasta to see what's what in the morgue. Interesting."

Ram glanced at Thorn. He cocked a brow. "Huh?"

"I'd share, but I want your take on her news first."

Ram scrubbed a palm across his jaw. "Is it a coincidence we have a dead incubus, two demons attacked, and humans waiting at a portal? I mean, things usually get psycho in the Big Easy during party season, too much drinking, pheromones colliding. I guess I'm a suspicious guy."

Galena kicked her boots off the desk. "Not enough intel yet to say if the incidents are connected or not. In the meantime, parents need to lock down their portal jumpers."

"That's my read," said Kole.

"Now what, Comm?" asked Thorn.

Kole laced his fingers on the top of his head. "As of now, the three of you work this together. Ram, you run point. Go hear Lacasta and stay tight on fun times in New Orleans."

"What about Tyr?" asked Ram.

"I'm lending him to Nace. His Northern Stronghold is running ragged chasing small cells of dealers selling nasty shit. He's also keeping up with the day-to-day while we're otherwise occupied. Speaking of which. Anyone seen Dax? I want him riding shotgun with the warlock."

Heads shook.

"Bounty," yelled Kole. "What else is popping?"

"Nico and Sabine are on duty at an Arisen Dawn warehouse today."

Kole nodded. "Yeah. No proof yet, but this new organization raises my hackles. We're gonna keep an eye on them. By the way, where's Dax?"

"Do I look like I know everything about everybody?" She paused in the doorway, arms crossed.

Kole glanced at Bounty, whose response was more snarly than usual. Then he shooed her out with a wave.

"I got an idea." Galena rose from her chair to balance on her long legs. "Denim, my New Orleans human partner during Mardi Gras, happens to be visiting me. How about if she tags along? She can act as our Alliance liaison. She was with me when the incubus's body was found."

Ram pushed away from the wall. "No."

"Stuff it, satyr. You wanted to get tight with her last night. I didn't see you so picky then." Galena went nose-to-nose with Ram.

"A quick hump in a backroom at the Shed is one thing. Working with a human is another. They're breakable."

Thorn ignored Ram's glare. "We could use an Alliance liaison to work Earthside."

Galena shook a finger in Ram's face. "Your biases are showing, satyr. It's her time off. Should be her choice." Galena did an about-face. "What's your input, Comm?"

"Thanks for including me," said Kole. "I don't give fucking input. I give fucking orders. But if it's her wish, I'll get her re-assigned to us for the time being." He fixed his fiery gaze on Ram. "Before you object to my call, think twice. Now you kids go yak somewhere else. I've got work to do. Keep safe. Stay in my good graces."

"Yeah. My pleasure." Ram's fist powered through the wall before he exited.

Kole chuckled. "Hey, Bounty. The satyr put a hole in the wall. Call the sheetrockers."

Hands on hips, Bounty stormed into his office. "I've got them on speed dial. Whaddya do to piss him off?"

"Why am I blamed even when I didn't do shit?"

She glanced at the big hole, frowning. "Yeah, whatever shit you didn't do caused him to box with the wall."

Chapter Seven

Sabine crouched behind Nico in the woods beyond the warehouses. The facility was a few old brick buildings surrounded by high barb-wired fencing. The only access was one gate.

While he used the binoculars to glue his sight on the entrance, she stared at his beefy biceps and broad back where firm muscles stretched a black T-shirt. A male like him should be forced to cover up with a jacket. The thick thighs and tight ass shown off in his cargos weren't bad scenery either.

What's wrong with me?

Delicious rock-solid males strutted nude in front of her all the time. After all, the Firebrands shared a locker room. No one, including herself, was shy about baring their private bits. Yet she never drooled over her *frerons*. Why was this asshole different?

Sabine sighed.

Nico snapped narrowed eyes in her direction. "Bored?"

No. I like ogling your hard, drool-worthy body, imagining it on top of me.

"Yes."

He returned his glasses to their position, twisting his attention back to the warehouse. "Here comes action. Looks like an M-35 cargo truck."

A grey vehicle pulled up to the gate. It stopped. An electronic device must have opened the gate, letting the truck roll through.

She and Nico observed a flurry of activity. Three males exited the main building to greet the newcomers who stepped out of the truck. All of them unloaded crates of stuff.

"Food," said Nico, still holding onto the binoculars.

"Yeah. Canned goods and other supplies from Aerilon. I recognize the markings."

Sabine didn't need field glasses to read the print on the boxes. Her nymph eyesight, stronger once she joined the Scion Firebrands, was more than enough.

Once the vehicle was empty, the driver and passenger slid back into their seats and pulled out, returning by the same road they had driven in on.

Nico and Sabine continued to observe for some time. The three males returned to their building. No activity. All was quiet again.

"Raise your hand if you want to get up close and personal." Nico held his arm high, like a schoolboy.

"Hell no," Sabine hissed, grabbing for his shoulder. She missed.

The idiot human broke free, racing from tree to tree until he neared the open field. He glanced around, dropping to his belly. To get to the chain-link fence surrounding the warehouses, he crawled. Elbow. Elbow. Pull. Repeat.

Sabine muttered curses but followed the lunatic. She was going to strangle him when they got out of here.

Stick a knife in his belly. A big knife. Watch the life ooze out of his eyes. Send him to the Evermore with one deep slice. Let whoever runs things there deal with him. Yeah. Good luck with that.

Nico dragged himself along the fence line until he reached the spot with fewest windows facing his location. He stood, toed into and climbed the chain links until he reached the barbed wire strung across the top.

He sprang over the top and landed softly on the other side, running for the protection of the building and keeping his back against the wall, sidling along it.

Sabine had no choice but to climb the fence to join him, imitating his moves.

A deep wound would lay him out, causing the most pain.

He flipped his gaze to her, raising his brows and nodding forward. She shook her head so hard her brains rattled, wisps of blonde hair falling loose from her braids. A lot of good that did. He flattened out and slid around the corner, back against the bricks, heading for the door. Once there, he opened it, fell into a fighting crouch, and crept in when no one was in sight. She was right behind him, frowning all the way while thinking of new ways to maim him when they got out of this.

The main building was huge and sectioned off inside. Hundreds of empty cots stretched out in one area. Dining tables, a refrigerator, stove, and all the makings of a kitchen kitted out another open space.

Stacked crates of food and other supplies were piled high in another section. Arisen Dawn was well stocked.

Ahead were stairs leading to a balcony and a door. A light shone out of an office through a large window. Nico signaled he was moving closer.

Having accepted his idiocy as normal behavior, Sabine tapped her ear.

"What?" he mouthed.

"Voices," she mimed.

Step-by-step he climbed the stairs, creeping closer. He made a good warrior, not a sound from his boots to alert the enemy. When he reached the top, he slid along the wall, out of sight of the window. He signaled Sabine.

Totally into the mission now, she followed up the steps, putting herself between Nico and the door into the office. The move earned her a big scowl, but she shrugged, staying in place. Let him try to muscle her out of the way.

Holding her hand high while using her nymph hearing, she listened. She raised four fingers. He nodded. When she stretched an arm across his chest to hold him back, his glare turned feral. Ignoring him, she placed herself directly in front of the door and kicked it open.

As she did, Nico elbowed her out of the way as he launched himself between her and the four males inside. He charged forward.

"Damn you." She tore after him.

When the males came to their senses, their weapons whipped out.

Sabine left her Arkansas toothpick holstered but drew the double-bladed staff from her back to take on two Arisen Dawn members. She tapped one tip to the floor while she smiled. "Come on, motherfuckers."

When she spared a fleeting glance at Nico, he snatched a tomahawk from his belt with one hand and slid a Buck combat knife out of his triple holster with the other. She admired his fighting form along with his flexing muscles as he attacked.

Sabine made quick work of one opponent who was foolish enough to charge her armed only with a switchblade. She spun. On the turn, she drove her staff blade into his heart. Kicking his body aside, she motioned the other male forward. "Come on. Don't make me wait. I got a hair appointment."

Her challenger was a satyr whose neon green eyes could have meant he was going to feed from her, but since she wasn't aroused, she went with option two. He was on some drug which made him bat-shit crazy. Spinning again, she kicked forward. The tip of her blade followed her foot, nicking her opponent's shoulder.

"Shit. You're gonna pay," the druggie roared.

"Who's gonna make me? Not you. You fight like a sissy. My grandmam could take you down."

Because of her taunts, he swiped wildly at her, which was what she counted on. A hot-headed, mind-fucked satyr was as good as dead. She gracefully danced away from each move, bobbing, spinning, watching for an opening. Then it came.

The satyr lunged with his right hand thrust forward, leaving his other side completely open. That was all a trained Firebrand such as Sabine needed. She sent her spear into his side, withdrew it, and slammed home into his heart before he even realized he was in trouble.

Catching a breath, she rested her hands on her knees while she glanced around for Nico. One Arisen Dawn male was dead at his feet, his head nearly chopped off with the tomahawk. Now the human was dancing with another Aeternal.

"He's an incubus. Don't let him touch you," yelled Sabine.

"Thanks, sweetness. The only one touching me will be you."

She snorted.

"Did you hear, incu-bastard? No stroking me. The nymph wants the pleasure herself."

Nico was gorgeous in battle mode. He was light on his feet. Despite the chatter, he was fully focused on the other male. His muscles rippled with power as he shifted from one foot to the other.

The incubus landed a lucky cut with a knife.

"Fuck. Enough of this shit. I have a lady to impress." He raised his tomahawk, took aim, and let go. It sailed straight through the air with a *whoosh*.

The stunned incubus watched as it embedded in his chest, his look wide in disbelief just before he toppled.

Nico marched to him. He put a foot on his abdomen, withdrawing his weapon from the Arisen Dawn male and wiping the Tomahawk's blade on the guy's shirt.

"It's important to keep the edge clean." Nico twisted toward Sabine. "I see you made fast work of the other two. Aren't you glad we dropped in?"

Sabine shook her head to clear away the thoughts of how spectacular Nico looked with his dark boyish hair, five-o'clock shadow, sultry eyes outlined with thick lashes, topped with black brows. *Wait.* She squeezed her lips together, remembering how they got inside this building to begin with. "You're a fucking idiot. We never should have come into the warehouse or attacked. It was dangerous, immature, downright crazy."

"Maybe, but look at all this great shit." Nico was standing over the desk, shuffling maps and papers. "This is a treasure trove of info. Give Kole a buzz."

"I can't work with you. You take unnecessary risks. You don't follow orders. I won't have a mission compromised. Plus, it was my job to keep you safe. You compromised that, too." She paused, touching her wrist to initiate a call.

"Yeah? Did you think I might not want you keeping me safe? Maybe I think it's my job to keep you safe." He was shouting now.

She sputtered. Nobody shouted at her. Of all the arrogance. "Your job to what?" Her attention strayed from the human. *Send at least four backups. We have to clear an Arisen Dawn compound.*

Nico ran fingers through his hair. "I want off this goddamn merry-go-round. I'm heading Earthside."

She grabbed his arm. His attempt to shake loose was useless. She was stronger. "You can't."

"Sweetness, I want another handler. One not quite so committed to the job of keeping me safe. I won't have a woman throwing herself in front of me."

A woman? Did he really just play the gender card?

He didn't respect her as a warrior. *Okay.* That hurt. When an unbearable pain shot through her heart, she hauled back an arm and slapped Nico. "Of all the misogynistic assholes, you win the prize. I can take care of your request."

He wiggled his jaw. "Good."

"Great."

"We agree."

"Finally." If Sabine wanted free of the bastard, why did she feel so sad?

****

Director Alarik of the Ministry of Well Being pushed back his chair, unfolded from his seat, and cleared his throat as he gripped the lapels of his black suit jacket. He glanced around the table at the best Aeternals he could gather for this task.

His half-sister Indigo was beside him where he could keep an eye on her. His Firebrand son Rein sat on the other side of her with Braelyn next to him. His ministry's department heads filled the other chairs.

"Thank you for coming. First, a reminder. Keep using the cover story designed for our investigations. We are writing a new history. Ostensibly, it is a genealogy of two species and our connections. Humans and Aeternals. Such will be our narrative as we search for descendants of the Blood Coven."

Indigo popped her gum as she raised her hand. "I need a potty break. May I be excused?"

Alarik was the offspring of the rapist and ex-Firebrand Voxel, an incubus. His older half-sister Indigo was a full-blooded witch, the product of the legitimate mating between their mother Adriana and the warlock Tor. Despite his less than honorable birth, she'd raised him, Tor and Adriana dead. She fed him, clothed him, and trained him as a warlock. She was his mother. She was quirky, sometimes wild, but her heart was kind and her love for him fierce.

"Yes. Leave now, dear."

"Start without me, brother. I'll use a spell to listen in. Of course, I'll probably miss out when I flush the toilet."

"This room is warded, Indigo. You won't be able to hear us."

"Oh. Pish-posh. That's so easy to get around."

Alarik bent forward, picked up a pen, and jotted a note to call his warding experts to see if Indigo was right. If she was, they would need to create a more secure spell.

He glanced at Rein, who tilted his head to the side. "Auntie may be ... flighty ... but she is rarely wrong."

Alarik nodded and continued speaking to the assembled group. "My son represents the Scion Firebrands."

The realm's warriors were an essential component in the drive to find descendants of Blood Coven mages before Cerberus did. They were also necessary to clean up the previous mess left after the megalomaniac kidnapped and brought human candidates to Scath.

His son Rein, a powerful vampire-warlock-incubus mix, skated the edge of the bludfrenzy before the Phoenix called him to the Firebrands and before he found his mate. He still radiated danger, enough to make the participants sit up and take notice when he spoke. "As you remember, Cerberus's flunkies, Silas and Aisen, kidnapped certain humans, bringing them to Scath. We shut down their operation, but they'd already sold off the Earthers who didn't prove to be Blood Coven descendants. Jarek's command is searching for these slaves. Though his warriors have already rescued quite a few, more are out there. Cleatra's been working with his Southern Stronghold on the search."

The tawny-skinned witch with mystical lavender-gray eyes gestured in the air as if she were waving away a cloud of vapor. "I'll keep scrying."

Rein scooted back in his chair, cocking an ankle over a knee. "I'm based at Kole's Eastern Stronghold in Covenkirk. Our assignment is different. My father's healers find Earthers with witch or warlock DNA markers. Hopefully, before Cerberus does. If they do, we accompany the healers to obtain a blood sample from the humans so it can be tested. If the test proves they are from one of the Blood Coven lines, our job is to bring them to safety. At this time, we have secured four. One we know of is out in the cold."

"Four safe and one in the wind?" Echo, Alarik's chief historian, posed the question. "I thought we found only two."

"Things change."

"What about this Cerberus?" asked Echo.

"Cadmon's assigned my stronghold to hunt for the ass ... er ... individual," said Rein.

"Any progress on finding him?" asked the chief historian. "Do we know if he has any Blood Coven descendants?"

"Nope to both."

"Too bad. I might as well bring you up to date on my department's role in the search for descendants." Echo, a pride demon, rose, adjusting the folds of her robe. "We are plodding through genealogies of

Aeternals. As part of the cover story, of course. Thanks to the records already archived at this ministry and the ones coming in from families who responded to our call for help, we are progressing. Slow work, though. Some Aeternals have painstakingly over the centuries kept records of humans in their bloodlines. I laud their endeavors. Whenever Earthers in their family trees have witch or warlock ancestry, I give their names to the healers responsible for getting their blood samples to test. To the best of my knowledge, none has proved to be a Blood Coven descendant."

Giving her brother a thumbs-up, Indigo breezed back into the room. "Just in time for the juicy stuff, I see." She took her seat, punching Rein on the shoulder.

Echo's lips formed a tight, disapproving smile as she continued. "Sad to report, those few families who are related to the original coven of thirteen maintained sparse genealogy records. Not one human noted in their trees. Which brings me to another discovery." She looked at Alarik for permission to reveal this information.

He nodded.

"Bring it on." Indigo blew a large bubble. When it burst, it left gum on her lower lip. She took the wad out of her mouth and dabbed it to get the dregs. "I hate it when that happens. Don't you?"

Wrinkling her forehead, Echo shifted her gaze from Indigo to scan the room as if she prepared to drop a big bomb. "Allias ... you might all know him ... is my most relentless researcher. He found the obscure reference to *Custodes Templii*, a secret society in the late 1800s and early 1900s. Then they disappeared. Here's the thing. They may have existed much earlier, and they may have kept genealogy records on Blood Coven descendants. Braelyn, I understand you've pursued this avenue."

Rein's mate flipped through the pages in her notebook. "I've confirmed the existence of the group, and it might still be active. The info came from a possible Blood Coven descendant I've mentioned before. Miller is currently on the run. Rein and I met up with him in a restaurant, but he gave my mate the slip."

She returned Rein's glare with a smile. "Of course, the guy was very slippery, being ex British Special Forces and all. My father's tabloid, *Strange But True*, is still offering a reward to anyone who can prove witch or warlock ancestry. No believable takers since Miller Nash, but thanks to Alliance agents we continue to monitor the phones. I wish the paper could do more."

"Indigo? Anything from the river?" Alarik asked.

Of all Aeternals, his sister was the only one who could read the River Am. The trips to its banks showed on her face, though. Creases jutted from the corners of her puffy, weary eyes. She wasn't getting enough rest. He hated forcing her to return to the river time and again, but the knowledge gleaned there was vital to Aeternals. Alarik hoped it was not too much to ask.

"Miller Nash is the key to the lock. The missing piece of the puzzle. The ring which decodes the secret message. The combination to the vault. The…"

"That's good, Indigo, dear. We get the idea," Alarik interrupted when she got too excitable.

"To summarize, he's *muy* important, playing a role in many potential futures." Her hand came up to tug on the dark curls hanging about her face.

Alarik clasped onto her fingers before she yanked out strands of hair. "Thank you. Your task is troubling but vital."

"Wait, bro. There are more beans in the enchilada."

"What, dear?"

"The River Am is changing."

Attention flipped toward Indigo. Despite her odd ways, her power was without equal among witches and warlocks.

"It is always changing, but I suppose you refer to something more propitious." The warlock Eliphias was Alarik's chief scientist. "Is it altering course? Is it deeper? Is it wider? Be specific. I'm a scientist, not a poet."

"Oh. Pish-posh. That's the word of the day. It means I've got it handled." She returned to twirling a strand of hair around her finger while she gazed out the window. "One more thing, Rein, tell Margo to increase the beds in the barracks during the rehab. She should have two spaces, each with fifty beds. Th-th-th-that's all, folks."

Rein's brows tightened as he stared at his aunt. "What rehab? We're not remodeling the stronghold."

His aunt grinned. "You will be."

Alarik continued around the table, knowing when to give up. "What about you, Eliphias?"

The warlock chief science advisor rose, facing the entire group. "My people perfected the BCA Variant Test. Simply put, once the healers bring in a blood sample from a candidate, the test detects if the human has a Blood Coven ancestor. The hang-up continues to be the initial search of Earth medical records for those with ancient mage DNA. The process is slow and hit-or-miss. My department still has not found a faster way to identify these humans. We're stymied. We haven't been able to create a spell which draws them to us. We have searched for a plant or talisman only descendants might react to. No luck. I hope this *Custodes Templii* group works out. Before you ask, Indigo, we tried Karmas Root as you suggested. When one of my researchers broke out in hives, we dropped the investigation."

"I bet he got a nice high, though. Or so I've heard." Indigo's lips curled into a smile as her head bobbed a few times.

"He was in too much pain to notice. Anyway, we are still working countless hours and will not give up."

Alarik leaned back in his seat, not cheered by the progress of the group, but these get-togethers to share information were necessary. "Right now, our most promising lead, aside from the laborious task of searching hospitals, labs, and doctor's records for humans with witch and warlock DNA markers, is to find *Custodes Templii* so we may access their records. If they exist and if they have genealogies. Thanks all."

Chapter Eight

Ram frowned as Galena rushed in arm-in-arm with Denim.

"She agreed to join us." The Amazon gave him a suck-it-up grin. "Hey, Thorn."

The shifter nodded.

"I'm a damn good agent, Ram. You won't be sorry."

He *hmphed* as he opened the door into the morgue, slamming it against the wall hard enough to dent sheetrock. "Hey, Doc. We hear you have news."

The autopsy lab was all shiny steel, high tech monitors, wicked probes, and sharp instruments. Four bodies were lined up on steel tables in the sterile, cold room. Must be the refrigerated corpse drawers acting like air conditioning.

A female wearing a white lab coat was leaning over one corpse. "I'm not a doctor. Just a witch who is the director's medical examiner. You may call me Lacasta." She moved to stand near the subject they came to see.

"Lacasta." Ram winked. A little harmless flirting usually helped get more information.

"I do have news. Remarkably interesting results." She drew back the sheet covering the incubus, revealing his mutilated body and unattached parts.

Ram studied the mangled cadaver bits with interest.

He glanced up at Denim to see how the human was handling the gruesome sight. Surprise. She was bending close. No sign of revulsion on her face. No indication she might barf on the evidence.

Denim caught his stare. "Blood and guts don't

bother me. Besides, I saw him on the street."

"Given the injuries the body suffered, I hadn't thought of sedatives. Glad you suggested the possibility." Lacasta shoved her hands into her lab coat's pockets.

Everyone looked at Ram.

"It was an outside chance. The demon Hannya who was attacked in New Orleans complained about being sleepy. I didn't think it was anything, but … there you go. Sometimes you have to follow your gut."

"Good organ to heed," said the examiner. "So, the results of the test. Knives and mutilation were not cause of death. He died from heavy doses of a sedative delivered in bullets. Afterward, they cut him into pieces."

"Sedatives? You're sure?" Denim puzzled her brows.

"Ram asked me to check for tranquilizers. When I found them in the body. I called Alarik's science wizards. They investigated the site where the incubus was killed, finding evidence of sedative-laced bullets. Our male here had a shitload of the stuff in his system. Gorilla biscuits. Enough to take out a questing beast or sand leech. No question he died from an overdose. Hard to kill one of us that way, but this stuff's chemical construct is powerful. The locations where your demon was hit also showed evidence of tranqs."

"What is the shit? Is there an antidote?" Thorn crossed his arms over his chest.

"None I know of, but I gave the chemical makeup to Alarik's lab techs. They'll concoct an antidote."

"This stuff can kill us?" Galena frowned, her gaze fastened on Locasta.

"Enough of it can. I'd be careful out there."

"Here's a question." Ram cocked his head to the side. "Why was the incubus shot with tranqs rather than regular bullets?"

Denim shrugged. "If we were talking about lions or hippos, I'd say someone wanted a capture, not a kill."

"Yeah. Maybe they just used too much." Galena smoothed a hand down her straight black, shoulder-length hair.

Thorn scuffed a boot on the floor. "Curious, though. Did the shooters know this male wasn't human? And if they did, how did they know about him or the portal?"

A smirk curled Ram's lip. "Okay. We have a link between the attack on the young demons and the murder of the incubus. Since Tyr and I chased humans at the scene, let's assume they're responsible for both incidents. Also means Earthers know of two portal locations in New Orleans. Is the crack Alliance agent glad she joined us now? If these tranqs took out an incubus, what do you think they could do to you?"

A fist popped to Denim's hip. "I'll take care of myself. As always. Thanks for the concern, though."

****

After the morgue visit, Denim drew the short straw, teaming up with Ram. They walked their portal assignments in the French Quarter, covering the first three while the satyr groused about her being on the mission. He complained he'd be spending more time protecting her than doing his job.

"Is there anything you do like about me or humans?" She reached behind her to tighten her ponytail, bristling from his comments. "Better yet, is there anything you like?"

Ram didn't even pause to think. "Fighting. Sex with a female. Sex with more than one female. Sex with my hand. Sex while I'm fighting."

Denim shook her head. "Figures."

He started spouting shit about how humans were

weak, human females still weaker. He closed off with "Facts are facts."

Denim gave him the silent treatment for the next two portals.

As they detoured toward Rampart to catch the newest Krewe, they dodged a lot of people wearing swag. Since the enthusiasm of the Mardi Pardi was infectious, Denim got into it.

Caught up in the energy, she paused to wave at passengers on a float. She couldn't stay angry at the satyr even if he was a bastard. Galena claimed it was his breed. She said he probably controlled only ten percent of his assholishness.

When a mini-skirted tramp riding a decorated flatbed saw Ram, her mouth dropped open. She rotated around, bent forward, and wiggled her ass.

Denim rolled her eyes as the satyr Firebrand shrugged, handily catching beads the besotted, brazen woman tossed at him after she straightened, faced him, and did a little shimmy.

Tart.

"What's a satyr to do? She wants me."

Behind the float was another. The masked krewe aboard had strapped dildos to their hips, each covered with a jock warmer. One fur, one velvet, one knit, and another in New Orleans Saints' colors. When the vehicle stopped in front of Denim, the guy with the fur accessory waggled his added appendage in her direction.

Denim popped a fist to Ram's arm, laughing at the antics. "He's hung." She regretted the words immediately, prepared for a barrage of lewd comments.

Ram grinned on cue. He threw a beefy arm across her shoulder. "Doll, you have no idea what hung is. Let's run a comparison test?" He reached for his zipper.

"Don't be crude. Keep it in your pants." She

slapped at his hand.

"You can't handle the truth." He chuckled as if his movie quip was original. And hysterical. "No, that's wrong. I'll let you handle it. Stroke it. Lick it. Suck it."

She wiggled out from under his weighty arm. "Disgusting."

Ram followed her when she headed toward the portal near Jackson Square.

He caught up and walked alongside, pushing Mardi Gras partiers out of his path. "You're right. I shouldn't have told you how big I am. My size will just ruin other males for you. But let's not forget, you've already copped a feel. So you know."

Denim couldn't help it. She dropped her gaze to Ram's crotch.

He caught her. "Made you look."

Her cheeks warmed. "I wasn't looking."

"Liar." He pulled her into a doorway away from the crowded street and blocked her in with a forearm on each side of her head. She was caged between two steel bars.

Denim planted her fists on Ram's chest and pushed, but he didn't budge. Her lashes flipped up as she locked onto his beautiful eyes. She parted her lips, grabbing a fistful of T-shirt and yanking him toward her. When he dipped his chin, drawing closer, she pressed her mouth to his, tentatively. He responded. His tongue swept inside with little effort, plunging in and out as he aligned himself so his arousal pressed into her stomach. Her fingers tangled in his silky, loose hair.

Ram was big. And firm. No lie there.

She melted into the kiss, his hair caressing her hand. His hips ground into her as she moaned.

Before she completely collapsed against Ram's hot length and succumbed to his numerous charms, she regained some control and pulled back. She whispered, "Stop. Please, stop."

Her shallow breaths turned to gasps as she pushed harder against his chest. "Let me out, now. Now!"

Ram stepped away, allowing Denim to escape, but she stumbled when she slipped under his arms.

He grabbed an elbow. As she turned around, her eyes wide with fear, he snapped his hand back. "Damn, female. It was just a kiss. What's wrong?"

"I don't like to be trapped." She inhaled and exhaled in a slow, calming rhythm. Just a kiss? His lips were heavenly, but she panicked. Just like... No. Ram was not Steven. She needed to stop thinking every man was an abuser like her ex.

Ram's arms hung loose at his side. "I'm sorry."

"We're partners. No kissing. Ever." Denim shook a finger at the satyr.

"Ever?"

She steadied herself, able to think more clearly without the dangerous-but-gorgeous Firebrand pressed against her. "Do you kiss all the female Firebrands?"

"You're not a Firebrand." He grimaced. "I might have kissed a few from different strongholds. Never from my own."

"You're a lost cause, *cher*." Her boots thumped on the sidewalk, leading away from Ram.

"Aw, come on. Give me a break here."

****

What a dumbass move! But her lips were as soft as Ram imagined. He didn't have to work too hard to get into her mouth either. Her tongue tangled with his willingly, and he smelled her arousal. No masking the sweet scent of hot-to-trot. The kiss was not one-sided.

Without thinking, he'd fed from her. Just the sampler pack. She was delicious. He might be up for a seven-course meal despite the fact she was human. Just once would satisfy his curiosity. Afterward, he could move on. Would Denim consent to a one-night deal? 'Cause it was all he had in him.

Alone with his thoughts since his partner was silent, he went on alert as they neared the last portal site off Jackson Square, the one where he'd run into the three human males.

At the entrance to the alley, Ram threw out an arm, shoving Denim behind him. He flattened her between a brick wall and his body. When she struggled to move around him, he applied more pressure while he peered around the corner.

"What is it?" She pushed against him. "Move."

"No. Don't know yet, but I'll check it out."

"I should be the one. I'm less intimidating. Plus, I have the added benefit of not being an Aeternal."

He popped around in her direction. "No way. I go. I can hide in my satyr mist, cloak, be invisible."

"Sure, but you can't ask questions."

True. Besides, he was certain the minute he cloaked himself and rolled out, Denim would fly into the alley behind him, unprotected.

Dilemma.

She spoke in a harsh whisper. "Use your head. I'm the smarter choice."

"You think I'll let you take a bullet for me?"

"What?"

Now she sounded pissed. Given how often people responded this way to his statements, it wasn't a new experience. Ram ignored her.

He pulled rank. "As lead for this mission, I'm ordering you to stay here."

She sputtered, but he knew she'd obey the order.

Before he could cloak, four males staggered

along the center of the alley. Holding each other up, they stumbled out the entrance and continued along the street. Just drunken revelers. He listened while he scanned the area. Nothing else. He signaled they could enter.

Denim slammed a hand into Ram's chest while she started with the finger jab. "What the hell do you think you're doing?"

Tap. Tap. Tap.

Nothing was more annoying than a female doing the digit dance on your chest. "Going to the last portal." He grabbed hold of the offending finger, knocking it away.

"That's not what I mean. Don't shuck me off. I was the better choice to go into the alley. I was in the army, a sharp-shooter and boots on the ground. I was a cop before I joined the Alliance, where I'm a top-notch agent. Stuff your protective urges. I'm as able as you are." She clenched her fists at her sides.

Ram shifted his translucent stare toward her. "The fuck you are." His angry gaze traveled from the toes of her shitkickers to the top of her head. Despite the tight athletic body she obviously took good care of, he let her know he wasn't impressed. "You may be a hotshot human female, doll, but I've got over one hundred pounds on you, many years of experience, and a variety of satyr powers. You want to arm wrestle me to settle the question?"

What he didn't say was that he would never knowingly put this female in harm's way. He bristled at the thought she was in such a dangerous job at all.

Hell. Didn't the Alliance have any non-lethal jobs? Paper pushers? Desk jockeys?

"You arrogant ass."

"That's Mission Leader Ass to you." Ram grinned.

"Let me be clear. If you ever use an arm to bump me behind you again, I'll break it off."

"I will not let you risk your life. Discussion *fini*."

Her brows arched as she stared in disbelief. "Is this how you treat female Firebrands? They must love you."

"Of course not. They're warriors. They're stronger than you. Better trained." *Shit.* The statements just slipped out before his brain engaged.

"Better trained?"

He shrugged.

"Really? It's because I'm an Earther and female? Obviously, a bad combo. You don't think humans, especially women, have any business in the field. Boy, are you behind the times. Father doesn't know best, and Fonzi's grown up. The fifties are over."

"I lived in the fifties, you know. It wasn't such a bad time."

Denim stomped off, heading for the busy street and a passing parade.

****

Ram shifted from foot to foot while Denim broke it down for Kole in his office. She listed all the whys and wherefores as to how the satyr Firebrand was a crappy partner.

Shaking his head as she stuttered, Ram stepped in to shoot himself in his own foot. "She might be right."

Denim wrinkled a puzzled forehead while she nodded hesitantly. "He makes crude comments."

"True. My mouth sometimes runs faster than my brain." When Denim raised her brows, he added, "Just saying."

Funny, he noted, she didn't mention the kiss.

Denim waved her hand dismissively through the air, talking without taking a breath. "I can deal with all the sexual innuendo and the hits. He'd likely rabbit if I took him up on his offers."

Before Ram could speak, she mimicked zipping her lips. "I've been working with good ol' boys my entire life. I can hold my own and return zingers. But you took me out of the action. I understand chain of command. I know you're in charge of this mission, but your calls need to be the right ones. I'm an Alliance agent. I won't be treated as an inferior. I worked hard to get where I am. I deserve respect. I served my time in the army. Do you know what it takes to qualify for such duty?"

She paused for a breath, shooting a disgusted look at him but giving him no time to reply. "A lot. And I was a damn good cop until I joined the Alliance. I'm used to calling the shots, taking charge, not being shoved behind some muscled male body to be protected."

Ram wondered if being in charge and calling the shots meant she wanted to be on top. That was fine by him. "Just to be clear. You don't want me to save your ass if it's in danger?"

"Sometimes I might need a save. Sometimes you might. That's not what this is about. You made a bad decision because you thought you needed to protect me. You should have sent me into the alley to do recon, to ask questions. I was the best for the job."

They were getting nowhere. Ram sighed, deciding to go for the big plunge. "Give me another chance. I can be a great partner. Next time, I won't interfere until you call my name when someone has his paws around your neck, choking you while you gasp for oxygen."

"Really? No. I want a new partner."

No way was Ram sending Denim out with anyone else. *Hell.* What if she got hurt?

Where did the protective loose-screw notion come

from?

Ram scrubbed a fist across his jaw. "I'm an ass. Aren't I, Kole? Tell her."

"You're finally including me in the convo?" His gaze popped up but immediately returned to the paperwork on his desk.

"I was the sensible choice to send into the alley." Denim popped fists to her hips. "Wasn't I, Commander?"

Kole glanced up again, but he didn't look happy. Fire danced between his fingertips. Already one of the most powerful demons of his breed, his gifts exploded when he was called to the Firebrands. His flame-throwing digits were always ready to flare. Passion, anger, or sometimes just being mildly pissed brought his gifts roaring to the surface. "Okay, we're really doing this. Denim, he's an ass, but he's also a satyr with a shitload more experience. He outweighs you by at least a hundred pounds of packed muscle. Sure, very little of it's in brain matter, but there ya go. Maybe you could do the thinking, and he could be the shield. Then I don't have to send you back to the Alliance in pieces. But she's right, satyr. She was the smart choice to step into the fucking alley."

"As I rethink my actions, Commander, I agree."

"So happy I have your approval." Kole's attention returned to his desk.

Denim faced Ram, waving her finger in his direction. "Don't ever restrain me again."

"I promise I won't restrain you. Unless you want me to. I added the last part just to show I'm open to any suggestions from you."

She sighed, tossing her hands into the air. The gesture showed her body to advantage. Lean but curvy.

Keep your head in the game, satyr.

Sabine and Nico stormed into the office before

Denim could resume yelling at Ram.

Kole leaned back in his chair. "This is going to be a fucking awful night."

Ram greeted his nymph *freron*. "Hey, Sabine, tell Denim I'm an ass."

"He's an ass." Sabine did a double take at the human female. She arched a brow.

Reaching around Ram, Denim offered a hand. "Hi. I'm staying with Galena for a bit. On vacation. Alliance agent. Partnering with the ass here on an assignment."

"Welcome."

They shook as Ram resumed pleading. "Tell her I can learn from my mistakes."

Sabine seemed to ponder the statement for a moment. "He's capable of learning. Whether he will or not is up for grabs."

"Thanks for the support, nymph."

Sabine ignored Ram when Nico crossed his arms over his chest and blurted out his concerns. "Enough with their bullshit. This is important. I want you to put someone else on me. Preferably no one."

"Somebody is going to be tight on your ass, Abello. Now, tone down the attitude. What's wrong with Sabine?" Kole fixed on his nymph Firebrand.

"I'm not having this ... I mean, anyone ... shove me to the back of the action like I'm some fly weight rookie."

"I hear ya." Denim peeked around Ram. "This lunk did the same to me."

She and Nico both nodded as if they were in the know.

The human acted as if he was suddenly aware of the other *Homo sapiens's* presence. "Nico Abello, by the way. An Alliance ex-agent. Kidnapped, brought here, and assigned a nanny. A fucking nanny."

Sabine sighed while Denim nodded a greeting.

Ram pressed his lips tight together. "I'm still sorry, do … Denim." He stopped himself short of calling her "doll."

Learning happening right here and now.

"It's her job," Kole said to Nico.

Sabine rested a palm on her Arkansas toothpick hilt. "For the record, Comm, he's crazy. He ran right into the Arisen Dawn warehouse. Without my permission."

"Your permission? Why do I need your permission to do my job?" Nico's eyes blazed as his volume increased.

"I can clear this up," interrupted Kole. "Because I fucking said you do." He shot out of his desk chair, checking it out as if he might chuck it across the room like the big-ass demon he was. "Son, I know your world's been turned upside down, but I'm your fucking commander now. Not your life coach. The unapproved raid on the warehouse was stupid. Watching and waiting would likely have bagged us better intel. Nobody understands rash moves better than I do. Still, not a smart idea for an experienced agent. Get your shit together, or I'll ground you from all action. On the plus side, and the only reason you're still standing, the stupid move netted us a shitload of information and cash. Seems Arisen Dawn is recruiting. Don't know why. Disobey me again, though, and you'll see how scary I can be."

Kole let fly a stream of fire which sizzled across Nico's left ear.

The human's hand flew to his singed lobe. "Shit."

Kole slumped back into his chair. "Just a sample. I could have aimed for your dick, lighting it up like a tiki torch. And Immagonnadothat if you don't see things my way. This shit is boring, and boring and I don't get along.

Denim, can you still work with Ram now that he's reformed?"

She stared at the satyr. "As long as he treats me like an equal. Like a professional."

Ram winced, but not one stupid word crossed his lips. He could have repeated all the skills he possessed but she lacked. He didn't.

Learning happening again. I am having such a growth spurt. Pretty soon I'll be ready for a guest spot on The View.

"Okay. Here's the solution to both problems. If Ram acts out, Denim, stab him or shoot him. Anywhere. I don't give a fuck. Sabine, you are sticking with the human warlock. Not dissolving your partnership either. Hell, shoot him, too, if he dares to disobey a command, but do not kill him. Just graze him. As Blood Coven, he's protected property."

The four of them stared dumbfounded at Kole.

"Yeah. Ya gotta love my solutions. Now. Get the hell out of here. Bounty?" he yelled out. "Did these four have appointments?"

"You don't make appointments."

"Exactly. So, how the hell did they get in? Nobody gets into my office for the rest of the night without one of those appointments I don't make. I've got a shitload of work to do before I can go home to my gorgeous mate."

Chapter Nine

Lizette awoke with Spear inside her. She squeezed her lids tight, turning her head to the side so his lips could not maul her with a kiss. His hips plowed up and down. The bed slammed into the wall, his grunts adding to the nightmare of her life.

This hut was a long way from the New York street where she'd been kidnapped before being shipped off to a dirty, dank prison run by vampires. Soon after they flung her into the squalid cell, her jailer sold her to this berserker.

How long have I been at Spear's mercy? Months?

Long enough that she was dry. No more tears. Crying prompted beatings, but more than that, she didn't want to give the rutting seven-foot monster the satisfaction of seeing her break.

His muscles tightened as he released inside her. When he pulled out, unwelcome moisture dripped between her legs. Lizette kept her expression frozen, hidden from her own personal monster. No frown. No grimace. No displeasure.

Survive. Survive. Survive.

She lived to escape this nightmare, faking her enjoyment of Spear's advancements. Once she was free, she'd kill him. How realistic was this thinking? He was huge. A mountain of muscle. And crazy as a poked grizzly.

Once a radio talk show psychologist at WMR in New York, she never would have used the expression "crazy." She would have said, "He is exhibiting sociopathic behaviors, likely a result of his upbringing." She would have lapsed into a description of his actions. Lack of remorse. Antisocial tendencies. Pathologic egocentricity. Specific loss of insight. Now she said things like "savage deranged beast," "wacked cretin rapist," or "crazy as a poked grizzly."

In her previous life, she would have spouted ways to deal with a sociopath. Stay cool. Stay calm. Resist the temptation to talk it out or change the person. Show them they don't have power over you. Consider avoiding the person. Keep your guard up. Now, she wanted to kill the monster, gouge out his eyes, or cut off his balls. She'd changed. She liked to think she was more pragmatic. It was possible she was just more bloodthirsty.

"Get up, female. Ready my breakfast." Spear's deep, gravelly voice assaulted her thoughts. Wrapping her chain around his palm, he yanked her out of their shared bed.

Lizette slammed onto the floor, scrambling for her shirt.

"No." Spear thundered a command.

She was exposed, vulnerable. Tired of the game she played to endure, she swallowed her pride, remembering she was naked but a survivor. If she refused his demand, he would hit her. She rejected starting the day with a headache and swollen jaw. Instead, she forced her lips into a smile, a pretense that she enjoyed Spear's assaults, a pretense she loved him. All to stay alive.

Lizette shuffled to the kitchen, the chain locked to a collar at her neck dragging along the dusty floor, leaving a pattern. She set the berserker's plate and utensils on the table. The outside door snapped shut. He'd probably left to pee.

She removed a dozen eggs from the refrigerator. They weren't from chickens, but she didn't know what kind they were. Likewise, the cured meat she fried in the pans on the stove wasn't ham or bacon. Similar. She didn't care enough to ask what it was. She cooked what he bought. Pancakes were next. About a dozen and a half would do. She set butter and syrup on the table.

The hair on her arms shot straight when Spear stepped back into the hovel. It was as if fear walked in with him. She could smell it like rotting meat. It was a gnat buzzing around her head.

Spear's chair scraped along the floor, sending a chalkboard chill through Lizette. Once he sat, she served his breakfast.

"Eat with me."

Pouring his coffee first, Lizette tilted the pot over her mug. She sank into the seat at the opposite end of the table, wrapping a hand around her steaming cup, drawing on the warmth. She sucked in a deep breath, controlling her voice and emotions. "I'm not hungry right now. I like to eat after you leave so I have something to do while you're gone. It makes the time without you pass faster. The coffee is good. Thanks so much for getting it."

Wearing ripped jeans and a dirty gray sweatshirt, but not looking any more civilized than he did in his pelts, Spear seemed to consider her statement for a moment. He grunted while he scooped an overloaded fork of pancakes into his mouth. Syrup dripped down his chin. He wiped it off with the back of his hand. Too late. A blob landed on his shirt.

His chair scraped along the floor again when he pushed up and stomped to the hook where his coat hung. He jammed his beefy arms into the sleeves. Reaching into the pocket, he removed a key. "You will fix the roast for my dinner. My potatoes will be the way I like them." He tugged his thickly braided, rarely washed hair from under his collar.

She nodded.

"Come. Outside." When he unlocked the chain

which connected to an eyebolt on the floor, he clipped another to the choker around her neck. Once he opened the door, Spear led her outside like a dog. She barely snatched a threadbare shawl from the hook and threw it over her shoulders before being pulled to the porch.

Spear stayed nearby as Lizette stumbled barefoot, walking as far as the chain allowed. At least she had some privacy behind a bush so she could go to the bathroom unobserved. Before leaving the shelter of the tall shrub, she inhaled. Pine. She smelled pine, and the air passing into her nostrils was crisp, pure. Somewhere others breathed in the odor of clean freedom. Were they close? She listened to the silence. The song of a bird interrupted. Maybe a meadow lark? Damned if she knew. She was a city girl. Never one for the rustic life. Then her neck snapped when the berserker hauled back her chain. He led her inside, re-clipping the indoor metal leash to her collar, securing the lock.

"I will have a kiss before I leave."

Lizette calmed her stomach, keeping the coffee down as she lumbered toward him, stretched onto her toes, and swiped her lips across his as he commanded. His harsh, prickly beard scraped her cheek.

"I have decided to keep you. No more talk of killing."

She breathed a sigh. Spear's fear of being caught frequently led him to consider killing her. Lizette became psychologically and sexually inventive in order to survive. "Thank you, my love. Have a wonderful day."

She waited once the door shut. The berserker sometimes peeked back in to see what she was doing. She lingered over her coffee. Her eyes focused on the cup in her hands while she recalled the smell of pine along with the crisp, clear air which carried the song of a bird.

The chain at her neck attached to an eyebolt in the floor, permitting her to reach the bedroom, the kitchen, and the small sitting area by the fireplace. It did not extend to the front door.

When Spear did not return for a surprise check, she slipped on a shirt and calf-length skirt. She kneeled on the dirty floor, bent low, and shoved her head under the bed. She reached a hand behind one of the large legs against the wall. Lizette's heart skipped a beat when her fingers did not strike her treasure. Once. Twice. She patted the wood planks, trying not to panic. When her palm finally smacked down on metal, she pulled out her prize. She smiled for the first time that day. In her grasp was a huge rusty nail she had scooped up from outside while Spear was not watching.

As she did all day, every day, except when it was time to stack wood in the fireplace, light it, and fix dinner, she jammed the nail between the eyebolt and the floor, wiggling it, trying to loosen the connection. Her plan was to jimmy the bolt until it broke free.

She made sure the wooden plank where the bolt was attached did not appear disturbed. Any time she created chipped wood or sawdust, she scooped it up, depositing it out of sight. When the fastener broke from the wood, she would be free to run. Where? She had no idea. Away from here. Away from Spear. She wasn't on Earth, but she knew she would run away from her nightmare Freddy Kruger.

Lizette sat on the floor, gouging, scraping, and wriggling. Her chore was slow, tedious, but it was her plan to escape.

When she worked at the radio station, every day she answered calls from people with problems. Maybe they feared intimacy. Maybe they were sex addicts. Had a drinking issue. Lived with an abusive husband. She always walked them through the same three steps. First, clarify the situation. Is your husband hitting you when he drinks? Second, devise a plan. Wait for him to leave for work, pack a bag, and go to a women's shelter. Third, carry out the plan. Just do it. Basically, she helped troubled people solve problems.

Her abduction, sale to a beast, and torture should have been an impossible occurrence, but she didn't believe in impossible. As long as she survived, she could escape. The current plan was to make the hole big enough so she could jiggle the bolt out. She would grab up the chain and run to freedom.

She had no idea where freedom was, but she recited steps one, two, and three again. Once she escaped, she would apply new steps to the new situation.

****

In the afternoon, the Aeternal Cerberus met Dante at a London gentleman's club, the building dating back to the early 1700s, the same century the Prince of Wales joined. They sat in a private room away from the hearing of human members and, more importantly, away from the sensitive ears of Aeternals. Of course, the club had never been aware of these special members.

Though intellectuals and the famous gathered in these grandiose meeting rooms to argue politics, philosophy, and the arts, Cerberus saw only pompous, abundantly rich humans with too much time on their hands. Ants beneath his feet. Instead of sand, they dug in massive piles of greed. He would bring them to their knees, where they would bow to their conqueror. All would be as it was fated to be. As the prophecy predicted.

In this club he first met Dante, a man distraught over the death of his daughter. Capitalizing on the Englishman's grief, Cerberus revealed the existence of

Scath. He invited him along with his vast resources into a plot. They discussed a plan to reunite Earthers and Aeternals, to open trade and relations between the two realms. Good business. Dante was in favor of it. Cerberus explained how descendants of the Blood Coven were necessary to open the portals between the realms.

From the beginning, however, Cerberus suspected the Englishman had another end. He suspected Dante sought to expose Scath, to wipe out Aeternals.

Tit for tat, Cerberus was not being honest either. His scheme within the scheme was tricky. His true end game was to rule Earth, to use humans as a food source for the breeds. He almost salivated at the challenge. The arrogant Englishman was far out of his depth.

So many balls to keep in the air. Cerberus was confident in his ability to be the best juggler in the three realms.

Dante leaned forward in the chair beside the fire to flick an ash from his cigar. "How are your two guests? Jace and Celene?"

"They are being taken care of nicely. They staged a hunger strike, but Lort, my new general, handled it. I have added a few more Blood Coven descendants to their small group. Since they can be difficult to manage, I keep them separate." He muffled a laugh.

Cerberus swished Scotch in the tumbler, sniffed the golden liquid, and took a sip. "Delicious." He glanced at Dante, wishing his need of the human was over. But it was what it was. For now. "The Ministry of Well Being is buzzing. My senses tell me it has to do with descendants."

"The hunt persists, though. My man, Mars, continues to monitor medical records, finding potential candidates for you to check out."

"Thank you. We test their blood as you find them,

bringing only verified descendants to Scath, where they are protected in lavish surroundings until I need them."

"How many of the twenty or so identified by Mars have panned out?"

"Several in addition to Jace and Celene." Cerberus did not intend to share the exact number. He emptied his tumbler and rose from the comfortable chair. Despite his smile, he was eager to return to Scath. Being among so many inferior humans weighed heavily on his mind. Bugs. No better than the billions of insects which crawled, flew, or swam in this realm. His glory was approaching. He could taste it as vividly as the Scotch. Perhaps, this self-important human would be one of the first to feed him. After his money was used, of course.

****

Denim's gaze shifted to the entrance as energy sizzled through the Blood Shed. A hand pushed open the exterior door. Owning the room, a male strode into the Firebrands' favorite hangout, his thick forearms exposed by the rolled-up sleeves of his black silk shirt. His face, a Greek god's chiseled in marble, forced every woman to lick her lips. His pale eyes scanned the crowd like a big cat seeking its prey. With sleek grace and power, he muscled through the mob who scurried out of his path when they sensed danger. Caramel-streaked hair caressed his shoulders as he pitched from side to side, stalking toward the bar.

He was dressed for attention in designer pants, shirt, shoes. The satyr was the total package. Sharp dresser. Killer smile. Lethal build.

When he reached his destination, women sighed but returned to their own business. Resting his elbows on the bar, he leaned forward. Once the bartender shoved a drink into his hand, he pivoted around as he had the first night Denim met him. A spectacular grin crawled across his lips when he caught her stare.

The DJ was playing Macklemore's "Firebreather." The words "Do you know who I am?" blasted out while the satyr scrutinized her. He was her kryptonite, her Achilles Heel, the chink in her armor. She could go on and on, but no matter how she fought it, her knees turned to Jell-O. Even though he was a misogynistic, egocentric A-hole with a huge need to protect her when she didn't want to be caged.

Denim dropped her gaze, the heat from his fixed stare too much.

He shoved off, heading her way while nodding at the DJ. The music changed from the heavy-beat rap to something slow and sexy.

Nods, heys, and pats on the shoulder from his Firebrand *frerons* met him at the table.

With greetings out of the way, Ram set down his drink. Unexpectedly, he reached out a hand to Denim.

She studied it.

"It's an apology." Ram waited, his expression irritating, confident.

She intended to refuse, but her heart pounded faster than the music. Louder, too. Finally, her fingers possessed a mind of their own. She slipped her palm into his. Her softer flesh contacted his calloused skin, formed from a lifetime of holding weapons, she guessed.

He pulled her to the dance floor and what she suspected was disaster.

"'Let's Get It On' by Marvin Gaye?" Denim took a little skip in her too-high heels to keep up with his long strides.

"A male can dream, can't he?" His voice was a husky whisper, heard above the din of voices.

"It's not very subtle."

"Hmm. Subtlety has never been my strength. You

won't mind if I lead, will you?" His arm wrapped around her waist.

"Not at all. As long as you don't mind if I step on your toes, *cher*." While Denim tried to keep her voice honeyed, dripping with sex, her words came out in a throaty rasp.

On the dance floor, Ram spiraled her around, rested her back against his chest. He began a sultry sway with his hips rolling from side to side. His arms circled her waist. Slowly, one hand rose to cradle her breasts while the other dropped to caress her stomach. She was locked firmly against all his sensuous power.

Her head drifted to settle just below his shoulder. He was a solid pillow of hard muscle, making her feel petite, desirable. Denim inhaled and exhaled to the rhythm of their movement. She was intoxicated, but it wasn't from the single beer she'd finished.

He twirled her. In his arms again, they were breast to chest. His palm glided to her lower back. When she stretched out her right hand to take his, he clasped it, kissing her knuckles. He brought it to rest against his heart.

Denim sighed, the warmth from his touch seeping into her bones.

A thick, muscular thigh drove between her legs, sending tingles from womb to toes, rubbing her sweet spot, drenching her. His undulating movements were pure sex on the dance floor.

With his arousal grinding against her stomach, his breath fluttered in her ear. Denim's knees trembled, nearly buckling.

Ram clasped her tighter, not letting her fall. "It's just a dance. I've got you, doll."

Damn. The arrogant Lothario. He knew she was wet for him.

Nonetheless, her head nestled into his hot, firm chest while her lips curled into a dreamy smile. She closed her eyes. His silk shirt fondled her cheek. He smelled spicy, woodsy, all man. Not man. Satyr. Her fingers crept up his neck to tangle in the river of his thick, caramel-streaked hair.

Steven didn't have this effect on me. So alive. So spinning out of control at the same time. Ram's like being in the eye of a storm. But I must remember he's only looking for a fast lay. One more notch on his active bedpost. He's a heartbreaker. Keep an emotional distance.

Chapter Ten

Ram came to the Blood Shed to throw back a few drinks with friends after another wasted day of checking out portals. He figured he'd get busy with a delectable succubus or nymph. He absolutely planned to ignore the Alliance female if she was there.

Yeah?

So why did his feet move in her direction? Why did he signal the DJ to play a great fuck song? Most of all, why the hell did his hand shoot out, inviting her to dance?

Reaching the table, he nodded at his friends, but his gaze latched onto Denim. She wore some sinful poured-on, hip-hugging tight jeans, a skimpy little top which displayed all her goods, and sexy tall-ass heels.

So what did he do? He stretched out a hand. When she put her soft fingers into his, he pulled her toward the floor, hoping the crowd would disappear. If they'd been alone, he'd have unbuttoned her jeans and slipped them down those shapely legs. She'd have rested her palm on his shoulder while she stepped out of them. He'd ask her to leave the heels on.

Hell. Yes.

Would he let her keep on her panties? *Nope.* They needed to go.

The snug little top hardly hiding her overflowing breasts would be next. He hoped she wore a bra with an easy clasp. Otherwise, it was a goner.

While he fantasized about stripping Denim, his thigh stroked the heat between her legs. The two of them swayed to the music. She didn't just dance to it, though. *No.* Denim made love to the beat. Her hips rolled. She moaned to the rhythm.

Ram took advantage of every movement, every sound. He molded his body to hers, pressed against her breasts until he could feel her nipples pulling into tight nubs. His swollen cock rode her belly.

With each sway and glide to Marvin Gaye's sultry sounds, he rubbed his leg against her pussy. Catching her arousal, he grew harder, hungrier. His satyr was always starved when Denim was nearby.

The fabric in her jeans whispered as she moved. Their feet swooshed, sliding on the floor in step with the music. Ram's nose nuzzled between Denim's shoulder and neck, taking in her scent. Fresh and citrusy. *Yep.* Her shampoo, maybe. He could get used to it.

The hand, which held hers against his heart, let go to glide alongside her breast. He kept traveling upward, sliding his fingers beneath her too-sexy shirt, slipping them under her bra. Molding his warm palm to her while he savored the feel of her flawless skin.

"Nice," he murmured in her ear. She didn't object.

Instead, she groaned, a sound which sent a jolt straight to his already painfully stiff dick.

He danced her further into the darkness. Dropping his unbusy hand from the hot skin at her waist, he cradled her firm buttocks. Again, no objections from the human.

With a little help from his palm on her tight derriere, she rode his thigh hard. *Oh yeah, doll. Come right now.* Up and down in time with Marvin.

"R-a-a-a-m-m-m?" Her voice was soft, drawn out, pleading.

"Yes?" He danced them into a shadowed corner, planting her against the wall. He roamed from her ass to cup her sex.

"Not out here. Oh, God. Never mind. Don't stop,

cher."

She was breathing harder while thrusting against his hand. He didn't plan to stop. Ram was having way too much fun enjoying the sounds she made. She moaned. Purred. Sighed. Like a good soldier, he kept the friction going while she drove faster toward an explosion. This wasn't about him. Now that was a goddamn puzzle. Not that he didn't pay back females with their own satisfying climax, but he was usually more concerned about jetting his own juice.

Then her body tensed. She pressed her mouth into his shirt, smothered a cry, and trembled as he helped her push through the orgasm. It was such a long one. He fed on it, shuddering from the intensity of her release.

Ram waited until she slumped against him, satisfied, mewling like a kitten. "Come with me, doll. I need skin to skin." Reluctantly he pulled his happy hand away from the juncture between her legs to lead her toward the back and a little privacy.

****

Denim and Ram tumbled into the room, her hungry mouth pressed to his. Their hands fumbled with too many clothes. His tongue set a frantic rhythm, plunging in and out, the satyr kissing like he fought. Hard. Aggressive.

She broke away from his crushing lips to flash on the surroundings. They could have been in any room at a Super 8 Motel. No frills but clean.

He clutched her hip while his other hand yanked her head back so he could attack her mouth again. Seeming not to care about the decor, Ram paused to drag off her top. Stepping away, he swallowed her whole with his gaze.

Denim was glad she wore a lacy bra, though it still wasn't what she would call sexy.

Ram didn't seem to mind, his eyes flashing neon green as his breath caught. He muttered, "Oh, yeah."

Denim leaned toward him, unbuttoning his shirt one slow button at a time. Exposing his flesh bit by bit, her fingertips brushed slabs of muscle and rippling abs. Each touch was like dipping cold toes into warm water. The pleasure made her want to plunge in all the way.

Once his shirt was open, she slipped the silk off his shoulders, letting it fall to the floor. Her palm glided along his brand, the wings of the Phoenix fluttering in her hand, sending shivers along her spine.

Ram reached behind Denim. Like the pro he was, he unclasped her bra. He tucked a finger beneath each strap to glide them down her arms.

She gasped when her breasts met the cool air and Ram's hot stare. His green eyes said a lot.

"I can't hide what I'm feeling, doll. I don't even want to."

He gently slid one hand onto Denim's back to tuck her close. His other hand caressed a heavy breast.

Denim moaned. "Yes, please."

"Yeah? Do you like this?" With his thumb, he stroked her nipple until she cried out, arching her spine.

When a tight bud formed, he lowered his head, licking around it, nipping. He took more of her flesh into his mouth, sucking hard.

With his wet lips drawing on her mound as he groaned, Denim was in heaven. She didn't care if this was their only hook up. She wanted him now. The total package.

Her hands explored the bunched muscles on his shoulders and dropped to his hips. Eventually, they landed on his buttocks where she dug her nails in. She pulled him in so tight his enormous erection pressed into her belly like a thick, solid rope.

When Ram moved onto her other breast, Denim moaned. "Fuck me."

The satyr backed away, growling, his eyes making another quick jump to green. "Lose your jeans." He unbuckled the belt on his pants.

Denim watched, swiping her tongue along her lips in anticipation. No way was she going to miss seeing a naked Ram for the first time. Her eyes followed the trail of light hair disappearing into his waistband.

Someone pounded on the door. A couple stumbled into the room, locked in an embrace. "Oops. Sorry," the guy said. "Didn't know the space was occupied. Carry on."

They slipped out, the woman giggling.

Denim flashed on Steven, his fists flying into her face. Every time things got good. Why couldn't she let go? Remembering her long recovery, she tugged on her snug jeans. "Fuck, no."

Ram doesn't break bones. He breaks hearts. I don't want anything broken.

Suddenly, he stopped, his pants already unzipped. "Now? You decide to get bashful now?"

Ram banged his fist against the wall, doing a little structural damage to the Blood Shed. Drawing a deep breath through his nostrils, he snarled as he buckled his belt.

Denim nodded, searching the floor for her bra. After she snapped it into place, she grabbed her shirt and pulled it over her head. This was so awkward. She tried for a light laugh. "Saved by the knock on the door. All's well, though. We have no business in a backroom getting a quickie anyway."

No answer. He snatched his shirt off the floor and covered up his delicious muscles.

Denim sighed. "We're partners. You're actually

my mission leader. Workplace romances are a bad idea."
Her previous one with Steven was a volcanic failure.

Ram's brows knit together. He quickly hid
whatever he was feeling behind his cocky attitude.
"Didn't seem to bother you a few minutes ago. I think
you were really into it. My hand, that is. Stroke. Pump.
Moan. Orgasm."

"Don't make this crass. Don't be that man."

"I'm not a man. Satyr here with a mega boner.
Thanks to you and your hormones jacking me up. To say
nothing of your pussy and tits. Let's face it, we need to
fuck."

"We do not."

"I think your body disagrees, doll." He leaned
toward her, sniffing. "Yep. It wants to argue the matter. I
smell lust. All the wet stuff in your panties is for me."

"Screw you."

She opened a door, stomping out. Ram grabbed
her elbow as he muttered something like, "Trying to."
Then he guided her the other direction. "Wrong way."

When she glared at him, he chuckled. "Kinda
ruins the exit, doesn't it?"

"Damn you."

"I was damned a while ago. You're too late."

****

Mars sat at a retro chrome kitchen table. He
tapped two fingers on the marred white top. When his
phone rang, the ex-military man extracted it from his
pocket

"You're meeting with the squad leaders this
afternoon, General?" Dante started without a greeting.

Not the Englishman's real moniker anyway, but,
then again, Mars was a code name, too. "I expect them
within the half-hour."

"Your men have captured nobody yet. My plans

are balls up unless you show progress."

Unaccustomed to explaining himself, Mars took a deep breath before he said something stupid. "They are learning, sir. They have been at this only three weeks. I admit, they're off to a rocky start."

"Rocky?"

Mars tapped harder on the table. "The doctor you hired got the dosages wrong. He said those monsters could handle several shots. Not true. My men plugged the alien with four bullets. He was hard to knock down. Turns out, it was too much tranq. He died. The doc now assures us their bodies will handle two shots of the new dose. Any more is iffy."

"If your task is too challenging, I can get another general."

Mars hesitated, choosing his words. "No, sir. I'm the right man for the job."

"Marvelous. What about the injections for our soldiers? Have you taken yours?"

"Yes, sir. Earlier today. I wanted to test it before my men."

"And? Do not make me ask."

Arrogant Brit.

"Hooah. Very effective. Though I am a bit jumpy. As if I want to pound on someone."

"Just make certain the someone is an otherworlder. How long did the technician say it will last?"

"I am told to expect a week. We'll report regularly to the lab for additional shots."

"Good. I want the team on the drug. I want my money's worth. Remember, I do not suffer failure. Get me a live otherworlder by high tea tomorrow."

Mars wasn't a stupid man. Disconnecting from the call, he caught the Englishman's implication. He needed to show a victory. As a retired military officer and later a mercenary in Africa, he liked wins. He also believed as Dante did. They were waging a battle for humankind.

Originally meeting with the Brit in his London home, Mars listened to his story. Fascinating but unbelievable. Crazy old coot with a snobbish cut-glass accent. Slowly, the military man began to think the story might be true. Now, he was sure.

The screen door swung open. The New Orleans native, an ex-Alliance agent with a grudge, stomped through. The guy proved helpful already. One of his old contacts turned out to be a tech at the organization with access to portal locations. Lucky thing the computer geek suffered from a severe gambling problem along with debts up the wazoo.

Dante's money also found a doctor who developed a sedative which could be delivered by a bullet. The aim was to target a fucking otherworlder, plug them with a tranq, and drag their ass back as proof. Proof these Aeternals existed. Mars put several three-man teams together. They checked the portals in New Orleans, trying to capture any Aeternals who used them. So far, bupkis. One dead and a miss.

An overzealous team emptied four loaded projectiles into an otherworlder creature. Too much juice. The other candidates escaped through a portal.

Mars nodded at the arrival, kicking out a chair with his foot. The ex-agent took the offered seat, lowering his body into it. He stared at the general, who continued tapping on the table.

Outside, insects, birds, and other critters broke the silence of the night. A car pulled in, its tires crunching gravel.

A red-headed, freckle-faced man strode into the

kitchen. He was only five-foot-six but sported solid muscles from hours of working in the gym. Mars chose him because of the number of missions they had gone on together. He was reliable. Vicious when necessary. The soldier was without a conscience, but he was loyal to a big paycheck.

"Manny."

"Hey. Look at you," he said, taking the other chair beside Mars. "Ben's right behind me."

The last squad leader came through the screen door, letting it slam after him. His face sported a scowl, but Mars didn't think he had another expression.

With all three present, the general rested his beefy forearms on the table, staring the men down, one by one.

"We're failing here. It's un-fucking-acceptable." He motioned at Ben first. "Explain."

"We took the guy down with too many shots. Now we know it was overkill. Literally. In our defense, the doc said they could take four."

Mars looked to the ex-agent.

"Almost got two. They're strong. They're fast. Scurried back through a portal."

The general squinted not because the lights were bright. He was pissed. He wanted a win. "Manny?"

"No encounters."

Mars opened a tattered case at his feet. He removed three syringes, slamming them down. "What I have here are equalizers. Straight out of Dr. Frankenstein's lab."

The men nodded. Ben licked his lips, looking eager for an upgrade.

Mars landed his fist with a loud thud, sending the table bouncing. "I want success. I want a creature. Now. You think the Firebrands are mean SOBs? You haven't seen me in action."

Dante had chosen him for his reputation. Relentless in pursuit of his target. Cruel and bloodthirsty when he ran it to ground.

A village in Africa was his legacy. They defied the warlord he worked for and paid the price. Every man, woman, and child. It was his job. And he loved his job. His new power was a perk.

"Line up and drop your pants."

****

Dax was MIA. Again. Bounty tried his D-chip and the private cell number only she knew.

No Dax.

She asked Ram and Brak to make discreet trips to his known haunts. The O blud dens on Scath.

No Dax.

She checked his apartment in Covenkirk.

No Dax.

She was about to invade his hide-away in Bloodhaven. No one else was aware of his cabin in the vampire region. He told Bounty about it only because he trusted her not to use the info unless there was an emergency.

Wasn't this an emergency?

When she crept lightly onto the porch, it creaked. Bounty stopped dead still, fearing she announced herself. She expected Dax to spring out in full attack mode.

No Dax.

She trod more carefully before she turned the knob. The door opened. *Strange.* The male was known to be paranoid. His security topnotch. Looking behind her, she glanced at three cameras. Those were only the ones she could see.

If he was inside, he'd already spotted her. She swung the door wide and dropped into a defensive crouch in case he came out fighting.

The house was still. Deep cave silent. No sounds.

Nothing could hide the smells, though. She caught a strong odor of blood. Fainter ones of leather along with rotting food.

Following the scents, she pressed her hand on a slightly ajar door leading into a bedroom. There on a massive four-poster bed lay Dax, clothed in his fighting leathers and a black Led Zeppelin Hermit tee. His feet were bare. Somehow, it made him appear fragile.

But he wasn't. His obsidian eyes stared right at her, casting a glare which would have chilled anyone else, sending them high-tailing it for the exit.

Bounty sighed. She walked in to stand beside the bed. She placed the backs of her fingers on his forehead. "Big brother."

He was so still she wanted to pinch him or shake him to make sure he wasn't catatonic. His brow was cold and damp, sweat glistening on his skin. His eyes were glassy but not shot with red-and-white streaks. A good sign.

"Sis."

He took a few deep breaths, dragged his two-hundred-and-fifty pound-plus body to a sitting position to lean against the headboard. Pushing his tangled long black hair onto his back, he pulled his lips into a snarl. "Not a good idea for you to be here."

"You don't look too intimidating right now. More like one of those popular movie zombies. What's going on?"

"I needed to take some time off. Get my act together and all that shit."

"Why didn't you call me for help?"

He waved his hand through the air. "Why would I want you to see this?"

Her neck swiveled when she looked around the

room. It was a disaster. A leather coat. Wet, soiled towels. His disgusting trophy necklace of vampire teeth. Cast-off bags of blood. Plates of dried food.

"Are you better?"

Believing it would look bad for Bounty, Dax wanted no one to know they were related. She blew their cover with two of his *frerons* recently when she enlisted Ram and Brak to help drag him out of an O blud den where he enjoyed sinking his fangs into opium addicts with tainted blood. It was a way for vampires to get a real, lasting buzz without a high risk of addiction. Her brother was fighting these demons.

His raspy voice sounded unused. "I'm not as thirsty as I was. So no bludfrenzy. I had a fever with sweats for days. Mostly gone now."

She held back tears. Dax wouldn't want them. Besides, she was afraid if she started crying, she'd never stop. Her brother was her hero. Her savior. A good male. If only he saw himself as she did.

"Kole is looking for you. You're supposed to be working with Tyr on an assignment at Nace's stronghold. Something about drugs."

A jarring laugh arose from Dax's chest. "The ironic assignment convinced me Kole has lost his fucking demon mind." He passed his hand across his chin, the sinister dusting of a mustache and goatee scragglier than usual. "I'll shower, dress, and give the warlock Tyr a call."

Worry crossed her eyes like a shadow. "Are you ready to do this?"

He swung his legs cautiously onto the floor. "Good as new. You can leave now. You've done your job."

"It's not just my job. I…" She was going to say, "worry about you," but it would have offended Dax. So, she settled for another truth. "I love you."

"Maybe you should love someone worthy."

"No one is worthier than you are, brother."

"Cut me loose, Bounty. You're dragging me down. Your love is a giant weight around my neck."

"Don't. You. Dare. Don't lay this shit on my doorstep." Bristling power slammed off the surface of her body as she sent a cold breeze toward Dax. "I love you, but you can be a real ass. Now get out of bed, shower, do your job." She spun on her heel, stomping out of his cabin, wiping tears from her cheeks.

Chapter Eleven

After Spear raped Lizette, part of his morning ritual, he unlocked the chain at her neck. *Snick.* He attached another to the collar, grasping the end of the links, pulling roughly. "Let's get outside before sunrise. After you do your duties, you'll return."

He threw a roll of toilet paper at her, which she barely caught. She lifted the hem of her shabby, soiled nightgown, moving like a dog on a leash.

Spear gave her his back while she hid behind a bush to pee. Though he assaulted her every morning, he closed his eyes while she did her "duties."

Such a gentleman.

When she walked from her cover, he yanked her into the cabin, re-attaching her to the sturdy chain which linked to the eyebolt on the floor. Just short of reaching the front door.

Breakfast passed as it did each day. She cooked and served the berserker. He ate like it was his last meal while she tried not to barf.

When he was about to leave, his hand snatched a hank of her hair. She flinched when he pulled her head back. His lips came down heavily on hers in his version of a goodbye kiss before he lumbered out the door.

Lizette spit on the floor. Running to the kitchen sink, she washed out her mouth, using a cloth and soap to remove all signs of Spear between her legs.

She scooted under the bed, reaching behind a leg to pull her tool from its hiding place. On the floor, she sat beside the eyebolt. With a towel wrapped around her hands, she wedged the rusty nail between the bolt and the wood plank.

Despite the towel, the constant friction chafed her

skin. So Spear would not notice, she made sure to fall at some point during their nightly excursions, marring her palms.

She shifted positions when she tired, curling both legs underneath. Using the other hand for a while, she continued to ram the long nail into the bolt's wood plank. The damage to the area was not visible from a standing position. Besides, Spear always disconnected or connected her chain at her neck rather than the floor.

Switching to her other hand, Lizette grasped the eye bolt to wiggle it. For the past few days, she'd felt the hardware give. The encouraging sign spurred her on. It was the first hope she had experienced since her kidnapping.

Though she hated to, she stopped, rose on stiff legs, and walked into the kitchen to eat lunch. Spear always checked to see what she consumed during the day. She took out two pieces of bread, some meat which looked like ham, and made a sandwich. Nearly choking on big bites, she chewed quickly before she returned to her task.

Singing Gloria Gaynor's "I Will Survive," she poked and prodded, further loosening the bolt. It wiggled. She stopped singing to stare at her work.

I'm almost there.

When the light changed in the room, she reluctantly pushed off the floor, making sure the dust and chips were swept into the gaps between planks. She could leave no evidence of her labor visible. She brushed a hand down her shoddy oversized dress.

In the kitchen, Lizette placed small chunks of timber into the wood-burning stove, lighting them with a match. Cutting up a chicken and carrots, she arranged them in a pot on the grates. Taking out flour, shortening, baking soda, salt, and milk, she made dough. Rolling it out, she cut circles with a glass before placing the biscuits onto a baking sheet. Once she popped them into the oven, she curled up on the large chair and grabbed the book on the table, turning on the lamp.

I was on page one-sixteen yesterday. By today, I would have been to page four-seventy-three. I read slowly because I do a lot of housework. Fortunately, Spear doesn't understand anything about cleaning since he lives in this sty.

By now, the room was dark because of the shutters on the outside of the cabin and the waning light, but Lizette sensed when the sun set. Soon he would be home.

Survive. Survive. Survive.

She bit her lip, swallowing a gasp when she heard the door rattle. Entering, the savage paused to check out the room, his seven-foot body barely fitting through the frame. His eyes took in everything. Finally, they landed on her. He stepped forward, swinging the door closed. After he locked it again, he stuffed the key into his front pants pocket.

He looked feral today, though he donned human clothes—jeans and a T-shirt. He wore his black hair in multiple thick braids like an ancient Viking. His beard was as dark as his hair, with similar tight braids woven through it.

Lizette forced a smile while she squeaked out, "Hello."

The berserker lifted her from the chair. When he allowed her feet to touch the floor, his hands began their exploration. One fondled her breasts. The other a hip, pulling her dress up until his fingers touched skin.

Smothering her revulsion, she found her voice. "You look tired. I bet you're starving. Let me get dinner on the table. I hate to see you so."

With his palm caressing her thigh and a grimy paw moving toward her sex, he paused. "Chicken and biscuits?"

"Yes. Carrots with the chicken. We have pie left from yesterday. I'll warm a piece after we eat."

She pushed a washcloth along with a towel at him. "Go clean at the river. Get comfortable while I put dinner on."

Lizette had no idea what Spear did all day, but when he came home, he was dirty and covered in blood. Early on, the odor made her retch, for which she earned a few bruises. As time passed, the smell became the least of her tortures.

Once he returned, they ate in silence. She cleaned the kitchen. Afterward, the dreaded nightly ritual began.

It always started out the same way. Spear said, "It is bath time, *kjaer*."

Bile rose in Lizette's throat, but she stifled a scream. The berserker released her from the restraint. He re-attached a leash to her collar. After stopping to gather a basin filled with supplies, he walked her outside.

He led her to a spot where the river was damned to form a pool.

His eyes aglow, he said, "Take off your dress."

While Lizette did as he bid, his chest expanded with his rapid breathing. His hand went to his trousers. Unbuttoning, he dropped them. He yanked on his disgusting penis, stroking himself while she stood naked in front of him, pretending she was somewhere else.

He stepped away from his pants, shucked off his shirt, and pulled her into the pooled water behind him. Lathering soap onto his hands, he washed her, every intimate part. He rubbed his hand across her breasts, closing his eyes. Spreading her legs apart, his fingers explored, cleaning her sex while he moaned in pleasure.

She no longer gripped her thighs together. This sick ritual was going to be completed. She simply stood still while she dreamed of her freedom. She saw the trees beyond the river, imagining cozy homes, warm fireplaces, happy families, some kind person who would take her in. While he bathed her, she fantasized somewhere pretty, someplace safe.

Finally, Spear walked her out of the river to dry her off. Once they returned to the hut, the nighttime horror began.

The next morning was like any other. Once the berserker left, she knew today would be the one. She changed clothes but didn't plan for dinner or lunch. She plopped down beside the eye bolt. In a frenzy, she resumed her task.

Despite the towel around her hand, it stung, bled. Yet she kept going. Jamming the nail into the hole, she gripped the bolt to shake it. It shimmied up until it slipped free from the floor.

She gasped, momentarily stunned. When she recovered, she grabbed the length of chain to wrap it around her waist. She ran for the biggest window, searching for a tool to break through it. Her gaze landed on the iron frying pan. Lifting it by the handle, she slammed it through the glass and exterior wooden shutter. Both gave. Lizette pulled herself up, dropping through the opening onto the ground below. She was bleeding from the shards scattered in the dirt, but she felt glorious.

She laughed. When tears streamed down her cheeks, she swiftly wiped them away. She shielded her eyes from the bright sun while watching a flock of birds fly overhead. Drawing a deep breath through her nose, she took a whiff of pine trees, jasmine, possibly approaching rain.

Freedom. This is the smell of freedom.

For the first time in months, Lizette Lee ran toward the river, toward the scent of survival.

****

While she lounged on the bank watching the River Am, Indigo idly stroked the lion-like tail of her gryphon.

"It's changed, hasn't it, Oskar? It's not just my overactive, albeit amazing, imagination."

The beast swung its massive neck, lowering its head to snort a puff of smoke. Her conjured gryphon was unique with the head and wings of an eagle, the neck and torso of a dragon, and the haunches and feet of a lion. Following its show, it pecked the hand stroking its tail.

"I'm petting you as fast as I can, Oskar. Don't be greedy." Her palm wandered to his neck, his green scales like those of a dragon.

The beast cast a petulant look in her direction.

Indigo gestured toward distant forks of the river, barely visible behind so much greenery. "See the possible futures, roiling upstream? Thrice more than usual. How am I supposed to scope out each? Evaluate which will become the present? Better yet, how am I to remember so many possibilities?"

Oskar snorted.

"Suck it up, you say. Don't be rude."

The witch tucked booted feet under her long, light-weight skirt before staring straight out into the turbulent water before her. The river crashed against its banks, formed whirlpools of concentric circles, and surged forward and backward at odds with itself. Stirring the waters like rage. Here, the countless streams of possibility fought to feed into the present.

Much further downstream, the river was calm. There, the present flowed into the past undisturbed.

The gryphon ruffled its wings.

"Just do it, you say? What are you? A Nike ad? I'm a lone witch. Truly incredible, of course, but nonetheless."

Oskar bobbled his head. His body shed feathers, scales, or fur in equal quantity.

"Glad you agree." She twirled a strand of hair around her finger, not convinced her beastly friend understood the complexity of her task.

In unison their necks pivoted toward the present, which was fed by only the winning futures.

The Gryphon squawked.

"I agree. It's a level ten white water rafting trip. Usually, where the future meets the present is a level two or three. What does it mean?"

Her conjured pet's tail swished back and forth vigorously.

"Hmm. Yes, disturbing events are an *au courant* reality, but we are unprepared."

Indigo glanced at her companion, whose neck was nodding again.

"Right. We need to fasten our life vests and prepare for a bumpy boat ride."

Oskar ruffled his feathers, rose, spread his wings, and took off. He circled the river, flapping, screeching so loudly Indigo was sure he could be heard in Covenkirk. After three wide loops, he swooped down to settle at her feet.

She rose onto her combat boots, brushed off her cobalt-blue spring skirt, and snapped her fingers before she climbed aboard. "File a flight plan for my brother's office, oh winged beast."

Her gryphon took to the air, Indigo on his back. She shouted to the skies, "Yippee-ki-yay, mutherfuckers."

****

Tyr swallowed his drink in one gulp when someone pulled alongside him at the bar.

Dax was dressed like the Grim Reaper at a funeral. Black on black. His midnight hair was tied back, falling nearly to his waist. His obsidian eyes were shot with red, a sure sign the bludfrenzy was knocking at his door. A dark, sinister goatee shadowed his chin while around his neck hung a necklace strung with fangs. Nobody knew the gruesome story.

The gnarly vampire tapped the counter twice. The bartender nearly pissed his pants while he rushed to pour a Demon Scourge whiskey, his hand shaking like a leaf in the wind when he handed it off to Dax.

Never having worked a case alone with the Firebrand rumored to walk the edge of sanity, Tyr wasn't sure he wanted to now. Still, an assignment was an assignment.

"Glad you could make it."

"I had something to do," snarled Dax. No other explanation followed as he tossed back his drink and tapped for another.

"Here's the short and sweet. A drug ring is operating. North Shelter has been assigned the take down, but apparently, it's a bigger task than expected. We've been ordered to lend an assist. I've got abso-fucking-lutely nothing." The warlock curled his pierced lip.

"Nace's terrain."

"His Firebrands are stretched. Lots of pharmaceuticals popping up. I hear tell the drug we're after is hell's own. It makes the user zombie-like, highly susceptible to suggestion."

"After chewing out my ass for disappearing, Kole hinted about what we would face. On my way here, I stopped to talk to an acquaintance, persuading him to give me a lead. He didn't have much to share, but we have a rock to flip."

"Is your acquaintance still breathing?" Tyr didn't really care. He only wanted to know if there was a body to bury. Leaving a trail of blood-drained Aeternals could get dicey, even if their previous inhabitants were scum.

A smile, more like Emperor Palpatine in *Star Wars* than Howdy Doody, crossed Dax's face. "Still alive. Maybe short a pint or two. Drink up. We need to find a shifter named Cage."

Damn. He's good. When I grow up, I want to be that scary.

****

Good to his word, Ram stepped back with a flourish, allowing Denim to enter the portal first. He was determined to let her die if it was her choice. It wouldn't be his fault. He also vowed to keep his dick in his pants.

She smirked but stepped through into the Whorl. Ram followed close behind, dropping low when he exited on Earth, resisting the urge to pull Denim to the rear. His hand rested on the handle of his Glock.

Denim glanced at him while they approached the roll-up door leading out of the parking garage. "Anyone around?"

The satyr used his superior senses to listen while he sniffed the air. He reached out farther. Only the sounds of party-goers on the street. The old smells of *eau de humans* wafted toward him. "No." At least, she realized he was better at something. Even if it was only sniffing or eavesdropping.

Ram awaited instructions while Denim squinted at him as if irritated. "Let's go then."

He drew upright, following her through the exit. His strategy with the female was to resist his natural inclination to protect her.

Big pat on the back.

So far, he was doing well. By the end of the night, he might be rocking a headache or sore muscles from restraining himself, but he was determined to treat her like a female Firebrand.

And no feeding. Stellar plans. I've ruled out sex, too.

"You're angry. You must agree a relationship will complicate our working together. Plus, I'm sorry I reported to Kole. Just stop trying to protect me. Let me do my job."

"I am. I was an ass before. Would you like flowers as an apology?"

"I'd rather have a gun. Nothing says sorry better than a firearm. You know, I wasn't asking to be in charge. You're the mission leader. You get to make the tough calls."

"Thanks."

"Be sure those decisions don't start with protecting the weak human chick."

Fine lines.

Ram reached out with his senses again. Nothing. "I won't overstep my authority."

Lie. I will.

Her shoulders rose and fell with a big sigh. "Look. I want a partner. Not a bodyguard. Not a minion either."

Before he piped off about his superior skills, he rethought his words, going with "I'm doing the best I can."

"I appreciate it."

"Can I still hit on you?"

Denim laughed. He loved the joyous sound.

"Not now. Maybe later."

"I'm holding you to it."

She was walking ahead of him, her human ass a spectacular display, a tempting sway to her hips despite the fact she wore trousers designed for a state patrolman. Her functional boots didn't make a sound on the cobblestone alley.

Denim glanced over her shoulder, her ponytail swishing side-to-side, giving Ram ideas.

"You can walk alongside me."

"No. I'm great here." The view was better. Besides, he'd make sure no one slipped up behind them. Of course, he didn't say that to Denim.

****

She didn't buy the satyr's big personality switch for a minute. Chauvinists did not change their spots any more than leopards did. Maybe she should have argued stronger for a different partner. *No.* She didn't want a different partner. The contradiction made her head swim.

She was attracted to Ram. Taken in by hot looks, a fantastic body with rock-hard muscle, a kissable mouth, massive amounts of charm, beautiful hair, and a big dick. What wasn't to like about him? *Oh, yeah.* His philandering eyes. He wasn't relationship material. Still, she wasn't in the market for a boyfriend.

Right? Headache.

Near a small dead-end street leading to a portal they'd been assigned to check out, Ram grabbed her elbow, bringing a finger to his lips.

She put her back against the wall, mimicking his move. He turned, sliding his body in front of her, chest to chest, letting a dense fog encase them. He pushed tighter against her.

His arm circled her waist. The other rested high on her back.

He shushed her again until a mist spread around

them both.

When she squirmed against his hold, Denim felt the thick, steely length of Ram's erection on her belly. She whispered, "What the fuck is that?"

He shrugged. "The one thing's kinda obvious. The other is my camouflage. Satyr skill. I just cloaked us, made us invisible. We have visitors. Hush." His finger rested on her moist lips.

She hoped nobody else saw the glow from his bright green eyes.

Denim stopped twisting to get out of his arms. Turning her head in the direction of the alley, she tracked three men. They were armed, tell-tale bulges sticking out from under their jackets.

All of a sudden, one bent his knees, springing from the ground onto the roof of a building. The other two followed.

"Are those guys humans?" she whispered.

"Through and through." Ram fixed on the men who streaked across the rooftop.

He released Denim, the cloak fading.

"Take me with you up there."

"Grab hold."

She latched her arms around Ram's neck as he leaped to the top of the building. When he set her feet down, they sprinted in the same direction as their targets. Jumping across three rooftops with the satyr's help, she observed the men disappear over the side of a brick structure in the distance. By the time she and Ram arrived, they merged with a crowd of Mardi Gras revelers below.

With her hands on her hips, she stared at the street. "That's not normal."

"Damn straight."

"We lost them. My fault. If you didn't have to

carry me, you could have caught one of them."

"You're my partner. You go where I do." He inhaled, his gaze on the activities below. "These weren't the same three males Tyr and I bumped up against. I wonder how many teams they've got at our portals."

She shrugged. "I hate being outsmarted and outmuscled, *cher*."

Ram scrubbed the back of his fist across his chin. "*Cher*? Doesn't it mean 'darling'?"

"No. Yes. But we call everyone '*cher*.' It's a local thing."

When he grinned, her heart skipped a beat.

She waved her hand dismissively. "It means nothing."

"If you say so, darling."

"Stop it." She couldn't help the silly smile curving her lips. *Yep*. He was charming. "Explain something."

"Anything."

"Why do your eyes go from translucent sea-glass-green to neon?"

"Hmm. A lot of reasons. Strong emotions. Feeding."

She stood still. "So, Galena was serious. Feeding? As from arousal?"

"Uh-huh."

"I wasn't aroused when you cloaked us."

"Doll. You can lie to yourself, but it won't do any good to lie to me. You were a full-course meal. Including dessert and after dinner drinks. Throw in the appetizers, too. A quick taste is second nature to a satyr."

Ram clutched her waist and dropped them into the alley where he tapped his wrist. *Hey, Kole. I've got more news about our humans. Not only are they using tranqs, but they are faster than a speeding bullet, more powerful than a locomotive, and able to leap tall buildings in a single bound.*

When he disconnected, he relayed his telepathic conversation to Denim. "What do you think?"

"Shit's getting strange."

"I'd say so."

Chapter Twelve

Skyler gazed through the window, following the morning work traffic. The soundproofing at the Alliance was terrific, but she still heard the gentle hum of automobiles below. She'd always loved the sounds and sights of Chicago, her Windy City.

More recently she learned to appreciate Lucifer's Forge in the Knife's Edge region, the ancestral home of her demon mate. Its red rocks, its sandy desert, breathless nights, stars which brightened the sky, sounds of animals as they scurried around the sagebrush, and the rich sultry perfume of the wild air. Someday, it would become their home. Once the Blood Coven was safe. She looked forward to it. Strange she would find such beauty as well as a home in another realm with an animus demon, a male whose powerful body was a constant aphrodisiac and whose love was a warm embrace.

Turning from the window, she walked to the hand-carved cradle. She rocked the beloved piece of furniture Kole built for their child.

Suddenly, Skyler's palm flew to her mountainous belly as a wave of nausea settled there.

Here I go.

Her eyes lost focus. She heard no sounds, not even the chatter from the outer office or from the street below. Her skin prickled. But she didn't move or call for help.

When an image came into sharp focus, her mind's eye zeroed in to settle on a computer screen.

Once the disturbing scene faded, she was back in her chair, staring out the window at the Chicago skyline. Thankfully, she was seated because she was always a little dizzy coming out of a trance. At least, she now recognized when she experienced a vision.

Anna opened the door, chattering on about some contract Skyler was supposedly working on. Her eyes widened as she raced toward her boss as fast as her stilettos could carry her. "Brak," she yelled into the outer office, "get in here."

The administrative assistant pivoted the chair around, touching her hand to Skyler's forehead.

The summoned Firebrand burst through the doorway surprisingly fast for such a huge male. "What's wrong?" He stopped in front of the desk, his gun drawn while he surveyed the room. Finding no danger, he holstered his weapon. "Is it the baby?"

"No. I think she's had another vision. I hate those things. She's damp. Her eyes are still glassy. Skyler. Skyler, are you with us?"

Anna's voice came from far away. "Yes." Skyler's pupils riveted on the woman and the giant male.

Brak. That was his name. Her one-man security force. Damn. He was big.

Skyler shook her head, rested a palm on her heart, and was back. "Yes. I'm fine." She immediately glanced down at her huge baby mound, a possessive, calming hand there. Her trainer assured her scrying would have no effect on her unborn babe. Still she worried. Of course Kole was a raving lunatic about the whole issue regardless of assurances.

"You had another vision?" Anna put a hand on Brak's shoulder to let him know the emergency was over.

Both stared at Skyler as if two heads sat on her shoulders. Maybe three.

"Give me a minute here. I need to think."

The two didn't so much as twitch a muscle.

Skyler's eyes flashed around the room while she

considered what she'd seen.

"I need the new director of technology up here. Now." Skyler raised her voice, something she rarely did since her icy demeanor usually did the trick, but at this moment, she didn't feel cold and calculating. She was steaming mad.

Anna raced out the door.

"Do you need me, Skyler?" Brak asked.

"No, but you might as well stay."

He flopped his oversized body into one of the chairs in front of her desk, stretching out his enormous leather-clad legs.

A freckled redheaded guy bounded through the door with Anna right behind him.

"Everyone stick around but do close the door."

Three pairs of eyes latched onto Skyler when she opened the conversation. "Tell me about our records of the portals between Earth and Scath."

The new director of information services looked barely out of high school. References claimed he was top-notch. He'd replaced Sarah Jenkins. Cal, the assistant legal officer at the Alliance at the time, murdered her at the end of last year.

He pulled his brows tight in obvious confusion. "You mean how many we've got, where the files are stored, how they are secured, how we got the data? What are you looking for?"

"Let's start with how we obtained the data."

"Sure. Okay, then. Obviously much of it was already in a file when I came to work here." He waited for some response from Skyler.

There was none. So he continued. "I get new portal information from the Ministry of Compliance on Scath whenever gateways are added. I personally update the file with the new data."

"Why do you personally enter the data?"

"I figure the portals are pretty important stuff. By entering the new data myself, it's extra secure."

"So, you expect problems?"

"I always expect problems."

"How does the Ministry of Compliance send you this new information?"

"Through my e-mail."

"Is it secure?"

He snorted but saw Skyler's frown. "Sorry. What I mean to say is, my e-mail is beyond secure."

"How secure is the file documenting the portals?"

"Encrypted. Quite secure."

"But could someone other than you get in?"

He stopped fidgeting, sitting deadly still. "What's this about, Chief Maxwell?"

"We've been betrayed."

****

Celene drummed her fingers on the kitchen table. Unlike other prisoners, she and Jace didn't scratch the passing days on the mud wall of a dingy cell. *No.* They measured time in their hellhole by how many words they read. "Go get the next volume of *The Path*, roomie. I know you're dying to start it."

Jace jumped up from her chair to rush to the bookcase. Her fingers skidded over spines of titles, finally landing on the right book. "A new adventure."

"I'd rather be parasailing but whatever."

"Think of Ohngel's words, recorded by the Cambion, as a way to study our enemy. Come over. Get comfy." Jace snuggled into the sofa, opening the unread book to its first pages.

Weary from a lengthy truth-seeking journey, I, the Cambion from Wales, rested beside a late evening fire after finishing a meager repast. A nightchat flew from the trees, singing. The warbler-like bird trilled, chirped, and whistled, its raspy notes a message from Ohngel, the fire-winged assassin of the OneCreator, the male I would deem prophet and friend in the coming years.

Oft thereafter, Ohngel or the prophet-warrior's emissary, the nightchat, emerged from the thickets to tell a tale of hope, courage, caution, or enlightenment for the Aeternals placed upon this world by the Genitrix Gahya.

"Blah, blah, blah. Stuff we've read before." Jace skimmed the pages. "Here it is."

Disconsolate over Niviane's betrayal and the bleak future of my isolation from fellow mages, I sank further into despair, a most debilitating humor, any action too troublesome to undertake. But the assassin-become-friend, Ohngel, counseled and set me to new tasks. Between these labors, the nightchat continued to visit, singing its narratives. To take my mind off the child I may never meet, hold, or succor, the messenger told of the Aeternals' fantastical origins which I penned in Volume III: The Creation.

Jace closed the book, her fingers holding the place. "They're late."

Celene savored Jace's voice, memorizing it, knowing it might be the last time she heard it. She glanced at the clock on the wall. "Only a few minutes. Keep going."

For about a year, the women had been prisoners in this two-bedroom house. Jace de Vries was kidnapped returning home from her job at a New Paltz, NY, winery. She'd been locked in a cellar before being transferred here.

Celene Bailey, on the other hand, was an heiress hooked on extreme sports and near-death thrills. In fact, that was how she'd gotten caught. Having base jumped Angel Falls in Venezuela, she hit the landing zone only to have a bag tossed over her head. Next stop, monster central.

But they did not blindly accept captivity. With tap water running, the mixer whirring, and loud hip hop playing, they schemed. They developed their own sign language, a version of charades. Early in their captivity, they tried to overpower their guards. Not possible. When they failed, they went on a hunger strike. The revolt earned them a new warden and a few extra privileges. Now, they had an escape plan.

A digital ping interrupted Jace's reading. The outside door swung open.

Celene gulped.

Great. He has to be the biggest guard. Hope he didn't sleep well last night.

"Let's go," he grumbled.

Setting the book on the side table, Jace smoothed a hand over the cover.

The guard wasn't much on chitchat. What he lacked in that area, he made up for in size. He was a mountain of a man, thick necked, beefy shouldered, and no conscience.

The two women bounced from the couch, already dressed for exercise in the yard. Sweats, T-shirts, tennies.

Celene nodded at Jace, clasping her hand. Today was a go. They followed the guard outside where each woman took a deep breath of fresh air.

The hulk settled into his usual seat nearby as Celene set the pace for their daily run on the makeshift track, taking a long lead. In seconds, Jace caught up with her.

Two laps. Three laps. Seven laps.

Celene glanced at the guard who slouched in the chair with his legs stretched out, his lids closed.

Not breathing hard, Jace said, "Let's do thirty

laps today."

The hulk stirred, pulling up a little straighter, his hearing sharp but his head rolling back as he resumed dozing.

Celene marked his movements, hoping their inane banter would lull him into a deep sleep. "Thirty's great. What do you think of the parables in *The Path*?"

They fell easily into conversation about the book, using parts of it as code for their plans.

"I like the one which begins with 'Look north and see the way.'"

"Great one, Jace. I'm particularly fond of how the philosopher urges his followers to lift themselves up and overcome the obstacles before finding a new path."

"Are you sure, Celene?"

"Yes, I am. The Cambion talks of love. I love you like a sister, Jace. You're someone I depend on."

On the lap around the track, her roomie bobbed her head toward the eight-foot wall on the north side of their exercise yard. "Overcome your obstacles and move on. It is what Ohngel told the great warlock."

As part of the agreement to end the hunger strike, Lort, their vampire warden, added a gym where they spent hours lifting weights, strengthening their arms, building muscle. They chucked each other off the ground as part of a gymnastics routine. Just a step into a hand and up and over. They ran laps every day. Their legs were strong. Their arms stronger. They were as ready as they would ever be.

Today, as they ran side-by-side, Jace squeezed Celene's hand. "Keep reading until I come for you."

Now or never.

Jace had been a runner in high school and college. She'd even broken some state record. Celene was the natural choice to stay put. Having lived seeking danger, the next thrill, she could deal with the creatures while Jace sprinted to freedom. Her roomie didn't like the arrangement but eventually understood it was the right one.

As they rounded the bend near the north wall, Celene glanced at the guard who remained asleep. She nodded at her partner.

They blasted for the wall. Celene dropped to one knee, cupping her palms together. Jace stepped into her hands and was flipped up in nearly the same motion, tossed by her fellow prisoner to the top of the wall.

Jace barely caught the blocks, hanging on by fingertips. Struggling to get a foothold while straining her muscles, she pulled herself onto the uppermost ledge.

Celene didn't wait for her partner's escape. She charged toward the guard, prepared for him to awaken.

When Jace flopped to the other side, the hulk woke up.

Probably his super hearing.

Celene toppled his chair with a kick. She straddled his chest, locking her arms around his neck. Her goal was to hold him down by any means possible for as long as possible.

Jace had to make it to freedom. Since she was the faster runner, she'd do it. She'd taste freedom for both of them. Celene just had to provide her with time to get away.

At first, the guard was shocked, too surprised to free himself. When he began to fight in earnest, Celene held on. He landed a solid punch to her jaw, tears stinging her eyes from the sharp pain.

She held on.

He gripped both of her wrists, rising, her feet dangling in the air. The guard tossed her against the house, rattling her head when it struck the siding. Celene launched herself at him again, flinging her arms around his knees, taking him down.

The demon growled, putting a boot to her ribs once he stood. Celene curled into a ball, but the kicks kept coming. She passed out with only one thought looping through her mind.

Run, Jace. Run.

****

Galena dipped her fingers into the buttered popcorn, grabbing a handful, her attention on the TV screen. She was enjoying a rare day off. Hence, the movie marathon. "So, Ram?"

Denim answered but she fixed on Uma Thurman in *Kill Bill: Volume 1.* "What about him?" She stretched toward the coffee table for another fistful of popcorn.

"The two of you. Are there sparks?"

"That would make me pretty stupid. He's arrogant. He's emotionally unavailable. He's left a trail of honeys."

Galena giggled. "Those are his good points. Seriously. If you scrape away all his bullshit, he's a good male. For a satyr. Besides, all male Firebrands play around until they meet their mates."

"Whoa, girl. Mate? You know my story. The satyr and I will maintain a professional relationship. I've nursed a broken jaw. I don't need a broken heart."

"Sure," Galena said around a mouthful of popcorn, her gaze returning to the screen.

When her D-chip signaled, she groaned and tapped a wrist. "This better be good. The knife fight is coming up, and it's classic. … Yeah. … Gotcha." Galena glanced at her movie-enthralled, visiting roomie and arched her brows. Since the call was not from a *freron*, she spoke aloud, unable to talk mind to mind.

"What's up? Another incident at a portal?"

"No. A strange message." She picked up the remote, clicking off the TV. "We've been called to Director Alarik's office now. Heavy emphasis on the 'now' part of the convo."

"Both of us?"

"Especially you, it would seem."

"Who called?"

"The director's personal assistant, Zora."

"Do they need more blood from me? I already gave yesterday. Maybe they screwed it up. I'll bet that's it." Denim unfolded the leg under her and pushed off the couch. "I'll just check the mirror and put on some better-looking sweats. I don't want to scare anyone."

"I'm right there with ya. We'll go in five."

****

Denim squeezed Galena's arm to portal into the Ministry of Well Being. "I want one of those D-chip things so I can hop around Scath and anywhere else I please. What's the chance? My portal jumper's bulky and so yesterday."

"I can always ask. I doubt someone's going to embed one into a human's wrist and wire it to your brain, though."

A knock-out blonde was *tap, tap, tapping* on computer keys. The woman must be Zora. Did everyone on the realm have to be so good looking? Ram had probably already hit on her. *Hell*. Denim didn't want the picture in her head. Their legs tangled in the sheets. Them going at it like horny teens.

The buxom blonde slid out of her chair, revealing a tight sweater and tighter ass-hugging skirt.

"Succubus," whispered Galena, as if that said it all.

Denim nodded, feeling a bit frumpy.

"He's been waiting. It's inappropriate to leave the

director hanging." The bombshell sashayed toward the door, opening it, shooing the two females inside.

Denim's eyes surveyed the office. Alarik was seated behind a desk. He wore a black robe, along with a dark expression. Commander Kole lounged on the couch, an ankle crossed over his knee and an arm around a frosty, gorgeous blonde who looked familiar. Everyone stopped talking when she entered with the Amazon.

Not good.

Galena greeted her commander and strode up to Alarik, offering a hand. He rose, shook, and then indicated the two empty seats.

Denim barely had the wherewithal to nod. A million frightening thoughts crawled into her brain. Something horrible was happening with her.

They found evidence of a life-threatening disease in my blood sample. A friend of mine at the agency has been injured or killed.

"Relax, Ms. Quinn," said the director.

"Denim, please."

"Certainly. We received the results of your blood test." Again, he pointed to the seats.

Denim collapsed into one of the chairs. Her mother died of Parkinson's, but she'd had her blood tested years ago. She did not have the gene. At least, that's what she'd been told. It was obviously all a lie. Someone messed up the test. They'd analyzed the wrong sample. "And?"

Alarik resumed sitting. "I'll get right to the point. You have genetic markers indicating you are a Blood Coven descendant."

She let out the breath she'd been holding and chuckled. "Thank goodness."

"What?" Galena stared at Denim as if a loose screw was rattling around in her skull.

"I mean, the news is not so bad." She felt as though she'd dodged a huge disease-carrying bullet headed right for her brain. To say nothing of a hospital bed with years of agony in her future.

"Actually, Ms. Quinn … er … Denim, it's not all good either. I called Kole and his mate into the meeting to help explain what you'll face."

Calmer now, Denim flipped her gaze to the icy beauty sitting beside Kole. The woman wasn't too cold. Her hand was sliding up and down the fiery commander's leg, almost unconsciously.

She spoke. "I'm Skyler Maxwell, a descendant also. That's why Director Alarik asked me to accompany my mate. Believe me when I say it's good news and bad news."

The white-blonde, decked out in designer clothes and a fashionable chignon, could have stepped out of the pages of *Vogue for the Expectant Mother*. Denim would never peg her as the mate of the scary, heavily muscled, fierce demon commander. She should be on the arm of a lean Brioni-suited businessman driving a Rolls Royce.

Denim snapped her fingers. "Skyler Maxwell. I know who you are. You're the Alliance's chief legal officer. You're a Blood Coven descendant?"

A regal smile tweaked the corners of the woman's lips. "Yes. I am."

Here was a live descendant sitting in the same room. Though rumors about Skyler ran rampant through the Alliance, Denim discounted most of the gossip.

Wait a minute.

Alarik just told Denim she was one, too. "Good and bad? Give me the good first, Chief Maxwell."

Startling eyes like lilac ice met Denim's puzzled gaze. "Skyler, please." Her chin tilted up like a queen's. "Your life is about to change. You'll possess unimagined power."

"Power?"

"Yes. So far, each of us has a … uh … gift, or power. I am a seer, of sorts. I have visions of people or events. I'm called a scryer."

"Impossible."

"Not for humans, but I'm no longer fully human, Denim. Neither are you. It's hard to accept at first."

"Trust me. I'm all human." Denim pinched her arm as if her flesh was proof.

Skyler offered a polite smile which implied Denim was a damn fool. "I changed. So will you. When your gifts surface, you'll be assigned a trainer, a mage who'll help you control and develop your new talents."

Denim nodded, despite retaining a healthy dose of doubt. "Okay. Hit me with the bad."

"You'll be on Cerberus's hit list. We don't know why he wants us, but it can't be good. His men captured Braelyn, Rein's mate. I was attacked, but…" Her lilac eyes rolled toward her mate. "…they failed to capture me. Margo and Chay were kidnapped. Thankfully, they escaped."

"Which brings us to maybe-good-but-probably-bad news." Kole uncrossed his foot to lean forward. "You'll be moving into my stronghold until we snag Cerberus."

Denim held up a hand. "Whoa right there. I have a place in New Orleans, Commander. I have a job at the Alliance. You can forget about the move."

"It's not an option." Sparks jumped from Kole's tented fingers.

"Sure it is. I'm not relocating." Denim clamped her jaw tight, a message of pure stubborn determination.

When a flame shot from one of Kole's fingertips, she flinched.

Skyler, obviously unafraid of being scorched, wrapped a slender-fingered, manicured hand around Kole's much larger one. The sparks stopped immediately. He exhaled, relaxed his bunched shoulders, and drew in his temper. His mate tilted her head to the side while smiling at the huge, dangerous demon. "Tone down the alpha male, darling. You frighten people."

She twisted toward Denim. "This intimidating demon and I live at the stronghold, along with Margo and Chay. Rein and Braelyn recently moved in as did Nico Abello."

"Abello? Wasn't he an Alliance agent?" Denim remembered him from the meeting with Kole. He had aired his problems with Sabine while she hammered Ram.

"The same. He'll look forward to having another agent at the stronghold."

"I worked hard to get where I am. I'm not sacrificing my job. The move is a no-go." Denim crossed her arms over her chest.

Galena rested a hand on Denim's shoulder. "Think about it. Cerberus is a serious guy who wants his own set of Blood Coven mages for some reason."

"Nope. Got a life. Love it. Got the Alliance. Love it."

Skyler glanced at Kole. She arched a regal brow.

For a while, he held her gaze. Then he blinked, doing a double-take as if the lights just switched on in his brain. "No. Hell no. Not another one. I'm not doing it, Frisca. One blackmailer's enough."

"Doing what, Commander?" asked Galena.

"Taking on another fucking Alliance agent just because they're too damn stubborn or stupid to stay out of harm's way."

Denim eyeballed each person in the office until

the situation dawned on her. "Oh. Abello. That's why he works for you now? Blackmail?"

"Yeah, but one dumbass is enough." Kole snarled despite Skyler's pat to the back of his hand.

Denim grinned. "I bet two dumbasses would be better, Commander."

Could moving to this other realm be the fun Marta wanted me to have?

It sure might.

Chapter Thirteen

Dax signaled for Tyr to wrap a cloaking spell around them while they waited outside a cabin in North Shelters.

After a few hours, a coyote shifter rolled in on a Ducati, weaving all over the road. Engine off, he swung a leg over the machine and stumbled through the front door of his house.

"Nice crotch rocket. Wonder where he got the green for that baby." Tyr, a biker himself, was drooling.

Dax, a chopper owner also, agreed. It was a beauty. "A mystery. A good-for-nothing male like this with a sweet ride." He stepped out of Tyr's spell.

"Let's solve the puzzle." The warlock Firebrand advanced on the cabin door. The moonlight shone on his face, exaggerating the sickle tat below his eye and reflecting off the shit-ton of silver poking into his flesh.

Dax didn't understand why a male would want so much metal on himself, unless it was a weapon.

But live and let live. God only knows, I have enough problems of my own.

Tyr slammed a boot into the front door. They stormed inside as the shifter lounged on the couch with a dead-ahead stare. The male lurched to his feet.

"Cage, what's up?" Dax knew the bum. They hung out in some of the same blud and flesh dens where an Aeternal could partake of any perversity.

The obviously stoned shifter dropped to the floor, freeing his coyote. As he sprang onto four legs, his jaw morphed into a muzzle. The rest of his face stayed the same. His fur had a serious mange problem. His torso was a little flabby, mostly white skin dusted with hair. Hard to tell if he was humanoid or critter.

Dax's fangs cut into his lower lip. "What the hell?"

"Goddamn. Butt ugly," said Tyr.

When the partially transformed Cage attacked, Dax flashed behind him, grabbing his neck to fling him onto his back.

Holding the scruffy semi-coyote down, Dax arrowed a command into his mind. "Shift."

Cage's body trembled but remained unchanged.

Dax leaned closer, sniffing. "I compelled him. It should've worked, but no go. He smells wrong. Drugs, I'm guessing."

"Why would a coyote take a drug to do this?" Tyr curled an upper lip.

"Could be he's a fool. Could be he swallowed some experimental shit."

"Change." Once again, Dax invaded the shifter's mind as only a master vamp could.

Cage shifted to his human form while his glassy eyes whirly-gigged.

"Where did you get this drug?" Tyr bent over the coyote.

Instead of answering, he growled.

Dax growled louder. "If you're telling me to go to hell, relax. I'm already there. If you don't talk to us, you'll wish you were, too."

Cage gathered a deep breath. "Power … to … Scath." He recited the phrase robotically, haltingly.

"Who sold you the drugs?" Tyr fingered the silver bar through his brow.

"Power to Scath."

"Nice sentiment, but you're nucking futs. Here goes." Dax dug deep into Cage's mind.

Tyr tugged on the earring in his lobe. "This can work out well or turn him to mush."

Dax shot up, jumping away from the coyote shifter. "What the fucking fuck? His brain's fried. There's nothing there."

"What? Something's got to be in his brain even if he is a drugged-up, bat-shit-crazy loon."

"I mean, nothing sane. A single thought is bouncing around in his cranium. That's all."

"What thought?"

"Power to Scath. Over and over again. On a loop."

Cage trembled before he went into a full-on convulsion. When he did, he shifted into the hideous semi-coyote from before.

Dax flipped a scowl at Tyr. "Two fucking days to find him, and he's gone."

Tyr nodded.

The vampire Firebrand wrapped both palms around Cage's neck and twisted it off his shoulders. With no remorse, he tossed the head onto the couch. Walking to the sink, he turned on the faucet, rinsing blood from his hands.

"Let's go chat with my other lead," he said to Tyr.

The warlock shrugged. "I got your back, vampire."

****

Jarek planted the point of his spear into the ground as he did each morning when he exited his steel fortified yurt at the Encampment Stronghold to inspect his command. The gesture demonstrated his trust. He put his life in their hands. In turn, they offered him their loyalty. A just trade.

Being a Scion Firebrand was a legacy. The Phoenix called to service only those with an ancestor who had served.

His grandfather Anthive once marched with the legendary Ten Thousand Immortals. His father also reported to duty. Jarek followed in his ancestors' footsteps, protecting Scath, Darque, and even Earth. Now he was a commander.

At six-foot-eight with a solid build, his shoulders were as wide as most big-ass berserkers while his fighting skills inspired mythic tales. Few of his warriors dared to spar with him these days. Those who did wanted to improve their combat knowhow and didn't care if they limped away with broken bones, bleeding wounds, and concussions.

Jarek eyed his command, a ragtag bunch of misfits who dressed like the thieves, murderers, rogues, and assassins who roamed Scath. Some wore pelts of slain beasts in the manner of berserkers. Others wrapped desert scarves around their faces in the style of Arabs. The rest were bareheaded with long hair worn loose, pulled back, or braided. Scars as plentiful as their tattoos decorated war-tested bodies. They sent a clear message to those Aeternals bent on breaking the laws. *We are the meanest mutherfuckers in the realm.* Jarek counted himself at the front of the line.

Darius stepped forward. "Commander." His voice was low, hoarse. A scar ran from under his left brow, down to his jawbone and neck. A century ago, a berserker nearly severed his head, messing with his vocal cords. Darius hid the scar with a snake tattoo twisting along the path of the wound. The Firebrands obeyed Jarek's right-hand male without question. Nobody ever knowingly pissed him off.

Jarek nodded at his second. "I received a call last night from someone with intel on a female sex slave. She could be who Aisen is rumored to have sold minutes before his facility was raided."

While Aisen along with his vamp brother Silas worked for Cerberus, they imprisoned humans who had a splash of witch or warlock DNA hidden in their genetic markers. The captives not testing as Blood Coven descendants were sold off to Aeternals for a high price. All quite illegal.

Murmurs rolled through the gathered warriors.

Darius raised a hand to stop the chit-chat. "Where is she?"

Original intel on the locations of purchased slaves came from a loose-lipped satyr, captured in the raid on a stockade of Silas and Aisen's. The asshole traded the names of all buyers he could remember for less pain. Empty of additional knowledge, he met his death with his bowels intact along with most of his skin. Recently, Jarek's warriors relied on rumor and reports from citizens.

"The male caller said she was outside the berserker village of Longphort. In the mountains. He refused to say who has her."

One side of Darius's mouth warped into a sneer. "Let's pack up."

"When nobody talks?" Norum, a longtime berserker Firebrand, decorated his ears with the bones of his victims, his own brand of bling. "It's the village's MO. There is a standard among them. DNT."

The warrior braids at Jarek's temples slapped against his shoulders when he nodded. "I am aware of the do-not-talk rule. When we tire of the silent treatment from the locals, we start ransacking the berserkers' homes, tearing apart each room."

Someone shouted from the line. "Yeah. Toss the places good."

The thrill of a fight was already racing through the Firebrands, flood waters through a canyon. Soon, it would be hard to hold his warriors back.

Kara, an Amazon, wore the skull of a Darque were-tiger on her head. "Permission to open a can of whoop-ass if they aren't forthcoming with the info?" She grinned, shoving her thumbs into the rear pockets of her low-slung jeans. She licked her lips like a big cat who'd targeted a weak gazelle.

"Permission granted. Now if I may continue. We portal to the north edge of the berserker village, going on foot from there. When we get to the lodgings, we'll split up, each of us taking a different dwelling. I have a search grid already marked. Gather around."

When Jarek spread the map out on a tabletop, Darius directed the warriors to memorize their assigned areas. "When you have finished questioning the berserkers in your sector, start tossing their places if you suspect they're holding out. Clear?"

His words were met with grunts, nods, and yeahs.

Darius fingered the snake tat on his neck. "Keep in touch. If we have nothing after the searches, meet on the south end of the village."

Jarek pulled his spear from the earth, hefted it point up, and gathered his shield. "We will locate this female if she exists. We will find her among the living, or we will uncover a body to honor with the funeral pyre of the Cede. She will not cry out for help unheard or slip forgotten into the eternal night of the Evermore. We remember her." The djinn commander deepened his voice, his resolve firm.

He hated to think beings might be cowering in the dark with nowhere to turn. Nobody to help them while they're ravaged daily, used for sport, used for food. Even though they were humans, he cared. He recalled the torment of hopelessness. Despite his torture being centuries ago, his memory was long.

Darius spun his hand to signal a go. The Firebrands marched to their stronghold's portal, touched their wrists, and disappeared one by one.

****

Mars ushered another group of men into the doctor's lab. Each were directed to drink a full glass of water an hour earlier.

Dr. Messenger washed his hands before he opened the refrigerator to remove a vial of medicine. He signaled the first subject to take a stool. "Lay your left arm on the table."

His assistant, a thin man in his early twenties wearing a white lab coat, palpated the subject's vein. He prepared the injection site with alcohol and a rubber tourniquet.

Lifting a syringe in his hand like a pencil, point up, the doctor pulled the plunger back before he inserted the needle into the vial. He pushed on the plunger, holding the container upside down while he filled it. He tapped the syringe before he removed it from the vial, motioning his assistant aside so he could administer the proper dosage into his patient's vein.

The doctor prepared another dose. "Next."

The Messenger guy who had created this juice was a genius. A Mad Hatter but a genius.

The subjects would return to the lab weekly to get a new shot of superhuman strength. It was worth it. Energy coursed through Mars, making him something he'd never dreamed of becoming. Not invincible. Rather, faster, stronger. The jittery nerves, which accompanied a rise in aggression after the injections, were manageable so far.

Once each man finished, Mars directed him to one of the many cots in another section of the lab where a white-coat employee waited to help him settle in.

Dante's general would hang around for a bit while his men slept. Once he woke them, he'd accompany them to the gym and track for a workout. The effects would be felt gradually over the next twenty-four hours. Each soldier would gain speed, endurance, and strength. Not as much as the Aeternals naturally possessed, but a damn sight better than before. He'd warn them to keep a lid on the aggression.

Once his super army was ready, the units would move into a new compound with barracks, labs, dining hall, gym, and outdoor training grounds. Humans First was gonna take out those otherworld bastards.

****

Jarek pulled back a hide covering the doorway, ducked, and strode into the hut. Darius and Kara had bound a berserker and a female succubus to a massive bed made of hand-worked logs.

The abode was a disaster. Drawers and cabinets were open, items were tossed about and furniture upended.

The Firebrand commander slid his palm along the rail of the bedstead, stroking the peeled timber. "Nice workmanship. You?" His piercing gaze landed on the berserker.

"Yes, sir." Despite the captured male's size, he trembled.

Fear.

The emotion showed he was smarter than he looked but, possibly, guilty.

The more confident succubus, holding a sheet so it barely covered her breasts, said, "I'm only a visitor who spent the night." She glanced downward, the covering slipping, exposing a plump breast. "Oops."

Kara snorted. "Just because you have no modesty doesn't mean you're deaf and mute."

Darius fingered his snake tattoo. "Sweetheart, give the succubus a break. She's only spreading the love."

Kara flipped her gaze toward her *freron*, a smirk playing on her lips. "Spreading her legs is more like it."

"Jealous?" The succubus shot a deadly glare at the female Firebrand.

Jarek continued to stroke the bed frame. "Your love life and your tits mean fuck all to me. What is important is the human who is being held as a slave. Tell us about her."

The berserker exchanged a look with the succubus, both shaking their heads. The male, however, immediately cast his gaze downward. He was hiding something.

Darius shifted from one foot to the other, clasping his hands behind him. "Let's keep this friendly for a while. What're your names?"

"Luke. This is Rina." He pointed at the succubus.

"Don't waste my time, Luke. I'm not patient. If you try my nerves, you will suffer." The djinn commander let go of the bed, charged the berserker, and slammed a fist into his jaw.

The big male's head snapped back. He lifted a shaky hand to rub his chin.

Jarek nodded at Kara. "Untie him."

She moseyed over to Luke where she withdrew her knife, cutting the ropes around his wrists. "Here you go big guy. Good luck."

The berserker, nearly the same height as Jarek but flabbier in the middle, jumped off the bed, backing up until he bumped the dresser.

Jarek stood toe to toe. "What do you know about a human? I'd suggest you raise your hands to protect your face."

When he did, Jarek landed a solid punch to his gut.

Oomph.

The captive doubled over.

Jarek followed with an upper cut to his chin.

The berserker spit blood. "I don't know anything about a human."

Jarek's next jab put Luke on the floor. He wiped more blood from his lip while he curled into a whimpering ball.

Darius leaned against the wall with his arms folded across his chest. "We have us a crier."

Kara approached the succubus, who stared at her nails rather than the violence taking place in front of her. Without warning, Rina jumped from the bed and grabbed Kara's hair, pulling hard enough to whip her around. "Don't even consider coming after me, bitch."

Darius unfolded his arms. "Shit. I guess I should have tied her hands tighter."

"Ya think?" Kara head-butted the succubus until she slammed onto the bed, whining.

Jarek put a boot on the chest of the berserker, holding him to the floor while he observed the two females.

Rina rose to her knees, making for Kara's hair again. The Firebrand Amazon easily twisted the succubus's arm, dragging her off the bed, spinning her around. She shot a foot out, planting it on her opponent's back while she face-planted her to the floor. When Rina popped onto her feet, Kara landed a one-two punch to her jaw, knocking her on her ass.

"Shit. You broke my nose." Rina pinched her nostrils together while blood gushed through her fingers.

Jarek tapped his wrist. *Kilem, get in here. We are in need of your talents.*

Luke spit on the floor.

"I've called my warlock," said Jarek. "When he digs into your head, it's going to hurt like hell. Wanna talk yet?"

"I have nuthin' to say."

Kilem strode in through the door, his shirt torn.

Jarek raised his brows.

"I ran into a stubborn SOB. Shit got hands-on. He didn't know anything, though. What's up?"

Darius spoke first. "Luke here knows something but is reluctant to share. The succubus might, too."

Kara wrapped her arm around Rina's neck to keep her from bolting, the sheet fully gone now.

Kilem's eyes widened. "Rina, nice to see you."

Kara snorted.

"You know me, Kilem. I've got nothing to do with this. I just stopped by for a quick fuck."

"Tough. Open your mind to me, Rina, so I don't have to hurt you."

"I'm open. If you'd drop by more often, I'd open a lot more."

Kara propped a fist on her hip. "Really, Kilem? Have you no standards?"

"None." His eyes captured Rina's for a few moments. "She's good to go."

Released from Kara's grip, she bent to pick up her clothes.

As she sauntered out, Kilem whistled. "See you sometime."

Jarek ground his heel into the berserker's chest. "Your turn."

Kilem held Luke's gaze.

The berserker's body jerked as he convulsed.

"He's resisting my probe," said the warlock.

Jarek nodded, bending near Luke's ear. "If he

can't get in, you're worthless to me. The next probe will get the information from you, but your brains might be scrambled. If you have any."

"Wait. I may have heard something."

"I'm waiting." Jarek grabbed Luke's upper arm, tugging him into a seated position.

"The last male who asked questions of the berserker never came home."

Jarek growled. "Who?"

"Golarg."

"I'm still waiting."

"Rumor has it Spear is buying enough food for two."

"Who's Spear? Where does he live?" Darius leaned toward Luke.

Kara grabbed a towel out of the bathroom and tossed it at the berserker. "Here. Clean up. You're a mess."

"Open your mind to Kilem." Jarek called on his Firebrand warlock again.

After a while in the berserker's mind, the warlock slumped against the dresser for support. "That's all he's got."

Jarek secured Spear's location from Luke. Tapping his D-chip, he sent Firebrands to the suspected berserker's hut.

By the time he arrived with Darius, Kara, and Kilem, the others were inside, but the hovel was empty.

Darius gestured at a hole in the wood floor, a chain hanging on a peg, the broken window, and the blood on the jagged glass. "Looks like we're too late. I'd say his prisoner bolted."

Jarek walked outside to the rear of the hut. "The captive traveled this direction. Not hard to track with the blood. Let's hope Spear ran the other way. I don't see his prints."

He pointed at several Firebrands in his command. "Find Spear. Don't kill him. We may need him for questioning. Darius, Kara, Kilem, with me."

After following the trail for hours, Darius knelt on the forest floor, examining a disturbance in the leaves. "The slave has stopped bleeding. She's sloppy about covering her tracks, though."

Jarek stood with his hands on his hips, looking uphill. "She's headed into the mountains where it will get cold. It's unlikely she is familiar with the area. Shit doesn't look good for her."

Chapter Fourteen

Ram strode into Kole's outer office as cocky as ever. He almost tripped over his own boots when he saw Denim on the couch chatting with Bounty. Galena perched on the edge of the executive assistant's desk. The females went all hush-hush at his entrance. He smiled, figuring they were talking about how hot and fearsome he was.

Sure.

Face facts. On a good day, the human could hardly tolerate him despite his ability to arouse her. Though satyrs could sexually excite anyone, they couldn't make the person like them.

Maybe that was why he was attracted to her. She was a challenge. But she was human. For him, it was a deal breaker. So why did he keep ogling her tantalizing breasts, luscious lips, and hot pussy while he imagined her all wet and waiting for him?

He shook his head, shattering the erotic thoughts while he burst into Kole's office. "You summoned, Comm?"

"Yeah. I did. Now take a fucking seat."

"Someone's in a good mood today. Does it have anything to do with the Alliance agent warming her pretty ass in Bounty's office?"

"It has everything to do with her." He shoved a rough hand through his close-cropped hair.

Ram paused for a moment, creases forming between his brows. "Wait a minute. I've been on my best behavior." He scratched his ear. "Yep. Absolutely best. I even let her help me chase those suped-up humans. What's she saying now?"

"This isn't about you, satyr. Tuck your guilty

conscience into your pants." When fire shot from one of Kole's fingers, scorching a piece of paper on the desk, the commander shrugged, letting the shit ash.

Animus demons were always one firecracker away from lighting up the sky on the Fourth of July. Ram scooted his chair back before his ass was collateral damage, ignited like a Roman candle.

"She pulled an Abello on me."

Ram's eyes darted left to right as he considered Kole's statement. "You mean she wants to be a Firebrand?" He shot to his feet. "Hell no."

"Sit down. I'm with ya, but she won't move into the stronghold unless I take her in like that other asswipe ex-agent made me do."

"Why would she move in here?" Ram set his butt into the chair again, but a crease still puzzled his forehead.

"Right. You don't know. She's a Blood Coven descendant. My fucking stronghold's starting to fill up with the damn witches and warlocks. Don't tell Skyler what I said."

The satyr Firebrand nodded. "Still doesn't explain my presence. Wait a minute. She's not fully human?"

"No. She's not. Why the fuck are you smiling?" Kole's palm scrubbed across his jaw. "Anyway, you're her partner, but things just got real. I want you training her. Needless to say, nothing … and I mean nothing … happens to her in the field. You have my permission to throw your body in front of her every time. Assign her a bodyguard when she leaves the stronghold unless she's with you."

Ram ricocheted from happy to hell-no in an instant. "Hold up, Comm. She gets all huffy if I even open a door for her. I can't win."

"Do I look like I care?" He yelled loudly for

Bounty. "Send in the baby witch. And put a call in to Skyler."

Bounty rested against the door jamb. "You've reached out to her every hour. She's pregnant not sick. You're driving her crazy."

****

With barely a flick of his hand, Cerberus changed his appearance. Whenever he met with his vampire general, he donned a disguise. No one recognized him. The time would come, though, when all would acknowledge him and tremble.

He waited for Lort on an island in Harrow Swamp in the demon region of Knife's Edge, surrounded by the putrid smell of rotting vegetation, cypress trees whose limbs pitched into the murky depths, and poisonous snakes who slithered through stagnant water.

When the vampire joined him, the insects, birds, and other creatures ceased their racket.

Though Lort was not a big male, he was taller than six feet with lean, solid muscles. His straight dishwater-blond hair rested on his shoulders. The grim line of his lips and brown eyes ringed with red marked him as a dangerous Aeternal.

He was what Cerberus needed to build his army. It was Lort's specialty. Once the Firebrands succumbed to his might, other Aeternals would fall in line.

"Thank you for coming." His vampire general bowed, his deference appearing forced.

A grin quirked Cerberus's lips when he pictured how Lort would grovel at his feet once he conquered all three realms. For now, a small arrogant bow was acceptable. "What did you need that is so urgent?"

Lort nervously cleared his throat, but he looked directly into Cerberus's eyes, unflinching. "The addictive drug designed to create followers who are … uh …

amenable to our cause is growing in popularity. Users are devoted. Even fanatical. If we ordered the addled motherfuckers to walk into a fire, they would. And a pack of shifters is happily distributing the goods. But there are kinks in the drug." Lort shoved his hair away from his face.

"Explain."

"It has unpredictable side effects. It must be perfected."

"Do so."

"Already being done. Another setback. One of the hostages has escaped. The one called Jace jumped the wall. We still have Celene and the others who aren't as difficult to manage."

The cypress trees swayed. A wind stirred through the swamp.

"What happened?" Cerberus agitated the debris at his feet.

As it swirled, Lort stepped away. "A guard let them out into the exercise yard. As you instructed, I gave them access to the outdoors. Jace climbed over the wall, racing to freedom while the other female fought the guard."

"I. Want. The. Guard. Brought. To. Me." Cerberus roared, thunder rolling across the sky.

Lort fought to stay upright in the storm caused by his demand. "The guard is dead. I took my time with him. Afterward, I searched the minds of others on duty, killing those who have been lazy or inattentive. Reliable replacements are assigned to Celene now. The rest of my soldiers search for Jace. We are scouring the forests nearby but are not picking up a scent. It's as if she has disappeared."

Cerberus grabbed Lort by the neck, squeezing, lifting him off the swampy ground until the general's feet dangled.

The vampire tried to pry the strangling hands loose.

"Have I been wrong about you?"

Lort barely spit out his answer, his fingers still plucking at Cerberus's palms. "I was not there."

Cerberus, his temples aching with sharp pains, threw the vampire into a tree twenty feet away and pressed his hands against his temples.

****

Lort's spine slammed into the trunk of a cypress. Sliding to the ground, he shook his head to clear it. One thing was certain. The male he worked for was not the incubus he pretended to be. Only a warlock could carry off a disguise or control nature.

"If we lose Celene or the others, I do not care if you are there or not. You will be held accountable. Now, what of new descendants?"

Rolling his shoulders, Lort straightened. "Miller Nash is still on the run. We almost caught him last week. He is proving resourceful, but I am more so. We will get him."

A deadly cold smile rested on Cerberus's face. "Do not promise me what you cannot fulfill."

"We continue to act on the list of names your human Dante releases to us. We are obtaining a blood sample from each candidate."

"I want good news!" Once more his shout stirred the wind, causing the swamp waters to ripple.

"Rumors say humans are moving into the Eastern Stronghold in Covenkirk. It may not be true, or if it is, it may be meaningless. Anyway, I am investigating."

"Hmm."

"I have expanded our hunt for Blood Coven descendants to the relatives, parents, siblings, and offspring of potential candidates. After all, these relations are potential descendants as well."

Cerberus nodded. "You are showing initiative."

"At your request, I have monitored Dante's movements. You are right. He is building his own army, called Humans First. They are watching portals. His aim, I believe, is to expose Aeternals."

"I suspected as much. The timing is early, but it may work in our favor."

Cerberus pinned his gaze on Lort's eyes.

The vampire knew his boss was assessing the strength of his bludfrenzy. The red streaks in his eyes were telling. "I control my disease. It has been with me for a century. Never have I given in to it since the early years."

"Silas allowed it to affect his reasoning. I will not put up with the behavior twice."

Lort was infected with blood lust, but despite his constant thirst, he had not killed to drink in a century. He wanted more out of his long life. He had goals. Nothing would stand between him and his goals. Not even his thirst. He would not kill his food source in an uncontrolled fit. Not until he subjugated Earth.

His boss picked at his nails. "I know about the blood slave you bought from Silas. He had better stay alive as proof you can control yourself and lead my army to victory."

Lort flashed on his smooth-skinned male. Though it was difficult to manage his thirst each time he held his male close, pressing hungry lips to the human's neck, he fought not to drain his meal. Did he keep his slave alive because he loved him or because letting him live proved he could control his overwhelming need? His reason was irrelevant.

The vampire general's chest expanded with a

deep breath, necessary to control the arousal caused by thoughts of drinking from his blood slave. He imagined his fingers tracing his human's firm buttocks while his fangs sank into the sweetest nectar imaginable. Anticipation rippled through Lort's body. Yes, he would take his human again tonight.

Lort would lead the greatest army in Scath's history. Errant Aeternals would fall into line, portals would fall, and humans would bow before their masters.

Cerberus would grant him thousands upon thousands of acres of land where he would keep herds of Earthers as ranchers keep cattle. He would never be thirsty again. Maybe then he would drain his beautiful human. There would always be more in his pastures.

****

Midday Jarek called in his best tracker. Clese. The grizzly shifter took his animal form to sniff along the ground heading up a mountain in the berserker region. Darius provided a piece of the female's clothing from Spear's hut.

The vegetation was sparse, the terrain rocky, but Clese kept his nose to the ground, lumbering upward.

Darius glanced around the area. "If the captive came up here, she's in trouble. The rocks are dangerous. There are few places to hide. While the sun is out, the heat is brutal. I don't see any water around. By nightfall, the cold could be worse."

Jarek flipped a thin warrior braid over his shoulder. "I agree. Let's hope we find her before it's too late."

The group climbed higher, the terrain steeper, less hospitable. They came to a stop. Clese spun in a circle, trudged one way and then another. When he caught the scent again, he continued forward, his nose to the ground.

Clese followed the bluff for a distance. When he stopped, he shifted. Brushing aside a few limbs, he exposed the narrow mouth of a cave. "She crawled in here."

Kara peeked into the dark entrance. "Let me go in. I'm smaller than you males."

"Sure, shorty. Just wiggle your little bits in there," rasped Darius.

Jarek rested on his haunches, peering in as far as he could see. Using his sharp hearing, he listened. Nothing. "If she's in there, she's pretty deep. I can't see or hear her." He rose.

Clese growled, sounding like the bear he was. "I smell her. Along with fear."

Standing near the entrance, Jarek propped his boot onto a small boulder. "Be careful, Kara."

"You got it, Comm. That's me. Careful."

Kilem chuckled.

The Amazon Firebrand dropped to her stomach and inched her way through the opening like a worm. Her boots disappeared from view.

The males waited at the cave. The only sound reaching them was Kara as she crawled through the tunnel.

Swish. Swish. Swish.

"How long before we go in after her?" Darius paced from tree to tree.

Jarek dropped his boot to the ground, brushing dirt off his pants leg. "A little longer. She hasn't called for help."

Clese returned to grizzly form to scent the area for other clues.

They waited.

"Someone's calling." Darius rushed to the entrance.

Jarek leaned closer to the opening.

"I need help dragging her out of here." The cavern muffled Kara's voice.

Jarek unstrapped his weapons, dropping to his stomach.

"Let me go in, Comm," said Darius. "I'm smaller than you."

"I'll fit." Jarek left no room for argument. One of his Firebrands in a dark, tight space was enough. He wasn't about to let two go in there.

He dragged himself forward on his elbows as he headed through the mouth. When his shoulders scraped the walls, he squirmed until they passed through the tight opening.

Shit. I hate being enclosed like this. Claustrophobia, here I come.

Continuing to slither like a snake, he drew deeper into the cave. Though light was long gone, his djinn vision adjusted. He paused when he reached a fork. He could go either way. He sniffed the air. His sense of smell was not nearly as good as Clese's, but it would do. He turned to the right, crawling along the path with only a little extra room.

"Comm, is that you?" shouted Kara.

"Yeah. On my way."

"Couldn't you find a smaller or less important volunteer to do tunnel duty?"

"Nobody's less important than I am."

Kara snickered. "Keep following my voice. I think you'll come to another fork. Go to your left."

"Got it." He squeezed his fear of tight places into a small ball, holding it in his gut.

After about twenty yards, he saw light from Kara's cell. "Almost there," she called out.

His elbows pulled him through the narrow

opening into a larger space where the Amazon sat huddled over a human who was curled onto her side. Unmoving.

Jarek stood, bending slightly forward. He glanced at Kara, who clasped the female's hand. "Is this how you found her?"

"Yes. She's alive but barely. I'd guess she's dehydrated and could use a good meal. Her elbows and hands are really scraped up. Probably from crawling into the tunnel. Lots of cuts on her arms, her legs. Maybe from the glass we saw at the berserker's hut. She's tight-fisting a piece of it, like a weapon."

Sure enough, she gripped a large, ragged shard of glass. Jarek pried it out of her hold. A long chain was wrapped around her waist, locked onto a collar at her neck. Must have been a bitch to crawl in here with the extra weight. He examined it, wedged his fingers between her skin and the collar, and snapped it. Together, he and Kara untangled the chain from around her. She didn't wake.

The Amazon said, "We'll have to drag her out. Feet or hands?"

Jarek left the decision to her.

"I'll take the hands. I think I can crawl backwards better than you can. Happy to say I'm not as bulky as you."

"Let's hope she stays unconscious during the long haul." Jarek removed his shirt and pulled it over the female's head, extra cushion for when they dragged her on her back. "The added layer could keep her from getting more scratches."

They began their journey. Kara scooted backward through the tunnel by wiggling her hips. Jarek assisted by pushing the female along, his hands gripping her thighs while he shoved forward.

When she cleared the entrance, Kara straightened and pulled the human all the way outside. Jarek crawled out.

Darius swept the female into his arms and rested her on a grassy spot, using his shirt as a pillow.

Jarek stretched, taking a big swig of fresh air, happy to be in the open. He retrieved a canteen from his pack. "She needs water." Cradling her head in his large hand, he dribbled liquid onto her lips.

No reaction. He tipped the canteen to her mouth. This time, she coughed but grabbed for his hand, squeezing tight. She gulped the water.

While he re-capped the canteen, her eyes snapped open. She screamed.

****

In the early evening, Denim surveyed the kitchen of her new stronghold apartment. "Stainless steel stove. Fridge. Microwave. Dishwasher. Nice." She fisted her hips, nodding an approval while she suppressed thoughts of how her life had taken a sharp right turn.

Tapping her friend's elbow, Galena led her into the hallway where she slid open a door. A stacked washer and dryer occupied the nook. "Ta da. You were worried you wouldn't have the full complement of appliances. This is a first-class joint."

"I'm pleased with the accommodations."

Someone knocked on the front door.

"I'll get it." Galena strolled to the entry as the *tap, tap, tap* continued. "Hold on. I'm coming."

Three females waited in the hallway, one peeking from behind a huge basket filled with goodies.

"Hey, Denim," the Amazon called, "your new coven kittens are here."

"Cute, Galena." Braelyn pushed past the Amazon to enter the spacious but unfurnished living room.

"We're the welcoming committee. Hey, Denim. I'm Braelyn, Rein's mate. This is Chay's mate. ... Set the thing down so she can see you. ... Margo brought a bunch of stuff in case you don't have much."

The redhead placed an overloaded basket on the wood floor near the entry while she eyed the apartment. "Great floors. Don't you just love the wood? Those," she pointed to three large bay windows, "let in terrific morning light. Fantastic. You need a few bright area rugs to make everything pop."

"She's a sculptor," explained Braelyn. "She talks a lot about color and light."

Skyler entered last. Unlike the others, she hung back, aloof. "Agent Quinn."

"Nice to see you again, Chief Maxwell, but let's call each other Denim and Skyler. Great to meet you all. You're my first guests. After Galena, that is."

The Amazon plopped onto the wood-planked floor near the windows. The other women followed suit, though Skyler needed help. Margo grabbed the basket before finding her spot.

"Here." The redheaded Blood Coven descendant sat cross-legged next to Denim, the welcome items in her lap. "Dish soap, a sponge, shampoo, conditioner, bathroom cleaning products, kitchen towels. Have at it. Go through the rest yourself." She passed off the gift.

As Denim picked through more items, she smiled at each visitor. "You really know how to make a girl feel welcome. Thanks so much."

Braelyn spiked fingers through her short auburn hair. "That's not all. On moving day, I'll fix your dinner and bring it over. Our apartment's out your door and to the right. In the corner."

Skyler sat with her legs curled under her. "You must be feeling pretty overwhelmed by now. We're here to answer any questions you might have."

"I do have a few. Mostly, now what?"

Denim figured Braelyn as the spokesperson. "First, we get you some furniture. This place looks like a tomb."

Denim set the basket on the floor. "If I could hire muscle, I'd retrieve my stuff from New Orleans."

"Muscle's easy," said Braelyn, "and they work for free."

Margo leaned against the wall. "Not for free, but we'll provide the incentive pay."

Skyler rolled her icy lilac eyes.

Braelyn braved patting the frosty CLO's arm. "Don't mind her. She's the newest addition to the I'm-mated-to-a-Firebrand thing. They're insatiable."

"Thank God," shouted Margo. "You'll be assigned a witch or warlock as a trainer for your gifts."

"Skyler mentioned gifts, but I don't have any. At least none I know about."

"You'll get some, once you're on Scath longer." The cool CLO of the Alliance smoothed her elegant blonde do, knotted low on her head.

"You bet," said Margo. "Mine started when Chay and I were imprisoned in a cramped little jail cell. Skyler's started while she was traipsing around Darque with the hot Commander Kole."

"It's not like we were on vacation, Margo. We were stuck there when a warlock working for Cerberus spelled our transportation devices."

Margo elbowed Skyler. "Sure, but look how great it turned out."

The corners of Skyler's lips turned up. "True. No complaints. My trainer works with me on scrying. I'm making progress."

"You're too modest," said Braelyn. "You're

amazing. My trainer works with me on mind control techniques."

Denim nodded. "What's your … skill … gift, Margo?"

"Chay calls it my wonky-thing. I mess with radio waves. Cool, huh?"

"What's Nico's?" asked Galena.

Braelyn's eyes widened. "Don't bring it up around him. Big, bad topic of conversation. He hasn't developed one yet."

"Wow!" said Denim. "What if the same thing happens to me? Are you sure we're descendants?"

"One hundred percent proof positive." Margo swept a lock of red hair over her shoulder.

"We believe some are slower to develop their gifts." Skyler rested a palm on her baby mound.

Braelyn jiggled her sandaled foot. "Anyway, you'll get a physical trainer, too. Of course, as an Alliance agent, you may not need one. I was sore for months."

"Chay rubbed my legs every night. I told him my ass was sore, too. He gave it added attention. A little rub, a little slap, and a lot of tickle." Margo's gaze swept the room.

"TMI," said Braelyn.

Though everyone grinned big time, they nodded.

"Like Abello, Denim is going to be working with the Firebrands. She'll be getting regular workouts with Ram. Probably won't need another trainer. On the sly, she's already been eyeing up the satyr for extra lessons." Galena tossed in her snark.

All the women laughed. Then they quieted abruptly.

"You're serious?" Braelyn wrinkled her forehead. "He's sizzling hot, but he hates humans."

Denim smirked. "Galena's kidding. I agree, the guy is bodacious. But there's nothing between us."

"He has a great tush, firm-like, squeezable. And all the luscious hair," said Margo. "Yummy."

The ladies' chins bobbed in unison.

Chapter Fifteen

Jarek lounged on a mass of floor pillows, one leg bent at the knee, the other stretched out. He eyed the unconscious female who tossed and turned, a sign she would wake soon. She'd slept over twenty-four hours.

In his oversized bed, a thick pallet made from a king mattress, layers of handwoven rugs, and a few homespun blankets, she seemed small, frail. Unable to avert his eyes, he saw her bruised, cut body when Kara removed the soiled, tattered dress to bathe her. She suffered enough indignities without a male ogling her dirty, abused form. Since he couldn't give her the respect she deserved, he left the room. After the bath, his Amazon Firebrand dried her off, slipping one of his T-shirts over her head as a nightgown.

She wasn't short. From hair to heels, maybe five-eleven, making her tall for a human female. After Kara lay her on his bed, he threw furs over her, not missing her shapely legs.

Jarek figured Spear had not fed her well. Her hip bones were knife blades. Her ribs jutted out of her thin torso. Despite this, her breasts were plump mounds which, under other circumstances, he might admire. With the grime washed from her hair, its rich midnight color shimmered as it fanned out beneath her resting head. Her lips were full, naturally pink. Her cheekbones were high, her slightly tilted eyes outlined with thick lashes.

Obviously, he wasn't good at being a gentleman. He looked on her longer than he should have. But something about her drew him to her.

Jarek had no idea why she fascinated him. They had never spoken. He knew nothing about her except she had escaped from Spear's prison.

Normally, he never obsessed over females. When he needed release, he brought a camp follower to his bed. They were enough. Plenty of them hung around. Yet this unconscious ex-slave seduced him. Was it because she had been enslaved? Was it because she had escaped her captor?

She stirred, kicking off her covers. Jarek rose, bent over her sleeping form, and resettled the animal hide to keep her warm. It was a chilly autumn in this southern hemisphere of Scath.

When she thrashed from side to side, the djinn commander tightened his fists, growling at the property mark on her neck. She wore a slave brand.

If Spear stood in front of him now, he would kill him with his bare hands. *No.* Not good enough. He would tie him behind a horse to be dragged until his flesh tore from his bones. Afterward, he would hang him by his feet to rot in the sun.

Jarek's shirt slipped off her shoulder, revealing bruises and scattered cuts. Pulling the animal skin up higher to hide the marks, he returned to his bedside vigil.

She flung her arms wildly while rolling onto her stomach. When she stilled, flipping onto her back again, she snapped her lids up. Searching the room, her rich dark irises landed on him.

Pedaling her feet backward, she propelled herself to the top of the bed as far from him as possible. Looking down at her clothed body, she fisted the animal skin to draw it to her chin. "Who are you?"

Though her breaths were shallow butterflies, her voice showed no fear. In fact, she seemed angry.

Good for her.

****

Celene picked over what remained of dinner. Though she hated the disturbing quiet of the house without Jace, she hoped her ex-roomie sprinted to freedom. Seeking the comfort of their routine, she removed The Path from its shelf, spreading it out on the couch. She opened the book to begin where Jace left off before the escape.

Though an oddity, the winged assassins of the OneCreator chose to live in Angor among those they had imprisoned rather than among their own kind in The Vast. Here in these territories, they thrived in the unpredictable environment. One moment sun, soft breezes. The next stormy skies, a place cold, icy, stark. Often, it was cruel like those it contained. But it was always honest, always just.

Landing in his atrium after a sanction kill, a true death, Ohngel fanned out his wings, the span from pillar to pillar, aglow with a blistering heat which vanished his kill's blood. With them snapped tight to his back, he stepped under the soothing spray of a shower to erase the weariness of battle.

Dressed in breeches of supple leather and a shirt of silk, he was about to consume a goblet of mead when Gahya summoned him to her abode in The Vast. She possessed news to share. He downed the contents of his glass. A fight. A capture. A hearty drink. A possible fuck. The day was getting better.

From the cliff behind her ethereal domus, he was stunned by his companion's announcement. Ohngel leaned against a large boulder, his thick arms folded across his solid chest, his fiery wings lashed against his spine.

Gahya gazed down on a narrow valley bordered by rugged mountains and smoking volcanos in a place named Earth. She directed Ohngel's attention to a pair of creatures she identified as incubus and succubus. The beings lay side by side in a thicket shaded by towering trees outside a stone dwelling.

"Behold. They are mine. When I rolled the winning combination in the game of Cee-lo, the OneCreator allowed me to fashion sentient beings, like us but less than. They live among the wildings of Earth." Her deep breath puffed out her already ample breasts. "I am now the proud Genitrix."

Her pronouncement was indeed interesting. "Who participated in this game?"

"The OneCreator set the challenge, but only Gabriel and I accepted."

Her creatures were beautiful. The female, with hair a luxurious spun silk, was tall, plump in the right places. The male resembled a warrior, his forearms strong, his shoulders broad. "How did you make them?"

"From a mixture of aether, a bit of my soul, and my unexplainable carnal desire for you, my love."

His gaze locked onto hers. She held it for only a moment before casting her stare to the ground. She knew she had crossed a line.

Ohngel's lips tightened. "The OneCreator will not be happy with you. Your soul and carnal knowledge should not be the material of creation."

She pouted, her mouth twisting into an unattractive moue. "Why not? The wager was his idea. I thought I was quite clever."

The OneCreator was not without vices. He possessed a notorious temper which on occasion burned hotter than the core of Angor, where the most serious offenders suffered in agonizing conflagrations. His other was a love of pitting his gods and goddesses against one another while stepping away, his arms akimbo while he awaited the shitstorm. Ohngel didn't blame him. A guy's gotta have fun.

"You are naive, Gahya. It does not become you.

You never should have used a part of your soul in their making or imparted carnal knowledge to your creatures."

Gahya's eyes slitted, her chin tilting upward in defiance. "My soul regenerated. I lost nothing. Besides, their sensual desire is their best feature. Are we the only ones allowed this craving for flesh?"

"He will eye your creations closely."

"It will do no good. My darlings are immortal."

"Unlike you and me, they can be killed." Ohngel angled his head toward Gahya, his gaze piercing.

"Under very rare circumstances. Most likely they will live forever. They are pure. Perfect."

But they were not self-sufficient. He and Gahya were. The OneCreator set that stipulation before the bet. They required sustenance to regenerate. Gahya, though, was clever.

Blood nourished vampires. Orgasms fed her demons. Power channeled from others for their spells strengthened the mages. Nymphs and satyrs partook of arousal. Incubi and succubi drew lifeforce. Ylves breathed another's soul. Djinn, berserkers, and Amazons thrived on the fear and excitement of battle while shifters required a taste of flesh. In these ways, her creations regenerated.

"Beware hubris," Ohngel whispered.

Below, the incubus rose, fastening his pants as he offered a hand to his succubus companion. The female allowed the assistance. Unfolding from the ground, she smoothed her peplos. A sated grin plumped her cheeks. With their fingers laced, the couple strolled along a path lined with scented flowers, the sun shining on the female's burnt umber hair, her skin rosy from the sample of her companion's lifeforce acquired when they joined.

"They are happy, Ohngel. What is wrong with their joy from copulation?"

"Desire runs strong in your creatures, feeding them, powering them. Do you not think this propensity for pleasure bodes danger?"

She trailed her fingers between her breasts and downward to stroke her abdomen.

Ohngel traced her movements, his lids growing heavy. He was a soft touch for a female's body.

She smiled. "I like my creatures to crave flesh. I enjoy when you hunger for mine."

Ohngel unlaced his breeches, shedding them to fist his aroused cock. Damn thing had a mind of its own.

With a raspy voice, Gahya offered, "Let me." She fluttered her eyelashes in feigned innocence, a coquettish gesture that hardened his already aching shaft.

He ceased stroking himself to sink onto the ground, rolling to his back.

Gahya threw herself beside him, her hand wrapping around his need.

Ohngel stretched his wings beneath him, spreading his thighs, kicking up a knee to give the Genitrix better access. When he folded his arms under his head, his biceps flexed.

"This pleases me," she said as she stroked him from crown to base, her lips moistened by her tongue.

Ohngel's eyes glinted like crystals, more penetrating than flint-tipped arrows.

With one hand still manipulating his solid flesh, Gahya tossed her hair over her shoulder, the gesture familiar to him. It spoke of self-absorption, vanity, and a desire to possess. "I make you feel, Ohngel. Give me that."

He squeezed his hand over hers, making her grip his shaft tighter. Together they pumped his phallus as he moaned, his eyes rolling in pleasure.

"I am almost there, Genitrix. Do not stop. My

balls are about to explode." His hips surged. He rocked, his release shooting into the air.

Surprised, Celene jumped off the couch, gripping the book to her chest when a demon guard burst through the door. He raced toward her, grabbing her arm while he snatched The Path from her hands. As he pulled her through the other room, she fought, biting, screaming. "Where are you taking me?"

Her jailer growled, snarled, but gave no answer.

Outside, another guard threw a black hood over her before he tossed her into the backseat of a vehicle. Doors slammed, the engine rolled over, and they sped off, leaving the house where they had imprisoned her with Jace. Just when The Path was getting good.

****

Nico slumped into the overstuffed couch at the Blood Shed, fisting a drink. With Sabine at his side, life was great. If only the nymph beauty queen could get loose. She was strung tighter than an ylve's bowstring. He'd kowtowed to Kole's orders. She was still his nanny. What more did she want?

They'd spent weeks tracking the movements of Arisen Dawn, though stakeouts were not his favorite pastime. Sure, he'd enjoyed his rash foray into the warehouse, but things were settling into the same ol' same ol'. He'd rather be investigating problems in New Orleans.

The only thing making his current assignment bearable was Sabine. He admitted, if only to himself, he had the hots for the female Firebrand. She could probably slam him against the wall. *Hell.* That sounded good. Against the wall. Body to body. His arousal grinding into her belly. Her Barbie porn-queen breasts punching into his chest.

"Are you listening to me, Abello?" Sabine

plopped her boots onto the table alongside his.

"Sure."

"Yeah? What did I say?"

"You said you're getting tired of trailing after Arisen Dawn and would rather be out kicking ass."

"That's not what I said. Just like a male. You never listen."

"You should have been saying that. And don't lump all males into the same shit hole."

She turned onto her hip to face him, her translucent green eyes giving him a stare down. Wouldn't you know it, his irises dropped right to her tits, which were plumping over the top of a body-hugging tank. He knew she was talking again, but *damn* he couldn't focus on a word she was saying.

"You're not listening. Remove your eyes from my boobs."

"You got me, Sabine. I can't concentrate on your lips when you're flashing your breasts at me."

"How would you like it if I stared at your dick all the time?"

"You do."

"What?" Her creased forehead said he irritated her. "Here. Do something useful. Get me another drink." She jammed a glass into his hand.

Nico clasped onto it and wandered over to the bartender. "Another for the lady and for me."

When the guy slammed the drinks onto the bar, Nico leaned close. "Tell me about the backrooms. Do you rent them? How does it work?"

"Which one you want? I'll put it on the Firebrands' tab."

"Which is the best?"

"Four has the biggest bed."

"It'll do." Nico sipped his whiskey on his way to

the table. Tyr, Brak, Chay, and Rein joined the festivities, chatting with his sexy partner. Setting Sabine's glass in front of her, he mulled over how to introduce the subject of fucking. He had to be quiet around these assholes with super sensitive hearing. After one hook up with the nymph, he was certain he'd be able to concentrate on his job.

Slamming his whiskey onto the table, he put an arm on the couch behind Sabine's head, leaned over, and whispered in her ear. He paused, waiting for a reaction. When he didn't get anything except an arched brow, his mouth crashed into her plump, kissable lips. His tongue followed the smooth move.

She jerked away, sending a fist into his jaw. The crack alone attracted every Aeternal in the bar, especially the Firebrands.

Nico might have been a little drunk, but he knew rejection when it hit him in the face.

"Man," said Chay. "She got ya good. Here's some advice. Quit hitting on her."

"Shut it," said Sabine. "I don't want help from mated ylves."

Chay raised his hands in surrender. "Just trying to give an assist."

"Do I look like I need it?"

The other Firebrands pinged their gazes from Sabine to the human. Show over. Then they returned to their conversation.

Nico put fingers to his jaw, wiggling it. "I get it, sweetness." His words sounded light, but his snarl contradicted them. "I won't make the same mistake a second time."

He tipped his glass to finish it off. Rising, he strode to the bartender again. After he ordered another, he put his back to the bar to survey the room. Grabbing his fresh drink, splashing dark golden liquid over the rim, he blundered toward a female target.

The Aeternal across the way was stacked, showing off her wares while she yucked with friends. When Nico approached, she stopped the chit-chat, batting her long, lacy eyelashes at him.

More like it. Yeah!

"You're the prettiest woman in this bar. I'm the horniest bastard. How about a trip to the back?"

****

Sabine closed her eyes, drawing in a breath. Nymphs, like satyrs, fed on arousal. Without the sustenance, they'd die. Lust and cupidity packed the Blood Shed. The perfect place to relax or recharge. With no direct touch, however, her need was barely topped off. What was worse, her set-to with Nico drained her. So, she continued with a little deep breathing, pulling the surrounding sexual excitement in through her nose.

In all her years on the job, Sabine had never slept with another Firebrand, despite most of them being ready, willing, and adept. Because she was a nymph, they couldn't help but desire her. Since sexual appeal was built into her breed's genes, she was born to be a porn-fantasy trigger.

Nico was like the others. *Right?* Instead of accepting the expected response from him, she was pissed when he made his move. She wanted more from him than a quick fuck in the backroom.

Crazy.

Her sex life wasn't as active as most nymphs, but it wasn't ho-hum either. Unfortunately, she had requirements. Males must respect her for more than a hot bod and off-the-chart pheromones. In turn, they must be of worth. Nico was a puzzle. Though he was a worthy male, she doubted he even knew she possessed a brain.

What was worse, she doubted he cared.

When he whispered in her ear, her sexual tension gathered into an explosive ball, heading straight for his jaw. She regretted the blow, especially with the other Firebrands having a front row seat.

What do I expect from Nico? Flowers, candy, sweet words? Never happening.

"Hey, guys. There goes our human. He's dragging a succubus into the backroom. You lost out tonight, Sabine. Way to go, Abello." Tyr adjusted his pants, his face jewels glinting even in the dim overhead light. "She looks fine."

Sabine's lashes flipped up. She caught Nico with his hand low on the female's waist, walking her through a door into the back.

"He recovered fast," said Brak. "S'okay. You've still got me, nymphette."

Her heart slammed into her chest, a squeezed lemon. "Yeah. Like I was holding out for you, demon."

Keep it light. Don't let them see.

"Hope your eyes aren't on me," said Chay. "I'm taken."

Rein held up a hand. "Me, too. And I never thought I'd say that."

"It's none of you losers." She chugged her drink. "I've got a real male. A big male." Her hands spread apart, showing just how large he was. "He's waiting for me, naked and primed. The longer he waits, the better he is when I come. Home, that is."

They laughed when she pushed off from the couch.

Like her *frerons*, Sabine tossed out smutty innuendo*s*. They all did it, not only because most Aeternals had exceedingly active libidos but also because it was how they coped with the job. Stress, sex, booze.

The triple play was hot-wired into them.

Sabine tossed a carefree wave when she headed out, never letting on how Nico crushed her when he took another female into the backroom.

Hoots and hollers followed her to the exit.

****

Nico returned to the table, another drink in hand.

How many was that? Who's counting?

He noticed Sabine had split. Good. He was doing nothing but fucking up with her. What he wanted was to be strong. To protect her. To be an asset to the Firebrands. Instead, he kept taking. He was never on the giving end of the biz.

"How was she?" The giant carnal demon straightened, rolling his shoulders.

Enough about the nymph who has my balls in a knot.

"I don't kiss and tell."

"Cause you're a gentleman," said Chay.

Nico nodded, splashing whiskey as he plopped onto the couch.

Tyr fingered the silver bar piercing his brow. "I might try my luck with your succubus. You didn't wear her out, did you? Wait. You're a human with a small prick. She probably needs a big warlock to get off good."

"We aren't going to whip out our dicks and lay them on the table, are we?" asked Nico. "Cause I'm pretty sure I'd win."

"Really?" Brak pointed to his crotch. "Carnal demon here. I'm hung like a Darque questing beast. Come to think of it, I'd make them a little jealous. Of course, my *frerons* have travel-size penises."

Rein shook his head as he kept drinking.

"Yeah? But rumor has it you can't get a stiffy." Tyr shrugged after the pronouncement.

"What? Who said it? It's not true. Hey, man. I can pop a chub whenever I want. I'll prove it." Brak went for his zipper.

Chay laughed, high-fiving the warlock. "Dude. Stop. So wrong. Do not whip out your weapon. Tyr's just pulling your … dick, in this case."

"Funny," said Brak. "I didn't really believe any female would say it. Back to the succubus, Abello."

"What'd I say? I'm not talking about her."

The four males pinned Nico with a stare.

Chay chuckled first. "You didn't do her, dude."

"Of course, I did her," slurred Nico. "I nailed her good."

"You're right, ylve-man," said Tyr. "The human was busting Sabine's chops by boning somebody else, but he couldn't finish her with visions of our favorite nymph in his brain. Or he was too drunk to get a boner. Which is it, Abello?"

Nico's glare was followed by a big sigh. "Damn. You pegged me. Too soused. No juice."

Brak leveled an observation. "Nope. It's Sabine. She shriveled your balls."

Chay added, "She took the air out of your tire."

"It was not because of Sabine," Nico snarled. Who the fuck did these guys think they were? Mouthing off about the nymph's effect on his limp dick.

"Dude, it's bad. When you're so hooked on a female you can't get your chubby to work." Brak shook his head. "It'll never happen to me. Must be horrible."

"You assholes need to shut the fuck up. What is this *The View*? Are we going to go weepy talking this to death?" Nico gestured with his glass, splashing booze on his shirt.

Rein said, "I will tell you this, Abello, and it's not on *The View*. Although, it saddens me you watch the show. You hurt our Sabine, and you'll have the four of us so far in your ass, you won't be able to fart."

"I don't need advice about my partner. Keep your noses out of my business. I'm outta here."

Before Nico exited the Shed, Tyr grabbed his elbow. "I'm gonna give you this bit of news about my friend, my *freron*, Sabine."

Nico glared at Tyr's hand before he shucked it off. "I said I didn't need advice."

"Yeah, you do. She's a nymph. While her breed is generally…"

"This is going to be earthshaking."

"Shut the fuck up. Stop interrupting. Here's what you don't know about the female. She's a mix. Her father's a warlock. Most nymphs choose a satyr for their baby daddy. Keeps the genes in the same breeds. Why Sabine's mom went wild, who knows? She's an independent thinker even for a nymph. Point is, the mage in question is in my family, a distant relation. I know what I'm saying. Sabine was raised by him. He didn't think her mother was a good role model. He was a Firebrand, by the by."

"Yeah. So?"

"I told you not to interrupt, human. She's more like him. Don't expect a hump and dump. She's got expectations."

"Thanks for the tip. Now, get the hell out of my path and my biz." Nico wasn't in the market for a long-term bed partner. If it was what Sabine expected, he needed to move on. Besides, he refused to chase a woman with a shitload of Firebrands for big brothers.

Am I? Fuck. I am if the woman's Sabine. Then why am I such a dick?

He'd held a prime position with the Alliance before the nymph and Tyr brought him to Scath because he was a Blood Coven offspring. *Yippee!* For his own good, they'd stuck him on this realm. Making the best of a shitty situation, he'd blackmailed the Firebrands into letting him hang with them.

So why am I looking for another chain—even if she has a knock-out sexy smile along with curves a race car driver would admire? Because she's more than a smile and curves. She's a woman who makes me want to be a better man. I best step up to the plate soon.

Chapter Sixteen

"What goes from this room?" Ram leaned against Denim's closet door in New Orleans.

"The bed. I'll take these off and get fresh ones." She popped off the top sheet.

Ram sniffed. "I don't smell a male. No sleep-over boyfriends, doll?"

She grabbed two stacks of clean linens, placing them into the half-packed box. "None of your business, *cher.*"

"That's what females say when they aren't getting any."

"I have a suggestion. Why don't you stuff a sock in your mouth?" She opened a drawer, tossing a pair at Ram. His arm shot up to grab them mid-flight.

"I have a better idea for my mouth."

"You aren't going to shut up, are you?" She snapped the bottom sheet off the bed.

"Probably not."

Rein tapped on the door frame. "Cut the shit, satyr. Let's get the bed out of here. Hey, some of you come help with this stuff."

Brak lifted the queen-size mattress with ease. Tyr took the box spring. He and Rein lugged the solid iron bed out with little effort.

In the parking lot, Ram called shotgun. "I'm not riding in the back of the truck. Come on, doll, seat of honor right next to me. Keep your hands to yourself."

Denim smirked, sliding in beside him. When she turned around for a last view of her New Orleans apartment, she sucked in a sniffle.

"Come on. No crying. You'll be back if you want when it's safe." Ram threw an arm over her shoulders.

"You're right. *Vivre la vie sans regrets*."

"Thatta girl. No regrets."

The group headed toward the Warehouse District in a big truck. Ram dropped a hand on her leg, shifting closer. Thigh to thigh. His lips curled into a roguish grin while he nibbled on her arousal.

Not too much.

Denim gave him a what-the-hell look. "Can you scoot over?"

"Nope. I'm a big guy. I need lots of space. I suggest you sit on my lap."

"Hah! Not happening. You're crowding me."

"Good."

She swatted at his hand before she grabbed it to stop its journey up her leg. "Stop."

"Stop what?" His mouth twitched.

"I hope Braelyn and I aren't this obnoxious when we argue. You two should just fuck it out. Talking doesn't work," said Rein.

Denim turned red, sputtering while Ram moved closer. "What do you think, doll? Have pity. Look at me."

She glanced down where Ram's hand adjusted a big bulge in his pants. Fingering the collar of her shirt, she asked, "Is it hot in here?"

Denim locked her gaze onto the street straight ahead.

Ram stared at her profile. She was part witch, no longer a weak human. Fair game. No harm in shameless flirting while he fed his satyr. She was a delicious appetizer. Enjoy. A little bump and grind, a snack, and a walk out the door when he was done. No entanglements.

Unfortunately, she acted like the kind of female who wanted entanglements. He didn't want long-term. He didn't want someone else to depend on him. It was a lose-lose sitch.

"The portal is inside the warehouse around the corner. Time for reconnaissance. Cut the satyr shit and get serious." Rein stopped the truck. "I'll hold here with the stuff until you clear the zone. If it's human-free, we roll on through."

Brak, Chay, Galena, and Tyr stepped out of the back end while Ram slipped from the cab.

"I'd feel better if you stayed in the vehicle, doll." Ram held out his hand since she insisted on a come-with.

Not only did she reject his offer of help, but she knocked it out of the way. "I'd feel better if you shut the fuck up, but we can't always get what we want."

A frown tugged at his lips. "Females."

"I heard you."

They prowled forward. Ram nudged ahead of her.

"I thought we'd settled the macho bullshit. It just pisses me off." Denim smacked his shoulder.

"Pissed off is better than dead. Kole changed the orders. You're precious cargo now. Besides, this way, you can admire my ass."

"I'm more likely to put a bullet in it."

"Ouch. You gotta curb your hostility. It might get in the way of my pounding into you. Though angry sex is good."

As they rounded the corner, Ram held up three fingers, IDing the number of males near the entrance to the warehouse's roll-up door.

Tyr nodded, signaling he was moving forward.

As Denim maneuvered nearer Galena, a piece of glass crunched under her foot. The sound shattered the silence. The waiting humans fumbled for their guns, obviously surprised to find action coming from the street rather than from the portal site.

Brak whipped out his butterfly swords, did a few

figure eights, and charged the biggest guy. Kole had warned them to keep noise down. No gun battles out in the open.

The human fired at the carnal demon who deftly bobbed, rolled, and weaved out of harm's way, all the while slicing through the air with his blades.

When the guy's weapon jammed, he threw it against the wall and extracted a knife.

He ducked under Brak's swords with fleet feet, avoiding danger with smooth moves of his own, almost landing a gut stab to the big demon Firebrand. When Brak's blades did their job, the human went down in a pile of dead.

Tyr called out a warning. "Watch it, satyr."

A guy sporting a classic Iron Maiden T-shirt stepped out from behind crates, taking aim. He fired wildly when Ram took off in a full-out run toward him.

Thud. Thud. Thud.

He tackled the shooter before the guy could scramble to cover.

Grabbing a handful of shirt, he planted a fist to the guy's jaw, driving his head into the concrete with a clunk. The punch should have laid a human out cold, but he shook it off. *WTF?* His jaw should be broken. His skull cracked.

Must be the superhuman shit.

They rolled, the Iron Maiden fan straddling Ram and narrowly missing his chin with a solid airborne fist.

Fuck.

Ram maneuvered to the top, spinning the human onto his stomach. He caught the guy's neck in the crook of his arm.

Despite being in a deadly headlock, the human threw off Ram's hold, barreling onto his feet and streaking off to join Baseball Cap, who was rabbiting.

The two human males paused at the brick wall, nodded at each other, bent their knees, and jumped onto the store's rooftop.

"Told you these guys were jacked up," muttered Ram.

He, Galena, Chay, and Tyr sprang onto the same roof with ease.

"There they go." The warlock pointed at a nearby building. "They're fast."

Tyr flicked his wrist to cast what Ram thought must be a holding spell.

Nothing.

"What's wrong with your hocus pocus?" The satyr jacked his speed up a notch.

"Abso-fucking-lutely nada. They're too far away for my spell to work."

The Firebrands pursued the human targets who leaped across a wide space and onto another rooftop, landing intact.

Galena took the lead as Chay jacked a bolt into the chamber of his *chu-ko-nu* while sprinting forward.

Ram hung back, pivoted, and checked below, drawn by a sudden urge to find Denim. He spotted her leaning against a wall.

What the hell?

Brak was bent over her.

Denim wrapped a hand around her upper arm. "It just grazed me. No worry," she shouted to Ram as he leaped from the roof, softly landing beside her.

He pried her fingers loose, ripped her sleeve, and exposed the wound. She was lucky. If the bullet had penetrated, the sedative in it could have exploded into her system. No telling what it would do to a human, even one with a dash of witch DNA. Some of the same shit killed a pure-blood Aeternal. A through-and-through made a female demon sleepy. As it was, his stomach busted a few flip flops.

"This is exactly why you should have kept your pretty cheeks planted in the truck." Pent-up anger bubbled to the surface, changing his translucent irises to flashing neon green.

Denim frowned. "Don't be an ass. I've gotten worse injuries than this shaving my legs." Her chin bobbed to her chest, her lids fluttering closed.

Brak shrugged. "I'll get Rein. We'll dump the body in the truck. Call in a cleaning crew."

Chay, Galena, and Tyr strode around the corner. Frowns all around.

"We lost them after they jumped to the ground again," said Tyr. "Too many places to hide."

"The male with the baseball cap dodged my bolt. No human can escape my aim." Chay whined, "Even Aeternals have trouble."

Galena scraped fingers through her silky straight hair. "You want to tell them, Denim, or should I?"

"I will." Denim slurred her words, but Ram got the drift. "The guy in the baseball cap is my ex."

****

After dropping off the dead guy, Ram stashed the truck in the garage. He strode into the stronghold's gathering room to a buzz of activity. Brak and Rein leaned against the wall, arms crossed, watching.

"What's up?" He followed the direction of the noise.

Rein pointed toward Margo. "As you can see, Chay's mate is tossing orders at a bunch of delivery guys. They've moved the same couch four or five times. I've lost count."

"Why?"

"The descendants say the stronghold needs a do-over. My Brae's leading the pack."

Brak snarled. "They better not fuck with the game room. All's I'm saying."

The Firebrands set up a game room on the other side of the winding stairs which led to the second floor where all the descendants' apartments were located.

Braelyn strolled by, a tray in her hand filled with soft drinks and goodies. "Nobody's touching the sacred game room slash man cave. All the boy toys are staying. We might add new furniture, though. Make it cozier."

"Not too cozy." Brak reached for an appetizer. Something wrapped in a crust.

Braelyn slapped his hand. "These are for the movers."

Rein stifled a grin, shrugging, when Brak looked to him for support.

Margo directed two of the males to drop the oversized couch onto a new area rug which was now lined up square with the wall. She had purchased the sofa, along with two others, a while ago. "What do you think about this arrangement, guys?"

They all nodded when the movers shot them pleading glances.

"Okay. Place the others. There and there." The feisty redheaded mate pointed. "The new big screen TV will go on the wall."

Brak pushed off, lumbering toward Margo. "Big screen, you say? How big? Where's it going?"

"It's staggering." Her eyes popped wide with enthusiasm. "Over 100 inches. With all the couches in this space, I'm thinking to put the TV there. What's your take?"

"Perfect." The big carnal demon was now interested in decorating. "We need a sturdy, huge-ass coffee table, one that'll handle boots and shit."

"It's on the movers' truck." Margo chuckled. "The boots-and-shit-huge-ass coffee table."

"Now you're talkin'. What about an Xbox console?"

"A low cabinet is waiting outside for under the TV. It's big enough to hold all the Xbox stuff."

"Hell yes." Brak fisted the air. "I'll hang out here all the time."

"Wait till you see what we're gonna do with the kitchen. We're tearing down walls, adding an eating area, expanding the pantry, bringing in a humongous refrigerator."

"If you keep it full, I'll definitely lodge my ass on a couch."

"Let's go, demon." Ram grabbed his *freron's* arm, walking toward Kole's office. "I'm starting to feel like we're in an episode of Queer Eye for the Straight Guy."

Denim came in on a run, her arm newly bandaged. She threw a thumb's up. "Great job, ladies. Looking good."

Obviously, she was already in on the remodel. Ram held the door, bowing with a sweeping arm gesture while she walked through in front of him. "How're you feeling?"

"Awake. Lucky the bullet only grazed me."

Already sitting at the conference table were Chay, Galena, Tyr, Dax, Thorn, Sabine, Nico, and Skyler. At the head, Kole thrummed his fingers on the tabletop.

As they entered, the commander belted out, "Tell me what the fuck's going on. Sorry, Frisca." He gave Skyler an apologetic grin.

Her brows arched, but she waved a dismissive hand.

Ram threw himself into a chair, flinging an arm

over the back. "Brak here killed one of the humans who were waiting at the portal. We dropped off his body with Alarik's lab techs. Maybe they can tell us what's powering them up. Two of them jumped from ground to rooftop. It's Denim who's got the big news, though."

She took a deep breath. "My scumbag ex-husband was one of them. But he's much bigger. I can also guarantee he never jumped so high before."

Kole took the news on the chin, barely flinching, no fire. "Any idea what's going on?"

"None, but I can reach out to a few of his old buddies. If they'll talk to me," said Denim.

Rein passed a hand over his military-cut hair. "We need to warn Aeternals to cross into New Orleans at extreme risk. We've been too slap dash about the situation."

"Yeah." Kole tented his fingers, a move everyone appreciated. "But the Ministry of Prosperity is squealing like a stuck wilding rhino-pig, proclaiming an economic crash if we prevent Aeternals from using portals. The Mardi-on partiers won't be happy either."

"We're going to listen to those pencil-dicked number crunchers or a bunch of kids?" Ram scowled. "With their new superhuman shit and tranq bullets, those humans, whoever the fuck they are, will capture one of us soon. A live Aeternal specimen."

Kole nodded. "Skyler has news. It solves part of the puzzle. Frisca?"

"The Alliance had a traitor in its midst, one who hacked into documents detailing New Orleans portal sites."

"Their agents picked him up, but didn't get much out of him," explained Kole. "He claims to work for a human named Mars. An alias. Described him as a military type. Buzz-cut hair, stiff jaw, cold eyes. Stick up his anal cavity. Average height. Bulked up."

"Big payments went into the traitor's bank accounts, but we haven't been able to trace where the money came from or where the guy sent the stolen documents. Our new tech and your Logan are both working on it. If anyone can find the information, they can," said Skyler.

Kole actually smiled at the Alliance's chief legal officer. Of course, she was his bedmate. If he wanted to get anything on, he'd better grin. Maybe it would be nice to have a permanent fuckbunny. Ram glanced at Denim. *Nah. What am I thinking? How would I squeeze a permanent female into my life?*

Rein spoke up. "We need new portals to the Big Easy, Commander."

"I know. So far, we're lucky the action is limited to the one city. Unfortunately, the traitor passed on intel about other sites as well. Maybe lack of manpower limits these humans to New Orleans for the time."

"I'm so sorry this happened." Kole's icy proud female slumped, but the commander tossed an arm over her shoulders.

Rein continued. "Still don't have an antidote for the sedative. Alarik needs more time to find one which won't kill us. I told him we're short on the commodity."

"Okay. Cadmon will broadcast a stronger alert to all Aeternals. Screw the Ministry of Prosperity. In the meantime, we wait. For an antidote. For the autopsy which might explain what's jacked up these humans. I'll call the Ministry of Compliance to demand a few new portals in New Orleans. It was already in the plans. Let's be sure your techie and Logan keep the whereabouts private, Skyler. Setting up this shit isn't simple. The magic of creating the portals isn't so complicated I hear, but the infrastructure Earthside is labor intensive. We can't just pop out anywhere. Secure places for the gateways, away from prying eyes, have to be constructed. Parking garages, storefronts, hangars, warehouses, or whatever. Right now, we'll have to use buildings already in place. I'm tired of reacting to this crap. We go on the offensive now. We need to snag a live Captain America, torture the hell out of him, and get intel."

Grunts, nods, and right-ons ended the conference.

Skyler rose and trailed her fingers up her mate's arm. "Sorry."

Kole wrapped her in his bear-like arms. "You have nothing to be sorry for, Frisca."

Ram watched the exchange, the warmth between the two. He was a tad jealous.

****

Thorn, the cowboy-booted Firebrand, shadowed Denim later in the evening when she went for groceries. He said something about "like glue" before he tagged along.

Denim paused inside the entrance of a gigantic market. "I think I'll be okay in here unless a rabid turnip or a feral steak attacks me. Why don't you do a little shopping for yourself?"

"Naw. I'm good. I eat out."

"Then help me." She reached into her pocket and unfolded a list. "I need milk, butter, bread, jelly, some thin-sliced turkey. You get all those. I'll get the rest."

Pushing the cart from aisle to aisle, she noted the shelves, amazed to find some familiar brands. Del Monte. Campbell. Others must originate on Scath.

Finished with her part of the list, she waited at the checkout for Thorn before putting all of the items onto the belt. As the checker scanned the groceries, she stared at Denim, frowning and sniffing.

"What's her problem?" Denim wheeled a shopping cart out the exit doors. She headed for Thorn's truck.

"You're human."

"Like it's a bad thing. Can't she tell I'm part witch?"

Thorn stepped back, eying her. "Nah. Your aura's pure Earther."

As the shifter's fingers caressed the red paint job on his truck, a sigh left his lips. The Ford Super Duty F-450 Platinum.

"Your girlfriend?"

Thorn gave Denim the look a guy gives a woman when he thinks she's said the dumbest thing ever. "The She Beast is much prettier and more reliable than any female. She hums and purrs when I start her up. And I don't have to buy her dinner or take her to a movie. Just look at her back end." He lowered the tailgate.

While they were loading the groceries, he yelled out, "Ram."

Denim's heart stuttered when she heard the name. She pivoted, spotting the satyr with a young child perched on his shoulders. The girls' legs hung down his chest, her fingers laced on his forehead. Ram had one hand against her lower back.

Looking a little sheepish, he approached. "Denim. Thorn. Meet Jonquil."

"Are they friends of yours, Daddy?"

Daddy? Was Ram married? With a daughter? Surely, Galena would have warned her.

"Hi, Jonquil. Nice to meet you," said Denim.

The child was definitely Ram's. She had his caramel-streaked hair and translucent eyes rife with mischief.

The dimples were her own, fitting her frilly pink

skirt, shiny black Mary Janes, and socks with ruffled tops.

"She's pretty, Daddy." He swung the child off his shoulders.

"Yes, she is," agreed Ram.

"Hey. What about me, little one? I'm handsome, don't you think?" asked Thorn.

She giggled. "No male's as handsome as my daddy. But you're funny."

"Funny's good. Nice to meet you. Heard about you."

Jonquil scanned Denim with eyes which were old for her age, which was probably about eight.

"We're going to get groceries for dinner." Ram was uncharacteristically soft spoken. No jokes with sexual overtones. "Come along, pest. See ya." He grabbed Jonquil's hand.

Denim and Thorn waved.

Tugging on her dad, the girl did a one-eighty. "Denim, do you want to come for dinner tomorrow? Daddy's cooking. He's a great cook."

"I'm sure she's busy, pest," said Ram.

"Please, Daddy. We never have dinner guests." She fluttered her thick lashes, giving him puppy eyes. Like any father, he couldn't refuse.

"Of course. What was I thinking? Denim, please join us for dinner tomorrow."

"Will your wife be there?" She cringed after the question stumbled across her lips, almost slapping a hand over her mouth.

Lame.

Jonquil giggled. "We don't have a wife. Please, Denim." She skipped around Ram, her fingers tapping his legs.

"We really would like you to join us. It'll be grill

night. Steaks. Corn on the cob. Some green vegetable we haven't picked out yet. If the pest behaves, we might even get a dessert."

"Daddy makes me eat green vegetables. I don't mind. They're good for you. Do you like green vegetables, Denim?"

"Asparagus. Love the stuff. My grandma made me eat okra. Not so fond of it."

"We can get asparagus. Huh, Daddy? And ice cream for dessert."

"Absolutely."

"I'd love to come," said Denim.

"How about me?" asked Thorn.

"You can come some other time," said Jonquil.

"Don't be rude." Ram corrected his daughter, but he didn't seem too upset. "Thorn, you're invited too. Bring the beer."

"You're gonna have to get your own booze, man. I'm busy."

Jonquil's grin spread from cheek to cheek. "Good. We'll see you tomorrow, Denim. About six, I think. Is it good, Daddy?"

"Perfect, pest."

Denim smiled. "See you then. How will I know where you live?"

"Galena will escort you. I'm glad you can come." Ram turned, slinging his daughter onto his shoulders.

When they disappeared into the market, a familiar warmth coursed through Denim's veins.

Damn. He's a father.

****

Inside the grocery store, Ram questioned Jonquil with an arched brow. "What's up?"

"What do you mean, Daddy?"

"You know what I mean. Your little nymph mind

is working on a plan."

"I don't have a plan, Daddy." Dimples puckered her cheeks when she shot him an innocent look.

"Yes, you do. You're cute and smart, but a schemer."

"The female's pretty. Isn't she, Daddy?"

"She is."

Denim's knit shirt hugged her breasts just right. Her pants hung low on curvy hips and showed off her long, luscious legs. Ram shook his head. Wrong time for these visions.

Damn satyr nature.

"It will be nice to have a guest for dinner. Another female."

"You're the only female I need, pest. You know that. It's just us. It's always been just us. And it always will be."

"Daddy. You need to get real. Someday I'll be out of the house, mated, or on my own. Who will take care of you?"

"It's my job to worry about you. Not the other way around. Besides, you won't be leaving me for a long time. You're stuck with me." Ram lifted a hand, lightly thumping the back of Jonquil's head.

"Ouch."

"Just a love pat, pest. Stop trying to run my life. Now, where's the asparagus?"

Chapter Seventeen

The next day Ram lumbered into the morgue.

"News, sexy Doc?" The Firebrand winked at Locasta, the blood smell tickling his nose. Not the fresh stuff. Plus, it was hidden under a sterile antiseptic odor.

Good thing I'm no vamp.

"I'm not a…"

"Doc. So you say. But you're smart, and I love a clever female."

"You're a flirt."

She led him to some machine which was spitting out paper. *Lab test results.* As if he knew what the printout meant. He glanced at several pages, shrugging.

Locasta returned to the body, flipped down her visor, bent, and almost buried her head in the open cavity. She straightened. "It's interesting. The human's chock full of weird chemicals, like steroids and amphetamines but unlike them, too. I've never seen these before. I trained at Johns Hopkins. So I know Earther cadavers." She sniffed. "He smells funny, too. What do you think?"

Ram leaned over, drawing the odor into his nostrils. "Hmm."

"Here's another fun fact. He's got more stretch marks than a pregnant hippo. Like he's gone through a growth spurt. Unknowledgeable about the effects of the chemicals in his system, I'm going to take an unscientific stab and say they're the cause. Sure, he might have been born with an athletic body and worked it his whole life, but I'm betting most humans aren't able to bench press a grizzly bear. I think this male was capable. You told me he jumped from the ground onto a roof. I'd expect to see evidence of the ability in his musculature. Bingo. It's there. It's abnormal for his species."

"How do you explain the anomalies?"

"Again, wild leap. I'm blaming those chemicals. I'm not saying they're the exact same structure as known amphetamines or steroids. Here's the puzzling part. They are close enough to be cousins. I found evidence of the substances in muscles, organs, the bloodstream, the nervous system. His heart's larger. His lung capacity is huge. See what I mean?"

"This stuff could do all that?"

"Possibly. I also found an injection site on his arm. He recently got a shot of something. A needle could deliver the drugs."

"Can you tell how long this shit would stay in his system?"

"No. Still, I can say it isn't permanent. It is already degrading. He would have needed another shot to stay this way."

"Good work, sexy."

Locasta snorted.

****

Denim stared at a long gravel driveway on Wildwynd, home of satyrs. A barn and a row of apple trees bookended the white, green-shuttered farmhouse. Circling the property, a fence framed a golf-course worthy lawn. To finish the idyllic picture, a front porch made her want to pour a mint julep, pull out a rocking chair, and enjoy the view.

Galena tagged along as her bodyguard or tour guide for the journey. "Nice. I pegged Ram for a city boy, living in a penthouse with minimalist furnishings. Decked out in black and gray. Typical male stuff. A place stocked with rotating women."

"You weren't aware of the kid?"

"I was, but Ram and child didn't jive in my

head."

Denim rang the doorbell. As they waited, she wiped her sweating hands on her dress, wondering if the case of nerves was brought on by the daughter or the father.

With a face lit by a broad smile, Jonquil flung open the door. When she saw the Amazon, her forehead wrinkled, the grin disappearing.

"Hi, Jonquil. This is Galena."

"You aren't planning to stay for dinner, are you?" asked the girl.

"Nope. I'm here to drop off the precious cargo. Have fun, kids. Call if you want company home."

"I won't need anyone. I'll pop into the stronghold when all is done." She tapped her wrist. "I have my new imbedded Flash Gordon watch now."

"Girl, we give them to anybody these days. I'm outta here."

Before Galena headed for the portal, Denim elbowed her.

She handed Jonquil a bottle. "I brought your dad a local wine which I was assured is the best on Scath." She passed off another item. "Also, here's a six-pack of what the grocer said was every kid's choice. Cream soda."

"I love this stuff. Thanks, Denim. Come in." The girl swept her arm in an elegant invitation. "Can I take your sweater? You look real pretty. Purple is one of Daddy's favorite colors. He likes pink, too. I wear it a lot."

Giving up her sweater, Denim tugged at the top of her sundress, which showed a more skin than she expected. It was, however, a stunning purple, sprinkled with little white flowers. She thought it looked great. White sandals had replaced her combat boots.

"Follow me. Daddy's in the backyard grilling steaks. Since he's been cussing, things must not be going well. He uses a lot of four-letter words when he cooks."

"I know the feeling." Denim trailed Jonquil through the kitchen. The door led to a stone patio. The lawn spread out about fifty feet behind the farmhouse before it dropped off, revealing a wide expanse of forested hills and valleys. Denim imagined Tuscany, lush, serene.

Ram was bent over the grill, inspecting the steaks, fork in hand. She licked her lips, admiring his firm ass in those pants. Her wicked eyes traveled to his trim waist and broad back where slabs of solid muscle rippled beneath a black T-shirt. A leather band tied off his long caramel-streaked hair. She blushed.

Just wrong to be ogling a kid's father right in front of her.

"How do you like yours, Denim? We go for rare. The pest and me." He turned around, almost dropping the steak on a fork.

When he whistled, she was pretty sure she fell in love. Denim blamed his admiration on the new sundress. If not the cause, she had paid a lot of money for nothing. "I'll have mine medium. You'd think you two are vampires. Rare and bloody, huh?"

Recovering with a smile, he pivoted back to the grill.

"Yes," said Jonquil. "Daddy says any other way makes the meat tough."

"The corn's ready." He plopped the cobs onto a platter, handing it off to his daughter. "Set this on the table. I'll have the steaks in a bit. We have to wait for the overcooked one. Seat our guest, pest."

Jonquil struggled with the plate while holding Denim's hand and towing her into the dining room.

"Here. Let me get that." Realizing the girl's dilemma, Denim took the corn from her.

At the doorway, Denim paused. "This is lovely."

A white linen tablecloth with matching napkins adorned the table. Blue stoneware dishes, two pale blue wineglasses, candles, and a vase stuffed with sunny daffodils finished the picture. Handmade name cards showed where each would sit.

The girl glanced up, wide-eyed, grinning. "Thank you. I set the table and made the place cards."

Denim fingered the one with her name on it. "You've drawn a beautiful flower."

"I'm good with daffodils. I put Daddy here at the head."

"As is proper."

Ram entered with a platter of steaks, forking them onto the plates. "I'll be right back." He raced for the kitchen.

Returning, he clutched the open bottle of wine in one hand and the cream soda in the other.

With a napkin over his arm, he leaned toward Jonquil. "*Mademoiselle?*"

She lifted her glass while Ram poured. He strolled over to Denim. "*Et vous, mademoiselle?*"

"*Oui, monsieur.* I would love a little … *vin.*"

After Ram slid into his chair, she cut a chunk of steak, popping it into her mouth. Her tastebuds danced a jig. "Wow! This is delicious."

"It's surprising what you can do with top choice meat," said Ram.

"Too modest. I think it's the chef."

Jonquil flipped her eyeballs from one adult to the other, her irises twinkling.

Denim sank her teeth into the corn. With the juicy kernels dripping butter, a stream dribbled down her chin.

Ram pointed as Jonquil laughed.

"What? Oh. It's delicious, but I'm a slob." Denim wiped the mess away with her napkin. She watched father and daughter. Their conversation was easy, sometimes silly. Like Marta's table, love ate here, a deep love. Family. Once again, Denim was only a guest, someone on the outside looking in. But she shook off the momentary sadness, choosing the joy of the moment.

Between bites of meat, corn on the cob, and asparagus, she squeezed in a few questions. "Do you have family on Scath?"

"My father is here in Wildwynd, but we rarely see him. My mother also lives on the island at the Sanctuary of the Maidens."

"Are they mated?" Denim asked. "Is that the correct term?"

"Right term. Wrong pair. While satyrs and nymphs often join to produce offspring, they don't always mate. They have other agendas. Ones which include fu ... having as many partners as possible." He glanced at Jonquil.

"Daddy, I understand these things. I'm not a child. My grandparents have lovers. Lots of lovers."

"What do you know about their lovers?" Ram's eyes were narrow slits as he stared at his daughter.

Jonquil looked at Denim, her glance saying another woman would understand. "He thinks I'm such a child." Her lips formed a pout.

Denim laughed. "I hear fathers are like that."

"My dear old dad retired from the Firebrands about a century ago. He heads up a village. Kind of a mayor. Mom specializes in parties."

"I love Gramma's soirees. That's what she says they are." Jonquil shot a quick glance around the room. "I can call her that, right? She's not here."

Ram explained, "Mom's not fond of being labeled grandmother or any form of the word."

"Anyway, Gramma's parties are the best. For my last birthday, she brought in a dozen vamponies. All the kids got to ride."

"Vamponies?" asked Denim.

"Think short horses with a taste for blood. I spent the night keeping them muzzled so they couldn't fang the kiddies. Great fun. What about your family?"

"I'm a foster home grad. My mother died of Parkinson's when I was young. I have only snippets of memory of her. No father I know of. At eighteen, I struck out on my own to join the army, where I found discipline and a purpose. When my enlistment ended, I did a stint with the New Orleans police. A Cajun grandma popped out of nowhere, having looked a long time for me, claiming to be my daddy's mom. She shared an interesting bit of family history about Aeternals and ancient bloodlines. I thought she was crazy until I checked out the Alliance at her request."

Denim sipped her wine. "She died four years ago. I miss her. I didn't know her long, but she was good to me. I loved her. So, I've only had family for brief periods."

"After you decided the Alliance was real and your grandmother wasn't crazy, you joined?" asked Ram.

"Once I told them my background, I was a hot commodity. They recruited me. Very persuasive people."

"I'm glad." Ram raised his glass in a toast.

"Me, too," said Jonquil, picking up a spear of asparagus with her fingers. Ram frowned when she slid in into her mouth.

Cutting another chunk of steak before stuffing it between her lips, Denim hid how insanely happy she was. "This is really good," she mumbled with a big bite.

While she ate, she watched Ram and Jonquil. They teased, talked, laughed. Like at Marta's she leaned back in her chair. There was love in this house. They were a family. And somehow this satyr dulled her memories of Steven's cruelty.

****

Ram watched his daughter jump out of her seat. She was still in plan mode.

Jonquil grabbed her plate and glass. "I'll clean up. You two go to the study."

Ram rose, clasping Denim's hand. "Get your wine. We've been ordered out."

"I should help with the dishes," said Denim.

"Oh, no. I've got this." Jonquil firmly planted her fists on her hips, her pose stern.

Ram led the way along the hallway. "Stop watching my ass."

Denim jabbed his shoulder. "Shh. Jonquil will hear you. I was not ogling your ass."

In the study, Ram flopped onto a well-worn mahogany leather sofa which creaked under his weight. He flung his sizable legs straight out while patting his stomach. "I ate too much. Must be the company or conversation."

When Denim eyed two chairs clustered around an unlit stone fireplace, he slapped the couch beside him.

"Here, doll." She was tempting tonight in the purple sundress. He hadn't expected such feminine attire, used to seeing her in fighting garb for the job or tight jeans at the Shed. Both of which he loved on her. The dress, though, was more than a satyr could handle. The swell of her breasts over the top. The narrow little straps he'd love to slip off her shoulders.

Not now. Not here.

Denim sank into the couch, kicking off her

sandals. She curled her feet underneath, looking comfortable and at home. "Your place is beautiful. I didn't figure you for something like this."

"What did you expect?"

"Glass. Chrome. Leather whips. Chains."

"Those are in the basement. I'll take you below later."

"Seriously. Why a farmhouse?"

Ram took a big gulp of wine, struggling with how much he wanted to reveal. *Fuck it.* Why keep secrets? "Long story. Here's the short version. Jonquil's mother was human. When we screwed around, I was careless with my prolific satyr swimmers. She got pregnant but died in childbirth. I brought Jonquil to this farmhouse because I thought it was a good place to raise a kid."

Denim fingered the rim of her wineglass. "I'm sorry."

Ram waved off her concern. "Eight years ago."

"Did Jonquil's mother know you were a satyr from a different realm?"

"Eventually, I told her about myself. I was doing my thing Earthside. Firebrands are required to go outside Scath to live now and then so we don't become insulated." He paused, chuckling. "I was a professional polo player. You may laugh."

Denim obliged him with a big grin. "I can see you riding a horse and swinging a mallet."

"She attended a match, we talked…" He took another sip before he put his glass down. "…and the rest is history. We never should have hooked up. Shit happens. Then you move on. No pity. The stuff shrivels my balls."

"Nonetheless, I'm sorry."

His gaze drifted to the side. He never talked about Jonquil's mother to anyone. Not even his parents. After her death, he returned to Scath with a baby in his arms and a don't-fuck-with-me expression on his face which said *ask no questions*.

"She deserved better. She was a sweet female, fragile, not independent or self-sufficient like you. We were going to be a family and bring our baby to Scath."

"Everyone claims you hate humans. How can you?"

"I don't hate humans. I just have a poor track record. Makes me a little Earther-shy."

"Because of what happened to your daughter's mother? You blame yourself?"

"She wanted a home birth with a midwife. Sounded good. Being a satyr, I didn't want to be any closer to an Earth hospital than necessary. So, I agreed. But there was a problem. By the time I rushed her to the emergency room... You know."

Ram sat silent, rubbing his thumb on his wineglass.

"Be careful, satyr. I'm starting to like you."

He wanted in Denim's pants, though he wasn't looking for long-term. "Don't. Satyrs aren't good relationship risks. I'm worse than most. I fuck things up. I'm a great Firebrand to have on your six, but I'm bad at anything else. I killed her. I might as well have stabbed her in the heart with one of my Scottish dirks."

"Not the same, Ram. Women die in childbirth. It's terrible, but it's true."

Ram swallowed the lump in his throat. "She depended on me to take care of her. It was my job. I didn't. I let her down."

"Look at Jonquil. You haven't let her down."

"She's still young." His daughter was his heart, and Gahya willing, he'd do a better job with her. He poured all of his love into Jonquil. Outside her, he was the warrior. The flirt. The horny satyr. Nothing more. He didn't want anyone else to depend on him.

"She's a terrific kid. Well, hardly a kid. She sounds so grown up sometimes. You are close, and she adores you."

He deflected. "Because I'm adorable."

"Incorrigible."

When he looked at Denim, his breath caught. She was so damn beautiful. His heart did a fast *thump, thump, thump* as he jockeyed her shoulders a little forward to loop his arm around them. He pulled her close.

"There. Better. Yeah. Too grown up. She thinks she has to manage my life. You know why she wanted this dinner party, right?"

Denim's chestnut hair was loose, falling in waves over her breasts, tickling his arm. As she peeked at him, hanging on his every word, her eyes bore into his soul. If he had one. He misplaced it when Jonquil's mother died. But the human made him feel as if it might still be there, buried deep, waiting to be claimed. He wanted to take her into his arms, race for his room, and lay her across his bed. He'd hike her skirt to her waist and pull down her panties.

No. We can't.

"No. Why?"

"What?" Had he spoken aloud? He didn't think so.

"You asked if I knew why Jonquil wanted this dinner party? I don't."

He laughed. "To get us together. She thinks I'm lonely."

"Are you?"

"I have Jonquil. I have the Firebrands."

"That's a non-answer answer. Explain something to me. You're a satyr. Only males are satyrs, and

Jonquil's mother was human. What's Jonquil?"

"All male offspring of satyrs are pure satyr. All female children, no matter the mother's breed or species, are nymphs. We shoot strong seed."

"I see." Denim lowered her lids, her lacy lashes forming a stunning fan.

Talk about emptying his nuts gave him an erection which rubbed against his pants. He shifted to get more comfortable. Except it was difficult to get loose with a hard-on and his daughter in the other room.

Ram always kept his lovers, or to be accurate, his one-night fucks, far from his life with Jonquil. Denim was the first female other than relatives or Firebrands who had come into this house. He wasn't sure how he felt about it. He was damn certain he didn't like having his dick stand up and salute with his young daughter a room away.

Denim is dangerous. She makes me want someone to sit with after dinner, to share stories with. How was your day? Shitty. Oh, baby, I am so sorry. How was yours?

Here he was, his emotions on his sleeves. How metrosexual of him. He almost sounded sensitive. A loud warning bell rang in his mind.

She took a sip of wine, shifted in her seat, and snuggled against his chest. "Have you gotten close to anyone else?"

"Never. No one except you has ever tempted me. I've been trying to get into your pants since I first saw you. I wish I had known all I had to do was wave my kid in front of you and tell a sad story," he whispered, hoping the pest didn't hear him.

"Are you always going for shock effect?"

He would be smart to keep a distance. He'd never been attracted to anyone the way he was to her, including

Jonquil's mother.

"Shock effect, doll. I'm about the shock."

"Stop calling me 'doll.' I'm not a wide-eyed fragile piece of china and stuffing."

"Don't I know it. I was thinking more like a female Chuckie."

Denim laughed. "I can go with that."

He adjusted the uncooperative swollen cock in his pants.

Denim leaned away from his grasp to set her glass on the table. "Answer a question."

"Sure."

"I may be out of line, but the answer's important to me. How often do you feed?"

His brows arched. "Every day."

"How have you been handling it?"

Ram leaned forward to stare into her eyes. "Fucking isn't necessary for feeding. I can touch anyone who's hot-to-trot. If it's a snack, I have to load up more often, but I don't need to screw. Fortunately, there are a lot of horny Aeternals running around. If a crowd gathers in one spot, I don't even need to go skin to skin to absorb the lust. The air is filled with arousal."

"So, you don't necessarily have sex when you feed?"

Ram drew a deep breath. Might as well let it everything hang out. "Denim, I haven't been with another female since I met you."

"Really? Why?"

Ram ran his hand along her thigh. "You tell me," he whispered in her ear, his tongue stroking her lobe. *Hold back*, he cautioned himself. Sex. Nothing more. Unfortunately, his emotions pinged from one chamber of his heart to another. He was in new territory, and he didn't like it.

When a soft knock sounded, he jerked away, his finger imitating a plug in a wall socket. Denim shot upright at the same time, both two guilty juveniles caught doing the nasty on Mommy's couch.

Jonquil peeked in. "Night. I'm going to bed."

Ram scrunched his eyes together. "Already?" Suspicion reared its head. Getting her to sleep early was usually a battle of wills.

Jonquil padded into the room to kiss him on the cheek. "I'm really tired." She paused, yawned, stretched her arms overhead, and leaned in to give Denim a peck. "Night. Thanks for coming."

Denim ran her fingers along her jaw where Jonquil had planted the kiss. "I've had a wonderful time. I'm so glad you invited me."

Ram thought he saw moisture in Denim's eyes.

"Good. You'll come again." His daughter flounced out of the room in her soft pink dress.

Ram's gaze followed Jonquil, who seemed pleased with herself. What an actress. She thought she was so clever.

Denim took Ram's hand. "I think you're wearing me down, satyr. If you proposition me another day, some other place, I might accept."

Her words raced to his groin, but he needed to be sure she understood. "Don't make more of this thing between us than what it is, Denim. You can't count on me. I'm not seeking a relationship. Can you handle the situation?"

"I don't need you to take care of me. I'm responsible for myself."

"We still work together. That bothered you before."

"Someone else could become my trainer."

"Hell no. Not happening. No males are going to

be laying their sweaty hands on you."

"Don't you have rules about fraternization in the Firebrands?"

"Nope." His eyes flashed green. "More wine?" He grabbed the bottle to pour. His cock said getting it on with Denim was a good idea. His mind told him he was in over his head.

Hell with it. Get her out of my fucking system. Right?

Chapter Eighteen

Ram made it all the way up the stairs without bumping into any familiar faces. Not that he cared. He set part of his load on the floor out of sight before he rapped on the door.

Denim answered in light gray sweats, a thin tee, white socks, and no makeup. Her hair hung around her face in a loose mess. She looked incredibly sexy. Like she hadn't been out of bed too long.

Ram kept a hand behind his back.

Tugging a chestnut strand over her scar, she smiled. "What do you have there?"

He pulled out a bouquet of flowers.

Denim accepted them with a halfhearted smile. "Thanks. I'll put them in water."

"Oh, and this." He bent to retrieve a package wrapped in foil with a fancy bow.

Clearly surprised, Denim set the bouquet on a table near the door before she snagged the gift. "May I open it now?"

"Yes. If I can come in."

She stumbled over a few words before she stepped aside to wave him toward the sofa.

Flinging herself beside him, she ripped off the bow and paper, nothing timid about her. Once she opened the box, she gasped. "A Glock G-19." Palming his gift, she pulled back the slide to check the empty chamber. "Why..." She laughed. "I told you I'd rather have a gun than flowers as an apology."

He nodded. "Silly, huh?" It was a joke at first. Somehow, the gift seemed more serious now. "There's more."

She rifled through the paper under the weapon.

Her mouth fell open when she spied a belt holster. A design was tooled in the leather. A colorful Phoenix, its wings spread, words beneath it. Denim traced the lettering. *Natis in Igne. Probata est in Sanquinem.* "What's it mean?"

"Born in Fire. Tested in Blood. You're a Firebrand warrior. I wanted to give you something to show how I see you."

Her eyes went all mushy on him. "It's perfect. Come here, *cher*." She pressed her lips to Ram's. "Hmm." Her fingers tangled in his loose hair, tugging his head down. She planted kisses along his jaw before she round-tripped to his mouth.

He licked the seam between her soft lips. When she opened, he explored inside before sucking on her tongue, slow, deep draws. Ram disengaged. "Where's your bedroom? I don't want our first time to be on a couch."

"That way." She jerked her thumb for directions.

Ram scooped her into his arms, carrying her through the hall to the door, tossing her onto the bed. He toed off his boots and slipped out of his shirt.

Denim sat up, warm chestnut eyes staring at him.

"Gahya. You're making me harder. Clothes. Off now."

She grabbed the hem of her tee, sliding it over her head, baring her breasts. *Holy shit.* He wanted to get his mouth on her rosy nipples.

Unzipping his pants, Ram shucked them off. To help Denim, he yanked on the toes of each of her socks and tugged her sweats down her legs along with her panties. All the time, she kept a lustful eye on his throbbing cock.

Beautiful.

Instead of crawling onto the bed, Ram froze.

Denim scooted up to lean against the headboard. "What's wrong?"

"Absolutely nothing. I've wanted you horizontal. Now that I have you here, I need a sec to enjoy the sight. Gahya. You're beautiful."

She swept her hair over the scar ending on her cheek. "I'm not."

"Denim Quinn, I see a strong, feminine beauty."

He prowled to the foot of the bed, his heavy length bobbing with each step. Crawling onto the mattress, he settled his hips between her thighs. Holding himself on stiffened arms, he kissed one eyelid before he moved to the other. Brushing her silky hair off her face, he slid his lips to the scar she tried to hide.

When she tensed, he kept kissing it until she relaxed. With a satisfied grin, he nibbled his way down her neck, capturing a nipple. He licked around the nub until it was a hard pebble. He traveled to the other breast to lavish it with attention.

When Denim moaned and arched into his mouth, he took more of her, nuzzling into her plump mounds.

While he enjoyed himself, Denim fisted his hair, pulling him tight. Her hips bounced off the bed, begging him for more.

Skin to skin, he closed his eyes. He sighed. Ram felt like a randy teen, ready to come before he was inside. "I'm not gonna last, doll."

"Foreplay's overrated, satyr."

"Holy Gahya. Wait. I have a shitload of condoms in my pants pocket."

"I'm on the pill."

"Satyr sperm is too potent." He jumped from the bed, rifling through his pockets until he found what he was looking for. He plopped the packets on the cabinet. Smooth.

He locked onto her lips again in a wild kiss, fucking her mouth with his tongue until he needed the real deal. He sat on his haunches to slip on the glove.

"Here, let me help." She took the packet from his hand, opening it, unrolling the condom a bit. Pinching the tip of it, she put it to the crown of his dick. He closed his lids, breathing deep as she unrolled it along his length. Wearing a glove had never turned him on this much.

Resettling between her thighs, he dragged his cock back and forth through her moist heat until he thought he'd die from the anticipation. She was ready for him. So luscious.

"Stop teasing."

He shifted his hips forward, his crown nudging her pussy.

"Yes, Ram. Now."

Shoving into her, he flexed his ass while her nails gouged his shoulders. Another inch. Her muscles gripped him, sucking him in. He pushed deeper, groaning. "Fuck, doll. A little farther."

Ram bent her knees, tilting her up to take more of him. He slammed into her, buried to his hilt. "Oh, damn." She was divine.

"Wait. Don't move. Let me get used to you." Denim's breath hitched.

The hardest thing in his life was to hold still rather than pound into this female like an animal, but he wanted her to enjoy the coupling.

Her ass rose from the bed as she undulated beneath him. He watched his shaft slide out of her before he plunged back in. "Oh, yeah. You take me just right."

"Harder, satyr. Faster."

****

Denim moaned when he molded a hand around

her breast, squeezing while his hips continued their assault. He latched onto a nipple again. He sucked, licked, nipped, his mouth full of her flesh.

He slammed forward. Inched his cock out. Glided in, touching all the right places.

Too much sensation. His wet mouth sucking on her breast. His shaft plundering her body. His rock-hard abs flexing as his rhythm got faster, more frantic. Flesh slapping flesh.

With his hair falling around her, a silky, sensual curtain, his lips deserted her breasts. She fixed on Ram's eyes, his irises solid neon green. He was feeding. Suddenly, his cheekbones were like sharpened blades, his jaw cut stone. Denim could swear short horns curled back from the top of his head, barely peeking out. His transformation and the intensity of her nourishing him sent her to the edge. She locked her ankles over his buttocks while she arched off the bed, taking the full force of his feral assault.

This was her wild, gorgeous satyr.

She was so close. "Yes, Ram. Oh, yes."

His hips plowed forward as her orgasm gathered slowly. It was fog rolling in, building until it was a storm. The mist ebbed. It rolled in again. With each new thrust from Ram, the sensation hit her anew. Stronger. Fiercer until it was a hurricane.

She screamed his name, clawing his back. Unable to come down completely, Denim gripped Ram's upper arms tight while he hammered into her, faster, harder, chasing his own release. When it struck, she was sent into one more orgasm.

While their heartbeats slowed, he held his groin snug against her. Then he clutched her ass and rolled them both to the side. "Doll, I don't think I've ever come so fucking hard."

His horns had disappeared. His face was softer when his steely arms wrapped around her. "How are you?"

She couldn't lift her head. *Hell.* "I can barely breathe."

"We're just starting."

"Did I hallucinate or did you kind of change on me there?"

"Change how?"

"Your face? Horns?"

Ram's breath caught. He hesitated. "It's a satyr thing. Only happens when... Well, never happened to me before."

Denim smiled against his chest, pleased she'd had such an effect on him. When she pressed against his thigh, he clasped her hand and moved it to his hard cock.

"See what you're doing to me?"

"I'm ready if you are."

"We don't have to be anywhere for hours. In the other good news department, I have a shitload of condoms. Spread your legs and lie back while I taste you."

Her sexy satyr began laying kisses on her stomach, the insides of her thighs, her sex.

Oh, yes.

****

Denim watched Ram out of the corner of her eye as she stretched her neck from side to side. Afterward, she did a few lunges. Thoughts ping-ponged in her brain while he leaned against the wall, his features frozen.

Holy hell. Look at him.

He wore loose-fitting black pants minus a shirt, showing off thick arms, bulging biceps. His caramel-streaked hair was tied back, his jaw clamped tight. And they had just come from the hottest sex match ever.

You're a warrior, fighting alongside the Firebrands. Cowgirl-up. Do your job.

Ram pushed off from the wall. "When we go Earthside, you'll be armed. A shitload of blades along with…"

"My sweet Glock with its personalized holster."

He grinned. "Always. Got it?"

"Got it."

"I believe you when you say you can shoot. What concerns me is everything else. Gotta be honest, you may have trained in Muay Thai, but you need to show more aggression, doll. We'll work on it, but for now grab a gladius."

She and Ram had already selected weapons from the armory. Four special-made combat knives, Eickhorns. The blades were an amalgam. Iron for demons. Silver for bloodsuckers or shifters. An upgraded Roman gladius. Its blade was sharp on both sides. Its point was designed for thrusting and stabbing. The great thing was, she could hold it in one hand.

Denim headed for the real things.

"Nuh-uh, doll. Those are take-home only. You might get in a lucky slice. Our practice weapons are duller." He snatched two swords similar to the gladius from the wall. After which, he tossed Denim a Kevlar vest. "Put it on for extra protection. Safety first."

When he winked, Denim blushed.

Ram rolled his shoulders and loosened his arms. He motioned for her to stand on the edge of the mats to watch his moves.

Taking position, Ram spread his legs, loose-kneeing it. He bobbed up and down a few times, bouncing left, then right to show Denim the advantages of his stance.

Holding the weapon outward, he used a trainer's

voice. "Swords are made for a variety of purposes. Some are hack and slash. Those are longer two-handers or cavalry kind. This blade is a thrust and slice. It's shorter. Easier for a female ... uh ... someone of your size to use. Hold it out in front of you. Like this." He demonstrated. "Not off to the side. Most of your kills will be with the point. You can do serious damage to your opponent. Do this." Again, he demoed the move.

Denim nodded while she gave her weapon a few stabs and thrusts.

"Good. Now come alongside me. We'll Fred and Ginger it. Follow along."

She positioned herself beside Ram, imitating his stance, mirroring his movements.

The satyr shot her a pleased glance. "I'm going to stand back now. You keep dancing."

She performed flawlessly, more fluid than ever.

"You're a natural. Elbow straighter, higher. Unstiffen those knees. Step. Lunge."

After a while, Ram raised a hand to stop her. "Here are four factors to remember. Timing. Distance. Reaction time. Reaction ability."

"This helps me how, sensei?"

"Being a smartass will not make you win. One. Predict your opponent's next move by starting yours before he starts his. Two. Keep a safe distance from your opponent until you strike. Three. Be faster than your enemy. Four. Your reaction ability is where I come in. I'll show you the moves you need. Of course, when all else fails, be more aggressive. Go for the kill. No hesitation."

Denim dipped her chin in acknowledgment. She flicked her arm, swishing the blade as he'd demonstrated. "The gladius feels good in my hand. Shouldn't I have a combat knife in my other?"

"We'll get there. Right now, I want you practicing with the sword. Are you ready for something other than air to fight?"

She smiled. "Bring it on, satyr."

His irises flashed green. "Overconfidence is not a good strategy, doll."

"Why not? It works for you."

"Again with the smartass. Prepare to be humbled." Ram bounced on the balls of his feet when he took position in front of her. He growled.

Denim lowered her sword, tilting her head. "Don't growl at me."

Ram lunged, tapping the point of his blade to her chest.

"I wasn't ready."

"Ding. Wrong answer. You must always be ready."

With her first thrust, he knocked the weapon from her grasp.

"That's a parry. Block your opponent's sword with yours. If you do it hard enough, you can kick it out of his hand. Lesson. Hold on tighter."

Damn.

She was gonna die in her first swordfight.

"Okay. I'm ready now."

He stopped, glared, and dropped his sword arm to the side. "Thanks for the warning. Few opponents tell me when they're set to go."

Denim didn't answer. She kept her eyes glued on Ram.

They waltzed around each other for a time, neither the aggressor. When Ram lunged, Denim side-stepped him.

When he fell for a fake, she sliced his bicep. "Nice, doll."

As he was talking, she charged, the point of her weapon glancing off his ribs. "Now who's distracted?"

He sprang toward her, but Denim parried to block his move. He almost lost his sword when they clashed blades.

They continued the blade play until she jabbed the point of her gladius against his chest, targeting his heart.

"Good," he said.

She spun, slashing, lunging, stabbing. Ram backed up, ducking, sidestepping her maneuvers. He barely dodged her quick blade.

When she charged, Ram slipped to the side and wrapped an arm around her, immobilizing her sword. Denim rotated out of the lock, flipping Ram ass over heels onto the mat.

"What the hell?" He popped to his feet.

"What the hell is right. I rock. Can you believe I did that?"

Ram scratched his head. "No. I can't."

Throwing her hands in the air, Denim hoofed it around the gym in a victory lap.

He stared in disbelief. "Doll, I've got a hard-on. Love a strong female. I may have underestimated you."

"I feel ya." She halted her Muhammed Ali prance. "I underestimated myself." She tugged on her sports top while she fanned her face with a hand. "Boy, it's hot as hell in here."

Water dripped onto her head, rolling down her cheeks. She glanced at the ceiling where a small cloud formed. Raindrops were falling from it.

Ram's gaze flitted from the raincloud to her eyes. "That's not all. You've got some sexy witch going on, doll. I think a meet with Kole is in your future."

****

Dax buried his fangs in the ylve, taking him to the floor. Since he was pissed it had taken four days to find the drug dealer, he drew hard, forcing the blood into his mouth, mindless of the pain he caused. His victim screamed, kicked, and struggled but couldn't shake the vampire Firebrand.

Arms crossed, Tyr waited in the corner, his bling shimmering in the light, the hard angles of his face making him resemble the devil's own.

Dax retracted his fangs and dropped the ylve. He swiped the sleeve of his black motorcycle jacket across his lips, wiping away the evidence of his snack. Leather was a great stain hider. "His blood has the normal drugs. No concierge compounds here. Nothing like what was in Cage."

Tyr planted a boot on the guy's chest after Dax backed away. "Have you run into somebody who sells something more exotic?"

Holding a hand to the gaping wound on his neck, the ylve glanced at Dax.

Tyr chuckled. "Hey, vamp. Tell him dinner's over. You're giving him the jitters."

Dax ran his fingers through his tangled black hair, pushing it over his shoulder. "I'm still hungry. I don't want to give him false hopes."

"Whaddaya need from me?" The ylve's nervous gaze bounced between the two Firebrands.

"Who's out there selling the exotic stuff? While the warlock's patient, I'm not so much. Hell, Tyr, let me rip his head off. He won't give us anything."

"Wait. Wait." The ylve squirmed on the floor, his shirt and jeans mopping up the dust as he wiggled under Tyr's boot. "You'll protect me if I tell ya?"

"Protect you from who?" Tyr punched down with his shitkicker hard enough to leave a print in the ylve's chest.

"I dunno, but the dealer's a shifter. His whole pack's probably involved."

Dax stroked his barely-there goatee. "Sure. We'll protect you."

"Okay. I did run across this hinky male. I didn't buy anything from him, though. He was a little too crazy even for me. Used too much of his own product. Get me?"

"Crazy how?" asked Tyr.

"He was a one-pony show. Saying crap like 'power to Scath' or some bullshit. I enjoy a fun high. Mellow's good. So's ready-to-party. This guy was intense, though. His trip didn't say 'havin' a fucking good time.'"

"Who is he?" asked Dax. This sounded like the same effect the drug had on Cage.

"Don't know. Some wolf. He works the alley outside Fang's."

"Is he a regular?" asked Tyr. "Was he having trouble shifting?"

"I've seen him before, but I wouldn't say he's a regular. No prob with his beast. Seemed normal there."

Grabbing the ylve's arm, Dax yanked him to his feet. "This is your lucky day. You're going to do a good deed."

The ylve kept his hand on his neck while blood oozed through his fingers. "Yeah? What makes it so lucky?"

Tyr smiled, his sickle tat bouncing with his grin. "You're gonna help us catch a bunch of bad guys. Be a good citizen."

"No. Nuh-uh. No way. No how. I don't want to get involved."

"Fine by me." Dax put both hands around the

ylve's neck. "I'd just as soon separate your head from your body. No biggie to me what you decide."

The ylve pawed at the vampire's hold.

"Give the poor male a sec, Dax. Big decision here. Help us or die. He might need a minute."

Dax started to twist. "Time's up. Pop goes the head."

"All right. Okay. I'll do it."

Stepping away, Dax mumbled, "Damn. I never get to kill anyone."

"Not true," said Tyr. "How about the coyote drug dealer? You did him in."

"Cage? He's dead?" asked the ylve.

"As a doornail," said Tyr.

"S'okay. Didn't like him anyway. Say, could you stop the bleeding now that I'm cooperating?"

Dax grabbed the drug dealer's arm, pulled him close, and ran a tongue along the wound to seal it. "Let's go to work. We'll pop over near the bar. The warlock here is going to cloak us in a spell while you wait for this shifter in the alley. Get me?"

The Firebrands dragged the ylve to a portal, touched their D-chips, and materialized in a gateway near Fang's.

"Here's what we want." Tyr fiddled with the silver bar through his brow. "Some of the product, its street name, the seller, and when to meet him again for more. Once you have the intel, you're done. Wait in the alley until we join you. If you cross us, Dax will find you... Well, you know the rest."

"I'm not stupid. Make a buy. Get the info. Stay put."

Dax patted the ylve's shoulder. "You're a genius." He turned to Tyr. "Keep us hidden until the exchange. Afterward we'll decide what to do. Maybe follow the dealer. Maybe get him alone in a quiet place later."

"Good plan. Start walking, ylve. We're with you all the way." Tyr shoved the male into the alley.

In an alcove where they could observe their spy, Tyr wrapped himself and Dax in a thick invisibility spell.

They waited at least an hour until a shifter came out the door of Fang's. He shot a look at the ylve. "You again?"

Their bait stuttered, twitching like a sonofabitch. "Sure thing. I changed my mind. I want some of your stuff."

"Why now?" The shifter's eyes narrowed on the ylve.

"Getting tired of the samey same. Ya know?"

"Smart move. Join us. You'll see things our way."

"Whose way?"

"Arisen Dawn. No other. We rule!" The dealer patted his pockets, finally reaching into the back one. "First time's free. Find me for the next hit." He handed the ylve a bag. "This is the snack pack. Snort it, or if you really like the stuff, mainline it later. Ya dig?"

"Yep. All's good. What's it called?" He took the pouch.

"Gold Dust."

"Where can I find you if I want more?"

"There'll be a next time. Trust me. Stuff's the shit. You'll join us."

"Uh-huh."

"Name's Karth. I'll be around here for a few nights." The shifter's glance took in the alley while he pivoted to return to the bar.

The ylve nodded.

Tyr dropped the spell. "Arisen Dawn."

"Yeah," said Dax. "They've moved into the drug business. I wonder if Sabine or Nico know this."

"There's more." Tyr jammed his hands into the pockets of his leathers.

"What?"

"Karth's in Thorn's ex-pack."

Chapter Nineteen

When the Alliance-agent-turned-Firebrand entered the outer office, Bounty rose, smoothed her fire-engine-red leather skirt, and flipped her blonde hair over her shoulder. "Do you wear anything other than BDU's or jeans?"

"I've been training with Ram. On a break." Denim glanced at her pants. "But yes, I do. Fact is, recently I got lucky because of a purple sundress."

They high-fived before Bounty nudged her toward Kole's office with a hand on her back. "Walk right in."

Pushing the door open, Denim expected a stream of fire to shoot her way. Instead, Kole was at his desk, head lowered, concentrating on some document in his fingers. He grabbed a pen and scrawled a hasty signature.

Glancing at her, he shoved the papers aside, giving his full attention to Denim. "You got something to tell me?"

She was about to share her story when two chuckling women flounced into the office arm in arm. Braelyn and Margo arrived.

Skyler entered a minute later, glancing at her watch before she strolled over to Kole, bent, and kissed him on the cheek.

"That's it, Frisca?"

She arched a regal brow. "For now, demon. I have to get back to headquarters."

"Pull up a knee." He cast a lopsided grin her way while patting his leg.

Not looking quite so frosty, the pregnant Skyler obliged him and curled her fingers around her mate's neck while the other women selected chairs.

"I'm here." Nico stormed into the office in full gear, a knife hanging from a hip holster, a long blade at his spine. He snapped his gaze toward Denim. "Holy shit. I'm pissed."

She fluttered the lashes outlining her rich, mauve-tinted eyes. They were no longer chestnut.

Braelyn propped her fists on her hips.

Margo took a minute to seize on Denim's new look. "You got all witchy, girl."

Skyler tilted her chin, staring at the Blood Coven descendant.

"When?" asked Kole.

"I was training with Ram yesterday when it happened. Something else, too."

"What?" Margo flipped a strand of red hair over her shoulder.

"I made it rain." She paused, waiting for a reaction. "Inside."

The room was hushed.

Kole cocked his head. "You control weather?"

Braelyn snapped her fingers. "Cool."

Everyone glanced at Nico as he batted his eyelashes in imitation of Denim. "Nope. Still shockingly sexy green. No warlock yet. You might as well cut me loose, Commander. I'm not one of your Blood Coven."

"The tests don't lie." Kole rested his palm on Skyler's thigh.

"You've been here longer than Denim has," said Margo.

"Rub it in." An angry shadow clouded Nico's face.

"What changed?" Kole swung his attention to Denim.

"Maybe fighting with Ram was a catalyst."

Nico tut-tutted the suggestion. "Can't be. I've

been in plenty of bloody skirmishes since coming to Scath."

Squinted eyes, clucks, and pursed lips indicated everyone was thinking hard.

Bounty leaned into the doorway, interrupting their concentration. "I hate to interrupt this party, but High Commander Cadmon is on the phone. Says it's urgent. Females, what do you think of this shade?" She fanned a hand through the air. "Bitches' Blood. Too much?"

"No. I love the color." Margo glanced at her own nails.

"You're right. How can anything be too much? Anyway, pick up the phone."

Kole reached for the landline. "All of you need to get together. Talk about what jumpstarts this thing. Meet with Alarik. His brainiacs can figure it out. It's obviously above my pay grade."

****

Lizette woke like a lazy cat, yawning, stretching, before she settled against the headboard. The menacing man sprawled on nearby floor pillows was a behemoth, bigger than Spear. His eyes, crowned with unswerving brows, were fierce, flinty, those of a predatory animal. They fixed on her. She should have been frightened. She wasn't.

His face was hard, cold stone. Only his lips looked soft. He extended his legs, an arm behind his thick neck, his head on a pillow while he studied her. Long, dark hair hung nearly to his waist, some strands woven into tight braids at his temples, making him resemble a savage warrior.

He wore loose-fitting black pants with no shirt, exposing faded tattoos on his chest, bulky arms, neck. They disappeared into his waistband. When she had asked the other day, he called them battle glyphs, explaining how djinn got a new one for every victory. The only colorful marking was a Phoenix on his bicep.

Unfolding from the floor with surprising grace to stand at least six-foot-eight, he approached with long, calm strides.

His eyes softened. "I mean no harm. I like observing you sleep. Forgive my intrusion, Lizette."

Though he clearly could break her in half with no effort, she trusted him. He had saved her. She liked when he watched over her while she slept, which she had been doing regularly since her body was repairing itself.

"I don't mind, Jarek. Stay. I feel safe when you're near."

He stared at her neck, the spot where the bastard had branded her with his mark. Ashamed, Lizette covered it with her hand.

"Do you want to talk yet? I can fetch Kara."

"Don't. I'd rather tell my story to you."

When she couldn't begin, he waited, his eyes expressionless.

Lizette focused on his lips. "I was in New York." She swallowed hard, having trouble gathering her memories. Finally, the words tumbled out of her mouth. "I left work at the radio station. I was walking to the subway when someone threw a bag over my head, tossing me into a van. The next thing I remember, I woke up in a cage. It was dirty. Cold. Other people were there."

"Sounds like one of the stockades run by Silas and Aisen."

"Yes. Yes. Aisen. I know the name." She pushed up straighter but held the cover tight to her chest.

"Then what?"

"Then Spear dragged me out. He took me to his

house. I couldn't get away. I tried." She slapped her palm across her mouth, refusing to allow the moisture in her eyes to fall as tears.

"My Firebrands and I were searching for slaves sold by Silas and Aisen when we heard one might be in the camp. By the time we got to Spear's hovel, you were gone."

Her arms fell to her sides, the pelt cover slipping, revealing the outline of her breasts beneath the thin white gown Kara had found for her. "I escaped. Have you located him yet?"

"No, but we won't give up. My promise."

"The cave. I crawled in there to get out of the rain. To sleep. I remember little else." She hesitated, dreading his answer. "Please don't be offended, but I have a question."

"You could not offend me, Lizette. Ask."

"At the jail, the guards weren't human. Neither were some of those who visited. You told me you are djinn."

He did not hesitate to answer. "Correct."

She liked that Jarek was direct, that he didn't coddle her. "I don't know what a djinn is."

"We are warriors, soldiers for hire, much like mercenaries. At one time, we fought for the Persians. We've been part of the Varangian Guard. Centuries later some of us flew with the Flying Tigers. Wherever there are wars, we fight. Earth. Scath. It matters little."

"Scath. Is it another planet?"

"No. A realm. Separate from Earth but part of it."

"It sounds crazy."

He laughed, a deep rumbling but sincere tone. "Not so crazy when you are an Aeternal."

"Why was I kidnapped?"

"This story is going to sound crazy, too."

"Hit me with it anyway. I'm in a mood to believe nutty as a fruitcake."

Jarek sank onto the floor pillows, his legs stretched out. For such a large, dangerous man, he perfected serenity. "Your captors took only specific humans, those with DNA markers indicating a witch or warlock in their lineage. They were looking for descendants of the Blood Coven. We aren't sure why."

"You're saying I have these markers?"

"Yes. You probably had a mage ancestor. It's doubtful you are Blood Coven since you were sold to Spear. Did you have blood drawn in New York before you were kidnapped?"

She thought for a moment. "There was a blood drive. I donated. Do you mean something like that?"

"Yes. That's probably how they found you."

If she had received a phone call months ago from one of her program listeners who spoke about a witch in her family tree, Lizette would have pronounced the woman suffering from a break with reality. Getting kidnapped and taken to another realm by aliens altered her sense of realism. It wasn't much of a stretch to believe Jarek's story about why she'd been snatched. She accepted some strange DNA proved she was descended from a mage.

When Jarek leaned forward, his black silky pants molded to his immense thighs. The muscles in his forearms bunched as he rested his elbows on his knees, his legs crossed under him. It was strange how human he looked with his enormous bare feet showing.

Lizette lifted the pelt which covered her. She peeked down the front of her gown, checking her injuries. "The scratches are healing."

Beyond her control, an image flashed in her mind. Spear's heavy body hovered above her, his hips pounding against her as he raped her. She closed her eyes, willing the picture to disappear. Clenching her jaw, she said, "Other things will never heal."

"Do not say 'never.' Any wound can mend."

"No. The things I allowed him to do."

"You survived, didn't you?"

Lizette cleared her throat, refusing to allow tears to fall. "At what cost?"

"I can't answer the question. Only you can. I suppose the cost depends on what you do with the rest of your life."

"You don't understand." Lizette drew a deep breath before she continued. "I let him rape me. I encouraged him to put his hands on me. Hell. I did unspeakable things so he wouldn't kill me."

"Yet here you are. Alive. And soon, he will be cornered and dead." Jarek leaned back, tenting his fingers to study her.

His matter-of-fact, stoic response nearly convinced her.

But no.

"He branded me. With an iron. Like a fucking cow."

He nodded. "It's a slave mark."

"I'm not the same person I was."

"No. You're stronger."

"A fucking cow. Now I'll carry this piece of him always. You don't know what I did. I'm dirty." Her fingers flew to her neck. She clawed at the brand, drawing blood.

Jarek approached to sit beside her, the bed dipping from his weight. He captured her hands in his, holding both of them away from her body. "You escaped. I can have someone alter the slave mark. Make it something else. Something which tells the story of your bravery."

Lizette calmed when this gargantuan warrior with the feral, deadly eyes warmed her hands. She was safe with him. When he released her, cold seeped into her bones. Lizette grabbed Jarek, burying her face against his chest, sobbing for the first time since her rescue.

The djinn's huge hand cupped the back of her head, his fingers intertwining in her hair. He soothed her, speaking in quiet, hushed tones, rocking her. To. Fro.

Lizette's hands swiped along his shoulders, trailing downward, savoring the bunching of his biceps.

Still, he didn't realize what she had done to stay alive. "You. Don't. Know." She sobbed, pulling her head off his chest, wiping away useless tears.

"A great Persian poet wrote, 'The moment you accept what troubles you've been given, the door will open.' Let it open, Lizette. You will never heal until you let the door open."

"Someone as strong or powerful as you could never understand." She gulped down her sobs.

Jarek stared vacantly beyond her. "I understand cruelty and slavery better than you think."

****

He was born into a family with powerful enemies.

The preparation for his Awakening began at fourteen, an early age for a djinn, but he was a valiant, strong youth. On his fifteenth birthday, the Varior Dalir, his trainer, announced he was ready to assume the mantle of battle, to become a fully matured breed. Three years younger than usual.

Males in Jarek's lineage held the highest ranks among the djinn because of their fighting prowess. His grandfather, a fighter with the famous Ten Thousand Immortals, had taken Egypt for Cambysis II in 525 BC. Later, he invaded India for Darius. When the time came to produce offspring, his own father, also a fierce warrior, mated a strong Amazon to ensure his son's destiny was to be the most powerful Rostamian ever born. Jarek was just that.

Be warned, though: When the gods bestow immense powers, they can also take them away.

Another djinn family on Scath, the Farahmands, possessed a rabid jealousy when it came to the Rostamians. Their obsession became the tool of the gods.

Abbas I of the Safavid Persia Empire decided to attack the Ottomans to retrieve territories lost in a previous war. He petitioned the djinn to assist in the march on Tabriz in 1603.

Jarek volunteered along with other young fighters from the Encampment on Scath. The breed regularly participated in Earth battles to feed their hunger for war. They favored Persia whenever possible. Hassem Farahmand, the son of his father's greatest enemy, also joined. Jarek feared nobody. He was stronger than his nemesis, despite their age difference.

On the road to Tabriz, the djinn and Persians kept in shape by sparring. When put opposite Hassem, the warrior Jarek defeated him seven out of seven times. The young Farahmand's anger grew while the journey proceeded.

At night while Jarek slept on the cold, unforgiving ground, he awoke with a knife at his throat.

As the blade scraped his neck, Hassem said, "When the battle begins, watch your back, golden boy. I'll be there with my sword." He disappeared, slipping away quietly.

Jarek lay still, unafraid though knowing he must keep an eye on his cowardly enemy. One day soon, Hassem would die. By his hand. No Aeternal threatened him and lived.

When they neared the city, they encountered Ottoman Janissaries. Though fierce, the infantry fighters were no match for young Jarek, who took pride in killing his attackers.

Jarek fought with a shield and a scimitar, a sword meant for slicing not plunging. The curved blade with a sharp point was all about close combat, moving in with a deadly slash. The design of Jarek's weapon allowed him to use it one-handed, but to be effective he had to keep his wrist loose, flexible.

The young warrior quickly learned something about himself. Not only was he talented at killing, but he enjoyed it. Adrenaline shot through his veins as he sliced an opponent before moving on to another. His sword was a melody. It sang to him as he spun, locked blades, and slashed. He excelled at the elaborate dance of death.

On the field of battle, already covered in the blood of his enemies, he turned to meet an attacker, a fighter who wore a knee-length tunic with the unique bork hat atop his head. A jeweled ornament at his forehead, the long tail of material trailed down his back. Jarek blocked his opponent's first attempt to slice his chest open, countering by swinging his blade at the attacker's neck. Though the soldier jumped away, the move was costly. It allowed Jarek to twist his wrist and whip his weapon in a figure eight. He connected with his enemy, slicing through his neck.

As the young djinn stood over the dead Janissary, wiping the blade of his scimitar on his fallen opponent's pants, he fell to his knees, weak, shaking. His thoughts were muddled. He ran his hands over his body, checking for wounds. Anything which could cause this strange reaction.

Five Syrian males surrounded him. Jarek could not lift a hand to stop them while they dragged him from the battlefield and threw him onto a litter behind a horse.

As he was carried off, he caught Hassem's eye, knowing in an instant he had been betrayed. Hassem told these men about the djinn's most guarded secret. Their greatest weakness.

Pitchblende robbed a djinn of his speed, his strength, his endurance, and even his healing powers. Hassem did the unthinkable. He shared the secret with an enemy. In doing so, he caused not only Jarek to be captured but also others of his kind.

The men who seized him along with three other djinn must have each been carrying the black stone which was feared by all his race.

This action would not go unavenged. Jarek promised himself retribution while he lay helpless on the litter, his hands and feet tied, his strength stolen.

He recalled the ancient saying, "Before you embark on a journey of revenge, dig two graves." He would. One for his enemy's head. The other for his body. Hassem would be wise to begin running now.

****

"Yeah?" Kole barked, never pleasant when interrupted.

Glancing behind her as if a ghost were on her ass, Bounty pushed through his office door, closing it. She walked to the credenza where she turned on the radio.

Frazzled.

It was a new look for his secretary, or executive assistant.

Whatever the hell she calls herself this week.

"Cadmon's out there with a sire and his mate," she whispered in his ear. "They're upset. The male is Viktor the Lawgiver."

"Sounds like a shitstorm of fun. Send them in. I'm expecting them."

Bounty turned off the radio before she swung the door wide. "Please come in. The commander will see you now."

Kole got the chills when she sounded so professional. It was rare, always surprising him.

Cadmon, who wore the formal uniform identifying him as high commander of the Scion Firebrands, led the vampire parents into the office.

Fuck.

Kole stood to clasp Cadmon's forearm, hand to elbow in the traditional Firebrand greeting. "*Freron.*"

Cadmon returned the gesture. "Meet Dania, Viktor's mate. I believe you already know our esteemed lawgiver."

Kole dipped his chin.

"They are parents of Varik, a male only out of his Awakening by a year."

The vampire Awakening was more barbaric than the coming-of-age ceremony for the other breeds. Since Varik had gone through it, despite being young, he was an adult breed, able to handle most situations with the usual skills of his kind.

Kole shook hands with Viktor but did not offer to do so with Dania. Vampires had nasty tempers when you touched skin to their mates. Instead, he waved his hand toward chairs. "Sit."

Cadmon directed the parents to the two seats in front of Kole's desk, sliding another up for himself.

"Their son is missing." The ylve high commander did not share his breed's belief in small talk. Though he was now a brilliant diplomat, he had been an inspired military tactician. His strategies and exploits on the battlefield were part of every young Firebrand's training, one being the V-shaped-wedge attack. He was also credited with creating the first longbow.

Kole was an impatient animus demon, short on pleasantries. He wanted to shout, "So what? I'm a commander of Scion Firebrands, not a goddamn missing persons' private dick." Wisely, the words did not leave his lips.

"Yes?" He leaned onto his forearms, tapping his fingers together to prevent setting off sparks. Only Skyler could bring him back if he lost control, and she wasn't here.

Though Cadmon seemed to sense Kole's temperament, he proceeded. "They suspect he and a female friend went to New Orleans."

Kole's brows raised. Now he was attentive. "Why do you suspect this?"

Viktor answered. "Dania and I were young once. Fortunately, we never got into any serious scrapes. My offspring, however, is a trouble magnet. Also, a portal jumper is missing."

The mother nodded.

"He stole your jumper? Why not wait for him to return? No harm. No foul."

Dania, letting her regal vampire control slip, wept openly, gulping down sobs.

Viktor clasped her hand. "He hasn't been home since yesterday. Our son can be careless. Sometimes downright stupid, but he would never worry us like this. He would have come back last night or called."

"Which portal did he use?" Kole slitted his fire-gold eyes.

"The one in Bludhaven near the Strigodierna Chapel. It would be most convenient for them." Dania nipped her lip with a small, sharp fang.

"Do you have any idea where he and his friend would have exited in New Orleans?"

"None." Viktor rested his mate's hand on his

thigh.

"What bars would they visit in the city?"

The father shook his head.

"The Ministry of Compliance will trace the missing device. Is it registered to you or your mate?"

"It is mine," said Viktor. "Which is another reason I suspect trouble. He knew I needed my jumper today. I had an Earthside trip planned. He would have slipped it back in time so I wouldn't realize it was missing."

Kole pushed out of his desk chair. "Bounty has my contact information. Reach out to me if Varik returns or phones. When we uncover anything vital, I will call. What is the friend's name?"

Viktor looked at his mate.

"Norah, daughter of Ossar and Licia." Dania fixed on Kole's eyes. "Find my son, Commander."

Kole escorted them out. While Bounty shared numbers, he waited at her desk until they left the area. Afterward, he got things rolling. "Phone the Ministry of Fuck-All-Incompetence to see where the young stud exited in New Orleans. He used his dad's jumper. Don't let them drag their feet. If they give you any shit, have Logan hack them. Call Ossar and Licia to ask about their daughter, Norah. Is she missing? How long? Where is she? You're smart. Figure out the rest."

Kole tapped his wrist. *Rein. Get the fuck into my office. I want Thorn, Galena, and the human. What's her name? The damn new coven female who blackmailed me into letting her work with the Firebrands. ... Yeah. Denim. She's training with Ram. Bring him, too. Anyway, I'll expect everyone two minutes ago.*

Bounty kept her mascara-laden eyes locked on her boss.

"I've got a bad feeling about this." Kole shot fire

from a fingertip, hitting the wall, zinging by Bounty's left ear. "Oops. Damn."

She dodged the flame but glared at him.

Chapter Twenty

Sabine ogled Nico. Bulging biceps. Check. Tight abs. Check. Two big slabs of pecs. Check. A nice package in his pants. Check. Check. Check. Male perfection. She wanted to grab ahold and stroke his manhood.

Whoa, girl. Rule number one, you don't do partners. Rule number two, you don't do males who have no respect for you. Rule three, you don't do males who hit on you and then take another female into the backroom. Where is your pride?

Nico swung his gaze from the Arisen Dawn farmhouse they staked out to Sabine. He squinted. "What are you up to, sweetness? Your sharp little tongue keeps licking your lips."

The air around them sizzled, but Sabine couldn't do a thing to control the pheromones racing from her body like horses out of the gate. She tried to stuff them all back in, but they had their head and were not stopping until she took Nico around the track a few times.

He moved into her space, backing her against a tree. "Your inner nymph's showing."

"Is not."

Maybe she could fool him into thinking he was imagining the desire wafting out of her pores. He was human. He couldn't smell her pheromones as most Aeternal males could have.

"Is too." His breath was hot as he leaned forward to whisper into her ear. "Sabine, I didn't have sex with the succubus."

"You took her into a room at the Blood Shed."

"I didn't go in. I stopped outside the door because she was the wrong woman. I knew it the minute I walked her to the back, where I apologized before returning to the table."

What? Rule three is taken care of.

She needed to get her attention back on the job. They were here to study Arisen Dawn, to see why they were recruiting, and to verify their tie to a bothersome new drug. With his chest smashed against her breasts, his arousal thick and hard against her belly, it was nearly impossible. *Damn.* How long had it been since she'd had a male inside her? Long time. Nymphs weren't meant to go so long without sex.

That's what happens when you're raised by a warlock father who doesn't let you hang out with other nymphs in your formative years. You get silly ideas, such as boffing a fellow Firebrand is wrong. You skip feeding or avoid regular sex. Worst, you only bed males who respect you. Yeah. I was raised with some real warped ideas.

When Nico shoved a heavy thigh between her legs, her hips automatically went to work, grinding her sex against his leg like a nymph in heat.

Kissing her neck on his way to her chin and north, he said, "Let me feel how bad you want it." He crushed her lips, opening her mouth with a stab of his tongue, doing the in-and-out thing like he was fucking her.

Sabine's hands tangled in Nico's dark, silky hair as she moaned.

God, I'm weak when it comes to this male.

Their tongues tangoed, his taste masculine. Woods and spearmint gum. Gahya, he knew how to kiss.

His hands cupped her ass, lifting her, pulling her against his arousal. He wanted her here. Now. And she was willing.

Wait. Think about this.

Sabine wiggled out of his grasp, punching her fingertips into his chest, catapulting him away, one of the hardest things she had ever done.

****

When Ram hot-footed it through the door, his boots thudding on tile, Kole was wearing a path in the carpet. Whatever the fuck was going on was serious. Even if he couldn't read the commander's grim expression, he could count the new burn holes in the wall.

Denim bumped into Ram's back when he hauled up short. Her gaze followed the fire shooting from Kole's hands. As he jerked his head up, he touched his fingers together to contain it.

"Animus demon problem. Sit. I'm through scorching the place." He swiped a huge palm across his military buzz-cut hair, dropping into the chair behind the desk.

Rein sauntered in, crossing his arms over his chest. He settled against the wall beside Ram, nodding a greeting.

Kole opened his mouth to yell out the door to Bounty, but she beat him. "They're on their way."

"Hey." Galena ushered herself in ahead of the wolf shifter, Thorn. She took a seat next to Denim, popping her boots on Kole's desk until he shot a fire-gold glare in her direction. "Sorry, Comm." She planted her feet on the floor.

The claw mark on Thorn's face twitched as he clamped his jaw tight, situating himself alongside Ram.

Kole snarled. "You know what? I get damn tired of a crick in my neck. I'm going to be the first demon in history to get arthritis. The wall's not going to cave in. So take a fucking seat."

Rein was the last Firebrand to grab a chair. He

didn't look happy.

"Incoming," yelled Bounty.

Kole picked up the landline on his desk. "Yeah? ... Where did they exit?" He slammed the phone onto its cradle.

Bounty peeked her head through the doorway. "Other parents say the female vamp hasn't been home either."

Kole pursed his lips together. "Gear up. You're heading to the portal off Jackson Square. You've been there, Ram. Two young vamps haven't reported to Mommy and Daddy. Normally, no biggie, but with the shit going down in the Big Easy, we need to be on top of this. To make things more interesting, the young male is the offspring of Viktor the Lawgiver."

Brows raised on each face in the room, except Denim's. Ram filled her in with a whisper in her ear.

After Kole shared the rest of the particulars, his blazing stare latched onto the team. "Okay, children. Arm up. Fuck it. I'm coming along." He shot up out of his seat, but Rein heavy-handed his shoulder.

"Right now, Commander, this is a simple search mission. We're all thinking the bad guys finally got some live Aeternals, but we don't know for certain. The vamps might be partying. Let us gather intel. As it is, you hardly make it home to Skyler now. Too much on your plate."

Ram nodded. "You're working with Alarik on finding the identity of Cerberus. You're keeping tabs on Tyr and Dax as they investigate the shifters' drug problem in North Shelters. You're getting intel from Sabine and Nico on Arisen Dawn. You're monitoring our ride-alongs with healers looking for descendants. Let us check this out first. Could be nothing."

Kole sat back in his seat, but his lips curled into a snarl.

Ram led the Firebrands out while Rein stayed to talk to Kole about the mission.

They headed to the armory, loading up with sharp things and guns which went boom. In the hall when he saw no one was looking, he brushed a hand across Denim's curvy ass. "Would it do me any good to ask you to keep this nice thing behind me at all times?"

"Absolutely none, but I appreciate the compliment about my ass." She rested a hand on his arm. "I'm starting to believe you can't control your nasty protective streak. Hell. It kinda warms my heart. Here's the thing, though. I'm going. It's my job."

"Yeah. I'm trying."

"I sympathize."

"For my sake, duck when you come through the portal. We might have a lynch mob waiting."

She raised a brow. "Do I look stupid?"

Ram's gaze crawled from the top of her head to the toes of her boots. *No.* She looked hot enough to simmer his satyr blood, two short blades strapped across her breasts and two swords jammed into sheaths on her back. The Glock, in its special holster, rested on her hip where her low-slung tight-assed BDUs rode. He'd like to drop her right here and take her hard and fast.

Weapons. Foreplay. Yeah.

****

Nico almost landed on his ass, digited there by a hot-cold nymph. He was tired of their song and dance. He wanted his old self back, the one who took what he wanted before he moved on. What was wrong with getting a little dry hump action? They were both fully clothed. Besides, she had been all in favor there for a while. What was her problem?

"Damn, woman. You light up like a Christmas tree. Then you go all virgin nymph."

"I must be such a bitch." She smoothed down her top even though it wasn't wrinkled.

"What do you want from me?" Now he was mad. He did not confuse messages from chicks. She was asking him to relieve an itch. He was willing. He was able. He was hard.

Nico could tell she was about to snap back with something bordering on snide. Instead, she punched a pin in his anger balloon.

"Honestly, I don't know. I've never met anyone who messes with my head as you do." Sabine continued to pat out imaginary wrinkles.

She threw ice water all over his temper. Nico's glower softened. "What do you mean?" He stepped in close to throw an arm around her waist, pulling her against him but not letting her feel his arousal.

What's with this uncharacteristic urge to be a gentleman?

"How would I know what I mean. You can be an asshole, but I felt your kiss as far down as my toes."

Nico grinned. "I'm your asshole, sweetness. It's why you find me charming." A hand slid up from her waist until it rested under the weight of her perfect breasts.

"I don't find you charming."

"You do…" Suddenly, the door on the ramshackle farmhouse flew open, and a male dressed in all black from boots to neck except for a red insignia on his shoulder peeked out.

Holding it open with his foot, the guy exited, accompanied by another Arisen Dawn member in a similar uniform. They propped a man between them, holding him under his arms, dragged him into the yard, and crossed to a tree. Winding a chain around the victim, they secured him to the trunk.

"What is he?" Nico whispered to Sabine, all business, dropping his hand from her breast.

"A warlock. A weak one. I don't feel much power coming from him. The other males are ylves. What's with their black uniforms?" Sabine pulled a double-bladed staff from the sheath on her back.

"This is the first time we've seen these shitheads dressed like paramilitary. Like they're ratcheting up the game."

One of the ylves backed up while he withdrew a bow. He nocked an arrow and pulled back the string.

"Wait," yelled the treed warlock. "You got it all wrong. I wasn't gonna talk. I just want out."

"Only two ways out. One, you're toe-tagged. Two, you're… No. I'm wrong. Only one way out," said the bigger ylve without the bow.

"We need to stop this." Sabine lifted a boot, prepared to walk.

Nico grabbed her arm. "Yeah, but it would be nice to hear more first. Of course, if we go in to save the warlock, maybe he'll spill. Okay. In it is."

"Watch the arrows. Ylves are deadly accurate."

"You care about me."

"No. We have a conversation to finish." The nymph flashed her translucent pale greens at him.

Nico smiled, whooping a war cry before he charged from his cover, heading straight for the bigger ylve. The Aeternal was slow to react. With surprise in his favor, Abello took him down, planting a fist on the guy's jaw hard enough to remove teeth like a dentist.

The ylve shook off the pain, shot his knee up, and tossed Nico overhead. When the guy got to his feet, he drew a blade, flipping it from hand to hand.

Fisting his own knife, Nico sprang from the ground. They circled each other. The Aeternal lunged.

When Nico side-stepped the move, he avoided a stab to the gut but took a shallow cut on his lower arm.

The ylve's pleasure was short-lived. When he charged Abello again, he ended up in a headlock with a blade shoved into his chest deep enough to draw blood.

"Fuck, human. Watch it."

"Shut up, wimp. It's a short trip to your heart. Drop your weapon." *Thump*. It hit the dirt. He looked around for Sabine.

She was holding her own with the other ylve. While Nico watched, her foot connected with the guy's jaw.

Ouch. That had to hurt.

Abello squeezed his arm tighter around his Arisen Dawn opponent's neck.

Ack. Ack.

The guy loosened Nico's arm. He rasped, "Air, asswipe." Then he swung a foot behind him, trying to topple the human Firebrand. The strategy failed. Nico squeezed harder until the guy stopped moving, his knees buckling, his body limp-dishragging it.

Oops. Too tight.

Nico dropped his opponent's body and eyed Sabine, his arms crossed over his chest. She was beauty in motion, spinning, kicking, weaving her double-bladed staff through the air like an artist. All woman. He wanted her under him now.

"Hurry up," he shouted. "I got a hard-on waiting for you."

Sabine did a three-sixty, her blade following her pivot while she separated the ylve's head from his body. One part tumbled into a tree while the rest collapsed at her feet in a heap.

"Only you can think about sex when we're in full fight mode."

Sabine's eyes widened. She sprinted toward Nico, pushing him aside. Swinging her staff, she beheaded the awakened ylve who was about to stab Nico in the back. Cleaning her blade on her pants, she said, "An Aeternal isn't dead for sure until his head is severed."

"Lesson learned. Thanks."

"You're injured." Sabine approached, gentle fingers touching his wound, those big translucent eyes soft with concern.

"This little thing? It's nothing. Kiss it to make it better."

Sabine *tsked*. She removed the scarf holding her ponytail, wrapping it around his arm. "This will make it better."

"I'd rather you kissed it."

She smirked. "Recon the outside. I'll take care of the quarters. Make sure there are no surprises."

For once, Nico did as she ordered, biding his time while she cleared the house. She strode out the door, tight leather pants, snug belly shirt, combat boots, and blonde hair swinging, wisps of it brushing her cheeks. Her swaying double Ds begged for his attention. He rushed her, grabbing a hand. "I can't wait any longer, sweetness."

Nico pulled Sabine into the shelter of a grove of trees. "Strip." Fight lust rolled through him as he tore off his blade holster, ripped out of his shirt, kicked off his boots, and shucked his pants.

"But our prisoner. The warlock."

"Going nowhere. I already checked. He'll be hugging the tree until we get back to him." Nico glanced down at his swollen, aching shaft. When Sabine shrugged out of her tee, toed off her boots, and shimmied out of her pants, he froze. "Oh, holy hell."

His nymph was naked. She was perfect. He was

as breathless as a virgin teenager about to do it in the back seat of his car for the first time.

Sabine was trouble. But she was his trouble.

****

Denim tapped her wrist, rocking her implanted D-chip. "This is fa-an-tastic." She and the other armed Firebrands exited the portal near Jackson Square without incident.

"You're a kid with a new toy, girlfriend." Galena shook out her black shoulder-length bob, so chic it settled immediately into place.

Denim nodded. "You guys don't appreciate this little gadget."

"Every day we're thankful." When Rein smirked, his fangs popped into view. "If we can get down to business, we'll split up to hit the hot spots. Question all Aeternals. If they shouldn't be here, tell them to head home but to stay in a big group with their eyes peeled. We can't babysit them tonight. What we want is intel on the baby vamps. Do they know them? Have they seen them? Could Varik and Norah still be partying over here?"

Galena jabbed an elbow into Thorn's rib. "Got it, Lieutenant Commander."

"You fucking call me that again, Amazon, I'll lay you out cold." Rein was famous for his control, but Denim guessed he didn't appreciate Galena's giving him a title.

Her friend shrugged but didn't wipe the smile.

"Thorn and dumbass, you're a team. Take the joints between Canal and St. Louis. Denim and Ram, search the spots from St. Louis to Dumaine. I'll be on my own from there to Esplanade."

Once the others headed for their sections, Denim locked her arm through Ram's. "Come along, *cher*.

You're in my neck of the woods again. We'll find the kids."

"I'm all yours."

He gave her a sexier-than-hell satyr grin. She almost shucked her pants to get it on with him.

Focus.

"How about a quickie in a back alley?" asked Ram.

They were on the same wavelength. Which was scary. "We're on a mission. Stuff it."

"I'm trying to. Stuff it in your…"

"You are annoying me again. Keep your mind on the job."

"How are you feeling?"

"Different. Stronger. More alive. Like my body's flipping on switches."

"Not about your witchiness, doll. About yesterday."

"Oh. Good."

"Good?"

Catching his squeezed down brows, she added, "Okay. Great. Fantastic. You were terrific. I'm still having fantasies about you."

"Are you blushing?" Ram pulled her to a halt, his palm locked around her upper arm. "That's so cute. You are blushing."

"Shut it."

An arrogant satyr smile spread across his face until his attention shifted to Muriel's. "Doll, wait a sec." Ram ducked inside the restaurant's bar.

Denim crossed her arms over her chest, humming while she hung ten.

He came out gripping two gigantic golden drinks, shoving one into Denim's hand. "We gotta blend." He rotated his body, noticing a group off to the side.

"Excuse me again."

Ram tapped a guy's shoulder, said something, and slipped some bills into his hand, taking *beaucoup* beads from around his neck. Afterward, he hit up the guy's friend for the same. Returning to Denim, he slid a handful over her head. "Perfect."

"Sure. If only the weapons weren't such a give-away."

"Hey. Everybody's too smashed to see past the beads. Drink up. I get better looking with each sip."

If he got any better looking, Denim would be all over him like a succubus in heat.

"So, you're having fantasies, huh? You want to talk about them?"

She had no chance to shake her head because Ram pointed ahead with the drink in his fist. "Look. A crowd of Aeternals. They're young enough to know our vamps."

"Can all Aeternals read auras to identify breeds?"

"Yep."

"Will I be able to?"

He shrugged.

They pushed their way nearer the curb where the youths grouped to watch the parade. Like the humans around them, they were drinking, yelling, yucking it up. No one would guess they had stepped over from another realm.

Ram looped his arm over the shoulder of a shapely, tall female. She eyed the satyr, boots to silky hair, her gaze making a final landing on his Phoenix brand. A stab of jealousy hit Denim.

"Damn. Firebrands." Her words were one thing, but the young female had flirt written all over her face, her tongue darting over her hot red lips, her eyelashes fanning Ram.

Denim reined in the urge to lay her sexy ass out cold. "We're not here to jam you up, *cher*. We need info."

"Anybody know Varik and Norah? Vamps. What do you say, little succubus? Do you know them?" Ram continued to prop his arm on her, his fingers too close to her boobs.

She shook her head, rubbing her hip against Ram's thigh.

Damn. He could move over.

A towering male beside her spoke up. "What's it to you?"

Ram separated from the succubus. Before he launched himself at the lippy kid, Denim blocked his path. When in doubt, go with the truth. "They could be in trouble. You've heard the warnings about the portals being compromised. The vamps haven't made it home."

Ram must have agreed with the truth route. "Yeah. It's possible humans are hunting Aeternals. Despite the alerts, you are here, mostly 'cause you're young and stupid."

"I saw Varik and Norah yesterday." The heavily pierced vampire speaker was familiar.

Another of his breed with blond spiky hair jabbed his friend. "We know you. You're the hot chick who was with the Amazon a while back. Are you stalking us? You re-thinking doin' us?"

Ram stepped forward, towering over the youth, outweighing him by a good fifty to sixty pounds of hard muscle. He paused, a grin spread from cheek to cheek. "Doll, were you thinking about doing these tiny-dicked males? I thought better of you."

"Don't get your leather pants in a bunch, *cher*. They're not my type."

"True. You like big-dicked satyrs."

Boy. Do I ever.

"Back to Varik and Norah." Denim rested a hand on her new Glock.

The spiky-haired blond spouted off again. "When I saw them last night, they were headed home."

Ram crossed his arms over his chest, his biceps flexing. "I bet, since Varik wanted a little bone-storming action, he decided to spend the night grinding his goods in a hotel."

The pierced vamp laughed. "Not Varik and Norah. He's into another chicklette on Scath. She'd take a strip of his hide if he got it on with Norah. They're just buds. Nope. Very def. They were homebound."

"Thanks, *cher*." Denim turned to the other youths. "You guys take it easy. When you go back, go in a big group. This is serious shit. If you spy humans near a portal, get out of there. Head to another one."

"Will do." The blond showed some fang. "You wanna hang with me?" He made a humping motion with his groin.

His eyes flashing neon green, Ram bumped chests with the kid. When the vamp had the good sense to reverse his gears, Ram moved in on him again.

Denim intervened, but Ram held up a hand. "I got this, doll." His fist tapped the kid's chest. "No. She'll hang with me."

"Whatever."

As Ram and Denim strolled off in search of other Aeternals, the group returned to fulfilling their roles as Mardiers by raising their drinks until blue liquid splashed out of their glasses, spilling onto the New Orleans street.

Denim should have been insulted. Her partner had gone all satyr he-man on the horny young vamp. Instead, warmth tickled her skin. *But.* "He was only a kid."

Ram gentled a hand on her arm. "He's a male vampire who survived his Awakening. Don't underestimate him or any Aeternal who has transitioned." He grinned. "Besides, he's got a dick. I'm the only one with that particular appendage who gets to flirt with you."

Now she was a volcano shooting lava.

Chapter Twenty-One

Jonesing from the fight, Sabine eyed a naked Nico.

Holy shit.

He was all male. His dark, thick cock jutted out between his legs, his fist going from tip to root. She and Nico had been waltzing around each other for months. It was time to erase him from her system. "I want you inside me now."

He came at Sabine, a loaded mining car rolling down a mountain, picking up speed. He dropped her to the ground and covered her with his heavy, muscular body.

"Wider." He growled, pushing her legs apart with his thigh. She didn't need the order. Sabine willingly opened for Nico.

She obeyed, loving his bulk on top of her with her hands running up and down his arms, giving her a chill while at the same time making her blood boil.

He crushed her mouth. He was a warrior, taking the spoils of war. It was a need as old as time. Sabine understood it. His tongue ravaged her, thrusting hard, exploring her wet, hot mouth. She shivered with anticipation when he drew back from the kiss, his lips trailing down her neck, heading for her breasts.

She cradled one in her hand, offering it to him. Nico obliged by sucking the nipple into his mouth. He licked until it pebbled.

"Yes, Nico." She offered him her other breast. He took advantage.

He pushed up on one arm to search for her sex with his fingers. He stroked through her folds two times. "Wet for me." Pumping one finger into her core, he withdrew it only to plunge in a second. He found a rhythm while he used his thumb to stroke her clit.

"That feels so good." Sabine arched into his hand. "Don't stop."

"Not nearly as good as this." He pulled out, grabbing his shaft. He stroked himself twice while Sabine licked her lips.

No more preparation. Nico nudged her sex with the tip of his cock before driving into her pussy in one stroke.

"God, yes, sweetness. I knew you'd be perfect."

He withdrew almost totally. Then thrust back in. His shaft glistened with her moisture as he buried himself deep. He withdrew. Again.

Sabine watched him slide in and out. His hips rolled forward. Jerked back. She dragged her nails along his tight ass, enjoying the feel of his flexing muscles.

Nico gripped her legs, shoving them onto his shoulders, burying himself deeper.

"I'm going to come." His breaths were shallow, fast.

She tangled her fingers in his hair. "Right there, Nico." The friction built. "Yes. Harder. Deeper."

Her ass planted in the dirt with rocks chafing her skin, she caught sight of the beautiful male straining above her. Lost to passion, he slammed into her like a piston. She gripped his forearms tight as an explosion rolled through her. She shouted his name.

He thrust faster and faster, his biceps bunching. His abs clenched as he pounded into Sabine. She hung on for dear life until he stiffened. His release spread into her like fire. With his weight off her, he pressed his groin into her for what seemed like forever.

When he collapsed, he rolled to his back, planting Sabine on top. "Damn. I promise next time I'll do gentle.

All night long. I so needed this, sweetness."

Sabine was in trouble. He was not out of her system. She worried he might never be.

Damn human Firebrand.

They lay in silence for some time, Sabine enjoying Nico's arms wrapped protectively around her. "You know we have to do something with the warlock who's still tied to the tree." Her breathing was ragged. Her heart a thumping beat against her ribs.

"I don't want to move. How about round two?"

She rolled onto a hip to glance at him. Sure enough. He was ready.

Holy hell.

"I think we better take care of the warlock situation first."

Nico grinned. "My situation's more fun."

"No. Yes, I mean, but the Arisen Dawn problem is critical." She rose, bending over for her pants.

Nico whistled. "I love your ass." He held a hand in front of him. As he twisted his wrist, a visible wave left his fingers. It headed for Sabine's dagger, which flew out of its sheath.

When it beelined for Nico, he caught it, blade first.

"What the hell did you do?" asked Sabine.

"I don't know. I wanted you. Instead, I got your Arkansas toothpick."

"It's like your body's magnetic."

"You say the nicest things."

Sabine shivered and damn if she wasn't shooting out pheromones again. She glanced at Nico's eyes. "Holy shit, warlock."

****

Ram tapped his wrist to contact Rein. *We ran into some young ones who swear our targets headed home last night. ... Sure. We'll meet you there. When?* He tapped again to sign off.

"Rein?" Denim had her eyes fixed on the crowd.

"Yeah. We'll rendezvous at the jump point after he investigates a lead. Galena and Thorn met a demon who spotted Varik and Norah near Jackson Square last night, definitely going back to Scath. This shit just got real. It's likely the two were snatched."

They walked the streets in silence, sidestepping raucous partiers as Ram considered the implications of two kidnapped Aeternals in the hands of humans.

He pulled up short. "It's long past dinner. I either find solid food, or I feed from you. Your choice."

Denim drew down her brows. "Oh." Her mauve irises flashed with understanding. "We're on a mission."

"Okay, food it is. You've talked about a Po'boy until I can taste one. Be back." He dodged cars as he maneuvered across the busy street to an old building where a faded menu was painted on the window of a restaurant.

"Tell them two shrimp, dressed and hot, *cher,*" Denim shouted at his back.

He waved fingers over his head.

When Ram returned, he was cradling two steaming sandwiches in his palms. He handed one off to Denim, unwrapping the other for himself.

Rather than take a bite, she watched Ram open his mouth to chomp down. "Well?"

Her eyes widened, expectant, as if she had asked him to unzip his pants and take her into the alley for a good fuck. Did everything about Denim make him think of sex?

Yep.

His lips spread into a grin. "It's almost as good as an orgasm. No lie. The best."

Smirking at his answer, she unwrapped hers and bit into it.

When she opened her mouth, Ram's mind took a U-turn. Now she was on her knees, her lips wrapped around his cock. Talk about a mouthful of sandwich with secret sauce. *Damn.* He needed more coital time with the human witch before his balls exploded.

When a blob of mayonnaise landed on her lower lip, it started sliding toward her chin. Ram stepped closer to swipe it off with his finger. He figured it was better than using his tongue, which was what he wanted to do. He sucked the coated digit into his mouth. "Yum."

Denim's rush of arousal made him hungry to touch, to feed the satyr. When she laughed, the sound went right to his dick. *Gahya. Soon.* He had needs. *A little touch. A little taste. What could it hurt?*

He wrapped an arm around her shoulders, getting the usual jolt as he snacked on her sexual stirrings. Unfortunately, it made him hungrier. What he wouldn't give for the full-course Denim meal.

Wrong time. Wrong place.

They both dumped their empty wrappers in the trash before they rounded the corner leading into the alley near the portal.

"Rein Man." Ram greeted the Firebrand's icy blue stare.

"Where are Galena and Thorn?" asked Denim.

"They're still walking and talking. It's only us for now. Let's search the area, see if anything points to what happened to the vamps. I'll take this…"

A bullet pinged past Ram, traveling to Rein's shoulder.

"Fuck." The vampire Firebrand grabbed the wound as blood spurted from it. "Grab cover." He raced to the other side of the alley, finding a deep alcove.

Ram couldn't help it. He shoved Denim to his rear, forcing her behind a huge green trash dumpster while more bullets whizzed by.

Pursing her lips, she smacked Ram's arm. "Knock it off."

"Why? Are you bulletproof?" He peeked around the edge of the cover, ducking back again when ammo glanced off the metal. "Can you see them from your angle?"

"No. Damn. I think one of them is shooting from the doorway."

Rein must have spied the same shooter, because he barreled toward the guy, rolling out like a tank. But he was three times faster, four times deadlier.

Ping. Ping.

Two shots hit the vampire Firebrand, his body jerking each time as he charged forward.

Ping.

Again. He dropped to the ground, imitating a rhino blasted by hunters armed with elephant guns.

"I've got to get Rein before they grab him. Cover me, doll."

Denim laid down a shower of bullets as Ram blurred his way to Rein with satyr speed. Clutching under his shoulders, he pulled him behind their dumpster.

"Is he alive?" asked Denim.

Ram refused to consider any other alternative. He touched two fingers to Rein's neck. "Still pumping blood, but his pulse is thready. Let's make fast work of these assholes."

Denim fired at three gunmen, one in the open doorway, another behind some crates at the end, and a guy behind another dumpster. She gave Ram time to cloak before he stepped into the action.

Invisible, the satyr sneaked up on dumpster guy.

Coming into view, he drew his blade, plucked a fistful of hair, and pulled back the shooter's head. He made a clean, quick slice, blood spurting from the guy's throat. He glanced out from behind the cover, showing himself to Denim, who jerked her chin up.

When doorway guy broke away, gun blazing, Denim fired twice, hitting him once in the leg and once in the chest.

Bam. Bam.

The guy's weapon fell to the ground.

Ram had no time for the gleam in her eye to register. She was about to do crazy shit. She rushed from cover to kneel beside her downed target.

"I got one. He's dead, though," she shouted, moving her fingers off his neck, rolling, then popping upright. She ducked into a doorway, bullets pinging on the frame.

"Haven't we talked about your doing stupid shit, doll?" yelled Ram, as the remaining gunman sent bullets his way.

Denim ignored the satyr's comment. "Only one left, behind the crates. Cover me."

Damn female.

Ram threw up a hand to surround himself with his miasma, preparing to charge forward.

Too late.

Denim sped in the direction of the crates. When the guy showed himself, he spread his legs as he straight-armed his weapon. She threw out a hand, a bolt of lightning traveling along her arm, out her fingers, and to the gunman. A weak but nice bolt. The male staggered, shaking it off, dazed.

Getting it together, the guy glanced up at the roof, bending his knees, preparing to jump.

Denim lunged for the shooter as he took to the

air. In a flash, she grabbed his leg, heaving him into the wall.

Ram skidded to a halt, uncloaking. Tilting his head back, he watched the male soar overhead, smacking into the side of a building before he slid down it to land on concrete like Wylie Coyote.

"Damn, doll. That had to hurt like a bitch."

Denim snatched the front of the male's shirt. With her fist drawn back ready to smash into his jaw, she gasped, letting him slide onto the ground out cold. "Steven."

Ram eyed her, watching her reaction. "Nice job. I'll get Rein Man and your ex while you roll the two dead guys into the gateway warehouse for pickup later."

With Steven on one shoulder, Ram got Denim to heft the vampire Firebrand onto the other.

With two males in a fireman's hold, Ram said, "Feel Rein's pulse."

"Still just okay."

"I expect you right on my ass. Don't do something stupid again, doll."

Denim smirked. "Your ass belongs to me. Move out."

"Stay right on it."

"Like a tick."

He started his run as she tapped her D-chip.

When the gateway opened, they raced through. The entire time, Denim was arranging for medical and reporting to Kole.

On the other side of the portal, two gaffers as well as a healer waited for them.

Stooping beside Rein, the healer scrunched his brows together as he shook his head imperceptibly, his fingers on the Firebrand's neck.

"He's still with us. Right?" Ram swiped a hand

across his chin.

Without answering, the healer took the portal with Rein in his arms.

Ram stared past Denim, not seeing her. The two Firebrands clashed at times. *Hell.* All Firebrands were fiercely aggressive, but they were loyal and as close as brothers. He refused to lose Rein Man.

After the gaffers carried off Steven, Ram and Denim traveled to the Ministry of Well Being's medical facility. They waited in the hall outside a room as the over-tranquilized vampire Firebrand settled in for some intensive care.

In the doom-filled corridor of the medical facility with the action over, Ram realized how scared he was to lose Denim. There was no turning back now. She was the female for him. They were a team, out there and in his heart.

He slouched in the uncomfortable chair. "Gotta say, doll, not pleased how you put yourself in harm's way. Just sayin.'"

"I hear you."

"Yeah. Until the next time. You're gonna make me die before my time. My hair will turn white and I'll be rocking a heart attack."

Their heads turned toward the sound of someone running down the hall. Braelyn raced forward, Kole right on her heels.

"He's okay, right?" Her skin was paler than Ram had ever seen it.

Ram rose to fold his arms around Rein's mate. "They're working on him now. He's steel, Braelyn. You know that."

"How?" asked Kole.

Denim sniffed. "He took four of those tranquilizer bullets."

Ram exchanged a look with Kole, both knowing a shitload was in Rein's system.

Braelyn clamped a hand to her mouth, stifling a cry. She hurried through the door to Rein's room.

"Talk," Kole said to his two Firebrands.

"Three of them surprised us when we headed back. Rein took one to the shoulder. Afterward he did his arrogant shit, charging, taking three more bullets. Denim and I took the humans out." He waved a finger at Denim. "Actually, she took out the most. I grabbed Rein and the live one. Here we are."

Kole brushed a hand over his buzz-cut hair.

"With two down, things got interesting, Comm. Denim stunned the remaining guy with a jolt of lightning. When he shook it off, going for a super-human jump, she caught him like a high infield pop-up. Amazing."

"The man I snagged mid-flight, Commander, is my ex."

"Will it be a problem?" asked Kole.

Ram was as interested in her answer as his commander.

After a time, she said, "Not at all."

Kole nodded, striding toward Rein's room.

****

Jace leaned against the trunk of a white oak. It was partially obscured by thick bushes. She slid to the ground, exhausted. Her legs wobbled from having evaded her trackers for so many days. It was nearly night again, but darkness did not stop her pursuers.

She held her nose so she wouldn't puke. Yesterday, at least she thought it was then, she had rolled in pine needles, dirt, and some kind of animal scat to mask her scent. She couldn't stand her own smell, doubting even sensitive noses could sniff her out as the escaped human.

This forest seemed to go on forever. She had run through endless woods, trapped in some scary fairytale where she imagined trees reached out to grab her. Picking herself up after each short rest, she had pushed to keep moving for days.

Would it be too much to hope for a full moon tonight? Sure, her trackers would be able to see better, but they could see in the dark anyway. At least, she suspected they could. She worried about the nights. Despite her treading carefully, she could fall, break an ankle or a leg, not get up again.

She was hungry, having lived off only berries, fruit she recognized, and other assorted lucky finds. She discovered wild asparagus, dandelions, and a marshy area with cattails. All edibles. Thank goodness for the college class on survival skills. She never thought she'd use the information from a course she'd taken for an easy grade.

The lack of substantial food was affecting her stamina, though. If she didn't find help soon, she'd collapse. Water, at least, was no problem since she frequently crossed clear streams.

With her breathing under control, her legs steadied. Jace told herself this was just another cross-country race. She rose, threw back her shoulders, pushed away from the tree, and started running toward what she hoped was freedom. Celene depended on her. She couldn't let her friend down.

****

Seated in the corner, Braelyn fought the urge to touch her mate as four healers surrounded the bed where he was hooked to beeping machines.

Closing her eyes, she slid into Rein's mind using her gift. She'd been practicing. But what good was a power if she couldn't use it to help the male she loved? Like a many-armed octopus, she settled into his mind.

Don't you die on me, vampire.

She knew about the body found in New Orleans. The tranquilizer bullets could be deadly, especially four of them. An Aeternal had died from that many.

But Rein was made of stronger stuff.

Wasn't he?

Panic shot through Braelyn as her mate slipped deeper into unconsciousness, farther away from her searching tentacles.

Squeezing her lids tighter, she pushed commands into his brain. Love. Will. Desire. If he couldn't fight for himself, she'd fight for him.

Boots thudded on the tile outside when more Firebrands gathered in the hall, pacing back and forth, speaking in whispers. She ignored them. Her sole concentration was on her mate.

The icy chill accompanying witch spells wafted through the air, but Braelyn was relentless. She bombarded Rein's mind with commands.

Burrowing into every fold, she shored Rein up where he was weak. She regulated his heartbeat. She drove blood to his cells. She regenerated tissue. She breathed for him.

She had never asked this much of her gift, but then again, she had never had such purpose or resolve.

As one part of Rein's brain fell into a comatose state, Braelyn gathered her power to the site and re-awakened it.

Healers scurried about the room on soft-soled shoes. Tranquilizer bullets were removed. Open wounds were stitched, and blood was wiped up. Bandages were applied. The clock on the wall ticked off the passing seconds. Seconds became minutes. Minutes became hours.

Braelyn had no idea how much time had elapsed. Her gift bobbled. A jolt of fear made her gasp, but she was determined to continue to regulate Rein's responses even if it meant her own death. Even if she lost herself in the winding, pained, and shuttered alleys of his dying thoughts. She would not live without him anyway. He was her breath, her heart, her other soul.

No. No.

Her spell faltered again. She hadn't had enough time yet. He was not fixed.

One more repair. Then another and another.

Darkness was coming for her, pacing at the edge of her mind's eye, but she held it off. Eventually, it slipped through. *Not yet*, she whimpered, as the black night swept her away.

Braelyn slept despite her own screams.

Wake up. Wake up.

Her awareness returned slowly. A warm arm pillowed her neck. Her lids fluttered open. Arctic-blue irises stared back. A body curled around her while she nestled against a warm chest. She smiled.

The most beautiful lips in the world moved. "Hey."

"Hey, yourself."

"You were rattling around in my head, witch."

"You nearly died, vampire."

"I'm not complaining about the assist. Thanks." Rein bent to place a kiss on her forehead.

Still too exhausted to sit up, she twisted to look around the room. One healer stood at the bedside. Kole slept nearby in a chair, his chin sagging on his chest. Tears began to stream down Braelyn's cheeks. "I thought I would lose you."

Rein pulled her in tighter, sharing his strength,

wiping away her tears with his thumb. It was his turn now. His turn to keep her safe. That was how it worked. Her cold, controlling vampire was her strength, but she was also his. "My mate's too stubborn to let me die."

"Right back at you. I had a really good peek inside. You're pretty stubborn yourself."

"I keep telling you."

Kole rose, stretched, the tension on the demon's face relaxing. "Welcome back, Rein." He rested a hand on his warrior's shoulder, a demonstration of love for his friend and fellow soldier. Braelyn understood it was a rare gesture between the two males who prized each other but would never put their feelings into words.

Their unspoken affection brought on another round of tears from Braelyn.

"Everyone will want to see you," said Kole.

"I'll share him for a while." She wiped her wet cheeks.

Several Firebrands at a time entered the room, Denim and Ram first.

Braelyn kept a close watch on Rein during the visits, but when his coloring paled and his lips clenched together, probably from stupidly braving the pain, she took control of the situation. "Now, get the hell out so I can have some alone time with my mate."

Chapter Twenty-Two

Braelyn balanced on the edge of Rein's desk in a short green leather skirt and four-inch heels which made her crossed legs look even hotter. She wished her mate would drool. If he were the drooling kind. Even hypothetically. Which he wasn't. He was more the attack you, throw you on the ground, and rip your clothes off kind. Anything not requiring much conversation or drooling.

Against her wishes, a healed Rein reported to the stronghold the morning after he had nearly died in the medical facility from a tranq overdose.

He stared at Brae's bouncing leg. "You're reacting to my near death. That's why."

"That's why what?"

"Why you're so horny and want me to fuck you on the floor." He paused and waved his hand around the space.

"Possibly." She gulped out her words. "You almost died on me."

"But I didn't."

The leg bounce started again. He did seem completely healed from yesterday's ordeal. "Do you think this whole mate stuff is starting to get boring?"

His blue gaze flipped up from reading a report, his brows pulled down as if puzzled. "Boring? Are you crazy? I can't get enough of you. Have you no memory, female? Three orgasms in lieu of breakfast each morning. Nighttimes of special pleasures. I confess to letting you down yesterday. I wasn't up to the task."

"I'm sitting here wearing your favorite skirt and a top which shows off my belly button. My boobs are pushed up to twice their size. My damn shapely gams are swinging like out-of-control scissors while all you do is read shit. Either I'm losing my touch or you're getting bored with me."

When Rein popped up, his chair flew into the back wall. He stalked to his mate. He palmed her knees, pushing her legs open wide, sandwiching his hips between them while her skirt rucked higher. His hands grasped her ass as he pulled her in tight. "Feel me?"

Braelyn's hand went to his crotch. "It's lovely. A big, hard bulge. Is it for me?"

"Only and always. Now unzip my pants, take me out, and ride me."

Her neck pivoted as she glanced around. "Are you kidding me? This office is filled with windows. Everyone will see us."

"Brae." His hips ground against her sweet spot in a suggestive rhythm.

She moaned, about to come with both of them fully clothed. Pausing, she flat-handed his chest, pushing him away. "No. Later."

Rein scrubbed a hand over his close-cropped hair. "Did you just come down here to give me a boner and run?"

"No. I came down here to tell you to get your ass home early so we can play Vampire and Witch Do the Nasty in Every Room. It's my favorite game."

Rein strode to his desk, his glutes tight, his steps determined. He shoved papers into random drawers. "Since I'm still recovering, I should leave early."

Before she could answer, Braelyn's cellphone buzzed. She leaned onto a hip and removed it from her back pocket. The caller was unidentified. "Maybe it's Miller Nash." She pressed accept. "Hello."

"Braelyn?"

"You got me."

"It's Miller."

"I figured. Are you on another burner?"

"It's the only way."

"You need to come in where we can protect you." Miller was on the run, a descendant and possible member of *Custodes Templii*. He had responded to Braelyn's lure published in her father's tabloid. Now they kept in touch by phone.

He let out a dignified British snort. "Not happening. I have questions, though."

"Shoot." Braelyn glanced at Rein. With his vampire-sharp hearing, she knew he picked up Miller's end of the conversation.

"I know I'm a descendant. I know you are. I know you're on Scath along with the muscle-inflated Firebrand bloke."

"Okay." She mimed to Rein. *I don't think he likes you.*

"What I don't know is this. You told me you have three other descendants under lock and key. I want names."

"We need something from you first," said Braelyn.

Rein nodded.

"Bollocks. You want me to trust you, but you won't trust me."

Rein mouthed a question for Braelyn to ask. "Are you a member of *Custodes Templii*? Do you know who all the descendants are?"

"I might be. I'll tell you this much. I have access to their information."

"Then here's a deal. Check on the living offspring. When you find out who's missing, give me a call." She disconnected.

A deep crease formed between Braelyn's eyes.

"Did I do the right thing by delivering the ultimatum and hanging up?"

"Yeah. I'm tired of being jacked around by him. Let's see what he really knows. So far all he's told us is he's descended from the Coven and *Custodes Templii* exists. Let's assume he's a member and they track Blood Coven spawn. If it's true, he'll give us the names of the missing. Then we'll compare notes. If we're feeling he's trustworthy, we'll tell him who we've got. We'll also have the names from him of descendants Cerberus might have in custody."

"Miller Nash may be the break we need."

Rein pulled his mate off the desk, wrapping an arm snug around her waist. "Let's head home. Later, I might need to sit in on an interrogation of Denim's ex. If he ever recovers. She really wiped his clock. Sabine and Nico also brought in a mage with ties to this group Kole's after. Arisen Dawn. The gaffers are softening them both up now."

His fangs dropped into view along with his predatory smile. "I'm hungry. And I know what I want to eat."

"Ooh. Lucky me. I'm on the menu."

Before they escaped, his D-chip interrupted plans. "This better be an emergency."

It was. Alarik called a meeting, one with all Blood Coven descendants.

****

Denim whispered in Ram's ear. He was in a chair beside her at Alarik's conference table, the director of the ministry having called a hasty meeting for Blood Coven descendants. "I told you. You didn't need to come with me."

"I said I was coming anyway. So, here I am."

"I can handle this myself."

"No doubt. I'll feel better with eyes on you." He leaned close, his gaze sweeping from her shiny chestnut hair south to her breasts where it lingered.

Denim shook her head, but a smile curved her lips. She should be pissed about his playing babysitter and ogling her. She should push back. Of course, with Ram she'd have to push back with a sledgehammer. But she no longer minded his over-protective nature. He cared. Whether he admitted it or not.

Rein and Braelyn sat across the table, most likely playing footsie or fondle-the-crotch because she kept punching his shoulder while she giggled. The controlled Firebrand's expression remained bland as he shrugged his shoulders, implying he had no idea what his mate meant.

Kole strode in with an arm clasped around Skyler's waist. He nodded at something she must have said. They chose the two seats next to the director of the Ministry of Well Being.

As loud laughter drifted in from the outer office, Margo shot through the doorway in front of Chay, who pinched her ass. She shot a frown over her shoulder at her ylve mate.

Behind them, Nico entered with his hand at Sabine's lower back.

That's when all conversation halted. Violet irises shot with dark purple specks shone below Abello's thick lashes.

"Ha!" Braelyn diverted her attention from Rein. "Finally. Not another word about whether you're one of us."

"No doubt." Nico plastered a smirk on his face.

He pulled out a chair for Sabine, and she plopped into it.

Rein glanced around and voiced what Denim was

thinking. "We're all here. What's up?"

Alarik held up a hand. "Not everyone. I invited someone else."

At that moment, a deadly man with waist-length black hair, thin braids framing his face, ushered in a strikingly beautiful woman. Her straight and shiny dark hair bobbed at her chin and swished from side-to-side like a swath of silk. A slight tilt to her dark eyes gave her an exotic look. The man nodded, leading the woman to her seat amid hushed stares. From the expressions around the table, no one had met his guest.

Alarik nodded, addressing the male. "Commander Jarek, I suppose you know why I asked you here with this group."

The male's gaze traveled the room. "I do."

The director continued. "None of you know her, but this…" He gestured toward the woman beside the djinn commander. "…is Lizette Lee. She is a Blood Coven descendant. When we found out this morning, I called Jarek about her test results."

Margo grinned, flipping a lock of red hair over her shoulder. "Greetings." She tapped near her own violet eyes.

"Not yet," said Lizette.

"For those of you who don't know our other guest, this is my sister, Indigo." Alarik pointed to the far end of the table.

She wore an off-the-shoulder peasant blouse, twirled a strand of hair around her index finger, and cast furtive glances at the faces, as if memorizing them.

Denim's brows furrowed, giving Lizette a puzzled look. No one new had moved onto her floor. "Will you be joining us in Kole's stronghold?"

Jarek didn't give the woman a chance to respond. "No."

"Okay." Braelyn spiked fingers through her short auburn hair. "What's your story? We all have one."

Before she answered, Lizette studied Jarek. He rested his hand atop hers on the table. "I was kidnapped, taken to a jail of sorts, and then sold to a berserker. Jarek and his Firebrands found me."

"You were sold?" Kole puzzled his brows. "Who sold you?"

"Aisen. I now understand he was working with a vampire named Silas."

"They gave all their captives a blood test. It should have told them who you were. They never would have sold a Blood Coven offspring. Selling you goes against every theory we're working on," said Kole.

"I think," answered Jarek, "they had run out of time. The Firebrands were on to the operation, and the two vamps wanted fast bucks. They sold her before her test results came through."

Braelyn leaned onto an elbow, her chin cupped in her palm. "We're graduates of the same prison system. Sounds like I lucked out, though. How long were you with this berserker?"

Lizette cast her gaze downward, pausing. "Too long."

Clearing her throat, Skyler reverted to her role as administrator. "Why are we here? Though it's nice to have us all together, what is the reason for this meeting, Alarik?"

"Nico called me about his recent transformation. That's when I suspected something was wrong with my original supposition. Once I saw Lizette's bloodwork results, I was certain I had drawn an unscientific conclusion. Scath cannot be the catalyst for the surge in your powers. It may be part of it, but whatever is turning you into witches and warlocks is something else. So, what is it? What do you have in common?"

Fourteen pairs of eyes pinballed around the table.

"We can rule out gender," said Skyler.

"Same with hair color." Margo fluffed her red curls.

"Our cities are different," said Nico. "Skyler and I are from Chicago, but Braelyn's from Seattle and Margo from Cincinnati. Denim's from the Big Easy. What about you, Lizette?"

"New York."

"How about Alliance connections?" asked Denim. "Nico was an agent. So was I. Skyler is the chief legal officer."

"Radio psychologist," said Lizette.

Braelyn raised a hand. "Paranormal journalism hack. Of course, my father's on the Alliance's board of directors."

"Sculptor," said Margo. "So that's out. Besides, we changed after we got to Scath. For some, it happened faster than for others. Explain that."

"Maybe we all metabolize something at different rates," said Braelyn. "Nico took a long time, but Lizette hasn't changed yet."

"I was on Scath with the berserker a long time. Could it be something in our diets?"

"There's the obvious." Indigo stood, leaning forward, her fingers splayed on the table. Then she straightened and flipped her black hair over her shoulder.

"What's the obvious?" Alarik stared at his sister.

Indigo chuckled. "I can sum it up in three letters. S-E-X. On Scath, of course."

Lizette swallowed hard. "That can't be it." No one probed.

Indigo sighed. "I have another option. The purple-eyed mages are all doing a little dinky-tickling with a Firebrand."

Skyler arched her brows while Kole swung an arm over her shoulders, drawing her to him. His smile morphed into a full-on guffaw with his head thrown back and sound erupting from deep in his chest. "So true. Well, regularly, and with success, as you can see."

"Kole!" Skyler rapped his arm.

"Hard to deny, Frisca."

Alarik glanced around the room. "Though my ever-shy sister may have expressed it somewhat crudely, can anyone deny it?"

"Of course, they can't deny it. There's enough sex in this room to ignite a blazing bonfire at a nymph rutting party. No offense, Sabine."

Sabine A-okayed Indigo.

Chay fisted the air. "We need T-shirts with a motto printed on them. 'Fuck a Firebrand. Jumpstart Your Inner Mage.' This is so cool."

Margo pinched his arm hard enough to make him wince. "Really, ylve?"

"Oh. For heaven's sake. Let's just hang out all our laundry." Skyler glowered at Kole. "Some of us turned before we fully consummated the relationship."

Even a dropping pin would have been too noisy for the silence which hit the room after Skyler's uncharacteristic outburst.

Kole broke the quiet by releasing another hearty laugh. "That's my Frisca." He kissed her white-blonde hair. Even Skyler chuckled before she buried her face against her mate's chest.

Jarek stroked one of his warrior braids. "Lizette and I have not been intimate." When he glanced at his companion, she cast her eyes to the floor, but her lips curled at the corners.

"I take it," said Alarik, "she has shown no signs

of being a witch. No change in eye color. What about gifts?"

"None," answered Lizette.

Indigo jumped out of her seat and rushed to the couple, hugging them both. "Don't worry, dear. Mark my words. He'll get in your pants yet. I know the future."

A blush crawled up Lizette's pale skin.

Rein pushed his chair away from the table, crossing an ankle over his opposite knee. "Auntie, that's not true."

"Spoiler alert. My boyo is throwing wet rags onto the fire. Okay, I confess, I do not know the exact future, but it is logical to assume the two of you will be rutting like bunnies soon enough."

Denim glanced at Ram, not knowing if she should comment on the extent of their relationship. It must be obvious.

Ram settled the matter. "Denim's eyes kinda speak for themselves."

She grimaced. "Well put, satyr."

The group around the table buttoned up, thinking. When eyes turned to Nico, he met their stares head on. "Hell no. Sabine and I are none of your damn business." His grin was a give-away, though.

Breaking in, Rein drew them back to business. "Let's say our fucking good times are catalysts. Don't you think it's odd we've been brought together? Firebrand and descendant."

Indigo scooted forward in her seat. Raising a finger, she pointed. "I saw you and you and you and you and you in the river. I didn't see anyone doing the nasty. So, relax. But you are all playing a role in this miracle play."

"What role?" asked Margo.

"Don't know yet. The river's a little murky on

that one." She jumped up, continuing to twirl a strand of hair around her finger. "Maybe we should send out all the single Firebrands to see which humans they boink. We might find more Coven descendants."

Braelyn chuckled. "I bet they'd be willing to soldier up. But I think we have a faster way, Indigo. Our best bet is Miller Nash and his *Custodes Templii* connections. We need their records. Besides, maybe the jumpstart is less about the sex and more about deep emotions binding a Firebrand and descendant together."

Denim interrupted, "This whole fate thing gives me the heebie jeebies. Are we implying our feelings for each other aren't real? Some cosmic force is bringing us together? That's disturbing."

"I agree." Braelyn tapped a finger on her chin. "It reeks of being a chess piece, moved around by some unseen hand. I don't like it." She glanced at her mate.

Rein's jaw set like stone. Pushing out of his chair, his muscles tense, he grabbed Braelyn's hand. With her jerking along behind him, he spoke over his shoulder. "We're not some damn pawns." They strode out the door, his anger palpable in the air.

Kole quirked his head toward the exit. He and Skyler strolled out while he smiled down at her. "Don't worry, Frisca. We chose each other."

Alarik pinched his lips together in serious-scientist thinking mode. "It's hard to think your choices are controlled."

Margo stroked Chay's leg. "I don't care. I love my ylve no matter who brought him to me."

"Damn straight, Red. Fate the matchmaker. Could be a Broadway musical. I'd go to it. This has been fun, but it's my day off. So, my little pawn and I have some unfinished business."

Led out by her Firebrand, his hand on her lower

back, Margo chuckled.

Jarek, with a hand to her elbow, gentled his companion to her feet. "I am a great believer in destiny showing us the best road. If fate has something in store for Lizette and me, it's a path I will gladly travel."

Lizette squeezed his hand as they left the meeting.

Nico snarled, his eyes narrow squints. "Fate does not have me by my balls. If something is happening between Sabine and me, it's because we want it to happen. Get me?"

"I get you, warlock." Sabine rested one hand on the ex-agent's forearm.

"Screw fate. We do what we want, sweetness."

"Damn straight, cuddles."

Once Denim, Ram, Alarik, and Indigo were alone in the conference room, an uncomfortable silence wrapped around them.

Clearing her throat, Indigo said, "That was interesting. I guess no one liked my idea. I know a lot of Firebrands would be happy to boff a bunch of humans. A prophet in her own land and all that crap. I'm outta here. See ya, bro."

Alarik nodded.

"What do you think, doll?" Ram stared at Denim.

"I need some time to deal. Destiny shit doesn't sit well with me."

****

Back in their apartment at the stronghold, Rein made it clear he didn't want to talk about any destiny crap. "What do you think he'll do?" Rein figured Braelyn knew who the "he" was.

"I think he'll do the right thing." She snuggled into Rein's solid chest, letting her fingers roam freely under his T-shirt, along his pads of muscle and on to the ridges of his abdomen.

"If Miller gives us the right names, we have to tell him they're safe with us in the stronghold."

"It's only fair. If he names humans not with us, it means Cerberus might have them."

Rein shivered. Destiny had no hand in making Braelyn's touch stir his erection into action.

He believed in an individual's will. Will had pulled him from the abyss of the bludfrenzy. Will had made him a strong Firebrand. Will had allowed Brae to survive the Bludhunt mating ceremony. Destiny was for fools.

Rein snatched Braelyn off the couch and threw her over his shoulder, ass up where he could smack it.

"Where are we going?" She rotated her neck until she was talking to the back of his head.

"To take a shower. I'm going to make sure you're clean. Very clean."

Chapter Twenty-Three

Ram sprawled on Denim's couch at the stronghold while she paced the room. "What's rolling around in your head?"

"What if you don't really want me at all?"

Ram pointed to the bulge in his pants. "I do."

"Not that way. You're a satyr. Galena said you have a hard-on for every female." She paused her back and forth to lob the slam. It may, however, have been somewhat deserved.

"While it's kind of her to notice my junk and where I'm putting it, she might have exaggerated a bit."

"If this is about destiny, you would have gotten stiff for any descendant who showed up."

"I saw Braelyn. I saw Margo. I saw Skyler. Hell, I saw Nico. Nothing. At least, nothing which made my cock twitch."

"But this was all so easy, so fast. I mean us and… You know."

Ram's brows raised as Denim lifted his legs to sit. "What was so easy? You? Damn, female. We have different ideas of easy. Easy would have had your hand down my pants the first time I saw you at the Shed. You would have dragged me to a backroom. Or you would have done me right there on the couch. You would have unzipped me, wrapped your sweet lips around my dick, and fucked me with your mouth all to some heavy beat rap. I don't need to remind you none of that happened. Sure, you squeezed me a little because you were pissed and going for the shock effect. Now, how about being easy for a change?"

He swung his feet to the floor and pulled Denim onto his lap, crushing her lips with his mouth. His dick was straining to get out of his pants, rubbing against her tight ass. But he had something else to clear up before his joystick took over. "What we feel, what I feel, isn't just sex, Denim."

She tangled her hands in his long hair. "Really?"

"Really. But I'm still a fuck-up." Ram wasn't ready to say more. He was a shitty catch.

Denim sighed, pulling Ram in for a gentle kiss. When she opened for his tongue, he thrust inside, hungry. In and out, he savored the hot, wet feel of her. Each plunge filled the air with the scent of her arousal. His fingers grasped the bottom of her shirt, ripping it over her head.

Ram paused, his eyes feasting on the lacy bra hidden under the not-so-sexy shirt. "Damn. You are beautiful."

He leaped up with Denim bouncing in his arms and sprinted for her bedroom.

About halfway down the hall, he dropped her to her feet. "I can't wait."

He yanked off his shirt but fumbled with his BDU's, finally unzipping and letting them fall to his knees. Denim was having the same problem. So he tore her pants open and shoved them down her legs.

Ram's shaft jutted out, painfully hard. He slammed her against the wall, slipping his fingers beneath the lace of her bra, flicking her nipples with his thumbs. Extracting his digits to complete the job, he unhooked the back clasp. With her breasts free, he licked his lips. "Those are kissable."

Her chest rose and fell with deep breaths, her nipples all perky.

Ram cupped one breast, squeezing it in his hand. As she moaned and stroked his arms, he dropped his head to take her flesh into his mouth, licking, teasing, and sucking until a tight bud formed. He moved to the other breast.

With her back pressed to the wall, she was at his mercy. Just where she belonged. His erection prodded her belly, his mouth working her succulent breasts.

Ram slid into her panties. One digit glided back and forth through the moisture between her folds. His thumb circled her clit. When he clamped his teeth around her nipple, he thrust a finger into her channel.

"Oh, God." Denim trembled.

He stabbed two fingers into her pussy, whispering into her ear, "How's that?"

"Oh, yes. Faster."

"You are so demanding."

The speed picked up while Denim pounded against his hand in a frenzy. His fingers punched in and out. When his thumb found her clit again, he circled and taunted.

"Come for me, doll. Let me feel you fall apart."

"Oh, Ram." With her shout, her body froze.

"Let go." Buried in her hot moisture, he helped her ride out the orgasm.

Withdrawing slowly, he brought his fingers to his mouth. She watched, her eyes wide, as he sucked them into his mouth. He grinned and licked his lips. "I'm gonna need inside you before I explode."

"You brought condoms?"

"Plenty. I don't go anywhere near you without a supply."

"I love strategic planning."

"Let me lose these." Ram had prided himself on being a smooth lover. With Denim, he was all thumbs and awkward moves. Too excited. He fumbled with his pants, shoving them to the floor, stepping out of them. Searching the pockets for condoms, he found one, ripped open the package with his teeth, and rolled it on while Denim busied herself disrobing. Once he was naked but gloved, being a gentleman, he helped tear off her panties.

He cradled her ass to lift her. "Legs. Around my hips." Fisting his cock, he nudged her wet pussy.

The female was strong. She locked her ankles, yanking him forward.

Both hands clenching her hips, he drove inside. In one hard thrust he found heaven. Pulling out almost entirely, he plunged back in, flexing his ass. "So good."

"Ram. Fuck me." Her nails drew blood on his shoulders. "I need you to move."

"Oh, yeah." His hips undulated. Every squeeze of her muscles killed him, the friction intense. He felt a twinge as his damn horns shoved through his scalp to lie flat against his head. His satyr's beast came out only for Denim.

With her face to his chest, she sucked and bit on his nipple, sending a jolt of pleasure through him.

Hell yes.

He tilted her chin up with a finger and brushed his lips across hers, his tongue invading her, pushing in, sliding out, keeping the same rhythm as his hips. Tongue and cock together. It was a fucking harmony of rapture.

Then, because she was the only female who brought his satyr beast to the surface, she did what no one ever had. She gripped his horns to urge him on. With her palms stroking them, Ram drove toward a release. His hips slammed forward. Back. His shaft pistoned into her, hard as steel. His balls slapped against her flesh. The wall shook when her back thudded against it while he ravaged her.

Denim cried out, "Yes. Don't stop."

Her muscles squeezed him mercilessly. As he felt her orgasm build, his satyr fed from her arousal, gorging on her passion. She nourished his soul, bringing light to the darkness, lifting what had been heavy.

She cried out his name, her body shuddering, tightening on him like a vise. He pulled out to his tip and thrust in hard and deep, grinding, pounding into her, every stroke a pleasure. "Yes, doll. Oh. Yes." He clutched her hips as he exploded.

Once Ram's muscles relaxed, Denim's legs started a slow slide toward the floor. When her hands dropped from his horns, he felt them retreat.

"Okay. I might be permanently ruined." She lazed against the wall.

"Stay right here." He retreated to the bathroom where he disposed of his condom. When he returned, Denim still had a sated look on her face, her eyes half-masted. "I'm not nearly finished with you." He clasped her hand, leading her down the hallway to the bedroom.

They right-turned it to enter. Ram barely glanced around before he tossed her onto the bed. "Do you know where I want you?"

"No."

"On my mouth, doll."

She crawled backward, blushing. "This is so…"

With his hands on her ankles, Ram yanked her toward him, pushing her knees up, spreading them. "So beautiful?" He used his two thumbs to part her folds. Dipping his head, he lapped along her slit. The groans and moans erupting from her were his reward.

When his mouth found her clit, Denim's back arched. She pushed into him, her hands clasping his temples, leading him where it felt good. "Please, Ram. Right there."

He paused to fix on her eyes. He could feel his own shimmer neon green as he watched her hooded, aroused stare.

"That's what I want to see," he said.

"Damn. Don't stop."

Ram resumed the task at hand. He invaded her channel with his tongue. In and out, he thrust, fucking her.

She tensed as she squeezed his head tighter, crying out his name. "God. Ram." Her body trembled as she pressed harder.

Again, he fed from her arousal.

She was so good. He had never tasted sweeter.

She stilled, her hands flopped to her side, seeming unable to move. Her breasts popped up and down with each ragged breath.

Crawling alongside Denim, he tugged her into his arms, holding her to his chest. "I needed this."

"Me, too."

He scented the sex which permeated the room. Her head moved up and down as he inhaled and exhaled.

Peace. This was peace.

After some time, she spoke. "Are you sure you don't feel as if we were shoved together?"

"What we have … I am sorry to say … I never felt even with Amelia. Nobody's shoved me. I fell when I first saw you at the Shed, but I didn't know it. I could have walked away, but I chose not to. Me. I chose to hit on you."

She sighed, resting on his pec again.

"And you know what? Even if fate chose to put us together, I have no complaints. Destiny's got my back. Excellent choice. Now come here. I'm in favor of Indigo's idea. Let's boff."

"How can you be ready again?"

Ram pointed to his erect penis. "Horny satyr. Stiff as a board. Give us a little relief." His hand patted the bedside table, searching for another condom. Denim helped out this time. Appropriately dressed, he rolled between her thighs and crawled up her body until his cock found its prize.

****

Denim stretched her arms overhead, unashamed to show her breasts above the sheet while she watched Ram stride back to bed naked, glorious, and totally arrogant. His proud cock jutted out, hard and tempting.

"You are so sexy, doll. The sight of you goes straight to my dick."

A reflex, she pulled a strand of hair over the scar on her cheek.

"Stop. It's part of what makes you beautiful." He sank onto the bed, on his back, his arms crossed under his neck.

Believing him, she combed fingers through her hair, pushing it off her face. "I know how to satisfy an insatiable satyr's appetite." Denim gripped his thick, proud length. Straddling him, she stroked his velvety hardness, loving the feel of steel under the soft flesh.

Ram settled a pillow under his neck, pointing to his crotch. He tilted his hips up. "Don't be gentle."

Denim bent forward to lick the crown where pre-cum beaded on the end. His hips hammered up.

She chuckled. "You like that, satyr?"

"Yeah. I like." His hands rested on her temples.

She flicked her tongue in a circle around the tip of his shaft.

"Oh, doll."

Ram's palms pressed tighter to her head as he inched deeper.

She listened to his groans, enjoying her control over his pleasure. Fisting the base of his arousal, she glided her hand up and down while her mouth worked the rest of him. She found a rhythm, sucking, licking, and stroking.

He tasted so good, his flesh firm, his shaft pulsing in her mouth.

He jacked upward, sending himself to the back of her throat. She gently feathered his balls with her fingertips.

"Really squeeze them, doll." She did. "Damn. I'm going to come."

Ram grabbed her shoulders, trying to drag her up his torso.

She resisted. "Finish." She licked her wet lips, puffy from having sucked him.

When she returned her mouth to his cock, Ram didn't last long.

Afterward, Denim couldn't stop smiling. "I loved tasting you."

"You can suck me anytime." Ram leaned against the headboard, Denim's arms wrapped around him, her head on his pectorals. "I hate to bring up bad tidings after such a superior performance, but it's time to interrogate your ex. Are you going to handle it okay? If not, you stay here. I'll oversee the proceedings."

"He's an asshole. It won't bother me at all, *cher*." She lifted her eyes.

Ram trained his penetrating translucent gaze on her. "How bad did he hurt you?"

Feeling the satyr's muscles clench when he asked the question, she realized something. In part because of Ram, she was healing. All men were not Steven. For the first time, she wanted to share the incident which bruised her where no one could see.

With a deep inhale, she began the story. "I was home packing to leave the jerk. He was supposed to be at work but returned to our apartment early. Drunk. When I told him I was divorcing him, he slammed his fists into my face, kicked me, raped me, and left me lying bloody on my own sheets."

Ram snarled, his eyes flashing neon green. In anger now. Not passion.

She stroked the ridges of his abs to calm him because she couldn't stop now. "My Pottery Barn sheets. They were expensive." Her lips tilted into a smile as she refused to give in to her emotions.

Ram was quiet, but his chest rose and fell with each breath. "You won't have to worry about him again. When we're done with him, I'll castrate the asshole. For free."

She continued to rest on the satyr, liking the feel of his warm skin, the rhythmic beat of his heart. "He put me in the hospital. A couple broken ribs, a cracked jaw, lots of black and blue..." Denim fingered the visible evidence of Steven's cruelty. "...and my scar."

He waited when she paused, somehow reading her as no one ever had. "That's your visible scar. What's your invisible one, Denim?"

She sighed before continuing her story. The next part was a hard lump in her stomach, a never-ending ache in her damaged heart. "I was pregnant. I lost the baby. It was a girl. She was one of the many reasons I was packing to leave. I could never allow a child to grow up around him. He was a monster. I reported the incident to the Alliance. They fired him. I hired a lawyer, toying with the idea of filing charges but decided against it. I did get a restraining order, but it's as helpful as a second appendix."

After the story, she did something she'd never done. Safe in Ram's arms, she cried for her lost child.

When she was sobbed out, Denim cleared her throat. There was more. She didn't want Ram to think she was a victim. She wasn't one then and wouldn't be one now.

"Anyway, I left the hospital, nursed my wounds, and sneaked into his motel room one night while he was asleep. I handcuffed him to the bed, made him suck on my Beretta. I told him if he ever broke the court order to fuck with me again, he better kill me. If not, I would come for him, cut off his balls, stuff them in his pants pocket, and then shoot him. I meant it. He obeyed the order. Until this recent stuff."

Ram remained silent.

"I never told anybody about the baby or going to Steven's motel. Not even Marta. I hooked up with her Safe Haven place after a while but kept my story close to my heart."

A tear leaked onto Ram's chest, her cheek caressing his silky skin.

"I'm sorry for your loss, for the hole you'll never fill. But you got partial payback, doll. You showed him you're tougher, stronger than he is."

Ram was a man who understood Denim's eye-for-an-eye world of biblical justice. Early on, she had pegged the satyr as someone who could break her heart. Now she was sure he could.

Please, don't let him.

****

Miller made a call. "Harry. It's me, mate. Listen up. I only have a few minutes."

He glanced at the number of another burner cell in his possession and gave it to his second at *Custodes Templii*.

"Call me at that number. Give me a list of the next twenty burners you buy. Use each one only three or four times. Then destroy it. Stay on the move."

"Gotcha."

"Phone each tracker. Ask if anyone in their

bloodline is missing. Not dead. Missing."

"Why? And what do I do if they say yes?"

"We break our own sacred rule. Ask the name of the missing. Pass it on to me."

"Why this unprecedented action, Miller? We're sworn not to do this. We only know our own bloodline. We never share our list with other trackers. How do I know you haven't been compromised?"

"You don't, but as you are aware someone tried to kidnap me. They failed."

"Yeah. All the British Intelligence shit paid off for you."

"For now. Here's the thing. I met with Braelyn James and her mate, the Scion Firebrand from Scath. You told me she's one of yours. She was captured and imprisoned. The guys who nabbed her had a jail stocked with other possible descendants. The blokes were looking for Blood Coven offspring."

"Holy hell."

"Yeah. Downright barmy. I think the Firebrands are protecting a few descendants, but they won't share names with me. They want me to cough up proof first."

"Like?"

"Like names of descendants we know are missing. If they recognize a name, they'll know I'm legit."

"Then what?"

"Then they'll identify the descendants they're keeping safe. Of course, if I give them someone they don't recognize, we'll know the bad guys might have the person." Miller exhaled into the phone. "This is why we were created in the first place, Harry. We have been warned to watch for this very situation."

"I get it."

"If the trackers are missing an offspring, give me

the name. I will share with Braelyn and her Firebrand."

"Do you trust them?"

"I do. For now."

"What do we get out of it?"

"We get to know if the bad guys have rounded up a few of us or if they're safe on Scath."

"It will take me time to contact all trackers."

"I expected it to."

"Communication may take longer since I'll be calling from unknown burners. It could be months before they can check on every one of their descendants."

"I know. Be as fast as possible. Our *raison d-etre* has come into play."

"Gotcha."

"And Harry."

"Yes?"

"Stay safe." Miller disconnected and walked into a dark alley, removing the battery from the cell he had used. He tossed it into a dumpster. Once he smashed the phone under his boot, he retrieved the sim card, giving it an extra foot-grind. He pocketed the remnants, planning to toss them into two other dumpsters far away.

Miller Nash, ex British Intelligence and leader of *Custodes Templii*, felt destiny breathing down his neck and she was a bitch. She had lain dormant for nearly fifteen hundred years. Today, she was eager to come out and play.

Ready or not. Here I come.

Why the hell did she have to come on his watch? He had the feeling everything was about to fall arse over tit. Right now, though, he was knackered and needed a bit of a rest.

Chapter Twenty-Four

The outer door banged against the wall when Ram sauntered inside, Denim's hand in his. "This is the Cubes." He tamped down his rage for her sake. If he had his way, he'd kill Steven outright.

Denim glanced around. "Scary."

Galena perched on a stool, bent forward with her elbows resting on her knees.

Cells lined the perimeter of the Cubes while the center was an industrial cavern with a concrete floor and several strategically-placed drains for blood and other fluids. Chains dangled from the ceiling. Various medieval torture devices sat around not collecting dust. Some with cranks. Aeternals often employed mechanical encouragement to loosen their tongues. One was a cringe-worthy chair with spikes on the back and arms. Saws and axes littered nearby tables.

Ram led Denim to the Amazon.

"Scary? It's cool. Look at that thing." Galena pointed to a contraption against one wall. "The gaffers strap a prisoner to it, tie his spread legs to one end and hands to the other. After he's trussed, they turn the handle. Snap, crackle, and pop. Bones and ligaments. 'Course, our jailers don't have to use machines or tools. They can rip a body apart with their gifts. But where's the fun?"

Denim tilted her head, staring for some time at her friend. "You've got a sadistic streak I've never seen before."

"You think? I dunno. Sometimes I have erotic dreams. You know, me strapped up there on the hooks with some berserker hunk going down on me. Anyway. Pull up a stool. Front row seat."

"I'm serious. You might be sick." Denim skidded the stool along the floor until she was beside Galena. Ram stayed on two feet.

Rein slammed into the room, accompanying a tall, skinny gaffer who dragged in the prisoner, the tops of his feet dusting the floor. His dark hair was matted, his body limp, his eyes rolling around unfocused. He was the poster boy for a Russian KGB interrogation.

Denim's hand clasped over her mouth, but she didn't look away.

It had to be hard on her. This was the man she'd once called husband. This was the man she had loved. This was the man who had beaten her, left her to die in a pool of her own blood, and killed their unborn child. This was the man responsible for nearly killing Rein, him, and Denim. But still…

The tall gaffer pointed to a hook which hung from the ceiling while he talked to the older jailer. "Bring it down. Use the big chains."

The guy lowered the hook and dragged out a few chains. As they clanged along the concrete floor, they left a pattern in the sprinkling of dust. Once the tall gaffer dropped the prisoner onto the ground, the older male bound his hands. The other chain went around Steven's feet and linked to the hook. The gaffer hoisted him upside down.

Her ex choked back sobs. "Assholes." The male cried, his tears and snot leaking onto the floor.

"We are." Rein smacked a hand to Steven's chest, pushing so he swung back and forth.

"I'm gonna throw up."

"Oh, man. I hate it when they puke." Ram pulled up a stool next to Denim and patted her thigh. "You don't have to be here, doll."

"This is where I belong."

He nodded but let his palm linger.

With another push, Steven's screams echoed through the Cubes.

"Pussy." Rein looked at the females. "Apologies. I love pussy. Just one now, of course."

Galena winked, but Denim's forehead creased. "You're all enjoying this."

True.

Ram stroked her thigh as he whispered in her ear. "Remember what he's done. This is justice. Besides, we have two innocent vamps to save."

Steven focused on Denim, his black-and-blue eyes swollen. "Help me."

She slid off the stool and approached her ex. Fisting his dirty hair, she bent, bringing his face nose to nose. His lids flicked up and down as if he was trying to have a look-see. He almost smiled but winced when he tried to curl his cracked lips. "I don't care what they do to you, sonofabitch. In fact, I might give them a few ideas. Like to cut off your useless, shriveled sacs. Tell us where the two vampires are, and I'll ask them to go easy on you."

"Nice one, Denim. My blade's sharp. Let me." Galena drew out a knife, holding it point up until it glistened in the overhead lights.

With the fistful of Steven's hair, Denim rattled his head. "Did you hear her?"

Steven sobbed. "Don't know."

"Then I'm sorry for you."

Denim returned to her stool. She waved a dismissive hand. "Do whatever you want to him. He's a pig. If he can't tell us where the two are, he's useless."

Rein signaled the older gaffer. "Got anything for this pussy male?"

"My favorite. We got Mung Beetles from Darque.

They like to crawl into any opening. Ears. Asshole. Mouth. Eyes. After they nest, they eat your organs. Nasty shit. I'll be back. We keep them stored in a terrarium under a heat lamp."

Ram scratched his ear. "Why there?"

The older male smiled, his mouth a slash of grim pleasure. "They like to live where it's warm." He left the room.

Trying to wriggle out of his restraints, Steven shrieked, his legs jerking, his body undulating like a worm. "No. No. Ask me questions."

"Okay. Here's one. Who's calling the shots?" Rein caught the prisoner's head between his hands.

"Mars."

"His real name?"

"I dunno."

Rein yelled into the backroom. "Got those beetles yet?"

"I don't know if that's his real name. I don't. It's the only name I've heard him called. Dark buzz-cut hair. Cold eyes. Like yours. Ex-military."

"Who signs his paycheck?"

"They don't tell us shit like that."

By this time, the older gaffer had returned.

"Let loose the beetles," said Rein.

The gaffer opened the jar and dumped the contents onto the prisoner's chest. As they crawled on his body, he jumped and gyrated, rattling the chain. "No. I told you everything I know."

"Not enough." Rein shook his head as if he really gave a shit.

Denim turned to the side, drawing a deep breath before she resumed watching the torture session.

Steven screamed as a beetle reached his neck, heading toward his ear.

Ram kept a sharp eye on Denim. When she clasped her throat, a shiver rocking her body, he looped an arm over her shoulders. Giving her a fast squeeze, he stood. "Hey, dead guy. I think there's a bug headed for your nose. Another behind him is beelining for your ear."

"Get 'em off. Oh, God, please."

"I'm not touching them. They're nasty. You should sneeze about now." Ram took over the interrogation, Rein stepping into the shadows.

"Please, man. I already said I'd talk."

"Your lucky day, Steven. The one by your nose veered right and is headed for your eye."

"What else do ya wanna know?"

"Let's talk about the jack-up juice." Ram decided to go through one topic at a time.

"The what?"

"The stuff which turns you into a superhuman?"

"Come on. I can feel something crawling on my cheek."

"What is the stuff?"

"Don't know what's in it. We get shots once a week." Steven squeezed his eyes tight as he shook his head to dislodge the vermin.

"Why are you doing this to us?" Ram asked the prisoner while brushing a bug off Steven's cheek.

Even in pain, the sonofabitch looked confused by the question, his brows squeezing tight. "You're not human. What else we gonna do? Get those fucking bugs off me."

"We'll see. Back to Mars. Who is his boss?"

The prisoner screamed as he flopped his body. "Wait. Wait, you asshole. Help me."

Ram cocked his neck to the side. "I'm a little new at this game. Not sure of the rules. Pretty sure you shouldn't be calling me names, though. Not when you're hanging upside down with organ-feasting bugs crawling all over you. I think one headed into your jeans."

Between sobs, Steven gulped words. "Dante. That's a name I heard."

Rein, Ram, and Galena exchanged looks.

"There's a name we've heard," said Ram.

The prisoner screamed. "It's in my ear. I can feel it moving. Get it out. Get it out."

"Uh ... sure. I'll get it out." The older gaffer shrugged.

"Back to Dante. Is this guy an Aeternal?" asked Ram.

"No. He's human. Our group's called Humans First. Motherfucker. Get the one in my pants."

"I am not putting my hand anywhere near your junk. Why do you think he's human?" Ram grimaced.

"Mars let slip he's an Englishman. Like from England."

"Here's the million-dollar question. Where are the vamps?"

"Best I know, they're in the lab." Steven jack-knifed his body, trying to shake off the bugs.

Ram grabbed the prisoner's shoulders to steady him, swatting several bugs off. "Got them." He stomped the ground. "Can you draw us a map of how to get to the lab and its layout?"

"Yes. Just get rid of the bugs." Steven's screams, punctuated with sobs, bounced off the walls as he jerked his body back and forth.

Denim sneaked up behind Ram and clutched his arm, whispering in his ear. "Please, stop."

Ram scrubbed his free hand along his chin. "Okay. Take him back to his cell. Give him some paper so he can demo his artistic skills. And get the creepy-ass bug out of his ear."

The older gaffer arched a brow.

Denim sighed as her body relaxed. She slumped against Ram. "Thank you."

When Galena stepped alongside her, Denim leaned over to whisper into her ear. "Do those bugs do what he said?"

"Yep. Gives me the heebie jeebies just thinking about it."

"Come on, doll. Let's get out of here." Ram led her to the door where he stopped. "Wait a sec. Be right back."

Out of her hearing, he huddled with Rein and Galena. "See if you can find out more about these Humans First nut jobs. After Denim's ex draws a map of the lab and we verify it's legit, you can kill him."

"Don't think we'll have to, satyr." Rein wiggled a finger in his ear. "The bugs will do the trick. Death will come slowly, though. Days. Weeks."

Galena nodded.

Ram grinned. "I'm okay with that."

****

Celene awoke in another new bed with fresh sheets and a thick blue comforter. She nestled into a generous pillow. After lying still for nearly a half hour, she tossed the covers aside and touched her feet to the floor. Large dark planks of wood. The bedroom where she had been moved to soon after Jace's escape had been carpeted.

Padding to the closet on the hard surface, Celene donned her familiar robe, glancing at the clothes on hangers. *The same pants and shirts.* Her gaze dropped. *Same shoes.*

She didn't bother brushing her teeth in the bathroom. Washing her face or showering required too much effort. Though her fingers caught on tangles in her hair, she lacked the energy to find a comb. Instead, she turned the doorknob and slogged into the kitchen. A coffee pot sat on the counter, but she was too tired to care. She opened a cabinet where a box of Frosted Flakes rested on the shelf.

Not hungry.

Four doors led from the new room. One was the bedroom she had exited. The other was the bathroom. Behind door number three was an exercise room. She twisted the knob on the closed door. Locked. It probably went to the guards' station.

Pulling out a chair, she slumped into it, leaning her elbows on the cold metal kitchen table, propping her head in her hands. She twisted her neck to gaze at a clock on the wall. Seven. AM or PM? She had no idea. She chose to believe PM. It felt right.

Continuing to scan the room, she jumped up, punching a fist in the air. *Yippee!* The books were back. New bookcase. Old, familiar books. She glanced over the titles until she found *The Path.* She fingered the volumes.

Pulling out her favorite book, she was thankful it had been returned. She had just gotten to the good part when she'd been tagged and bagged the day after Jace's escape. Celene flipped through pages until she reached the spot where she had left off. Burrowing into the overstuffed chair covered in a worn plaid, she kicked her feet onto an ottoman. Gahya had summoned Ohngel, and while he seemed to have a problem with her, he had no problem screwing her brains out.

His flesh still hard, Ohngel rolled onto an elbow, demanding, "Disrobe." He gazed with hunger as Gahya unpinned the fabric of her peplos from her shoulders, giving Ohngel better access to her flushed and heavy breasts. He molded his hand to them, squeezing, pinching her nipples until they were tight pebbles.

Twisting the goddess onto her back, he bunched her skirt at her waist, baring her to his view as his fingers sought the folds of soft moist skin at the V of her thighs. When he rubbed her slick cleft, she rewarded him with a moan.

Ohngel slipped one finger inside the Genitrix's wet channel. "So warm. So ready."

She rocked her hips against his invasion. "Yes. More." With breathless gasps, she rolled her head from side to side.

He withdrew and re-entered her body with two fingers, her whimpered pleas encouraging him to plunge in and out.

"I want you inside me." Gahya palmed his aching need, guiding it toward its destination.

He lowered himself between her thighs. "Open to me," he commanded. When she lifted her knees wide, he gripped his shaft and shoved into the anxious depth between her legs.

Gahya cried out, her heels clasping onto his buttocks, her clawed nails drawing blood on his back. "More, my Ohngel."

He growled but adjusted the angle and thrust of his swollen erection until he seated himself deep within the Genitrix's sex. With a savage desire, he pounded into her, slamming her against the ground. Ohngel took what he wanted with uncompromising force while she stayed with him push for push. He took. He assaulted. Attacked. In and out. No mercy.

Just as she liked it.

His lips captured her mouth as he spiked his tongue inside like a sword seeking the kill, each plunge fiercer than the last. This was what her creatures experienced, what she gave them.

"Yes. Yes. Ohngel."

With her shoulder gripped between his teeth, he pistoned his hips forward, faster and faster, harder and harder.

She bucked against the warrior a final time, shattering the silence with her pleasured screams.

As Gahya cried out, Ohngel's eyes blazed, his wings snapped out, and he threw his head back to shout. Once his seed filled the Genitrix, he stilled.

Moments later, the goddess unclasped her trembling legs, dropping weakened arms to the leaf-strewn ground. "This is good."

Ohngel twisted onto his side, raising onto an elbow. With furrowed brows, he contemplated the Genitrix. Regardless of the carnal pleasure offered by her body, he remained guarded, possessed of a bone-chilling distrust. Though passion is hot, scorching the bearer and the recipient of the emotion, his wariness was not so. It was cold, frigid. Freezing all who touched it. "It is satisfying. The need to fuck you again rips me apart. Is it good?"

"You are mine. I am yours."

"You are forever faithless, Gahya. I mean this as no insult. It is what it is. You are not mine, nor I yours. Once, I could have been. No longer. Let us not make too much of fucking. You will be off to a new male tomorrow."

"And you?"

"I'll have a different female in my bed by tonight."

Sitting, Gahya lifted her peplos, re-pinned it at her shoulder, and smoothed the skirt down her legs. Her brows knitted together. "You have grown cruel."

Unfolding his lethal body from the ground, he slipped on his shirt and laced his breeches. When clothed, he bent at the waist in a deep bow. "Such is so.

And I apologize if the truth has offended the Genitrix."

His form dissolved as he left Gahya's abode, aware she would summon him again. And he would come.

Celene jerked her eyes from the book when a key snicked in the lock of the door opposite the kitchen. The vampire who called himself Lort strode in. Because he rarely visited, she feared the news would not be good.

"Where is she?" he demanded, his eyes streaked with red.

The vampire's question made Celene want to cheer. With two changes in prison locations, no windows to see if it was dark or light, and drugs distorting her sense of time, Celene was unsure how many days had passed. Maybe five or six. They had not found Jace. "How the hell would I know? I don't even know where I am."

So fast she could not track him, he was beside her chair, his fingers wrapped in her hair, pulling her head back, hard enough tears welled in her eyes. "Where is she?"

"I don't know, asshole."

His grip unbreakable, he wrenched her neck farther, her spine arching. Then he released her. "You get no walks outside. These rooms will be your cage." A cruel snarl contorted his face, his fangs cutting his lower lip.

She lifted her hand and threw Lort a middle finger.

That felt good.

****

Slipping into an alcove off the street, Miller drew his cell phone to his ear. "Harry. That was fast. What did you find out?"

"First, I need to get this out there even though

you already know. This task is overwhelming. Some of our trackers have lists of over a hundred names. It's not like they can check on them daily. And, of course, their people are spread out all over the world."

"I do understand, Harry, but *Custodes Templii* has waited centuries for this event. Our legacy. The time of the prophecy has come. We can't neglect our duty."

"Not saying we can. Just taking my frustration out on you."

Miller could almost see Harry running his fingers through his messy hair.

"Some of our guys are asking for more time. They're all doing the best they can. They're renting private jets, using up money like water. Hope we've got plenty."

"We do, mate. It's been accumulating for centuries, racking up interest for such a day. You're in charge of the books now."

"Okay. Two of the trackers with the smallest numbers hit me immediately because they already had people they were worried about. One of Solemnia's has gone missing. She's a sculptor who lives in Cincinnati. She's a little flaky, our guy says, but she's never been off the grid this long. The apartment is still listed in her name, but one day her stuff is there and the next day it's gone. Anyway, her name is Margo Hunter."

Miller sandwiched the phone between his shoulder and ear while he searched for writing material. When he took a small notebook from his pocket, he reached for a pen. "Margo Hunter, you say. Solemnia's line. Got it. Who else?"

"One of our gals said her person isn't missing. The sitch is just weird. Skyler Maxwell, the chief legal officer for the Alliance, sold her condo in Chicago. The tracker doesn't know where she's living, but she's still with the Alliance. Here's the catch. She never leaves her office to go home at night. After work, she vanishes but shows up again in the morning."

"Skyler Maxwell. Whose bloodline?" He wrote her name in his notes.

"Anarai." Harry gave Miller three more names.

"I'll see what this info gets me with my contacts. I'll be back in touch."

He paused so long Harry said, "You there, Miller?"

"Yeah. We can't fuck this up. We need to account for our people."

"I know."

Chapter Twenty-Five

Kole thundered into the antechamber of the Temple of Justice, tugging on the neck of his purple robe with the insignia of the fiery Phoenix on its sleeve. He was not pleased to start his day here. Cadmon nodded a stiff greeting.

Hearing footsteps behind him, Kole shifted his hand onto his dagger hilt as he twisted around.

Nace entered, his eyes feral gold, his cat prowling close to his skin. "High Commander. Kole. You look as comfortable as I feel. I'd hate to fight in this get-up. Wearing it chafes my dick."

Jarek slammed through the door. "Down, *frerons*. Only me. What does the Temple want?"

Cadmon shrugged. "They summon. We come. They are interested in these superhumans and are requesting a status report on our other activities."

As high commander of the Scion Firebrands and, thus, director of the Ministry of the Shield, the ylve reported directly to the Temple of Justice. Kole didn't envy him the job of juggling the demands of the warriors and navigating political intrigues.

Nace patted the side of his robe. "I feel naked without my sword. Kole, I hear a lot of activity is going on over at your stronghold. You a hotel or what?"

He snorted. "Yeah. I'm hanging out a no-vacancy sign. A second Alliance agent named Denim Quinn followed in Abello's footsteps. She's now one of my Firebrands."

"Careful, demon. Soon all your warriors will be human," scoffed Nace.

"The fuckers keep blackmailing me. They may be weaker than us, but they are devious as hell."

Kole shifted his feet apart, clasping his hands behind his back. "And those newbie witches are turning my stronghold ass side up. They're doing what they call a retro-fit. Some shit they watch on HGTV."

The others moaned in what was likely sympathy.

Nace turned his attention to Jarek. "So, you've got your own Blood Coven witch under wraps."

"Lizette Lee resides at my camp. I wouldn't call her my own."

"You aren't having a go at the human, are you, djinn?" asked Nace.

"Who I fuck is none of your business, shifter. Mind your own sex life."

"What sex life? Haven't had one since I took over the North Shelters stronghold."

"This female is different," said Jarek.

Nace studied the djinn commander, his jag eyes amber. "Hell. Another Firebrand falls."

Jarek shrugged. "Not yet."

Cadmon stroked his chin. "No matter what the justices ask, stay as tight-lipped as possible about the Blood Coven descendants and the new intel on the Arisen Dawn group."

"Why?" asked Nace.

"My gut. It's kept me alive in many battles. So, I listen to it."

A black-robed demon opened the chamber doors to wave them inside.

Four of the most powerful warriors on Scath strode into the sacred chambers, Cadmon leading the charge. Their backs were ramrod straight, their eyes alert.

Kole scanned the room. He feared nothing and no one, but he would be a fool to underestimate the beings in front of him. A word from any of them could put his neck under the blade.

The rare eagle shifter Aras spoke from the high justice's elevated throne. On each side of him were four other representatives of their breeds. "Welcome, High Commander Cadmon, Commander Kole, Commander Nace, and Commander Jarek."

As one, the Firebrands pressed the palms of their hands to their hearts in a quick salute. "Justice and long life."

Aras locked a predatory stare on Cadmon. "Some of us have questions."

"Ask." Cadmon, his head tilted up toward the justices, used his words sparingly.

As he leaned back in his seat, Aras pointed at the warlock Dolph.

"We request a status report on the Scion Firebrands' current activities."

"Not we, warlock. You and the demon," interrupted Gilda. *Pffft.* "I trust High Commander Cadmon to voluntarily bring his concerns to us."

"As do I, Amazon. Please, Commander Nace?" Justice Dolph signaled the jag shifter to begin.

"The run-down. Absolutely. We're peacekeeping on Darque where a pot boils over regularly. But an uptick in drug traffic is eating up warriors and time."

"Why the increase?" asked Eron, pushing her long, black hair over the shoulder of her robe where the insignia of an eye with a dagger beneath it identified her as a justice.

The female demon was a recent addition to the Temple. Kole knew little about her.

"Not sure, but we're chasing it down," continued Nace.

Kole admired the jaguar's careful words as he heeded Cadmon's warning, not mentioning Arisen Dawn and its newly uncovered link to drug trafficking.

"Interesting," said Eron. "Commander Kole, would you like to fill us in?"

Hell no.

"Sure. We're assisting healers in the search for Blood Coven descendants."

"Have they met with success?" asked High Justice Aras.

He was the male to target the meat of a conversation. "Some," said Kole. "Of course, it's Alarik's ministry who has more intel on the subject. We are just the ride-along muscle." He strove to be accurate but limited his comments as Cadmon suggested.

Dolph tilted his chin in the haughty manner he pulled off so well. "How is the sweep for sex slaves going, Commander Jarek?"

"We have checked out all the captives named by the satyr guard caught in the raid on Aisen's Stockade. We found six dead. We erased the memories of the live ones, if it's what they wanted. Some actually joined the Alliance when they found out about their heritage. We arranged the contact. Now we're operating on rumor. We rescued a male from a succubus when a neighbor turned her in. Recently, we raided a berserker's place only to find a human female had escaped. We located her nearly boots-up in a cave but nursed her back to health."

"Commander, when your warriors tackled the recent New Orleans' problems, I understand you uncovered an interesting problem with Earthers. Explain." Ares fixed his sharp gaze on Kole.

"Correct. Humans are aware of several portal sites in New Orleans. They killed an incubus, attacked two young demons, and kidnapped a pair of vampires by using tranquilizer-loaded bullets. The male is Lawgiver Viktor's scion. They call themselves Humans First. Stranger yet, they're injecting their soldiers with a drug which makes them stronger."

"Is this related to Arisen Dawn or Cerberus?" asked the demoness justice.

"Doubtful. A man calling himself Dante, likely an alias, organized these humans. This isn't the first time we've heard this name. Uwrick, the warlock whose spell trapped the Alliance's chief legal officer and me on Darque, offered up the name when he was captured."

"Organized humans who are aware of our existence," said Eron, as she glanced at Dolph. "What do you plan to do?"

"We are set to raid a Humans First lab to rescue two kidnapped vampires. Our information comes from a prisoner in the Cubes." Kole checked the time on his D-chip.

Gilda, her eyes swirling with silver and green, bent forward on her elbows. "Do our portals remain impenetrable?"

Cadmon answered. "Minister Alarik claims they are strong, but as you know, a male known only as Cerberus hunts for descendants of the mages who created them."

Aras squinted. "Is this mystery male, Cerberus, connected to Arisen Dawn?"

Kole shifted nervously. He had asked himself the same question. "Why do you ask?"

The shifter steepled his fingers. "My eagle senses things. Too many coincidences."

Kole agreed. Too many. "Your guess is as good as mine, High Justice."

"Tell us about these Blood Coven descendants, Cadmon," said Dolph.

The high commander paused. "I am happy to report they are safe."

Aras cocked his head to the side, studying the

speaker with his sharp-sighted eyes. His lips curled slightly at the corners.

"How many do you have?" asked Eron.

Cadmon counted on his fingers. "Let me see." Pause. "Six."

"And where are they now?" The djinn Roshan kept his gaze on the paperwork in front of him.

Bang. Bang.

Aras pounded a gavel. "High Commander Cadmon has assured us they are safe. That is all we need to know. You are dismissed. Justice and long life."

Back in the antechamber before each commander returned to his own office, Cadmon touched Kole's arm. "Put extra wards on your stronghold as soon as possible. Jarek, keep your female well-guarded."

Before the djinn could object to the high commander's description of Lizette as his, Cadmon raised his hand to continue. "We've got Cerberus in the shadows on Scath with this Dante playing center stage Earthside. I trust no one but Firebrands."

****

After his visit to the Temple of Justice, Kole removed his stiff purple robe. Comfortable in BDUs and a clean tee, he leaned over the table to study a sketch. The prisoner Steven, Denim's ex, had drawn a layout of the Humans First facility. He claimed the two vampires were kept there in a lab.

Rein scrubbed a fist over his short military cut hair. "It's a simple floor plan. Three main hallways. Four teams. We should be in and out in minutes." Rein spread his fingers on the table. "He gave us the location. It's a warehouse in a deserted complex. We have a portal nearby. If it's dark, we should have no problem."

"How many soldiers at this Humans First place?"

"The facility is not large. He's never seen more

than twenty-five on site at one time. Some are soldiers. Some work in the labs."

"Can we believe him?"

"We brought in a gaffer who senses lies. He listened in and saw no problem. Of course, we can't be sure how much Denim's ex really knows about the headquarters. Maybe shit has changed since he was captured. Maybe he wasn't on site often enough to know the complete story. Maybe he only saw what they wanted him to see."

"We go before first light. Put me in a group. What's the plan?" Rein's growl pissed Kole off. "Don't even think about my staying here behind a desk."

"No way. I was thinking about using you as my shield. You can take the bullets. Brae gets cranky when I'm shot up. You've never seen her mean side."

"Smartass."

"You wanna lead a team?"

"No. I don't have time to prep with the group."

"I figure Ram's team deserves to free the vamps. Him, Thorn, Galena, and Denim will take this hall with the labs. Our prisoner says the Aeternals are kept there in cages or laid out on slabs for examination."

Rein tapped the sketch. "He says mostly scientists, their assistants, and a few guards hang out in those rooms. I'm assigning Jezzi outside in front with our two newbies. Sig and Bade. Good training. They'll keep unwelcome visitors out."

He dragged a finger along two other hallways. "A lot of the action will be here and here. The left corridor is where the offices and gym are. Dax and team will take it. I expect activity in this back hallway. Dining hall and quarters. I'll lead the group into this area. You're with me."

"Sounds good." Kole memorized the floor plan.

"It's the ifs and maybes I worry about, Rein." He strode to his desk chair. It squeaked when he parked his big body in it.

"Have you considered Skyler scrying? A fast look-see."

"Are you fucking out of your mind? She's pregnant. If I had my way, she wouldn't even use a portal. Unfortunately, it seems what I think is irrelevant."

Rein grabbed a chair and propped his shitkickers on Kole's desk. "If I didn't live with an equally stubborn female, I might feel sorry for you. What's the word from the warlock Sabine and Abello found at the Arisen Dawn warehouse?"

"He's a weak link. New to the organization. Still an outsider. Seems they wanted him to take a drug to make him more gung-ho. He declined, saying he wanted out. Might be the same shit Tyr and Dax have seen up close and live. Nasty stuff."

Kole shuffled through papers on his desk, picking up a note. "Gold Dust. They found a coyote shifter strung out on the stuff, half-shifted, and ranting about world domination."

****

Sabine side-by-sided it with Nico on one of the new sofas in the gathering room at the stronghold, his boots and her sandals propped on what was now called Margo's huge-ass coffee table. She'd changed from her all-business Firebrand garb into a rare dress.

Nico licked his lips as if he was hungry for more than just dinner. "We have time to go back upstairs, sweetness."

"No. We don't. Margo said dinner promptly at eight o'clock. She and Skyler have gone to a lot of trouble. Your coven will be here. Jarek's even bringing Lizette."

"This whole coven thing is still new to me. Not feeling the love yet. I'd rather be upstairs with you." He palmed her thigh, inching her dress up.

Sabine laughed. "After dinner. But we'll have to be quick, cuddles. Rein says we're outta here before sunrise." Her hand clasped his to stop the action.

"Quick's my middle name." Nico squirmed in his seat, looking like he was struggling with a thought.

He'd been acting strange, more silent than usual, since they'd made passionate love in one of the rooms in his upstairs apartment. No. Two of the rooms.

"Spit it out." Sabine expected him to say something like, "We should slow it down. Maybe see other people." She held her breath, waiting for the emotional blow. When she could wait no longer, she said, "We're moving too fast, right?"

His dark brows pulled down tight. "What? Fast? No. We've been jerking each other around for months. I think you should move into the stronghold. You know. Permanently."

What a surprise. Shock more like it.

How to respond? Keep it light until I'm sure.

"Really? Do they have an extra room here for me?"

He brushed a stray lock of hair off his forehead. "No. With me. Unless of course you don't want to." His gaze shot to the floor.

"What's my incentive?"

When his head bobbed up, a smile tugged his lips. "All this, sweetness." A wave of his hands indicated his huge, muscular, sexy body.

"What if I need more, cuddles?"

"More than this? Impossible."

Sabine got serious. "Not everything's about sex, Nico."

The usual stray lock of hair fell over his eye. Persistent. "This coming from a nymph? I'm shocked. What more do you need?"

She combed it back with her fingers. "Words."

"Like nouns, verbs, adjectives? You need words?"

"As a matter of fact, I do." Sabine locked her fists in her lap so he wouldn't see her tremble.

Nico swung his feet off the table, twisted toward her, and took her hands in his. "Okay. Here they are. I hope I don't fuck up what I want to say. You're smart, you're a great fighter, and you're beautiful. I think about you from the minute I wake in the morning until I go to bed at night. There. I've used the words."

"Not the right ones."

"Damn, sweetness, you're tough."

Sabine arched a brow, Nico still holding onto her.

"I love you, Sabine. I have for some time, but I have a fucking crazy way of showing it. I will always love you. You're it for me."

"It's always bothered you that I'm stronger than you."

His lips curled high on one side. "Here's the thing, sweetness, you may not be tougher than I am since I got my warlock on. But if you are, great. I want you to be powerful enough to protect yourself. Hell, you'll have my back while I'll have yours."

She released a loud sigh. "That wasn't so hard, was it? I love you, too." She leaned in and kissed him, hot, deep, lots of tongue, pouring her feelings into it.

Of course, Nico being Nico, he highjacked the kiss, palming her breast and squeezing. When they broke apart, he grinned from ear to ear. "Great. Now what about moving in with me? I'm neat. I don't snore. I am a horny bastard when you're around. So you can expect to get jumped regularly. Often."

"All pluses. I will move in. Maybe one drawback."

"What?"

"My father will want to meet you."

Nico held a palm high as he stiff-spined his posture. "Whoa. I'm not good with parents."

"How many have you met?" Sabine caught her breath, a stab of jealousy to her heart.

"None."

"To be clear, there'll be no other females like the one you propositioned at the Shed."

"I told you, sweetness. I was drunk. I was pissed. I was stupid. I took her as far as the door outside a room and stopped. She wasn't you. I apologized. Walked her back. There won't be a repeat. Ever."

Sabine nodded, her lips clenched tight. "Back to my father. I'm afraid he'll insist on meeting you. And I'm not keeping our relationship a secret. Either we are open or I'm outta here."

Nico's arm came around Sabine as he hugged her to his chest. "I always knew when I fell in love I'd be a forever kind of guy. I'm in this for the long haul. I want everyone to know I was lucky enough to snag you. My stud creds will skyrocket. Other males will spit green when they see you on my arm."

"I believe in forever with you, Nico." She snuggled into his bulky, solid pecs.

"I'll meet the dad. How bad can it be?"

"Not so bad."

Such a lie.

Her ex-Firebrand warlock father was a terror when it came to Sabine and males. No one had ever been good enough. She had left home a century ago, but he still kept close tabs on her. She had to be the only nymph on Scath who was required to justify her hook-ups to her father. At her age. *Who did you see tonight? I've heard about him. No good. You need someone solid.* Those were his usual responses. Of course, she didn't pay attention to him. If she had, she'd be cloistered in a nymph nunnery.

If she didn't see him weekly, he phoned. Nothing slipped by him either. She suspected he used truth spells on her.

Once, he told her she would always be his baby, no matter how old, how strong, or how independent. He loved her as much today as he had when she was young, when he had bandaged every scrape, wiped away every tear, and taught her how to fight.

"Actually, he's a lot like you."

One of Nico's hands popped into the air. "Holy shit. He's gonna cut off my balls."

Margo and the other descendants, in the throes of remodeling the stronghold, had purchased an iron-based lamp. It sat on a side table in the gathering room. Well, it had. Suddenly, it shot across the room, landing in Nico's quick grasp. He returned it to its spot.

"I gotta work on this magnetism thing." When he resumed sitting beside Sabine, he lifted her chin with his finger and took her lips in a passionate, invasive, toe-curling kiss.

Somebody yelled out, "Dinner" and feet thudded in from the game room and down the stairs. It was about to get crowded. Everyone was here for a meal before the big raid on the lab early tomorrow morning.

Chapter Twenty-Six

Before sunrise, the armory buzzed with activity. Firebrands Denim didn't even recognize loaded up with weapons. A knife here. An axe there. A sheathed sword. A gun slipped into a holster. The warriors were prepping for the kill. She yanked out her Glock to re-check the magazine.

Yep. Full.

Over two hundred muscled pounds of gorgeous satyr planted his chest directly in her line of sight, tucking his fingers under the strap of her cross-chest blade holster. He tugged on it. Then he jerked on the scabbard at her spine.

"Do I pass inspection, Ram? Again?"

"Is your Glock loaded?"

"No. I thought I'd try it without them. Of course it is. Just like it was the last two times you kicked my tires."

She must be a bullet shy of a full chamber. Ram's over-protective behavior wasn't irritating anymore. She loved that he cared. In fact, she loved...

Oh no. Don't go there.

Did she use the *L* word? Even in her head it was crazy. *But yes.* She was in love with this gorgeous-but-dangerous satyr with his body of hard muscles. The sexy caramel-streaked hair flowing down his back like a river didn't hurt.

"Sorry, doll. I respect your skills. It's my problem. I own it."

"I get it. I do, but knock it off, *cher.*" She stroked his arm, feeling all those corded knots bunching under her fingers.

He nodded. "K. Good to go. Stay safe."

She motioned for him to bend toward her. When he did, she touched her forehead to his. "You, too."

"Always. Safe is my go-to space." He grinned.

Her heart skipped a beat. "I…"

"What?"

"Nothing. It can wait."

She couldn't drop the *L* bomb on him here. Now. Besides, how long had she known Ram? Not long. He'd freak. After all, he'd warned her he wasn't a keeper. Still, she'd fallen in head over ass for a man who was unavailable.

Can I say 'broken heart'? Yeah. Shattered. Crushed. Stomped on. Cracked in two.

Thoughts of love faded when Rein thundered into the hall, dropping orders on the fly. "When you exit the portal, go low. Prepare to take fire. They're looking for captives. So stay away from those pellets. If one of us falls, bring the warrior home. Once we enter, follow your team leader. You know your jobs."

Kole entered behind the vamp-mix Firebrand. Armed, he leaned against the wall, letting Rein take the lead. The gazes eventually fixed on him. "I'm only a warrior along for the ride."

"What about the supposed antidote?" asked Jezzi.

Rein smirked. "Alarik said it would kill us. He claims the sedative bullets are safer than the cure."

"Play dodge 'em when the ammo flies your way." Rein adjusted his chest harness filled with three long-bladed US Marine Raider Stilettos. "If we find no resistance at the portal, we double-time it to the warehouse lab. A reminder. Dax's team goes left, mopping up the gym and offices. Mine charges along the same hall but heads to the mess and the bunks at the rear of the building. Ram's team sweeps right, taking the hallway with the labs and shipping room. Jezzi, your group holds the perimeter, particularly the front door. Don't let any surprises inside. What's the goal?"

In unison, the Firebrands recited the mission objective. "We snatch the vamps. We kill anyone who gets in our way."

Rein's lips curled, his fangs sharp, visible points. "Damn straight. Gear checked?"

Nods all around.

"Abello, Denim, you get how the D-chips work? No verbal comm. Chatter's in here." Rein tapped his head.

Denim locked eyes with Nico. "We've practiced. Good to go."

The vampire shouted, "For duty."

His words were met with another shout. "For honor."

Along with the others, Denim touched her wrist, floating, dipping, spinning through the Whorl. The ride was a bigger thrill than the pre-Katrina Mega Zeph at the old Six Flags. Besides, she was going into battle. The excitement rocketed through her.

Unlike portal jumpers, which allowed no more than five to use a gateway at once, the Firebrands' D-chips got them all through.

Stepping out of the portal, she dropped into a crouch. No opposition in sight. Ram landed in front of her. He nodded at his group. They raced toward the lab.

Ram signaled for the action to begin. Thorn put his shifter strength to work on the door, breaking the lock. He swung it open. The satyr barreled through, Thorn, Galena, and her on his ass. They broke right, charging along the hallway toward their destination, each room with multiple doors. One opened to the hall. Another connected the rooms. They expected the young vampires to be in a lab.

No problem. A short distance to the corridor on the right. Denim heard the other teams of Firebrands move into position. Still no opposition. They passed the shipping room along with the first two labs.

The strategy was to hit the farthest target initially, sweeping back toward the entrance after they cleared each lab. Too quiet. The only noise was the muffled thud of their boots on the concrete.

Ram glanced over his shoulder at his team, his brows slammed tight, gun out when they neared their first objective. The far lab.

A man popped out of the doorway. He pierced the silence, sending a bullet whizzing by Denim's ear. Headfirst, sliding on her belly, she dove into an alcove formed by another entry door. Shooting upright, she scanned for Ram. He must have cloaked himself in his satyr mist.

Thorn sped to shelter with Denim while Galena hustled to a space further down the hall. Team members accounted for.

Ping. Ping.

Bullets smashed into the wall near the Amazon.

Damn. Denim heard Galena's words as clear as if she was standing beside her. *I'm eating paint chips. I think this is real ammo. Not the tranqs.*

Ram was the Firebrand who replied. *Don't take a chance.*

Now the ammo was flying. Denim peeked around the corner, ducking back when shots pelted the metal frame. She turned to Thorn, at the last minute remembering not to speak aloud. *Shit. That guy's got us stuck here.*

Ping. Ping. Ping.

Wait, Denim. Fate rewards those who are patient.

She tapped her D-chip. *What are you now? A*

guru?

He gave her a wolfy grin. A barrage continued to ding the metal near their hidey-hole.

Where is Ram? How long can he cloak?

Wait for it. Thorn prepared to shoot around the corner of their spot. He didn't get a bullet off before she heard a grunt followed by a *thud.* Sounded like a body dropping.

Denim tapped her chip. *Way to go, satyr. Check off a shooter. Possibly more in the labs.*

With the obstacle removed, Galena, Denim, and Thorn darted into the lab after Ram, zigzagging to avoid potshots from guys who sprang from behind turned-over lab tables.

Missing their targets, the humans scurried through a connecting door to the next room.

Denim plastered herself against the wall. She peeked through the side exit. A hail of bullets sent her scrambling backward.

Cover me. Thorn charged through the doorway to crouch behind a metal cabinet.

Galena and Denim both fired in rapid succession.

I'm hit. The Amazon slapped a hand to her upper arm. *Only a flesh wound. Not drowsy. Real bullet. Not a tranq.*

Ram uncloaked to take out a human while Thorn's gun sprayed ammo, giving Denim time to race into the lab where she turned over a stainless-steel gurney. She spotted three guys firing. *Shit. Sorry. Unnecessary chatter.*

"Amazon, on your ass." Denim forgot her D-chip, shouting her warning.

A man charged out of hiding to end-run Galena, but she drew her axe, whipping her arm overhead, launching the weapon into his chest. DOA.

A guy's head popped up like a jack-in-the-box behind a tipped metal bed.

Ping. Ping.

He was aiming for Thorn.

Denim didn't have a clear target until the shooter jumped up again. She fired. A hole between his eyes oozed red.

Ram flanked the humans. He had two guns blazing. Wyatt Earp and Doc Holiday, move over. Knocking a table onto its side, he avoided painting a bullseye on his forehead.

Galena winged a guy who squealed like a cat with a stomped-on tail.

Ping. Ping. Ping. Ping.

Bullets sprayed the area where the satyr hid while he fired off a few more rounds at the humans. Then he cloaked, reappearing behind a shooter. A shot to the head. Dead guy on the floor.

"It's him," shouted a Humans First soldier. "I recognize him from the drawing. Big money for tapping the satyr."

Thorn darted forward, discharging bullets when he ran, but the humans ignored him to fire on Ram.

The action was aimed at her satyr.

When several of the shooters hightailed it into the next lab, Ram took off in pursuit.

Is he crazy? Denim eyed the door he had raced through.

Yes. He is. Galena duck-walked to a counter nearer Denim. *Let's go.*

When Denim charged into the room, Ram was behind an overturned table, leaning out into the open to fire. This larger lab was loaded with shooters, more than the three guys who'd just run in. They targeted Ram, bullets spraying his cover like a meteor storm.

Galena moved in closer to a Humans First guy, taking him out with a pop-pop to the chest. Thorn felled another.

Still, the guns pointed at Ram. They sacrificed men to keep the heat on the satyr. It made no sense. And how the hell did they claim to recognize him?

Denim laid down fire. She lifted a foot to take off in Ram's direction. When Galena grabbed her arm to try to stop her, she threw an elbow to her friend's chin, shrugging off the Amazon's hold. Denim darted from one shelter to another until she crouched alongside Ram.

His scowl had no effect on her. Together they fired at the attackers while she muttered, "Why the hell do they want you?"

A lucky shot grazed her arm. She collapsed to the floor, unable to move, paralyzed. When a shooter who moved into the open had a bead on Denim, Ram threw himself over her, protecting her with his body.

But he took one to the back because of his stupid save. A different soldier fired. Ram clutched his leg. Another bullet hit his shoulder. He buckled and fell to his ass. He was stiller than Denim, silent.

While she was woozy from the sedative-laced through-and-through, bad guys cropped up to drag Ram out the connecting door toward shipping.

The remaining shooters held down Thorn and Galena, spraying ammo to cover the escape.

Denim was useless while her *frerons* were hamstrung by a barrage of gunfire.

Though she was out of ammo, her arm flopped uselessly at her side when she tried to grab another magazine. No go.

Ducking heavy fire, Galena and the shifter braved the tranq bullets to charge the shooters. Some ran. Some dropped to the ground. Dead. The Amazon took out two soldiers as Thorn raced after the satyr.

Denim shook her hands, regaining a little feeling. She stumbled to her feet to follow the shifter, limping after him. Thorn was in the middle of the empty shipping room. The rear slide-up door was open, the loading dock deserted.

When Galena joined them, she and Thorn raced out and down the ramp. Denim bumble-footed after them, still in a haze. Outside, Jezzi, Bade, and Sig faced them with weapons drawn.

When they spied Galena, the Firebrands dropped their arms to the side.

"See anybody?" asked Denim, blinking her foggy eyes.

"Nobody." Jezzi's sleek dark hair flipped from side to side.

Tires squealed.

Denim, Thorn, Galena, and Jezzi jerked toward the sound. Their targets raced out of an adjoining warehouse in a black SUV. Ram had to be with them.

"Another exit." Thorn threw back his head and roared, his wolf surfacing, claws popping from his fingertips. "Where the fuck did it come from?"

Sig, one of the new Firebrand recruits, raced out of the shipping room. "There's a hidden door behind a cabinet in there. It leads down some steps to a tunnel. A garage at the end."

Lightning shot from Denim's hand, cracking the concrete at her feet. A fierce wind kicked up, so strong the Firebrands struggled to stand upright. Thunder clashed. Thor himself couldn't have spoken louder.

Kole and Rein rushed to her side.

Containing the storm she created, Denim pointed toward the road. "They've got Ram."

"Jezzi. Thorn. Shift. Follow the scent." Kole

tapped his wrist. When he disconnected, he explained he had asked Logan to do a GPS trace on Ram's D-chip. Fire shot from his fingers. "Tyr. Rein. Do your shit."

A cool breeze ruffled Denim's hair when the males raised their arms, palms out. Swirling dirt traveled along the same road as their spells. They remained still for some time, eyes closed.

When the panther and wolf returned, Thorn took to two legs and shook his head. "Sorry. After a while, a car mutes the scent too much."

Denim sensed lightning building in her toes, moving upward, and trying to exit through her hands. She controlled it. The two warlocks dropped their arms and faced her. "Sorry," said Rein. "We lost them a few miles away. Tyr and I will portal there. See what's what."

She ran a palm over her hair. "Please."

He and Tyr touched their wrists and disappeared. They threw their own gateway, something Denim had not learned to do yet. Ram had told her it was used in emergencies only, too draining on a D-chip. This was an emergency.

Kole clenched his jaw, grinding his teeth while his demon flickered. He tapped his wrist. "Logan says the satyr's chip is inactive. As if they took it out of commission. What happened in there?" Kole growled, tapping his fiery hands together.

Rapid words fell from Galena's mouth. "The humans tranqed Ram. They dragged him out through a hidden tunnel before we could reach him. It led to a garage. A car musta been waiting."

Kole listened, his fire-gold eyes set on the road the SUV had traveled.

"They targeted Ram." Denim took a deep breath to keep from choking up, still unsteady on her feet.

"They recognized him. I heard them talking. Some picture they'd seen."

Dax's team came out of the raided warehouse. "We've swept the place. Only dead bodies left now. Looks like they were packing to leave before we arrived."

"They wanted Ram." Denim's palms were sweaty and her breathing shallow as she waited for the two warlocks to return with good news.

Tyr and Rein materialized from a temporary gateway alongside Kole.

The young warlock Firebrand crossed his arms as the glow from a streetlight bounced off his piercings. "We got there. It was an airfield. The SUV was abandoned. We couldn't get a fix because they probably took to the air. Likely in a chopper."

"I agree." Rein's eyes flashed arctic blue.

"Damn satyr. Always trying to protect me." Denim clenched her fists, wanting to hit something as lightning crackled and clouds rushed in with a fierce wind.

Galena stepped behind Denim, stroking her arms, gentling her, calming the storms. "We still have our prisoner, your ex. He might have some idea where they'd take our Ram."

Denim nodded, her shoulders slumping, her emotions as scattered as the stormy weather she'd created. She should have told Ram she loved him.

What about Jonquil?

She would check on her. "Now what?"

Kole shot a stream of fire, blackening the concrete at his feet. "Now we bring our warrior home. Mark me. We will get him back."

****

While Lizette piled Jarek's plate high with eggs,

bacon, and buttered toast, her eyes sparked with anger. She slammed his breakfast onto the kitchen table. "What gives you the right to tell me what I want?"

The djinn's calm demeanor was frustrating. Unnatural. Despite his size and savage power, she itched to shake him until he displayed some reaction. Anything. Anger. Hatred. He was always so rational.

"I am telling you that killing a being, even a sadistic asshole, is a hard thing to do." Jarek cut his eggs with the side of his fork, slipping a bite into his mouth. "Delicious."

"Thanks. I'm telling you I want Spear to die. Do you need jelly for the toast?"

Damn. He's got me doing it.

Lizette was still living in Jarek's yurt. In his bed. When he told her he had readied her own quarters, she refused to go. She was being unfair, but she felt safe with him.

"No thanks. He will. It is my promise." He sipped his black coffee.

"I want a hand in it." Lizette flopped into the chair across from the djinn commander.

"And we are right back where we started."

Finally, a reaction. The feral slant to his lips would have deterred most warriors from arguing. Not Lizette. He didn't scare her one bit. She'd seen a real monster.

"Killing in cold blood is hard, *atashe delam*." His sexy mouth curled around another bite of egg.

Lizette shook her head to erase a vision of the commander kissing her with the same mouth. How could she even think about a sexual act after what she had been through with Spear?

"Obviously, you haven't met many New Yorkers. We survive everything. Subway and garbage strikes.

Cabbies who try to run over us. The worst disaster of all times, 9-11. We're strong. We're resilient. We're bloodthirsty. I want him to die painfully. Slowly. Death by a thousand cuts."

"Aah. Lingchi. A respected Chinese method used as capital punishment. It is a cruel death."

"I want to be cruel. You know what he did to me. How can you deny me my revenge?"

"I do not deny you revenge, but allow me to be your blade." He motioned toward the refrigerator. "I will have some of the jam. I shall hunt him and kill him."

Lizette's lips curled into a sarcastic grin when she rose to fetch his strawberry jam, slamming it onto the table in front of the infuriating man. "While I appreciate the alpha male wanting to take care of the little woman, it won't happen. I will be with you. I will exact my own revenge. By my own hand."

"We have been through this, *atashe delam*. Murder served cold destroys your soul. I shall not allow that to become your destiny. Have you already eaten breakfast?"

"Yes. I awakened early. You are not in charge of my soul. I am. I need to do this. To move on with my life. You may help me hunt Spear down, but I will hold the blade of justice. Accept it. Are you finished?"

Only one brow arched. "Yes. It was delicious. Thank you."

Yes. Frustrating.

"You didn't send someone else after Hassem, did you? How can you expect less from me?" Lizette cleared his plate, pleased with her final response on the matter.

****

The housekeeper leaned close to whisper in Dante's ear. "Guv, the phone in your study keeps ringin.' Some bloke must be miffed."

"Thanks." Dante dabbed his lips with his napkin. He excused himself from his four dinner guests, walking unhurriedly to his office.

He sat in the leather wing-back chair beside the two phones. Only Cerberus had the number to one. Only Mars had the number to the other. Whoever it was would keep calling until they reached him. He waited only a few moments before a landline rang again.

"Yes."

"Dante, it's Mars. I have news. The two vampires are settled into our new facility. They're ready for your interrogation. I assume you want to be in on it?"

"I bloody well do wish to be there."

"The better news is, I possess a satyr. The right one, by the looks of him."

Dante's heart pounded against his chest. Words caught in his throat, refusing to come out.

"How long until I can expect you?"

Dante looked at his watch. "I will leave early tomorrow morning. Figure thirteen to fourteen hours thereafter."

"I'll soften them up first."

Dante was aware the injections which gave his men greater power had side effects. Those impacts grew worse if a shot was missed. A soldier who had neglected to get his regular dose attacked and killed another for no reason. He would not allow Mars to unleash his aggression on their captives. "Under no circumstances should the vampires or the satyr be impaired when I arrive."

"Understood. Do you need my assistance to get here?"

"No. Everything has been pre-arranged. Are my quarters ready in the new base of operations?"

"Yes."

After Dante disconnected, he phoned his chauffeur. "Prepare my jet for an eleven-hour trip. I'll tell the pilots where when I arrive. They should plan to wait for an undetermined amount of time at our destination. Pick me up at five in the morning."

Disconnecting from the call, he punched in a number in New Orleans. When the phone was answered, he said, "This is Dante. Be at my hangar before four in the evening. You may have a one-hour wait or longer. I require a ride."

"Yes, sir."

The Englishman grasped the photo of his daughter, running his thumb across her face. "It has begun, my lovely. Finally, I will avenge your death." Tears escaped his eyes.

Chapter Twenty-Seven

Miller looked over his notes, memorized the names, and took out a lighter, setting the paper on fire. When his fingers nearly burned, he dropped the ashes to the ground where he spread them out with his boot.

Time to call, he thought, dialing the number he had for Braelyn James.

"Greetings, luv. This is your favorite member of Her Majesty's Royal whatever."

"Miller. What's new?"

"So far, I've got five names for you, but let's review the agreement. I give you what I know. With all that out of the way, I will have passed my test. If you have them or know their whereabouts, you inform me. I tell my guys to scratch them off their watch lists."

"If I can verify the names you give me, I will tell you who we have."

Miller sighed. The usually chipper Braelyn sounded down. "Something wrong, luv?"

"Nothing concerning you."

"Okay. Let's meet."

"Name it. When and where. Remember, where I go so goes Rein."

"Yeah. Yeah. Bring the steroid-dosed bloke. I'm in St. Louis. Can you meet in two hours at Mama's on the Hill? I'm hankering for Italian."

He heard Braelyn chit-chatting, the sound muffled as if her hand cupped the receiver.

"We'll be there unless Rein gets called to duty."

To kill time, Miller wagged off by walking the streets for an hour. Centuries had passed since the forming of *Custodes Templii*. They had one job. To track and protect the descendants of the Blood Coven while they waited for the bad part of the prophecy to kick in. At least, it was the Kool-Aid they'd been sold. Why on his watch? Still, the action made life knees up. And he wasn't one to ignore a little excitement.

Traveling from city to city, Miller not only stayed one step ahead of Cerberus but he tracked his own bloodline, looking for those who might be missing. So far, everyone was in place.

Ten minutes before the meeting, he walked through the door of Mama's, choosing a table in the shadows. With his back to the wall, he eyeballed the door. After about five minutes, the beautiful Braelyn walked in, tucking her sunglasses into her shirt, hand-in-hand with the huge, cold Firebrand. Miller could do without the bodyguard. Did she say mate? Anyway, he wouldn't mind some one-on-one time with the lady. Not happening with the big bastard glued to her side. Besides, he wasn't into poaching.

As his visitors approached, he kicked out two chairs.

Rein waited for Braelyn to sit, his eyes prowling the restaurant. When he took a chair, he glared at Miller. "You slipped out on us last time, mutherfucker."

"Sorry about that, mate. It was necessary."

"I'm not your mate, asshole."

"What's good here?" Braelyn was probably trying to tamp down the testosterone.

"Toasted raviolis, luv."

"She's not your love." The Firebrand's arctic-blue eyes were as icy as his frown.

All talking stopped while the waitress took their orders. When she walked away, Braelyn opened the chat. "Let's focus on our common problem. What names can you give us, Miller?"

He jotted the names on a napkin, sliding it to

Braelyn.

Rein twisted toward his mate, his nod almost non-existent.

"Skyler Maxwell and Margo Hunter are with us," she said. "We don't know the other three."

Miller scrubbed a hand across his chin. "I'll let my guys know to stop worrying about Skyler and Margo. There's my *bona fides*. Now tell me who you have safely stored so I can tell my trackers to mark them off. I'll let you know who else pops up as missing. My people are still checking. Then you can see if this Cerberus might have them."

"We can help you protect your charges," said Rein.

"While I'm chuffed as hell about that, here's the thing. First off. We have thousands on our watch lists. Second. No. You can't. Each of my trackers manages one bloodline. Nobody else knows the names on another bloke's list. It's very hush-hush."

The waitress returned with a bottle of Chianti along with three glasses. When she left, Miller said, "Changing the procedure will take discussion and time."

"Here are the people who are with us. You can tell your guys they are safe." Braelyn took a piece of paper out of her pocket, wrote down names, and handed it to Miller. "You must contact us immediately if anyone else is missing."

"We'll continue the chit-chat. You have my word." Miller studied the list, got out his lighter, and turned the sheet to ashes, both Braelyn and Rein arching their brows. "Good memory."

After the waitress brought them each toasted ravioli, they dug in. Between bites, Braelyn asked, "So, you guys live to check on Blood Coven descendants?"

"Right-o."

"What about money?" Rein swallowed a large gulp of wine.

"We've got it handled. Course, I discovered a few necessary tweaks when I had to run. I'm good for now. May need to hit you up later."

Braelyn chewed on her bite of ravioli, closing her eyes as if savoring the dish. "Must get boring."

"Not really. Lots of travel."

"How did you come to be?" She set down her fork.

"After the Schism, *Custodes Templii* organized. The names, the job, the duty passed from tracker to tracker. That's the way it's been."

"Doesn't answer why." Braelyn sipped her Chianti.

"Because this day was predicted nearly fifteen hundred years ago by the Cambion from Wales who created our group."

****

On the front porch of Ram's farmhouse, Denim rang the doorbell, shifting nervously from foot to foot. She wanted to go to bed, to hide her head under the covers until Ram returned. Or she wanted to go on a killing spree until she found him. Neither avenue was open to her nor productive. Instead, she was here, about to break a little girl's heart while the Firebrands interrogated Steven again.

The door swung wide open. Jonquil greeted her with an inviting smile, as sunny as her namesake.

"Hi, kid." Denim swallowed hard.

The girl grabbed her hand, bouncing toward the kitchen as if she had a prize in tow. "Come meet Mara. She's my demon nanny. Not that I really need one. Daddy is overprotective. It's a Firebrand thing."

"Of course." What should she tell Mara and

Jonquil? She didn't want to lie, but she didn't want to scare them either.

"Mara, this is Denim. She's Daddy's girlfriend."

Denim cocked her head at Jonquil. "That might be an exaggeration."

Mara dusted flour from her hands, brushing aside a lock of hair. "Nice to meet ya."

"The same."

The nanny was a tall, curvaceous Scath version of Sophia Loren.

Great. Ram has his own food stash right at home.

Mara returned to her task. "Join us. I was finishing with the biscuits for dinner. A nice roast beef from Aerilon is in the oven. Potatoes and braised carrots are next. A pie for dessert. The satyr should be here in about an hour. Then I have to be somewhere tonight."

"What?" *Panic time.* Denim tried to keep her voice calm. "Can you hang around for the night? Ram kind of sent me with a message. Since his job got a little complicated today, he won't be home."

Mara did not glance away from the biscuits. "No. Usually I can when he gets detained but not this time. He knew it. This isn't like him."

Jonquil's little fists snapped to her hips. "Daddy promised me we'd do some fun things while he was off work."

Denim nodded. "Uh, I think this was unavoidable. A last-minute thing."

Mara punched a fist into the biscuit dough. "Humph. I'm going with my mate on a trip to Knife's Edge for a few days. Ram was going off rotation for the time. When will he get back?"

She has a mate. Good.

"Not sure. Tell ya what. After dinner, Jonquil, we'll pack a bag so you can head to my place tonight.

How about it? We'll watch movies, stuff ourselves with popcorn and candy, and rack up some coin with poker."

Clapping her hands together, Jonquil gave a little hop. "What's poker?"

"It's a card game every girl needs to learn. It's how you get cash from guys. I'll teach you. You'll be a natural."

Mara cast a curious gaze in Denim's direction but kept kneading biscuit dough, every so often wiping a wisp of hair off her face.

Volunteering for kitchen duty, Jonquil and Denim peeled tiny potatoes and sliced big chunks of carrots.

"Mara says I need to know about what I put in my stomach. She is very scientific about food. You know, vitamins or stuff."

When the nanny stepped out for a few minutes, the girl cupped her mouth with a hand, lowering her voice. "But I'd rather not eat carrots."

Denim lapped an arm over the Jonquil's shoulder. "I don't like them either. When I was quite young, I fed them to my dog under the table."

"I don't have a dog."

"In times like this, one would come in handy."

Mara returned to stand at the stove, lifting a cast iron lid in her hand, smelling the roast. She twisted her neck around as her vivid green irises met Denim's.

The nanny was a younger version of Marta. The same sharp gaze, knowing glances, keen perceptions.

Mara turned nonchalantly back to the pot. "Jonquil, while we wait, you go pack."

When the child skipped to her room, Mara set the spoon on the stove, tapping her foot on the floor as she asked her question. "Spill. What's really going on?"

Denim glanced toward the doorway, approaching the nanny to whisper. "Ram was grabbed in a raid."

She heard a gasp from the hall. "Daddy's in trouble?" Jonquil rounded the doorway, obviously spying on them.

Damn.

"Come here." Denim led the girl to a chair, pulling the other out for herself. With their knees touching, she took Jonquil's hands in hers.

"It's kind of like he got lost for a while, but his friends are going to find him. Right now, our job is to wait... Do you pray, Jonquil?"

"I'm a nymph. I make offerings to Gahya."

"Who is Gahya?"

"The Genitrix. Can we visit her? Her temple is here on the Isle."

"You'll have to tell me what to do."

"My grandmother makes me take fruits or vegetables."

Once she had prepped everything for dinner, Mara left to join her mate after exchanging numbers with Denim. She and Jonquil ate, forks clinking against plates and knives pinging the butter dish, but the mood was somber.

After clean-up, Denim peeked in the fridge. "You have apples, oranges, potatoes, carrots..." she called over her shoulder to Jonquil.

"No carrots."

"I agree."

After a portal ride, followed by a short walk, they carried a basket of goodies to a white-columned temple straight out of a Greek myth. Denim kneeled on the stone in front of Gahya's marble feet while Jonquil offered the basket of apples, oranges, potatoes, green beans, and zucchini to the goddess. Returning to kneel, her small hand searched for Denim's. They laced their fingers together, gathering warmth, comfort from each other.

Ram needed their help. If their prayers would get him home, if they would give Jonquil something to do to get her daddy back, Denim was all for chatting with a stone statue.

The child cast her eyes toward the cold goddess. She whispered prayers while Denim, who regretted not telling Ram she loved him, squeezed her lids together to offer her own pleas.

Whoever is listening. Bring Ram home. Please. Home to Jonquil. Home to me. I miss the warmth of his body, his cocky smile, his innuendos. Even his crass comments. Hell. I miss everything about him.

****

Jarek had met with Kole and Nace about the Covenkirk raid. He followed the meeting with another to prepare his warriors for the action to bring a Firebrand home.

It had been six days since Lizette had first awakened in Jarek's yurt. Most nights when he returned from a mission or his duties, she awaited him with drinks and a tray of food. Those had become his favorite times.

They stayed awake, discussing serious matters or nothing. Tonight, however, it was long past midnight. She was already asleep in his bed. No matter the hour, he checked on her before he retired to the spare room. He had offered her a place of her own, but she had refused. He was happy about her decision.

Watching her rest eased his mind, listening to her purrs, seeing her dark hair spread like silk on the pillow.

Sometimes she dreamed about her captivity. Asleep in his own room, he would awaken to her screams. At those times, his heart broke. He would rush to her side, shaking her, containing the terror. He would cradle her in his arms, murmuring to her in his old language.

Tonight's sleep was restful. He leaned back onto the scattered floor pillows. Stretching out his legs, he crossed one ankle over the other while dropping his head back to slumber. Although her dreams were pleasant, the memories of his own past disturbed his peace.

The young Jarek had no idea where his jailer kept the other three djinn who had been captured with him. He was in a lavish bedroom decked out in colorful rugs, pillows, and wall paintings. He was not chained. There was no need. He was too weak to be of any danger, even to the slightest human. He could barely drag himself to the chamber pot or the basin to wash. The door was locked. He had tried to open it.

Substantial meals appeared regularly. For breakfast, he was given a sweetened tea, bread, and yogurt. For lunch rice or lentils. Dinner was sometimes lamb or chicken with a vegetable like eggplant. Figs or dates when lucky.

He tried to keep his strength up, fighting the pitchblende. No matter how often he exercised or for how long, the weakness never left. At first, he thought those who entered his quarters carried the debilitating stone with them, but then he realized it must be in the room because it remained a constant drain on his energy.

Bit by bit, he began a systematic exploration.

His captor visited, a short man with a bulbous nose and well-fed stomach. He sat, leaning back on pillows, his pig-like eyes cast on Jarek.

"You'll bring in much money." He scratched his balls while he continued to leer. "Men and women alike will pay for your services."

Jarek rose, stumbling toward the door. He turned the handle, but it was still locked.

The man laughed. "I am not so stupid."

Jarek lunged for the male but could not wrap

fingers around his neck strongly enough to block air. Instead, when the human fell, he pushed the young djinn to the ground, straddled him, and stuck a hand into Jarek's pants, grabbing his cock.

"Ah. A fine member. Let's see if I can get it to respond?" He stroked the djinn rhythmically.

Jarek was a healthy young male with an active libido. Despite what he wanted to happen, he began to be aroused. He felt his shaft grow and stiffen in his jailer's hand. He fought the urge to thrust against the male's fingers.

"Oh, yes. You are a big one. I imagine you fantasize about a female, her sweet lips surrounding you, sucking on you. Her wet tongue licking up and down. Her teeth lightly grazing your dick. Yes, that's it. Pump into my hand. Let me help you release."

He squeezed Jarek until it almost hurt. Stroke. Stroke. The young djinn couldn't help himself. He froze and erupted, his seed spilling into the jailer's hand.

"Yes. You'll be most valuable."

When he left, Jarek rushed to the corner. He vomited, over and over until nothing was left in his stomach.

The next day, a veiled female entered. Two males accompanied her. One grabbed Jarek's arms. The other disrobed him.

The skinnier of the two looked his body over, licked his lips, and said, "My lady, should I ready him for you?"

"Thank you but no." She spoke quietly, almost demurely. She dropped her veil and stood in front of Jarek. Her hands began to explore. His chest, his biceps, his hips. Her fingers trailed along his abdomen, traveling to his manhood. It took very little for her to arouse him.

She pushed him back onto the bed and sat astride

him. She lifted just her skirts. With her hand, she guided Jarek's engorged shaft to her opening. She sank down on him and began to rock up and down. At first slowly. Then more quickly. She moaned, stroking his chest.

"Here," she said. "Fondle me here." The lady drew Jarek's fingers to her clitoris. "Play with it like a good boy."

When he did, she thrashed, screamed, and slapped Jarek's face until his teeth rattled. Then she stilled, slumped over his chest. She dismounted, patted her skirts down, and re-fastened her veil. She knocked on the door. When it opened, she exited.

The female returned many times.

He was always too weak to stop her. His member was always solid and alert, though. She wasn't the worst. Not by far. Other females visited. And males.

A grey-haired male came in with the same two guards who brought the lady in. "Hold him over those cushions," ordered the man. When they did, they pulled his pants down.

Jarek struggled despite being weakened by the pitchblende. He punched the fatter guard in the stomach, twisted around, and pulled up his pants. The skinnier guard clasped both arms behind his back while the male he had hit began to use his fists on his cheek and his jaw.

"Not the face," shouted the visiting male. "Don't ruin his face."

So, the guards threw punches to his gut. Eventually, they subdued him, dragging him back to the pillows where they once again pulled down his pants.

The man touched Jarek's ass, spreading his cheeks. He then took his cock and rammed into Jarek. He rutted, grunted, pounded until he stopped. The rest was a blur for the young djinn.

That's the moment Jarek changed.

No matter how much the stone drained him, whenever he had a visitor he fought back, hitting his guards, hitting his visitors, male or female. He didn't care.

Eventually, they chained him. When he resisted, they yanked the chain to control him.

After each visit, he emptied his stomach onto the floor in the corner. In time, he no longer did.

He made a lot of money for the pig-eyed man. Perhaps his visitors enjoyed his rebellious spirit. He didn't care what they liked at all.

One day he found the stone. Under a rug amongst other rocks. Now he had to get it out of his room. Afterward, he would kill them all. Afterward, he would find Hassem, who would wish for death.

Jarek turned most of his anger inward, however. He reserved his greatest hatred for himself. No matter how hard he fought, each time a female came in to use him, he became aroused. Despite his revulsion, when some of the males raped him, he found himself engorged with lust. So much so, he often had to relieve himself. If only he could control his own reaction, he could despise himself less.

When a guard was distracted, he buried the pitchblende in a stew he had not finished. The guard unwittingly removed it in his left-over dinner. He waited. He watched. He grew strong. When the time was right, he slayed all the guards, the pig-eyed owner, and any of the visitors he could find. He freed the three djinn who had been captured with him.

****

"It's time to talk again, luv."

"I didn't expect to hear from you so soon, Miller. Hold a sec," said Braelyn. She nodded to Rein, her hand muffling the mouthpiece. "Are you headed out?"

"Yeah. Gotta go. Call if he has important info."

Braelyn stood on her toes, clutching Rein's neck, brushing her lips across his. "Stay safe, vampire."

"This is just a little recon."

"You heard me." She nodded and returned to Miller. "I'm back. What's up?"

"I have a name for you. My contact heard from a tracker. He gave me a name which isn't on your list."

"Who is it?"

"Jace de Vries. She should be in New Paltz, New York where she works in a winery, but she hasn't been there for months. It's not like she would have skived off the job. One day she simply didn't show. The winery is a bit miffed."

"Did she make a habit of not showing for work?"

"My source said the winery claimed she was the ideal worker. Always on time, never out sick, hard worker, smart. Our tracker also went to her home. The place has been vacant for a while. Neighbors are worried. Apparently, she's always been the pleasant, sociable sort."

"We don't have her. I'll ask our IT guy to check out hospitals, blood tests, and all that stuff. See if she could have been found by Cerberus. If she's in those records, the news is doubly bad." She paused. "Before you go, I have a few more questions."

Miller cleared his throat. "Why not. I've got nothing else to do, luv."

"You know our bloodlines, right? Which mage we each came from?"

"I know the bloodlines. Sure."

"Do you know about me? Spill."

"Niviane. You're from Niviane. After the Schism, she and the Cambion apparently had a falling out. She married a human bloke and had a child. You're from her line."

"You said *Custodes Templii* formed right after the Schism?"

"Maybe fifty years or so."

"How does it work?"

"One descendant from each line is a tracker. Well, all lines except the Cambion's. He has no descendants. Strange. So, I'm not sure how a full coven can be assembled. Anyway, each tracker takes a solemn vow to watch those in their bloodline."

"What about when trackers die?"

"Amazing, huh? We each have multiple backups in case of an emergency or death. It has worked this way since the beginning."

"Are any of your charges missing?"

"I'm doing my rounds. Not an easy task since I'm also in hiding. So far, all are in place."

"Are your trackers safe?"

"Thanks to your info, they are. Those who think they might have exposed themselves through their medical records are hiding out also."

"Stay safe, Miller. I'd feel better if you'd come in and let us protect you."

"Look, luv, this is a dangerous game. I stay alive because I don't trust anyone. I've learned over the years to depend on myself. Ta ta."

"Call once a week or right away if you find out anyone else is missing. We could use all your records, Miller."

"I couldn't live without hearing your cheerful voice, luv. As far as the works, I'm going to have to mull that a bit. Cheerio."

Chapter Twenty-Eight

"You returned late. I tried to wait for you." It was early morning and Lizette sat in bed, her back against the headboard, her gaze on Jarek, who had fallen asleep nearby on the floor pillows.

He leaned forward, his eyes feasting on a sleep-rumpled Lizette.

"What were you dreaming about?" she asked.

"How do you know I dreamed?"

"You have tells."

"Revenge."

"You must share." She patted the bed beside her. Though she threw back the cover, Jarek put it back over her legs and crawled atop the hides. "What happened after you escaped?"

"I rejoined a djinn unit. I was older and stronger than ever. I trained every day in camp, always challenging the bigger, faster males. Sometimes I got my ass handed to me, but most often, I won. Eventually, I was the victor every time. Soon, no one accepted my challenge."

"Was the camp better than what you had before?"

Jarek threw back his head, his laughter a glorious deep sound. "Battle camps are not resorts. The general's tent was lined with the hides of conquered foes."

"But were you better off there?"

He propped his head in the palm, his elbow bent, his earnest gaze on Lizette. "Yes. My life was in my own hands. The camp djinn were rapists, murderers, and thieves, typical mercenaries, but the general required fair fights for dominance."

"What if you won your fight?"

"I had my choice of companions for the night."

"And when you lost?"

Jarek grinned, his smile breathtaking. "That was only early on."

"But?"

"The victor had his choice of me or some other companion to fuck."

Though Lizette hesitated, she asked anyway, her curiosity getting the better of her. "Were all companions male?"

"No. We had ample female camp followers."

"How did you avenge your enslavement?" Her eyes dropped, but her pulse sped up.

Thump. Thump. Thump.

"Hassem was with General Rashon by the time I escaped my slavery. They still fought the Ottomans. I stole into camp one night and injected Hassem with a sleep serum. I hauled him to a cave in France where I had prepped for his torture and death."

Lizette nodded, her fingers trailing along Jarek's naked chest. "I want the details."

He withdrew his knife from a sheath at his waist, the metal shimmering in the light. "I honed my blade until it was a razor. I sliced off his genitals. I split him from groin to throat. I slipped this tip just under the skin, careful not to cut into the body cavity. You get the idea. I removed his flesh. After I skinned him and treated his hide, I slept with Hassem against my flesh each night as a reminder all who betray me die." His savage gaze fixed on Lizette.

"What? You expect me to be horrified. I'm not. Did he scream?"

"Loud."

She narrowed her eyes. "Good. I want to do that to Spear. Show me how."

"No. Doing such to another being will destroy

your soul."

"My soul wants revenge."

"No, it doesn't." He rested his palm above her breast. "Your heart wants revenge."

"And I want to castrate him before I kill him."

"I will do that." Jarek sighed.

"How did you get here?" She waved her hand around, taking in his yurt. "How does a young djinn ex-slave eventually become a commander in the Scion Firebrands?"

He pointed to the brand on his upper arm. "He gets this mark burned into his flesh. The pain brings a grown male to his knees. Worse than anything during my enslavement and worse than anything the djinn camp could deal out. Serving is an honor passed from an ancestor to a descendant. Hence, Scion Firebrands. Like my father before me, I assumed the gauntlet, rose in the ranks, and eventually became commander of this unit."

"Because you're the best?"

He laughed again. "Because I'm the deadliest."

****

Dante settled into his seat, strapped in, leaned against the headrest, and closed his eyes as his private jet went wheels up. Memories flooded his thoughts.

By the time he had been summoned, it was too late. Too late to say goodbye. He had not been phoned when Amelia's labor began. Officials told him she had eventually been admitted into hospital once the delivery became difficult. They tried to save her but couldn't. The infant lived, but the mother died.

So sorry.

Then hospital attendants informed him the child was missing. The infant, his granddaughter, had been stolen from the nursery by the father.

So sorry.

They assured him their security was top-notch. Nothing like this had ever happened before.

They were sweating a lawsuit, but he satisfied them by saying he had no intention of resorting to the courts. Their sighs of relief were infuriating, but he had more important things on his mind.

Revenge was at the top of the list.

Because of Dante's money and power, the commissioner as well as CID were present at the crime scene. Scotland Yard was on the job. The less than one-day-old baby would be found. He told them he would meet with them tomorrow. They shook hands politely.

So sorry.

He left the hospital, preliminary arrangements made for Amelia's burial. He saw no reason to hurry. After all, the otherworlder, the father, had taken the infant. Dante did not share the last bit of information.

Yes. Dante knew his daughter's lover was an otherworlder. Amelia had been young and much in love. With all the adoration bubbling to the surface, she spilled everything to her father once she learned she was pregnant. She told him the handsome polo player who had gotten her with child was from another realm, that he was a different species, a satyr. Of course, Dante did not believe her.

She was impetuous, the spoiled daughter of a man rich beyond all dreams, wanting for nothing. He believed her ramblings to be flights of fancy from a girl who had not rubbed shoulders with reality.

Then he investigated, his curiosity and dread growing. Eventually, he invited the young man to lunch, grilling him about his nature and realm.

The handsome young polo player looked Amelia's father in the eye, assuring him humans and his kind mated successfully to produce offspring. There would be no problem. Dante remained wary.

Gripped by an uncontrollable grief, the distraught father, who had not yet become Dante, wound up at the gate to his private gentleman's club, not for comfort from fellow members but to get royally pished.

In this state of mind, he came to his club, asking the familiar bartender for his usual Scotch. Then another and another until he could not remember how many he had consumed. Those around him scattered as his rants grew crazier and crazier. Members quietly took their drinks to other rooms, suddenly remembered meetings, or looked at their watches, late for an appointment. He blathered about otherworlders among us all. Those who once walked Earth but now only visited from their realm.

During the Englishman's tirade, a large man sidled alongside him at the bar, also ordering a Scotch. The man gently touched Dante's elbow. "May we sit by the fire, friend?"

When the stranger finally persuaded him to take a chair, Dante continued his outburst as the man listened patiently, one hand resting on a knee. The attentive man set his glass on the table and thoughtfully pinched his chin between his thumb and a knuckle.

The Englishman continued to describe a realm called Scath as well as the species who lived there, revealing more and more, encouraged by the man who hung on each word. Since Dante was drunk, not stupid, he kept a lid on some truths, suspicions about his companion penetrating the alcohol haze.

His new friend sighed, asking how an English gentleman knew of such a place as Scath.

Dante explained about the polo player from Scath, the infant, and the death of Amelia. The bereaved Englishman would do anything to find this man and bring him to justice, to his death. The otherworlder had impregnated his daughter, knowing she would die with his spawn.

The attentive man, who called himself Cerberus, claimed Dante and he had met serendipitously. Their friendship would get them both what they desired. Dante could be free to enter Scath and search for this man if Cerberus could open free trade between realms.

The listener explained about the portals dividing the realms and how travel was limited since they were closed to all but the chosen. A group called the descendants of the Blood Coven could remove the spell and open the gateways for the business benefit of both Scath and Earth. Together the two of them could make it happen.

The father, who was not yet Dante, suspected he and the Aeternal were at cross purposes. While Cerberus strove to open the realms for his own reasons, Dante sought proof that Aeternals existed. With it, he could expose them to the British or American governments and avenge his daughter's death. He knew, despite being less than sober, his rants about the beings would not convince anyone of their existence. He needed proof.

Now he had it. Through Cerberus, he had discovered the Alliance and other bits of significant knowledge about Scath and its beings. Once he exposed them, they would be annihilated, including his daughter's lover. He felt nothing for the infant. After all, she killed his beloved Amelia also. If she was destroyed in the process, so be it.

Dante no longer needed the nefarious creature Cerberus, whom he suspected viewed all humans as inferior and dispensable. It was time to walk different paths.

He had hired an ex-mercenary, Mars, to build an army. Thanks to the scientists in his employ, these soldiers were nearly as strong as the otherworlders. They had also developed a tranquilizer which resulted in the capture of two vampires. And, possibly, his daughter's killer. His proof.

The jet glided onto the runway in a smooth landing. Once the steps rolled into place and the door opened, Dante exited the plane, a man on a mission, walking with the extreme confidence which came from money and power.

A black limo waited for him in the hangar. A chauffeur jumped out to open the backdoor. "Sir."

After Dante slid across the leather seat and poured a Scotch from the bottle in the bar, he spoke to the driver whose eyes stared at him in the mirror. He wanted to know where to go.

The Englishman phoned Mars, who directed him to the new compound rather than to the old lab. The base was now where his proof and his vengeance awaited.

"How was the flight, sir?" asked the driver.

"Uneventful."

The rest of the drive was as the Englishman wanted. Silent. They headed to a helicopter pad, the wealthy man boarding the aircraft.

Landing in the middle of the new compound, Dante stepped out, surrounded by armed, uniformed men.

"I'm expected." He handed the guard a card. On the card were two words. "Humans First."

The man examined it, the logo matching the HF on his uniform. He signaled for the men to make way. Dante followed the soldier into the building. Taking stock as he entered, he was greeted by Mars and two other men in Humans First uniforms.

"Where are they?" asked Dante. No greeting. All business.

"This way, sir." Mars led the way, the other men flanking the Englishman.

Mars escorted him outside to an exterior door which required a thumbprint for entrance. He stopped. "Go on, sir. Yours works."

Dante pressed his thumb against the pad. A click sounded. Mars opened the door.

In full view, strapped to a table, was a male vampire. His hair was matted with blood. His eyes rolled from side-to-side. He was naked and starved, if his elongated fangs were any indication. He growled, tugging so hard on his restraints his ankles and wrists were raw, bloody.

Proof.

Dante nearly cried. Let the military call him crazy now. With proof, they would rise to destroy the enemies of all humans.

It was the other table that drew his attention. On it lay the reason for his continued existence. His revenge.

****

After a string of phone calls, Dante paced, clenched his fists, took shallow, impatient breaths as he waited beside the helipad.

He had verified the identity of the unconscious satyr. He had seen the vampires. He had slept, though not peacefully.

Now, with armed men at his back, he awaited a skeptical American general and colonel. With the proof he needed, Dante had called his contacts in the British government who vouched for him with the American army.

These two military officers were about to understand what humans faced. Armed with the knowledge, they could marshal forces against the otherworlders.

Whap. Whap. Whap.

As the helicopter dropped to the ground, wind beat up dust, but the Englishman stood firm, impervious to its chaos.

Two men walked down the airsteps, holding onto their hats until they were out of range of the blades.

"General Lipton." Dante offered his hand.

"Isaac, please." The American military officer stretched out to shake.

"Colonel." Dante greeted the other officer.

"Mateo. We ought to be on a first-name basis given what we are about to do together."

"Follow me, gentlemen. I think you are going to be amazed. Astounded, actually. I've lived with this knowledge for some time but wanted proof before I brought you into my world. I have it now."

Dante led the way from the landing site, passing the shooting range and crossing the track. He paused at an outside door for a thumbprint. When it clicked, his hand clutched the thick metal. "I have three otherworlders waiting for you in here. One satyr and two vampires."

The officers eyed each other, shaking their heads, wary.

"I have to say, sir, when you first contacted us, I thought you were batty," said General Lipton, standing behind Dante.

"I'm not an idiot. That's why I offer proof."

They entered the sterile lab, Dr. Messenger waiting along with an assistant. Ten armed men, wearing Humans First uniforms, guarded the perimeter of the room.

The colonel's eyes pinged around the room, his expression showing dislike for Dante's private army of mercenaries.

The satyr on one lab table shook the chains and straps which had been required to restrain him despite an enormous amount of sedatives in his system.

On another exam slab, the female vampire struggled against silver bindings, her wrists and ankles raw and bleeding. She growled as her body jerked from side to side.

The male vampire lay on a third table, his chest slashed open for viewing. He was in a sedative-induced coma for the time-being.

"Dr. Messenger. Please do the honors. Start with this specimen."

"Wonderful choice, Dante. Sirs." With a flourish, the doctor walked toward the table near the center of the lab. "This is a vampire." He lifted the specimen's upper lip, exposing fangs. "These are not always visible, but his have dropped. We are finding that happens for a number of reasons. Anger. Hunger. Stress. Since we have not fed him blood for six days now, he is starving. His fangs have remained exposed."

The female nearby tossed her head, her own fangs punching through her gums, her guttural roars echoing across the room.

"Gentlemen, note his exposed chest. Here is his heart. It is larger than the comparable human organ. Same with his lungs. Here." He pointed with a rod. "Now this is interesting. Humans do not have one of these organs." When he tapped it, it quivered. "I am not sure how it functions. A thorough autopsy might reveal its purpose. If I could cut it open to examine the contents."

"Not yet." Dante angled his neck to one side, studying the vampire.

The doctor appeared to be thoroughly enjoying himself. He had a body, his pointer, and a captive audience.

"Astounding," said General Lipton. He shared a look with the colonel, their exchange brief but holding a touch of disgust. "You say they are stronger."

"Stronger and capable of magical actions. The female vampire shared information, hoping to keep us from examining her friend." The doctor's smile made even Dante cringe.

General Lipton walked toward the female, keeping a respectable distance from her teeth. He strode to Ram whose drugged, unfocused eyes tried to track him. As he neared, they flashed green. "What did you say this is?"

"A satyr." Dante stood where Ram could not see him. "But he's mine. You may interrogate him. We will give you ultrasounds, x-rays, and images once we open him. Nothing more."

"What do you want from us?" Colonel Mateo Garcia stood ramrod straight, hands behind his back, his legs parted.

"As I have already told you, they call themselves Aeternals. They live on Scath, a realm which can be accessed only via portals, some of which I know. They travel to Earth through these gates with devices called portal jumpers. My scientists are examining one of them. The satyr specimen had a travel implement imbedded in his wrist. We dug it out and are tearing it apart also. If lucky, we will be able to duplicate the gadgets and invade their realm. I am sure you agree we need to destroy the otherworlders before they kill us."

Ram popped the chain on his wrist, shifted his hip to snap the other. A soldier raised his rifle and fired. The satyr gripped his abdomen when the sedative struck. With his other hand, he ripped off the strap across his chest and the chains on his legs. After he swung his feet to the floor, he charged Dante, his steps lumbering and slow. Two more shots.

Ping. Ping.

Before he collapsed to the floor, he stared at Dante. Shock playing across his face. "You." With so much tranquilizer in his system, the word was slurred.

Humans First guards rushed him. As the satyr's lids closed, he slumped into their arms.

Dante patted one uniformed man's shoulder. "Good work, soldier."

****

Ram awoke slowly. Voices. Shuffling feet. Light filtering through his lids. Busy machines. Sobs from the female vampire. *What's her name? Norah. That's it.*

Varik moaned. Conscious again. Earlier, he had screamed. When his cries for help had quieted, Ram got the willies. He thought the vamp might be dead. Glad to know he wasn't. Yet.

How long had he been out? Hours? Days? He had lost track of time.

"The satyr's coming to. Get Dante and the officers. They want to talk with him."

Ram recognized Dr. Messenger's voice as the butcher responsible for the torture-fest. The guy enjoyed his job too much.

The door squeaked. Footsteps.

A shadow passed over Ram.

"Is he awake?" The voice was familiar.

I didn't hallucinate. Why is he here?

"Yes," replied the doctor.

"Look at me, bastard." The old Englishman from his past stepped into view.

Ram peeled up his sandpapery lids. Confusion. It was him. Amelia's father. He licked his cracked lips, his mouth dry, his throat raw. "You're not a dream."

"I am your nightmare."

Ram rattled the chains attached to his wrists. "I have to get back to your granddaughter." His biceps nearly popped from the strain. New chains. Stronger.

"I have no granddaughter. You may question him." He waved his hand at the two men behind him.

The human with stars on his uniform identified himself as General Lipton. "What are you?"

"Pissed."

"Why don't we know about your world?" The other military man wore a silver eagle, calling himself Colonel Garcia.

"Probably because you're dumb fucks."

A black-uniformed soldier rushed forward, throwing a fist to Ram's jaw, rattling his teeth.

"Don't insult them," shouted the fist owner.

"The Englishman told us about portals. How do we go through them to your world?" The colonel scrubbed a palm across his clean-shaven jaw.

"You don't. Look, this lunatic painted the wrong picture of us. I'm a Scion Firebrand. I not only defend my own people but also yours. We keep you safe from any of us who try to harm you." Ram tested the chains at his ankles.

Unbreakable.

Ignoring him, the colonel continued his interrogation. "What kinds of things can a satyr do?"

I give. They're all delusional.

"I can blow you up with a thought. You're all about to go boom."

The colonel's eyeballs flipped around as if he was waiting for an explosion.

The man calling himself Dante but whom Ram knew as Lord Ellington drew a deep breath. "I don't think so."

"What other kinds of creatures live in your

world? What did you call it? Scath?" The general decided to join in on the question-fest. "Do you have this extra organ like the vampire? What's it for?"

"The better to eat you with, asshole."

Whop.

Another crack to the jaw.

Dr. Messenger came into view, rubbing his hands together. "I can open him now to see."

Dante fingered his chin. "Yes. Open. A fast look. Close. We'll watch."

The prat-hat of a doctor signaled his assistant who rolled a cart across the floor.

Blump. Blump. Blump.

Ram inhaled. This was going to suck.

These assholes aren't going to hear a peep out of me.

As the blade sliced into flesh, he nearly fractured his already aching jaw by clamping his teeth tight. Then a saw powered up. Tears dampened his eyes, but not one scream rolled across his lips when his sternum was split.

Okay.

That was bad, but what came next was un-fucking-believable.

"I have to spread his ribs." The doctor sought Dante's approval. He got it.

Ram heard a metal tool clink on the cart.

"A retractor." The butcher showed the implement to the observers.

Ram squeezed his eyes closed, howling inside as the doctor snapped bones. Nausea punched his gut, like a feral cat caught in a bag.

Hold back the upchuck.

He imagined Jonquil, skipping rope in the yard, winning a card game they were playing, reading a favorite story. What was it? Yeah. *The Lion, the Witch, and the Wardrobe.*

When pain crashed through his mental barriers again, he slipped Denim's sundress over her head, unclasped her bra to reveal those luscious breasts, and slid her panties down long legs.

"There it is." Dr. Prat-hat held up his torture tool. "The same organ."

"We see," said Dante. "Close him up. Watch how he heals."

Stars flecked the black sky behind Ram's lids. Followed by a blissful nothing.

Having passed out for a few minutes or *hell* an hour, he awoke to a rush of noise. Ram twisted his neck to see the cause of the ruckus.

The vampire Varik snapped his silver chains. With one hand, he struggled to keep his intestines from spilling out his gut along with multiple organs. Grabbing a scalpel from the tray with the other, he faced Norah, his lids hooding remorseful eyes. "I'm so sorry. I can't handle this." He plunged the blade deep into his heart, enough to bury his fist, the tip of the instrument, and the handle. The damage was enough to take him to the Evermore.

As the female screamed, frantically shaking her bindings, her hips jack-knifing off the steel slab, Dr. Messenger and his assistant rushed to the side of the male vamp to save him. Too late.

"What a waste, assholes. He was no danger to you. He was a kid who came to New Orleans to have fun." Ram lifted his head to check out the wound on his chest. It wasn't healing and wouldn't until he fed his satyr.

Damn. It hurts like a mutherfucker.

Chapter Twenty-Nine

Three days after Ram's capture, Denim leaned against the bathroom doorjamb with her arms crossed over her chest while she monitored Jonquil, who brushed her teeth. "Good job, kid. Did you sleep okay?"

"I did after you came in." The girl spit toothpaste into the sink. "Daddy says I have to brush until the handle turns off. It's a long time, but it's good for my teeth."

"Your daddy's a wise man."

"He is smart. He's handsome, too. I think he would make a terrific mate. Don't you?"

Denim laughed. "You are quite the matchmaker."

She lightly pinched Jonquil's waist, causing the girl to giggle and jump out of reach. A brief but sweet thought wandered into Denim's brain. She imagined her own child might have been as bright and wonderful as this one. If only she had lived.

"I know my daddy has a dangerous job." As the kid stuck her toothbrush into a glass, she drew Denim's thoughts away from the past.

"You do?"

"Yes. He's a Firebrand. He keeps everybody safe, but who keeps him safe?" A tear trickled down her cheek.

Denim caught it with a gentle finger. "We do, Jonquil. You and me. And a bunch of really scary tough warriors."

The doorbell interrupted them.

"I'll be right back." When Denim opened the door, the tall, sleek, black-haired shifter stood in the hall. "Hey, Jezzi."

"I'm here for sitter detail. Like I told you, I'm off

rotation today." She pointed to her calf. "Pulled muscle. I tripped over a curb. Dumb move. But there ya go. After I shift a few times, I'll be as good as new."

Jonquil came out of the bedroom at that moment. "Jezzi. You look pretty as a panther."

"Thanks, little flower. I'm on boss detail while Denim goes off to do Firebrand stuff. Now, go get dressed so we can blow this joint. I need a run in the park. Put on some tennies."

When Jonquil disappeared back into the room, Jezzi leaned closer to Denim and whispered, "Kole has called a meeting in his office. Take along a shirt of Ram's from his locker."

"I'll put it in my bag." Denim waved her thumb at a duffel on the floor.

"How much does the kid know?"

"I told her he was lost. I didn't give the particulars, but she's worried. Apparently, he's never been gone this long without telling her." Denim picked up her bag, slinging it over her shoulder. "We've got to find him."

Jezzi patted Denim's arm. "We won't let the little girl become an orphan. And we won't let you be without your mate."

"Oh, I'm not…"

When Jonquil returned to the room, she shuffled up to Denim, her small fingers clasping onto the woman's larger hand. Ever so slightly, she squeezed.

Jonquil's voice trembled. "Find Daddy. He promised me he'd always be home. I don't want to be alone."

Denim dropped into a crouch, wrapping her arms around the kid. "I will. Your daddy is strong, fierce. He'll keep his promise. You're the world to him."

"I know, but sometimes other people won't let

you keep a promise."

"You don't know me well, Jonquil, but let me tell you something about myself. I am a stubborn woman. You ask your daddy when he returns. If I want something, I get it. I'm tough as a demon's claws. I've got more bite than a wolf shifter. I can be scarier than a berserker. Right now, I want your daddy home."

Jonquil took her hand again. "Good, but don't you get lost, too. Daddy and I wouldn't like that."

Yep. This kid is everything I wished my daughter to be.

****

Denim may have denied it before, but she couldn't now. She loved the satyr with the caramel-colored hair, flirty smile, and crass pick-up lines. With all his faults. *Hell.* He avoided serious relationships because he blamed himself for the death of Jonquil's mother. But he was wrong. He wasn't a fuckup. How could she make him see?

Lifting her chin, determined not to bawl, she stepped up her pace, stomping through the open door into Kole's office, her fists clenched.

The conference table was full. Rein. Thorn. Galena. Brak. Sabine. Nico. Tyr. Chay. And a few she didn't know but recognized from previous meetings and the lab raid.

Skyler was sitting beside Kole, drinking from a bottle of water in front of her. Each Firebrand nodded at Denim as Galena pointed to the empty chair beside her.

In a corner the scary male with long black hair, leathers, vacant eyes, and a string of vamp fangs around his neck leaned against the wall. She had seen him around. He'd led one of the teams on the raid, but she couldn't remember his name.

Kole rested on his forearms. "The GPS on Ram's

Dick Chip must have been cut out first thing. He was drugged, snatched, and shoved into an SUV. Likely, he was choppered out."

"We're assuming he's alive?" Nico swiped at a dark strand of hair which had fallen onto his forehead.

Hostile glances, spine-chilling frowns, and growls met his unwelcome words.

"What? It's not like asking the question can kill the satyr."

Sabine whispered in his ear loud enough for everyone to hear. "You can be so damn insensitive." He looked somewhat contrite.

"Fuck off, Abello." Rein popped fangs. "He's alive. He's one stubborn sonofabitching satyr. Too mean to die. Especially at the hands of some crazy-ass weak humans." He glanced at Skyler, Denim, and Nico, as if he expected them to argue with his description of their species. None did.

Denim cleared her throat. "What's the plan?"

Kole plopped another bottle of water in front of his mate. "We know the missing vamps, Varik and Norah, had been in one of those labs we raided. Thorn smelled them. Denim's ex, the guy being interrogated in the Cubes, spilled intel about a new base. We believe that's where they are now. The prisoner said the satyr was a high priority capture. He didn't know why. And about the new base? The human only knows it's in a swamp outside New Orleans."

"He doesn't know anything else?" When Galena shifted in her seat, her straight, shoulder-length bob swished across her shoulders.

"Nothing. I probed so deep his brain is oatmeal. Between my trip inside and the bugs, he's a dead man walking," said Rein. "Sorry, Denim. He's dust by now."

Denim shivered, but instead of seeing Steven as

he'd been when they married, she saw the man punching and kicking her, killing their unborn child. She didn't spare her ex another thought. She wanted Ram home. "Atchafalaya Basin. We should look there."

"We need more intel." Rein's normally blue eyes were killer dark.

"Straight up," shouted Brak. "Once we get it, we're good to go. Hey, Denim. Ram's too damn dumb to go out like this."

Her lips curled up weakly as she scooted her chair closer to the table. "Okay. The basin's big. How do we find out where this base is?"

"Scath's best scryers have been looking for its whereabouts. Mages have used spells. We've done fly-overs. Still haven't found it." Kole patted Skyler's arm, a frown tugging at his lips. "My mate, despite being pregnant and aware of the danger to her, insists she can find him."

She nodded, taking a sip of water. "I believe with my scrying and astral projection combination, I'm the best chance to find the base."

"Keep drinking your water, Frisca. According to your trainer and the healer, you have to hydrate. You brought something which belongs to the satyr, Denim?"

She picked up the duffel beside her chair. "Right here. I got a shirt from his locker. Is this good? If not, I'll get whatever you need."

"Perfect," said Skyler, setting a half-empty bottle onto the table. "Having something personal helps me focus."

Kole tented his fingers, controlling the sparks. "If my mate finds the base, Rein and Tyr will do recon. They'll locate the place from her descriptions and scope it out."

Kole nodded at his computer guru. Logan

straightened. "I'll be pulling up aerial views of the swamp, looking for heat signatures, the ushe."

"That's the plan for now. Once we have better intel, we'll figure out how to move in. Denim's ex says he was told the new base could hold upward of a hundred men. Remember, those injections they take have jacked them up into super-soldiers. And in case they've recruited, I've called in Firebrands from other strongholds to assist."

"The swamps aren't easy to move around in." Denim struggled to speak, her throat tight. "I've been there."

Kole scrubbed a fist over his buzz-cut hair. "We'll involve you in our plans. You'll look over a map after Frisca does her thing. For now, we go with my mate, Logan, Tyr, and Rein."

Fire jumped across Kole's hands, but he did nothing to contain it. "I don't have to tell you how important this mission is. Not only does this whacked group have one of our own, but they want us as specimens for some reason. They now have three. Wait for my call and be prepared to arm up at a moment's notice. It'll mean we know where Ram is."

The Scion Firebrands filed out of Kole's office, each one palming Denim's shoulder, offering assurances. The dark male in leathers who leaned against the wall was the last to approach her. He paused in front of her, his lips curled into a snarl. With his fangs exposed, Denim realized he was a vampire.

"The name is Dax. We haven't met formally. We got this. We never leave one of ours behind."

For some reason, hearing this frightening male with dead obsidian eyes speak these words comforted her more than any of the others' talk.

****

Jarek, Kara, Darius, and a few males whose names Lizette couldn't remember lounged on thick cushions around a fire with stars overhead and a light breeze fanning the flames.

Commander Kole had called on Jarek to lead his own Firebrands on a mission to rescue one of their own. Tonight was for relaxation before the fight.

A high wall surrounded the Southern Stronghold, enclosing hundreds of yurts. Some were homes. Others training centers, an armory, barracks, gathering rooms, kitchens, dining huts.

At first, Lizette thought the exteriors were wooden frames covered with animal hides, but they were too solid. Darius had explained how Jarek wanted the structures to look like his home of old. But impregnable. So, between the exterior hides and the inside walls were layers of steel.

"The weather is perfect." Lizette propped her bare feet close to the fire. She shifted on the cushion, tugging on the loose-fitting dress Kara had given her, an ancient Persian style. She loved the soft blue linen against her skin. Bracelets, also on loan, jangled on her arms. "It reminds me of my vacation in San Diego once. In the daytime, grains of sand glittered like jewels in a hot sun. At night, cool breezes drifted across the water. Have you traveled there?"

Jarek snorted. "Sea World," he said, as if it explained everything.

"Okay. That's not what I expected to hear." Lizette widened her eyes, interested to hear the story.

The commander pointed at Kara.

"It was my idea. I confess. I had read about Sea World and Disneyland in a travel magazine. Since I was dying to see the places, I invited Darius and Jarek along. Despite their constant griping, they had fun."

"You didn't invite us. You made us accompany you." Darius stroked the snake tat hiding his scar.

Lizette chuckled. Then she broke into outright laughter, stifling the sounds with the palm of her hand.

"What's so funny?" Jarek tacked onto an elbow, frowning up at Lizette.

"I would have paid to see the three of you on It's a Small World."

Kara smirked. "We missed it because they refused to go on it."

Lizette stopped laughing when a curvaceous woman in a gauzy, see-through dress strutted toward Jarek. Bangles on her ankles and wrists tinkled as her hips shifted from side to side. Reaching her goal, she trailed her fingers along his shoulders, bending to whisper in his ear.

He waved her away. "No."

Darius leaned toward Lizette. "A camp follower."

"What's... Oh."

"I loved the frozen bananas." Kara broke the uncomfortable silence. "No place here has them. Maybe we're due another Sea World-Disneyland jaunt."

Both Jarek and Darius shouted, "No."

"You're no fun." Kara drew her lips into a pout.

Chuckling again, Lizette glanced at the woman Jarek had sent away. She leaned against a nearby tree, glaring in her direction.

Kara rose, stretching her arms overhead. "Time for bed."

"Likewise." When Darius left, the other males near the fire nodded and took off.

Lizette wiggled into her thick, red-patterned cushion, making it more comfortable. She chewed on her thumbnail.

Jarek pushed higher on his elbow, tilting toward

her, touching her neck where the slave mark had once marred her perfect skin. "The ouroboros fits you. You chose well. It is an ancient symbol, the snake in a figure eight who eats its own tail. It means whole. That is what you will be."

Lizette had something else on her mind, though, and wasn't one to hold onto pressing thoughts. "You didn't have to turn the woman down on my account."

His thumb still caressed her neck. "What makes you think I did?"

Her spine stiffened. "Did you?"

"Yes."

When he settled back onto both arms, Lizette missed the warmth of the djinn's touch. She had grown to need him. *No.* She had at first. Now, she wanted him. Not as a crutch but as a man.

"Darius said she's a camp follower. Is that like a prostitute?"

Jarek relaxed against his cushion by the fire. "We don't think of them in such a way. They provide a necessary service. They give blood to my vampires, arousal to my satyrs and nymphs, orgasms to my demons."

"Sex."

"Of course. Where is this conversation going, Lizette? It's not like you to be indirect. If you want to ask something, do so."

"Do you use them?" As she rotated her head, the strands of her hair moved like a swath of silk. She liked her new bobbed cut.

The day before, she had awakened, gone into the bathroom, and studied her reflection. Something was off. The woman in the mirror with the long hair was not her. She snagged a pair of scissors and went to work, trimming it to just below her chin where she had worn it in New York. Surprisingly, her old self did not re-emerge. Instead, a new Lizette, a stronger Lizette, stared back.

"Yes. I use followers." Jarek brushed a warrior braid over his shoulder.

"Are you in a serious relationship with one of them?"

"No."

Lizette appreciated the djinn commander's directness. He never softened answers for her. "As a psychologist, I realize I am too close to my own problems. Denim and Braelyn came to visit me the other day. Did you know?"

"Yes."

She inhaled. "They shared their experiences in captivity, encouraging me to share mine. I did."

"I am glad."

She paused, her lower lip stiff. "I wasn't only raped, Jarek. That would have been one thing." She met his glare, knowing it to be directed at Spear, not her. "I participated in my own sexual abuse. I encouraged him. Sometimes I begged him to take me. I would untie his pants and wrap my hand around his disgusting penis. I stroked him until he came. I took him into my mouth. I let him ejaculate inside of me." She swallowed a gag before it rose. "One part of me understands what it means to be a whore."

Jarek shot back his response, no pause, no deliberation. "A whore? You? No. So what if you had to suck dick." He laughed. "You think you're the only being who's had to give a blow job? You think that makes me respect you less? There is an ancient Persian saying, my *atashe delam*. 'A river cuts through a rock not because of its power, but its persistence.' You are a persistent female."

"Is this how you see me?"

"Yes, because that is what you are." Jarek's hand grasped the back of her head as he pressed his mouth to her lips.

The kiss was gentle, warm, and inviting but not insistent. He broke away, sitting back, undemanding and unhurried. His lids hooded the desire in his eyes while his chest rose with a deep breath.

Lizette sighed. "Here's what I came away with after meeting the two women whose experiences overlap mine to some extent. I'm sick and tired of being a victim. So, no more of that behavior. I'm here. I'm alive. I'm me. True, with more experiences, not all of them good, but I am still me."

"Yes, you are. You won."

"I did. Now I'm claiming my prize." She rose from the cushion, the blue linen dress gathering at her ankles, her bracelets tinkling when she held out a hand to Jarek.

His eyes narrowed. "This is what you want?"

"Want. Need. Truthfully, I'm not sure which. I saw green when the camp follower touched you. Her fingers will not be the last ones on your skin tonight."

"I am not a gentle man, *atashe delam*. I have known only females like her for centuries. I take what I want. I'm not much on giving."

"Perfect. I don't want a gentle man. I want a man who'll make me forget. I intend to use you for that purpose. Now get off your ass and come fuck me."

The firelight caught the spark in Jarek's irises as his lips curled into a seductive smile.

The camp follower had ignited Lizette's possessiveness for the djinn. She wanted to erase Spear from her memory, but she also felt something for this fierce warrior.

"When you put it so sweetly, *atashe delam*. How can I refuse?" Like the predator he was, Jarek uncoiled, gathered her against him, and swaggered into his yurt.

****

That night, Tyr and Dax slipped away from the stronghold to follow a lead. If they needed to return for the big rescue, they could immediately.

The warlock swung a leg over the seat of his Harley CVO. He twisted to glance over his shoulder at Dax.

The vampire adjusted his leather jacket. "You know, your hog has 'I'm compensating for my small dick' written all over it."

"Don't bad-mouth my favorite lady." Tyr patted the fuel tank, resisting the urge to caress it.

Dax's Scath-made Tonkawa roared to life as he pulled out. They cycled from the Covenkirk stronghold toward the drug dealer Karth's place where they planned to play good-warlock-bad-vamp.

Tyr had warned Kole things might get sticky with Thorn's ex-pack possibly involved in the pharmaceutical game. Maybe his shifter *freron* had gone rogue on them. *Nah*. Tyr doubted it. Too much honor in the male.

The wolf Firebrand's brother Luka was alpha. The job should have been Thorn's, but he answered the call to the warriors, rejecting the top spot. Unfortunately, Luka's leadership style lacked Thorn's firm hand, sense of justice, and understanding of behavior. Rumors had leaked about the pack for years. Mistreatment of the females. Involvement in shady deals. Nothing the Firebrands could prove. All the while, the relationship between the brothers deteriorated.

He hoped Luka's problem was only a loose rein on the pack, not a drug trade sitch. Tyr wasn't eager to pump Karth and find out Thorn's brother was ass-deep in the biz. He didn't want the ensuing convo with his *freron.*

He and the bloodsucker rode the main highway from Covenkirk toward Karth's village in North Shelters. From the lowlands outside the capital city of the mage, they traveled toward the mountains. From there, they would proceed through a pass and into the shifter region.

Most times Tyr hit the road, he enjoyed the wind in his face. The warlock lived for speed, danger, and the blur of trees as he jacked up the mph. He slowed today, not wanting to leave the vamp in his dust. He imagined, though, the bloodsucker didn't mind knocking knees with death. Probably his favorite pastime.

Tyr turned to eye his companion. Dax's stony, dead gaze locked on the highway. No admiring the scenery for him. Might just as well be riding in a vacuum tube. The bloodsucker was business only, glare on the target and all that shit.

Sure wouldn't want him tracking me.

Then he saw something in his headlight. A lump on the road ahead. Smack in the middle. It moved.

Tyr braked, fishtailed, and high-sided it on his way to the pavement. Not bothering to check on Dax, he shot up and raced toward the injured Aeternal. It was a female. She curled into a fetal position, arms wrapped around her head. She was breathing. Barely. Even from here he could smell her. Pine, soil, and scat.

Chapter Thirty

Jarek understood. Sometimes fucking was less about sex and more about proving a point.

Once inside his yurt, he asked, "Are you sure?"

Maybe Lizette had PTSD. Earthers talked about such shit. He should go get Kara. Females were more sympathetic. He was no goddamn counselor. He was born to kill, not cure.

She chewed on her bottom lip. "I'm sure. But let me lead."

"I'm not sure how good I will be with that, but I will try to give you what you need."

Soft hands stroked his arms, his muscles twitching with her gentle touch. She continued to his abs and tucked her thumbs into the waist of his loose pants. "I want to see all of your glyphs."

Jarek nodded. "Just my glyphs?" After shrugging his pants down his legs, he kicked them aside.

Lizette smiled, drawing a sharp breath. She asked him to spin around. Her fingers traced the swirls of letters on his back, his ass, and thighs. When he faced her again, her gaze rolled from his neck to his feet, returning to his cock where it settled.

"They're even on your penis. Beautiful."

"I have no control over where they appear." Jarek growled when she wrapped her fingers around his stiff arousal, her thumb following a glyph's pattern.

"I want this inside me."

He wouldn't be fetching Kara. His shaft jerked at Lizette's touch. Making this strong, brave female forget Spear had become his counseling specialty. He was about to enjoy every moment of it.

"Lose your clothes." Jarek's voice was a hoarse

whisper.

Lizette unclasped her linen dress, letting it slide to the floor. Panties followed as she shimmied them down her hips. Her fingers dipped behind her where she unhooked her bra, allowing the straps to slip off her shoulders, exposing herself to Jarek's gaze.

His hooded stare paused on her rounded mounds of flesh with rosy nipples. She was exquisite. Her silken hair moved with her every motion. Thick lashes lined her brilliant dark eyes. Her full lips parted as her tongue flicked over them. Her body combined the best of soft and firm with a trim waist flaring into curved hips.

"Where do you want me?" Jarek practiced more control than he knew he had.

Lizette swallowed hard. "On the bed."

"At your service." He lay on his back, his legs spread, his hand circling his hard shaft.

She crawled alongside him, her nipples brushing his arm and chest as she caressed his skin, her feathery touches erotic.

"What's next?" His voice was a gravelly whisper.

Lizette pushed up to straddle his thighs. "Will you stop if I can't go on?"

"I will. No matter what."

Lizette bent forward. When her mouth touched his, Jarek deepened the kiss, his tongue opening her lips, exploring and thrusting while his fingers stroked her sex.

He separated from the kiss. "Does this feel good?"

"Oh, yes."

"Open wider, Lizette. Sit up on your knees a bit."

When she did, Jarek slipped a finger inside her channel, his thumb pressing on her clit. She ground into his hand. "That's it, *atashe delam*. You are hot and wet. Are your juices for me?"

Leaning onto her arms, her head angled, she groaned. "Yes."

"You deserve a reward."

He slid a second finger into her channel, pumping in and out as she moaned.

"Faster."

"Patience, *atashe delam*."

She bucked, taking what he offered, begging for more. She was slick with desire.

"Don't stop." She rocked her hips faster, moaning, her lips parted. She was tight but wet, eager to come. Unable to resist the temptation, Jarek lifted his head to taste one of her breasts, her nipple a sweet fruit begging to be plucked. As he nipped, she cried out his name, an orgasm rolling through her.

When she settled, Jarek smiled. "Surely you are not through with me, *atashe delam*. Is this all you desire? Finish what you started."

She rose higher onto her knees, fisting him and positioning the blunt tip to her entrance. Inch by inch she lowered herself onto him. Jarek fought the urge to rush her, letting her take the lead as he had promised.

With a drawn-out sigh of pleasure, she took him. Jarek lifted his hips, seating himself deeper, holding onto a snarl and a strong desire to grab her thighs while he fucked her hard. *Damn.* "You must move, Lizette. You are driving me insane."

She bit her bottom lip, arching her back. Her hands rested on his chest, her breasts bobbling. "I'm enjoying the feel of you inside me." She rose until only the tip of him remained in her body. Sitting down again, he disappeared inside her. Again. And again.

Jarek was mesmerized by the way she took his flesh, squeezing him with each motion. "Faster."

"Yes."

As her breasts bounced in front of him, he palmed them, enjoying soft, supple mounds.

"Jarek, I want more."

"I am at your service." He flipped her onto her back, inside her again with one long thrust. He lifted her legs over his shoulders, changing the angle of his penetration, plunging deeper. "Are you okay with me on top?"

"Yes. Very." She moaned, clenching his shoulders.

Scooping his hands under her ass for a better grip, he plowed in and out, listening to her frantic cries of pleasure, taking her faster.

Damn.

He wasn't going to last much longer.

She was ripe with need. She wanted to forget the berserker. She didn't want gentle. She wanted a savage djinn warrior. Here he was. He narrowed his eyes, his jaw clamped tight, his war braids brushing her breasts.

"You wanted my cock. All of it. Are you full?" He rocked his hips back and forth.

She nodded, her eyes hooded by her lids.

He withdrew to slam back inside. She was so damn tight, her greedy muscles flexing around him, trying to take his semen. This was pure animal need. Nothing more.

He pumped harder, rocking his hips until his balls tapped against her. A hand molded to her breast where he cupped a plump mound, caressing and pinching her nipple. Crushing his lips to hers, he took a savage, brief kiss.

She urged him on, clawing his back, drawing blood.

Jarek's hips pistoned in and out, faster, deeper. "Who am I? Who's fucking you?"

"Jarek." She met him thrust for thrust, lifting off the mattress.

"Come for me, *atashe delam*." Jarek rolled her nipple between his fingers and pinched hard. She shouted out in pain and pleasure as her body shook, her hand snaking around his neck, pulling him down.

He bit into her shoulder as her spasms warned of her release. Having satisfied Lizette, Jarek followed. His balls tightened. He punched deep. Hard. Once. Twice. "Yes, Lizette. Damn. Yes." He ejaculated into his female.

When he finally eased away, he kissed her forehead while pulling out. "Did I hurt you?"

Her chest bounced with her rapid breaths. "No. You were wonderful."

"This next one is for me." He spread her legs with his thigh and drove her knees up, resting her feet on his shoulders while he scooted down. Lowering his head, he found her slick folds, soaked with the evidence of their combined desire. He opened them with his thumbs. He licked up and back, lazily, tasting himself as well as her.

She moaned when he sucked on her clit, nipping and circling it with his tongue. He found her core and thrust inside.

Lizette wove her fingers into Jarek's long dark hair as she arched her back. "Don't stop."

Ruthlessly, he ground against her sex with his mouth.

"Jarek." She fisted his hair and stilled.

He rode out her demands until she was limp. Then he slid up her body, tugging her into his arms.

She stroked his brand, the feathers of the Phoenix fluttering. From there, her fingers trailed along the many breed marks on his chest and arms. She licked a path along one.

He shivered, the glide of her tongue once again thickening and hardening his arousal. "You, *atashe delam*, are a dangerous female."

"How so, Firebrand?" She paused.

Jarek wanted to comfort Lizette through the night. To say healing words, but the gentle side of him was broken. It had been for centuries. Who knows, maybe he was born without it. Maybe he was always destined to be a violent, bloodthirsty asshole.

He excelled at his job. He paid for anonymous sex. Rough, quick, no strings. Nothing better than a good lay and pay. No kind words, no cuddling, and certainly no shared feelings. When he tired of camp followers, he frequented succubus and nymph erotica houses because there he got what he wanted with no attachment. His hostesses always appreciated the money on the dresser. It made them more accommodating to his tastes the next visit.

But comforting words? No. He had nothing to offer Lizette except the harsh realities of life.

"What do you expect of me, female?"

"Whatever you can give."

Jarek stroked a thoughtful thumb across his lips. "What if it's nothing?"

"Then it's what I'll take."

"You deserve more."

"Yes, I do. So, what'll it be?"

"Why choose me?"

"You are a good man, Jarek. You found me and kept me going even when I wanted to kill myself. You encouraged me to talk about my captivity. I got up every morning because you demanded it. You never pitied me. I'm falling in love with you."

He twisted onto his elbow, fondling her breast with easy ownership. "See. This is why you are a dangerous female. You make me want to keep you in my bed. I enjoy watching you sleep, dress, cook, brush your hair, talk. It doesn't matter. Most of all, I respect your will to survive. When I see myself reflected in your eyes, I almost believe I am a good male. May the gods help you, but I'm falling in love with you, too. You make me whole. I thank fate for bringing you to me even though it was unkind to you."

Lizette's fingers stroked his cheek.

"Sleep, *atashe delam*. I will return soon. I must prepare my stronghold for our *freron's* rescue."

She grabbed his face between her hands. "Be safe, my djinn warrior. You belong to me now."

****

Unable to sleep, Lizette wandered outside the yurt, worried for Jarek. It was late, and she stretched her arms overhead to ward off sleepiness.

Out of the shadows came the camp follower in the long gauzy dress who had propositioned Jarek. Her kohl-lined eyes were narrow slits of derision. "You think he will keep you? Do not fool yourself. He will return to me and to others at this camp."

"That would be his choice. Wouldn't it?"

"Not as long as you have him spelled."

"Spelled? Don't be ridiculous. He is a free man who will choose for himself. But be sure of this. I won't kick him out of my bed." Lizette didn't dare turn her back on this woman with madness in her gaze.

"He will be mine."

"Listen to me. Once, my job was to counsel women who were brokenhearted after a failed relationship. Let me give you the same advice I gave them. Have some dignity. If he leaves you, he was never yours. Accept that. Accept the relationship is over. Be good to yourself. Move on. Someone will be there for you. I'm not sure my usual advice holds, but here goes. You could be shopping for groceries next week and bump into him with your cart. I don't know if this idea works on Scath, but you get the drift."

In truth, Lizette doubted Jarek and this woman had ever had a relationship. He saw it as sex. Obviously, she wanted more. Lizette could sympathize. He was an easy man to love.

"No. I will kill you first."

The woman withdrew a knife from the folds of her dress and stormed forward.

Without thinking, Lizette held up a hand, palm out, wishing for help. It came in the form of a Bengal tiger. Prowling out of a puff of smoke, it stalked the woman. When the beast snarled, its lips pulled back to reveal sharp canines. The camp follower pivoted and sprinted for the tree line. Seeming disappointed, the tiger faced Lizette, sitting on its haunches, cocking its head, as if a pet cat.

Her eyes wide, she spoke to the tiger. "Now what?"

It snorted.

Lizette flicked her wrist, watching as her beast evaporated in a funnel of smoke. After a few moments, her knees gave out and she sank to the ground.

Damn. That's some good counseling.

****

Pain.

Ram awoke, grinding his molars, his jaw clenched. The odor of antiseptic hung in the air. And blood.

Beep. Beep. Beep.

How long was this nap?

A white-coated human leaned in close with a needle and thread between his fingers. The guy's arm moved up and down. Needle in. Needle out.

Between gritted teeth, Ram snarled. "You're dead." Did he speak the words or think them? It didn't matter. These white-coats were cadavers walking.

The guy jumped back when Ram's gaze locked onto him. "He's awake. Fuck. Hit him with the sedative."

Another white-coat poked a syringe into the satyr's flesh. Sounds faded, faces blurred, and smells vanished like memories. Darkness set in again.

When the Firebrand surfaced once more, he tested his bindings. No give. *Damn*. A slab of metal chilled his ass. He bit back a groan, but the pain was bearable. He sniffed. Not as much blood. A band strangled his arm as a machine dinged.

Someone moaned. Norah?

Cracking a lid, Ram glanced from side to side. He was hooked to medical equipment. Wires led to the noisy machine. A cuff sheathed his upper arm. Pads stuck to his chest which was now stitched, but the red gaps in his flesh told him he wasn't healing. Of course not. He had to feed.

Through blurry vision, he made out the faded aura of a lump of flesh on another metal cart. A dead vampire. Varik.

The satyr clamped his lids closed as the door *whooshed*. Footsteps. More than one human. He flexed his wrists again.

Not dying. Nope.

He had promised to return to Jonquil. He could not let her down. And he wanted to try with Denim. Was it true? *Yes*.

The images of Jonquil and Denim faded when he remembered. Amelia's father was here. Dante. It's what he called himself.

Amelia, a sweet, fragile human gave her life to

bring their daughter into existence. Holding Ram's hand in her final moments, she had said, "Don't blame yourself. I was always free to choose, and I picked you. Let our daughter comfort you when I'm gone. Forgive yourself so you'll love again."

Her last words were for their child. "Tell her I love her. Take her home to Scath. Raise her to be a good person. Don't ever let my father near her."

Cloaked, Ram had crept into the nursery as asked by Amelia. Once home with the infant, he hired a nanny and grieved alone in silence. He hadn't loved the cheerful, kind Amelia enough. But he planned to devote himself to her and Jonquil.

Instead, she died, and he buried himself in the Scion Firebrands. They and Jonquil became his purpose.

He hadn't saved Amelia. He'd let her down, but he was true to his word. Their bright, sunny child was perfect. Despite long, unpredictable work hours, he always carved out time to share with his adorable daughter.

The familiar voice broke into his thoughts. "I've found you."

Ram tugged furiously against the chains. "Why?"

The human snarled.

"Why? What audacity. You killed my golden-haired, innocent girl."

"Amelia died giving birth to your granddaughter." Ram did have regrets. He never should have allowed Amelia to have a home delivery. He should have brought her to Scath for the birth. He should have rushed to the hospital sooner. He should have worn a fucking condom. He had let Amelia down, but he had not killed her. And she had wanted only his and Jonquil's happiness.

"I feel nothing for the alien you planted inside my

lovely child. That fetal otherworlder murdered her just as you did."

"Amelia was a bright light who dimmed too early. I made mistakes, but being with her wasn't one of them. I snatched Jonquil from the nursery because it was your daughter's wish."

"You hypnotized her."

"No. Never. I mourned her loss. Shouldered the guilt. Raised an extraordinary child."

In that moment, the satyr felt the darkness which had surrounded his heart for eight years fade. He accepted his role in Amelia's death, but he deserved happiness. It was time.

"You made her a mindless minion."

"You're crazy. Cut me loose. Stop now before it's too late. Your grandchild needs me."

Dante turned toward a male in a white lab coat. "Keep him sedated. He and the vamps are our proof Scath and otherworlders exist. The Americans may have more questions before they leave."

"We're not otherworlders, old coot. We're Aeternals. We were here long before your kind. We locked ourselves away in another realm to protect your species. Your asses are still on our to-save list."

Ram thrashed against his restraints, tearing out stitches, opening the incisions, as the technician prepped a syringe.

"Fuck no." Lights out again.

****

Once her assigned healer gave final approval and Kole stopped shooting fire, Skyler sat cross-legged on a gray yoga mat in a small empty room at the Covenkirk Stronghold. She rolled her head, stretching her neck. She raised her shoulders to her ears and lowered them. Vanilla-scented candles flickered. Soft music played on her MP3 player. Her mate had set everything as she desired. The rest was up to her.

Scryers used reflective tools—mirrors, glass, crystal balls. Skyler's medium was inside her. While she plugged into Enya's "Watermark," she closed her eyes and pictured a river. The water chilled. Little by little it froze. She imagined herself encased in the frigid cube.

Not correct.

She became the ice.

Skyler clasped Ram's black shirt to her heart. Though her lids opened, she couldn't see the stronghold chamber. She was elsewhere. A lab.

Voices sounded through an open door. She wandered into the room, invisible.

A man donned a white coat, talking and squirting liquid from a syringe. Four guys lined up in front of him, one by one getting an injection.

No Ram.

She slipped outside when a human in a black uniform with an HR logo on the shoulder exited. Leaning against the wall, she lingered near a huge, grassy field, a running track circling it. To her left was a shooting range and beyond a pad where a helicopter sat.

Skyler crossed her arms while she waited for a door to open. As the trainer had explained, physical laws no less real than Brownian Motion or Einstein's Mass-Energy Equation governed the Scrying Principle. More specifically, her secondary talent of etheric travel. Her body remained at Firebrand headquarters while its spirit, existing in air and composed of a gaseous substance, roamed the Humans First compound. Here was the catch. In that form, she could not use already occupied space. No passing through objects. No grabbing them. She could feel a chair, sit in it, but she couldn't move it. When she asked for a clearer explanation, her trainer clapped hands to hips, frowned, and snapped, "Just accept it." Still, it would be nice to float through walls.

While she marked time, men in uniforms entered and exited doors, gathering, talking, moving on. From the action, she identified a barracks. A mess hall. She itched to drift by, but finding Ram and the base's location were the mission.

An older man in an expensive suit breezed out a door.

Skyler sneaked in before it clicked shut, but when she scoped out the lab, her hand flew to her mouth. Gasping, she was relieved people could not hear her. Ram lay asleep, or unconscious, on a gurney, his beautiful hair matted. What had they done to him? His skin was sallow, not its usual color. His chest barely moved with each breath.

On another slab, the butchers had cut open the male vampire. An instrument stuck out of his heart. He was dead. Guys in lab coats peered into the body, chatting while they unhooked probes.

On a different bed, the female vampire sobbed.

"Damn shame we lost him," said a white coat. "Our visitors are gonna come back with Dante and start in on the big guy again. The otherworlder's time is short, though. I think the English guy will finish him off."

Skyler gasped, but she was unable to do anything. Needing to get a fix on the base, she cast around for evidence, paper with an address, a photo.

Nada.

The door clicked open.

"There they are now," said a white coat.

Three men entered, two in uniform. The costly suit must be Dante. Not staying to make sure, Skyler glided outside before the door closed.

If only she could float. High enough to view the

surrounding environment.

That's when she rose. Up and up. Over the compound and its wooden buildings which formed a huge rectangle the size of four side-by-side football fields. In the open center was the track, field, shooting range, and helipad.

As she soared higher, the shape of the island amid murky waters, green and brown with algae, formed. Huge cypress trees leaned into the encroaching swamp. Two intersecting highways and a river gave her reference points.

Her vision clouded as she began to dissolve.

"No. No."

Though not ready, she could never stop the fade-out.

Solidifying, she sat yoga-style on the carpet in the Firebrand headquarters. With her palm, she cradled her belly, her child. Pushing herself up on wobbly legs, Skyler grabbed the doorknob. Too weak to turn it, she tapped the D-chip Kole had insisted she have after they mated.

In seconds, her mate stormed in, catching her in his arms.

"Frisca. Damn it. I knew this was a fucking bad idea."

"I'm okay, Kole. The baby's fine. But the scene's bad. Ram was unconscious, chained to a lab table. Varik is dead. The female is alive. A lab assistant implied Ram didn't have much time left. And I think I spotted the Dante guy. He was with military types. A general and a colonel, if I remember insignias. I'm sure I can find the island on a map. Get a big one. Quick, before I forget."

****

Once Skyler identified the location of the Humans First compound on a map of the Atchafalaya

Basin, Rein grabbed Tyr. He pulled the warlock off med center duty where healers were working to save the human female he and Dax found in the middle of the road the other day. Denim filled them in on dangers in the swamp and possible problems.

Standing at the edge of the island, both Firebrands hid in a thick mist while they reconned the military set-up.

Rein analyzed tasks for the upcoming attack. What if they all portaled to a nearby central staging area first? Out of sight. He and Tyr could scout a spot.

After all boots were on the ground, a small team could wipe out the first-line defense. Spaced around the perimeter, snipers tucked themselves into the tall grasses. They were priority one. High guard towers pinpointed each of the four corners. The men who manned these were the secondary targets.

The task required mages with skills. Him. Tyr. Braelyn. His father. Aunt Indigo. One of the new recruits was a warlock, but Rein wasn't sure about his abilities yet.

Once that job was one-and-done, Margo was up next. She'd destroy communication signals, taking away everybody's ears.

Next, the warriors would storm the base. From Skyler's description, the lab holding Ram lay on the south side of the facility. A special team would proceed directly there while others handled the remaining Humans First soldiers.

All buildings opened onto a central field. Skyler figured several barracks, a mess, two labs, at least. There was the helicopter. They'd need to disable it.

Two tall, solid doors barred the entrance. Rein and Tyr had seen no one come or go from them, but they stuck around to observe the changing of the guard.

Fresh snipers came out. The guys in the grass switched with their replacements while new guards took over the towers. Rein glanced at his watch.

The operation was big with lots of moving parts.

He signaled Tyr, and they scoped out an area where the Firebrands could stage the action.

Chapter Thirty-One

Splash. Pop. Squish. Pop. Squish. Squish.

Several hours before nightfall, waterlogged swampland grasses slogged under boots as fighters from three strongholds unloaded from SUVs and trucks at the designated operation staging area out of sight of Dante's compound.

Kole's fiery gaze swept over the males and females, not only from his command but also from Jarek's and Nace's. Black leather, jeans, tees, and shitkickers were the dress of the day. Blades crisscrossed on chests and backs. Guns hung from hips. The Scion Firebrands were weighted with metal and fierce determination.

Though death's bell tolled with an uncertain outcome, their backs were straight and their heads clear. The air rippled with energy. *No.* Excitement. Anticipation. They were born for this. The Phoenix had called them for this.

No warriors were more impressive. None made Kole prouder.

Silence greeted the commander's raised arm and clenched fist. Even the swamp stilled. No birds, no frogs, no crickets sounded as if they had read the orders of the day. The usual bullshit banter among the Firebrands paused for the moment.

"You've been briefed, but once more for the dumbasses who didn't listen." A few snickers rolled through the group. "Rein, Tyr, Alarik, Indigo, and Braelyn will go in first to take care of the hidden snipers and guards in the towers. When they signal job done, we will all move outside the compound to our assigned zones. Margo will silence communications. From this point forward, we'll all be deaf. No D-chip babble even. Vampires, you have the advantage here if you're telepathic. Once Margo has zapped the airwaves, we go in and we go in fast. Hit them with everything we have."

Chay bounced from foot to foot, unable to harness his energy.

Brak punched his arm. "Stop with the war dance."

The ylve Firebrand grinned his comeback as he continued to bob and weave.

Kole ignored them to continue. "Dax, you're leading Denim, Sabine, Nico, and Thorn to the labs. First in. We hope first out. The rest of the Covenkirk stronghold is with me. We'll make a direct run for the helicopter, killing anyone in our way. Jarek, you and your Firebrands will secure the entrance and the south sector. Nace, take your warriors to the north."

Both commanders nodded, their vibes as palpable as those coming off their warriors. Since djinn fed off battle, Jarek's anticipation was expected. He needed it to survive. Nace? He was just savage.

"I know these are *Homo sapiens*, and we have spent a lifetime protecting them. Not these males. Not now. Remember, they are stronger, and they are faster than what you expect. Kill them all. They chose this battle. We leave no one behind who knows about us."

The Aeternals nodded.

"We do this for one of our own and for two innocent citizens being tortured by a madman. We do this for Gahya who created us. For the Blood Coven who gifted us with a home on Scath. We do this for the glory of the Firebrands who give us purpose. For the survival of our species. Do it fast. Do it well. And do it with a clean conscience. For duty. For honor."

When silent raised blades and spears paid homage

to Kole's words, he nodded at Rein and his group. They were on deck first.

****

Rein's Team One moved into position. When he, Braelyn, Tyr, Indigo, and Alarik flicked their wrists, the guards in the towers and the snipers hidden in the grasses grabbed their heads. Lights out. Put to bed with a thought. The mind-control spells wormed into the humans' brains, burrowed in, voraciously devouring tissue. No shots fired.

His robes replaced by black BDU's and a dark shirt, Alarik strolled to the nearest shooter. He touched fingers to the guy's neck, signaling no pulse.

Indigo kicked over a sniper, bending to whisper while she twirled a strand of hair between her thumb and forefinger. "You chose the wrong side, dumpling."

Rein fisted Braelyn's arm. "Retreat to stand with my father. Margo will join you when her task is complete."

"Sure thing." She rose on tip-toe, pressing her warm lips to his. "Be careful."

After he muttered a response, his thoughts drifted toward the fight. "I live for the battle, Brae. The rush."

When she caught his shoulders, he had no choice. He looked at her. Eyes soft, she gave him a quick hug. "I know, but watch your soul."

Firebrands rushed in behind them. Jarek and Dax's teams took point near the door. Kole and Nace's squads assembled to their rear. Recruits spread around the perimeter of the base.

On cue, Margo straight-armed it, holding her palm out to disrupt communication signals. Firebrands along with humans lost chatter. The airwaves dropped dead.

Bloodcurdling screams, thundering boots, blades

or spears pounding on shields, and guns drawn, the warriors charged through the front entrance in a blur of speed, taking out the doors as if they were *papier mâché*.

****

Kole's team along with Nace's warriors met resistance from Humans First mercenaries on the north side of the base, men pouring out of what must be barracks.

The battle took place in quick-time, the Earthers' jacked-up speed, their agility nearly matching the Aeternals. Nearly, but not completely.

A uniformed human blocked Kole's path. The soldier lifted his gun, but Kole shot a stream of fire. With the shooter incinerated, he slapped a hand to his side where he felt the sting of a bullet. He pivoted to face the guy, a pale-faced kid hardly out of puberty.

Kole sent a blast of heat to the would-be killer's gun, the young mercenary dropping it like a hot potato when it scorched his hand. The commander grabbed the kid's shoulder, letting loose 220-volts of shock and awe. Black around the edges, the kid dropped to the ground, smoking. The demon had no time to consider the uselessness of the inexperienced soldier's life choices.

He glanced at his command.

Jezzi, in her panther fur, gripped an adversary in her jaws. Nace, a jaguar, was tearing flesh from a fighter's body, feeding. Rein, having joined the team, spun in a circle with his hand out, using warlock powers to down charging opponents.

Plop. Plop. Plop.

They fell before they could fire.

Rein hunted for more blood action. He never stuck with the non-messy route. The mix-breed Firebrand drew back lips, his fangs popping sharp. His big set of pearly whites changed him from coldly handsome to feral. No denying it. He strode toward a soldier, allowing a wild shot. With fingers locked in the male's hair, he bit into the guy's neck, draining him. When Rein stepped away, the facade of civilization was wiped from his face. Blood dripped from his mouth. His eyes glowed red.

Satisfied everyone was on task, Kole thundered toward the chopper, flinging attackers out of his path. His demon was in control, its body leaving a trail of crimson flames. When he neared his goal, the helicopter's blades rotated. It lifted off.

Damn.

The ground shook with the chopper's power as it took to the air. The panther Jezzi, closest to the aircraft, shifted while she jumped for the runner, naked or not. The female was about the win. She held on while it gained altitude but dropped when it continued to rise. No holding back those engine horses.

A bullet whizzed by Kole's ear. He spun, straight-armed his Glock, and fired. Dead center forehead. One more dirt nap. With his gun holstered, he tossed out his hand, shooting flames at the next Humans First bastard.

****

Denim was with Dax's Team Three when it raced through the front door, a wide path cleared for them by Jarek's fighters.

While the Southern Stronghold remained to clean out the sector, their squad charged out the back, across a field, and toward the labs Skyler had described.

They met resistance on the way from soldiers, some in uniform, some in boxers with no shirts or shoes. The humans fired wildly, surprised or roused from sleep.

In a blur, Dax barreled into two attackers. He took one to the ground, twisting the guy's head between weighty hands. When the vampire Firebrand sped behind the other, he grabbed around the soldier's throat and sank fang. Blood splattered in Denim's face while she sprinted past.

Handy skill.

Denim fired off a shot to the chest of a soldier who bullseyed her. It was hardly fair since he was half naked, but she didn't care. Only Ram was on her mind. This asshole stood between her and her satyr.

Thorn turned wolfy, a guy's neck clenched between his jaws. Blood matted the shifter's fur.

Sabine and Nico disappeared into the first lab but exited, shaking their heads.

Denim raced for the second door. Locked.

Damn.

Dax pushed her aside, palming the knob. *Pop.* It opened, but they dodged to the side when bullets streamed out in their direction.

"Don't shoot." Denim grabbed the vampire's arm. "Ram might be in there."

"Fuck." Dax stormed in, ammo thudding into his Kevlar. He marched up to a white-coated male, firing point blank between his eyes. "Outta my way, mutherfucker."

Another guy in white crouched behind a turned over lab table. Denim rushed him at full speed. He fired, the bullet hitting her vest.

Oomph.

She fell to the floor, grabbing at the protective gear. "Shit. That hurts." Satisfied she was still alive despite the pain, she kicked out, sent the guy's pistol flying, and jacked to her feet. She planted her boot on his chest, lifting her Beretta.

Who lives? Him or me. I choose me. Bang.

Thorn took out another shooter. He shifted to his human form, bloody and naked. His golden eyes sought a target.

Sabine and Nico guarded the door, firing off rounds while they dodged bullets flying into the lab.

Denim's gaze flicked toward a steel table. Ram was strapped to it, his chest flayed open, his body still. An older man in a suit tapped a gun barrel to his skull.

Bile rose from Denim's stomach when she didn't see the satyr breathe. She had to believe he was alive or fall to the floor, a puddle of ineffective soldier.

"I'll kill him." The man's hand was steady, his thin lips curled into a snarl, his finger on the trigger. He was as Skyler had described Dante.

"I can't see if Ram's breathing." Denim shouted to anyone who'd listen.

A dust devil started small, swirling at her feet. It grew stronger, tearing her hair from its ponytail, whipping it around her. While the storm's circle widened, debris funneled throughout the room. Beakers and test tubes shattered. Papers whirled like a blizzard in winter. Airborne metal embedded into walls.

A bolt of lightning struck a counter, sparks shooting from one wall to another. Thunder rattled the foundation. Dax grabbed a table and rolled with it. Nico and Sabine clutched the doorjamb, the nymph's feet leaving the ground. Thorn flattened himself to the floor, gripping a desk leg. Ram's out-of-control gurney wheeled around the room, the man with the gun hanging onto the edge.

When Dante lost his grip on the cart, his weapon waved in his hand while shots pinged wildly off cabinets, carts, doorframes.

Caught in Denim's whirlwind, junk continued to roil. A shard of ragged metal lodged in Dante's neck. In order to stay the flow of blood with his hand, he dropped his gun.

In the eye of her own tempest, Denim stalked toward him. She was an untamed force of nature, her hair swirling around her head, her eyes stormy, lightning sparking from her fingers.

She forced Dante's hand from his neck, dispatching deadly jolts of lightning into his arm. Kicking his gun away, she willed the squall to calm. Though the air stilled, the residual energy pinged from steel table to table.

Dax rose, wiping dust off his leathers. Thorn pushed off the floor while Nico checked Sabine for injuries. Ram's cart stopped rocking and rolling.

Denim unfisted Dante's shirt, letting him fall to the concrete while she rushed to Ram's side. No pulse. "Get a healer," she screamed, trying to tuck the satyr's parts back inside, trying to piece his flesh together.

Dax and Thorn pulled alongside her at the cold, sterile slab. Sabine and Nico continued their watch at the doorway, firing into the courtyard occasionally.

A healer rushed inside and pushed Denim aside to work on Ram. She did a much better job of re-arranging his organs, re-aligning his split chest, and laying some quick stitches to his flayed skin. She touched the area of his heart. His body jerked. Again. His hips popped off the table.

Denim was helpless. She could do nothing to help Ram.

The healer shook her head.

"Again, damn it," shouted Denim, her loud plea sounding rattled. She grabbed Ram's hand, squeezing tight. "Do not give up, satyr. You promised Jonquil you'd be home."

The healer zapped him once more. This time, she nodded. "I've got a weak pulse." She faced his *frerons*. "This is a temporary patch. It'll last until we get him to the medical center. I need to wake him." She touched his temple.

Ram's lashes fluttered.

"That's a nasty cut, man." The claw marks on Thorn's jaw twitched. "Kinda goes from sternum to navel."

"Waited for you." Ram's lids dropped like a napping cat.

With shaky hands, Denim fumbled with the chains binding him. She couldn't speak.

"Here. Let me." Dax snapped them one by one.

The satyr's lids fluttered open. "Nice. I could have done that. If I didn't have the fucking wobbles. Female vamp next room."

"Nico, Sabine. Get her. Thorn, take door duty." Dax shot orders at the team.

Ram's gaze searched the room, a hand pressed to his barely patched chest. His head lolled to the side. "Too many sedatives." When he saw Denim holding his other palm, his lips twitched. "Doll."

"Don't talk." She stroked his arm, useless tears welling in her eyes.

Ram jerked his gaze toward the man bleeding on the floor. "Dante. Amelia's father. He did all this to make me suffer."

"Everybody at the compound dies," said Dax.

Ram nodded. "He's my job. I'll do it."

"You're not getting up." Denim held him on the metal slab. "You're lucky to be alive, you crazy-ass satyr. Stay put. We're taking you to the medical center."

****

"Not yet, doll." Ram snagged Dax's nine. Not an easy task when he was barely conscious. He rolled off the slab, holding his gut, stumbling toward Dante. Here was the man who wanted to kill him, all Aeternals, and the guy's own adorable granddaughter.

Denim and Dax reacted at the same time, latching onto his upper arms, steadying him, urging him back to the metal gurney.

Ram refused to budge.

Lord Ellington was conscious, but blood poured from his neck. He sat with his back to the wall and legs spread out on the floor, awaiting his fate. "Go ahead, you damn otherworlder. You killed me long ago when you entranced sweet Amelia, filling her head with fantasies."

Denim and his vampire *freron* held Ram upright. "I didn't deserve her. True. But in my way, I loved her. She gave me Jonquil. Great kid. Smart. Kind. Beautiful. You'll never meet her. Never hug."

"If I had seen her, I would have killed her. She's as much to blame for my baby's death as you are." The voice of the man who claimed to have loved his daughter was venomous.

"Amelia would never have chosen this." Ram's knees nearly buckled, but he stayed on his feet.

"Amelia was a besotted dreamer."

"She hated you, old man. Why do you think she turned to me? To get out of your clutches. She made me promise to keep Jonquil away from you."

"Liar." Amelia's father stared at him as if he were a monster.

"Now is not the time for lies. Only truth. Amelia got ripped-off. Bad husband. Worse father."

The satyr aimed the nine-millimeter weapon at Dante. As he tried to squeeze the trigger, the gun flapped like a flag on a windy day.

Dax gripped the barrel of the gun, taking it from his hand. "One last question, asshole. Where's General Mars?"

As Dante clutched the wound on his neck, his

mouth twisted into a sneering smile. "On a helicopter. He's in the air with your fate, two American military officers."

Dax fired. Dante died instantly as the bullet opened a perfect hole between his cold, hard eyes. "There. Done. No guilt."

The vampire Firebrand tucked the Glock into its holster.

For a moment, Ram pictured Amelia's father in other times, in front of a fireplace, smiling warmly at a daughter who had seen the ugly side of him. As Ram's feet buckled, he heard Denim scream, "Where's the damn healer?"

****

Denim flung Ram's arm over her shoulder. He was dead weight. If Dax hadn't been on his other side, he'd be face down on the floor. Damn stubborn satyr.

She and the vampire carried him back to the metal slab to wait for the healer.

Pulling up a stool, she tangled her fingers in his hair, needing the contact, a balm. She loved Ram even if he couldn't return the favor.

Two healers raced into the lab, carrying a stretcher. They transferred Ram to it. Denim grasped his hand, walking alongside as they ran for a truck the medics had moved from the staging area to the center of the compound. They'd drive it to a portal and on to the medical center.

Ram raised a hand before they loaded him onboard. "Varik's dead. He killed himself rather than face more torture. Two officers, one a general and the other a colonel, were here. I think they flew off in a helicopter with the vampire's body and Dr. Messenger. Mars could have been on it, too. All my fault." Ram's voice was scratchy.

Kole met them at the vehicle, other Firebrands gathered around. "Son. Glad to see you again."

Ram once-overed the warriors. "Any dead?"

Jarek said, "Three seriously injured, but healers are on it. They'll be fine."

"No bodies," said Nace. "Lots of minor injuries. Major ones sent to the experts. All's well."

Dax wiped blood from his jaw, his fangs still sharp and prominent. "Your Denim cooked up a storm."

The satyr's voice was slurred and raspy. "My fault. All my fault. Dante was my father-in-law, Jonquil's grandfather. This was about revenge." He paused while Firebrands shuffled their feet and whispered in surprise. "If I…"

"If, if, if. When did you become such a wuss, son? Where's the pig-headed, arrogant asshole we know and love? If you had never hooked up with the female, you wouldn't have Jonquil. She's a decent female. Could be Firebrand material one day. Any of us could have triggered our exposure. Fact is, we've lived a charmed life for fifteen hundred years. So, shut the fuck up and carry on. Now, I'm going home so my mate can kiss my boo-boos. Maybe it'll give her other ideas."

The Firebrands whooped, pounded shields, and banged spears on the ground, the noise swelling until it was a deafening roar.

Brak guy-punched Ram's shoulder. "Now, there's a pep talk to remember. One of Kole's best. You missed his gabfest before the attack. Brought tears to my eyes."

The satyr flinched.

"Sorry."

Denim squeezed Ram's hand tighter.

"I don't deserve you, doll."

"But you're stuck with me."

"It goes both ways. Did we get the female

vamp?" asked Ram.

"Got her," said Sabine. "A healer took her."

Ram eyed Denim. "Home?"

"Are you nuts? You're almost dead. Held together with chewing gum and tape. The Ministry of Well Being. I'll call Jonquil."

"No. She can't see me like this. Home." He glanced down at his chest, which still seeped blood.

"No. She's worried. We do this my way."

"Bossy female."

"Have to be with you. You never listen."

"In full disclosure, you need to know I'm about to pass out."

One of the healers shot her eyes to the sky. "Is the gabfest over? Can I get this male to the medical facility? He's not out of the woods. Are you riding along?"

"Try to keep me out."

When they loaded an unconscious Ram into the back end of the truck, the island returned to normal, birds chirping, insects buzzing, and bent cypresses stroking the surface of water.

Chapter Thirty-Two

Lizette's shapely ass, which his hands had cradled this morning while he pumped into her, swayed back and forth in front of Jarek. *Nice.* "Not too late, *atashe delam.* You can return. We will take care of the berserker."

She cast a smirk over her shoulder as she slipped on loose pebbles. "Try to keep up, Commander."

"Ah, a challenge." Jarek raced ahead, pounding dirt and dodging trees. He laughed.

When was the last time I played, laughed?

"Damn." Lizette picked up the pace, arms churning and boots digging into rock.

This female made him want to laugh. Had fate brought them together? Each had survived a past forged in a crucible of fire and cruelty. They found each other. Fate, the whim of the gods, or pure chance? He cared naught. The result mattered. The female was here and his forever.

I belong to her until the Evermore and beyond.

Jarek paused at the base of a steep, rocky cliff, shielding his eyes against the sun while he gazed toward the mountaintop. "Clese, you're certain he is up there?"

"The berserker's up where it's rugged. And running scared." The bear shifter slipped into furry skin, climbing easily with claws.

The trees grew sparse, the topography becoming rougher, more vertical. He, Lizette, and the Firebrands jammed boot toes into crevices and fingers onto small holds.

"A slide." Jarek warned the others while small rocks tumbled down the mountainside. As he covered his head with his arms, he snugged his body tight to the wall.

When he glanced below, he let out a breath seeing Lizette had done the same.

"I'm fine," she yelled.

Jarek started his climb again. Hand, foot, other hand, other foot. When debris clattered below, he dared a peep at his female.

Lizette struggled but continued toward the top. "I'm okay. Just a little slip."

"Move to your right a bit." He waited until she maneuvered in that direction, her foot and handholds gaining traction.

Jarek swung over the outcropping of rocks onto a plateau. He offered an assist.

Lizette accepted his palm, cleared the rise, and took to her feet, brushing dirt off her jeans. "I never thought of myself as an outdoor kind of girl. New York and all that. I'm re-defining my image." She swished her hands together. "Where is he?"

"There and fleeing. Let's go."

They took off at a slow side-by-side jog. "Look ahead. Spear's stirring up a dust cloud."

"I see. Hurry." Lizette kicked it up a notch.

Jarek shook his head. Using his djinn gift, he faded into smoke and caught up. Not fair, but a hell of a lot easier.

****

By the time Lizette arrived, Darius, Kara, and Clese, still in bear fur, had grounded the berserker.

Spear's braids matted together, dirt crusted his face, and blood dripped down his shirtless chest onto ragged pants. He had lost one boot, his bare foot mangled and swollen.

Curled into a fetal position, he hooked hands over his head while Kara kicked him. Clese circled, growling and slashing out with claws.

Here is my nightmare.

Lizette's chest heaved with rapid breaths as she stared at the object of her hatred, opening her mouth to speak. No angry words formed.

"Your tormentor is not such a big male now, is he? Sit up, asshole. Look into this honorable female's eyes. Show at least that much courage." Kara landed another gut kick.

Spear trembled. When he tilted toward Lizette, tears streaked his dirty face like wrinkles.

The bound male whimpered. *"Kjonner."*

Lizette's eyes hunted for Jarek.

"Slave. Maybe something kinder, but that's what it really means."

She nodded.

"I loved you, *min besettelse.*"

Once again, Lizette sought an interpretation.

"Beloved." The djinn commander snarled, his immense body pitching toward the berserker.

Lizette settled a hand on Jarek's arm. This cornered man was Spear. Studying his pitiful form, she shoved her fists onto her hips. "I am not your beloved. I was never your slave. Tie the freak to that tree, please."

"Gladly." Kara unhooked a thick rope she had fastened to her belt while Clese shifted to help secure the berserker. The ever-watchful guard, Darius cradled a long sword in his arms.

Lizette withdrew a knife from her sheath, the blade glistening in the mountain sun. The brightness reminded her of the day she had climbed out Spear's window. As she had done that afternoon, she listened. Birds sang on a nearby branch. Pine trees and gathering rain clouds scented the air. No jasmine.

She approached the berserker until her hiking shoes nearly touched his gnarled toes and remaining boot. He wasn't scary. He was a dirty, bloody, flabby-fleshed pervert.

Words gushed from her lips. "You dragged me by my hair from the cell. You beat me. You put filthy hands on me and raped me. You stuffed your ugly penis in my mouth. The baths at the river were the worst. I bet you don't know that, do you? Yes. Those were the worst times. You thought you were making me cleaner with all the soap and water. Instead, I was dirtier."

He gulped huge sobs, but with his hands tied, he could not wipe the tears. "I love you."

When Lizette found Jarek observing her, his eyes black with rage, she gathered the strength to continue. "No. You don't. Here's the plan. I will cut off your prick while you watch. Then I'll kill you."

Spear's legs kicked frantically against the bindings, his chest flinging from side to side, the rope chewing his flesh.

Lizette yanked the male's pants to his ankles, baring his flaccid shaft while tears welled in her eyes. For what seemed an eternity, she stood frozen. "I can't touch it."

"Let me." Kara fisted the crown of his dick and pulled on it, giving Lizette space to slice. "Better?"

With the knife in her fist, Lizette focused on completing the task, but she spun away. "I can't." She flung the blade into the dirt.

With desperate lurches, Spear snapped the rope. Once loose, he yanked his pants up while he ran, stumbling.

Lizette held up a hand. "He's mine."

She stretched out a palm and channeled power from Jarek. A cool breeze signaled a spell-in-the-making. The familiar Bengal tiger leapt from a tree, landing on silent paws. As the cat prowled toward Spear, it gained speed, the powerful muscles in its thick legs and shoulders flexing with each step. Its orange fur with black stripes ruffled in the air. When the beast caught Spear, it wrestled him to the ground. Its sharp canines clamped around his neck. Since Lizette did not call off the tiger, it bit through flesh and bone, severing the berserker's head from the body.

Jarek's brows arched. "An excellent gift."

Lizette's sensible and smooth chin-length hair yo-yoed as she nodded. "A handy one."

With a flick of the wrist, the tiger disappeared in a misty *pfft*.

"I practiced on your camp follower who thought I might share you. I convinced her it would not happen."

"Hmm. Remind me not to piss you off." As Jarek threw an arm around Lizette's shoulders, he drew her against his hard body. "Let's go home, *atashe delam*."

****

Denim dragged a faux leather armchair to the bed. She sat in it, Ram's hand clutched in hers. While he was unconscious, three healers worked on him, adjusting his organs, knitting his bones, mending his skin. He was stable, his heartbeat steady, but his still-bleeding wound was raw.

She had washed his hair, brushing it out as best she could. His face was clean now, a combination of rugged masculinity, dangerous warrior, and movie star perfection.

Ram was not Steven. He had raised a joyful, wonderful Jonquil. He had stepped in front of a bullet meant for her. Sure, he could claim he was like any satyr—sex with no commitment—but Denim knew better. She'd make him see.

When the door whooshed open, a healer popped her head into the room. "He needs to feed. I'll close the door for a spell." Her eyes locked on Denim.

"Okay. Um ... you mean?"

"Yes. I mean." The healer tapped the toe of a soft-soled shoe on the floor.

"He can't. He's injured."

She shook her head before stepping out. "Newbies. When he wakes up, you can either be his food source, or I'll hunt down a volunteer."

Hell no.

Denim fell asleep until the tap, tap, tap of shoes on the floor woke her. Jonquil rushed into the room, coming to an abrupt stop when she spied her father, his exposed skin sallow, his breath halting. Mara was behind her.

Denim wiped the sleep from her eyes as she kneeled in front of the girl. "He'll be fine."

"He needs to feed."

Denim clasped both of her small hands. "He will when he wakes. It's handled."

****

Tired of on-again-off-again naps, Ram steadied his breathing but clamped his lids tight. Soft-soled shoes padded on the floor. Machines beeped. Antiseptic scented the air. *Damn.* The whole rescue scene had been a hoax. His arms and legs scissored, tangling in the covers.

"Hey. Calm down, man. All's good."

A meaty, warm hand rested on Ram's leg, its owner's voice familiar. When the satyr popped his lids open, he stared into Brak's face.

Denim and Jonquil floated into his line of sight. Ram struggled to smile, but his lips were dry and cracked.

Jonquil's fingers touched his arm. "Is it okay if I do this?"

Denim answered when he couldn't. "Sure it is, *cher*."

Ram's gaze swung around the room. Firebrands crowded the space, some on the floor, some leaning against walls, some sprawled in chairs. They sprang to their feet.

"Satyr. Welcome back." Rein high-fived Ram as he passed the bed.

His fellow warriors tossed nods, shakes, and grins at him as they trekked alongside one-by-one, chattering about how they had hung around to make sure he was still kicking.

Kole rested a calloused palm on Denim's arm. "We'll leave now. Needless to say, Ram, you're off rotation for a spell."

"I'll be good to go by tomorrow."

"Idiot. Only you would say that. Gonna go. Got a human to check on down the hall." Jeweled-up and grinning, Tyr man-fisted Ram's shoulder before he followed the other Firebrands.

"Great idea. Leave me alone with my ladies."

"I should go, too." Denim pivoted toward the door.

Both Jonquil and Ram together said, "No."

The satyr stretched out his arms, pulling his daughter into one and Denim into the other. Jonquil squealed.

Ram loosened his hold. "How long have I been out?"

"The rescue mission wound up late yesterday. We brought you here, kicking and screaming. Okay. That's a lie. You were asleep, couldn't scream or kick. You've been out about eight hours." Denim flipped her wrist to check her D-chip.

"You don't look so good, Daddy."

Denim agreed. "Too many sedatives in your system. Them and the ... uh ... surgery they performed." Her eyes moistened.

Ram peeked under the lightweight blanket, lifting his hospital johnnie. An angry red slash ran the length of his chest and abdomen. *No shit*. Without feeding, he was in for a long recovery. "Memories are coming back. Dax said you let loose a big storm?" He glanced at Denim, trying to scoot into a sitting position.

"You'd be proud. I went all thunder and lightning. I'll need a witch coach soon before I do real damage. And don't move like that. Let me help." She pushed his shoulders flat to the mattress and levered the back of the bed up higher.

"Better. Thanks. How are you doing, pest?"

"I'm great, Daddy. I'm happy you're not lost anymore."

A smile curled the corners of his lips. Sounded like something Denim might have said. "Lost, huh? Who stayed with you?"

"I stayed with Denim. She says we're bunk mates."

The female bit her lower lip nervously, a grimace crossing her face. "I can explain. What else could I do? Your nanny or housekeeper..." She looked to Jonquil.

"Mara."

"Yes. Her. Anyway. She was leaving town for a few days. I thought it best if Jonquil roomed with me. I hope you don't mind. I might have crossed some lines, but..."

"Hey. Stop rattling. You did the right thing, doll."

"Really?"

He nodded while Jonquil eyeballed him and Denim with a wide grin showing a bunch of well-brushed teeth.

"How did you like your visit, pest?"

"I had fun. We played games, dressed up dolls, did each other's hair. We read to each other at bedtime."

"Hey. I do those things with you." He pasted a pretend pout on his face.

Jonquil chuckled. "You don't like dolls, and, no offense, Daddy, but Mara does my hair again after you leave."

He humphed. "How about you go out and get me some water? Give your dad some time here."

"You need to feed." Jonquil looked at Denim.

"I'm working on it, pest. Now, a little privacy, please."

When Jonquil left, a healer peeked into the room but backed out.

A grinning Ram shoved his blanket down and pulled up his hospital gown. He took his shaft in hand and stroked. "Come on, doll. Think of it as a big stick shift. I'll lie here and let you drive."

****

Denim wore nothing more than a satisfied smile when she slipped her shirt over her head and wiggled into her jeans again.

Ram's skin had a healthier tone, and his incision was less angry. "You know, I'll need to feed often to heal."

Denim fluffed her sex-messy hair. "Lucky me. I want to tell you…"

"I want to…" Ram pulled the cover up to his groin and rolled onto his side.

"You first," said Denim.

He patted the mattress. "Curl up here."

Denim crawled onto the bed and tucked herself against Ram. As she trailed fingers across his brand, his muscles bunched with each feathery touch.

The satyr kissed her forehead. "I love you."

"I love... What did you say?"

"I love you."

Tears welled in Denim's eyes. "I love you, too, Ram. I was so afraid I'd never get to tell you. And if I did tell you, I thought you'd run screaming."

"Do you think we can get a bigger suite at the stronghold, doll? One with two bedrooms."

"What?"

"I want to make an honest female of you."

"Jonquil and you would move in? What about the farm?"

"We'll keep it, but right now, you're safer at the stronghold. And wherever you are is where I'll be."

"Jonquil should have a say in this."

"No. She shouldn't. That you love my daughter and that she loves you is a big, big plus. But, doll, make no mistake. This is our biz. I want you for myself. As my mate."

"What?"

"So young. Is your hearing going?" Ram grinned. "What'll it be?"

"You told me not to make more of us than what it is. What happened, *cher*?"

"It was a dumbass thing to say. You'll probably hear more stupid shit come out of my mouth. Ignore it. Besides, horns don't lie."

"I don't understand."

"A satyr only sprouts horns when he finds the female who holds his heart. You're the one, doll."

"You didn't tell me."

"I was worried I'd let you down. Be unable to protect you."

"And now?"

"I'll probably fuck up on occasion, but loving me

as you do, you'll forgive me."

She laughed. "I will. And hell yes."

When Jonquil returned to the room with a bottle of water, a blushing Denim popped off the bed.

The girl smothered a giggle. "Here, it's cold."

"Good news, pest. Denim consented to be my mate. You're the first to know."

Jonquil jumped up and down, hugged Denim, and reached onto her toes to kiss Ram's cheek. "I knew it. I knew you were perfect for each other."

Ram propped his head on his palm, elbow resting on the bed. "How did you know?"

"When I first saw Denim outside the grocery store, she looked at you as if she loved you."

"I did not."

"You did. Your eyes got all sparkly when you saw Daddy. And his got all green when he looked at you."

"My satyr recognized what it wanted. A brave, strong, and beautiful female. You were right, pest."

"For the record, I'm getting a two-fer, kid. I adore you." Denim opened her arms. When Jonquil ran into them, she folded herself around the child.

"I love you, too." The kid's eyes moistened under thick lashes. "Can we talk about what I can call you? Denim doesn't sound like we're … you know, special."

Denim swiped a palm across her eyes before she got all weepy. "What would you like to call me?"

The girl got shy, a toe of her shoe tracing a pattern on the tile floor. "Mom."

Denim swallowed the lump in her throat. She glanced at Ram, who watched the scene, a satisfied smile on his face. When she had least expected it, Ram stormed into her life. And to think the gorgeous male came as a package deal. "Nothing could make me happier than to have you call me Mom."

Chapter Thirty-Three

Celene closed the shower door, steam filling the bathroom. She scrubbed a hand across the mirror, studying her blurry image. Her blonde hair was longer than she liked, and restless nights made her eyes puffy. She curled her lips into a fake smile, trying it out. Nope. It didn't make her feel better. Drying off, she donned warm sweats, a T-shirt, and fluffy socks.

In the kitchen, she poured her second coffee of the morning, spread butter and jelly on a piece of toast, and ambled into the sitting room with today's breakfast. She set the plate on the couch beside her, kept her finger curled around the cup handle, and opened *The Path* to continue reading.

Alone on a cliff in The Vast, Ohngel studied the beings Gahya called shifters. He was intrigued. While he did not agree with how she had made her Aeternals, they possessed a spark for life he envied. Did she visit them, guide them, nurture them as a mother should? He would ask when he next journeyed to her abode. For now, his gaze focused on the creatures below.

In thick woods filled with tall pines, leafy bushes, and mossy undergrowth, a large black-and-gray animal, shadowed by a smaller silver-tipped wolf, loped into a clearing, blood of a recent kill staining their muzzles and fur. So much so, they appeared to have bathed in their food's carcass.

When they assumed their two-legged form, the naked male strutted, his cock engorged and jutting outward. Need coursed through him as he cast furtive glances toward the female. She eyed her companion, her amber pupils glowing with anticipation.

Casting a glance over her shoulder, she offered

him a chase by turning to flee. The male wolf tackled her, throwing her to her hands and knees. "Stay very still," he snarled.

Though his muscular arm clenched around her hips, she struggled in his grasp.

He bared his savage canines and clamped onto her shoulder, immediately freezing her efforts. She would submit or be torn apart.

With a sense of survival and her own arousal growing, the she-wolf lowered her head, acquiescing to the alpha.

He took his thickness into his fist, pumping twice before he rubbed the crown through her moist thighs. With the tip at her entrance, he surged forward as she cried out in pleasure or pain. It was difficult to tell the difference.

Flesh slapped flesh while their sweaty bodies crashed against one another. When the male shifter unlocked his teeth from the female, he churned against her hips, his pounding frantic. In and out. Hammering her body. Relentless in his need to finish.

The she-wolf screamed his name. After a shudder rolled through her, she quieted.

But the male was not finished. On his knees, he pulled her hard against his chest, one arm curling under her breasts and the other low across her hips. He growled as he continued to ravage her with frenetic thrusts. With one final deep surge, he howled while his seed flowed into his companion. Finished, he dropped the smiling she-wolf to the ground.

Aroused by the scene below, Ohngel called a willing female to his chamber. When eager dainty sandals tapped across the tile outside his bedroom, he again wondered whether the OneCreator would be displeased that Gahya had shared carnal desire. Her

creatures were almost savage in their drive for nourishment and sex. And their needs were growing.
****

Once again Denim was on unpadded knees at Gahya's marble feet. This time, she wore a pale green gown the color of Ram's eyes with layers and layers of thin, frothy silk. A short train swept onto the floor behind her. The fabric of the long dress gathered tight at the waist and rose to hug her breasts. At her shoulder, a pin studded with sapphires, emeralds, rubies, and citrines fastened to a delicate strap. A gift from Ram, it depicted a Phoenix in flight.

Baskets of fruits and vegetables surrounded the goddess, sumptuous offerings dropped off earlier by Denim and Jonquil.

As the Blood Coven descendant rose in a surging mass of sea foam, she resisted the urge to twirl around like Scarlet O'Hara at a ball. Instead, she stretched onto her toes to whisper in the goddess's marble ear. "Thank you for bringing him home."

In a gold gown of similar light silk but topped off with a white sash at her waist and matching sandals, Jonquil was adorable. Denim had braided the girl's hair and piled it on top of her head with stray wisps feathering her angelic face.

The child repaid Denim by using the curling iron to create soft, shining chestnut waves which fell around her shoulders. She wore it brushed off her face, unconcerned about the scar. It was no longer the symbol of a victim. It was the symbol of a strong woman who had survived to build a better life.

All Scion Firebrands who weren't on duty, a few of Denim's Alliance friends, and Ram's mother and father along with their invited guests packed the Temple.

Margo, Braelyn, Skyler, Lizette, and Galena had

decorated Gahya's shrine with swaths of lavish purple cloth, weaving it in and out of the alabaster columns. The fabric fluttered in a gentle breeze scented with thousands of golden lilies from Darque. Candles filled the temple with soft, flickering light while music floated on the air, an otherworldly sound. Denim was the center of a childhood fantasy come to life.

Jonquil pressed a bouquet of the same lilies into Denim's hand. Woman and child walked through the draped colonnade along a path lined with Firebrands. Palm in palm, both smiling, Ram's females entered the Temple's *cilia*.

The satyr, alongside Tyr and Brak, waited in front of another likeness of Gahya, this one larger, towering far above the Firebrands but honoring them with a downward-tilting head.

Ram's long purple robe stretched taut across his wide shoulders. His caramel-streaked hair as soft as silk flowed like molten metal while his roguish smile outshined the glowing candles.

Her heart thudded against her chest as she relived the first night at the Shed. He had turned around, his elbows braced on the bar and his black sleeves rolled up to reveal muscular forearms, his translucent gaze fixed on her. When Ram had prowled toward her, sex in every step, he had captured her heart.

How lucky she was. This man... No. This satyr with the hard body and quick wit loved her. A good male. Devoted father. Warrior who fought for his people.

She squeezed Jonquil's hand. As they drew even with Ram, the girl released Denim, accepted her bouquet, and stepped to the side.

The satyr tapped a fist to his chest, held it there, and swallowed hard. He shook his head, his hair tumbling onto his shoulders. "Words fail me. You are so beautiful. Thank you for being mine." He dipped his chin.

If eyes were windows, then Ram loved her with all his soul.

Denim beamed. "This ol' thing, *cher*? I just threw it on. You, on the other hand, are breathtaking. I'll never tire of looking at you."

As they clasped palms, they kneeled at the altar, his eyes flashing neon green. Philomena, the high priestess of nymphs, entered from the side, clothed in a lovely gown. But it lacked a spectacular train, a color to match a satyr's eyes, or a colorful Phoenix pin.

In her hand she clutched a leather tie which she wound around the couple's wrists. Her fingers paused atop the symbol. The guests hushed as Philomena spoke. "Bound thus you will be for all time even unto the Evermore. Once tied, a satyr and his mate cannot be undone. Together in conflict. Together in peace. Together in disappointment. Together in joy. Together in what matters and in what little matters. Together in life. Together in death." She waited, her gaze skimming the audience.

Denim's breath hitched at the words, but Ram's eyes focused on her.

"Beyond the Evermore, Denim Quinn, this male will be yours. Do you accept him and all he offers?"

"Yes. I accept this male and all he offers. I will love him even unto the Evermore. I will nourish him as he nourishes me. I will be his strength as he is mine. I will be his ear and his voice." Denim had rehearsed the words.

"Beyond the Evermore, Ramirez the satyr, this female will be yours. Do you accept her and all she offers?"

"Yes. I accept this female and all she offers. I will

love her even unto the Evermore. I will nourish her as she nourishes me. I will be her strength as she is mine. I will be her shield and her sword."

Philomena raised her arms, her head tilted so she could stare into Gahya's face. "Your creations have come before you to seek your blessing. Denim, descended from the Blood Coven witch Morgana, and Ramirez the satyr. They choose to mate. Do you accept them and all they offer?"

Denim chanced a glance at the hard, stone goddess. In telling the story later, she would say Gahya's lips curled into a maternal smile.

"Let it be so." Philomena touched the leather strap.

It tightened until Denim thought it would snap. Instead, the band disappeared into their flesh.

Without warning, Ram's love slammed into her body, shooting through her bloodstream, sparking her nerves, the shock nearly stopping her heart. It was strong. Eternal. So powerful she trembled.

Her new mate steadied her with an arm around her waist when she listed to the side. "Now and forever, doll."

A slight nod was all Denim could muster. "Did you feel that?"

Ram nodded, his sexy grin on her. "The earth moved. If you play your cards right, I'll make it rock and roll again later."

She laughed, slapping a hand to her heart as her words slipped out breathy. "It's so amazing."

"No more than you deserve."

Jonquil walked behind the kneeled couple and put a palm to each shoulder.

Denim, her eyes moist, twisted toward the girl. "I'm a little shaky, kid. Nobody told me about the body slam."

Ram cupped her elbow with a warrior's hand, guiding her to her feet.

Jonquil placed small fingers on her other arm. "We're family. We help each other."

"We are, aren't we?" Denim straightened her proud spine.

Together, the Blood Coven descendant, the satyr, and the young nymph walked down the Temple steps where Scion Firebrands, some with their own mates, whooped and hollered. Denim wondered if the quiet sanctuary had ever heard such a splendid ruckus.

****

Skyler was about to hug Denim when she felt a trickle down her legs. "Uh-oh. Kole."

Her hand flew to her watermelon-size belly while everyone looked at the puddle beneath her feet.

"What the fuck, Frisca." Understanding came slowly to his fire-gold eyes. "It's time." He swept Skyler into his arms. "We need to get the hell out of here. Outta my way."

Kole raced for a portal, Firebrands, guests, and the newly mated couple hot behind him. He kept mumbling to his mate. "You're all right. You're all right."

She drew her lips into a circle, breathing in and out in short puffs as she'd been taught. She paused. "Of course I'm all right, demon. I'm having a baby."

Skyler bounced in his arms as he ran faster. "Shit. Don't remind me. I've got this." At the portal, he turned to his audience. "Back off. Give us some room. You can follow in a few secs."

She tapped his shoulder. "Kole, I think she's coming fast."

"Fuck no. You keep her in there."

Skyler cocked her head to the side, still puffing oxygen. "Don't be stupid, demon. She'll come when she wants. Now, get me to the med center."

They portaled into the Ministry of Well Being, Kole racing for the admitting desk. The healer took one look and grabbed a wheelchair. Her demon waved it off. "Point me to the room."

Kole set her on the bed. Another healer entered. "Commander, you'll have to leave."

"No way in hell are you getting me out of here." Flames shot from both hands, luckily aimed at the wall.

Skyler shrugged as best she could with labor pains shooting through her. "He won't leave. Give up before he sets the place on fire."

"Okay, but he'll be helping."

Kole tapped his fingers together, containing sparks. "What? No. I'll watch."

"Males. Let's see how far apart your pains are, honey?" The healer timed them. "Okay. You're close. Commander, walk Skyler around the room a bit."

"Are you crazy? She can't be on her feet."

"Kole, help me." She swung her legs over the edge of the bed.

"I don't like this." He shot a stream of fire at the wall before he snagged onto Skyler.

"The animus demons are the worst." The healer shook her head.

Kole held her waist, leading her around the room at a slow pace.

After a half hour, the healer motioned toward the bed. "Time to lay her on her side."

Kole did, staying to rub her back.

"That feels good."

The healer suppressed the pain, watching for any sign of a problem. But she was ready to push. "Prop her up on those pillows. Knees bent, Skyler."

Kole rested a warm hand on her shoulder to soothe her.

"Push," said the healer.

Mimicking her, the demon, his mouth a worried slash, muttered the same order.

Skyler obeyed. Waited. Followed their commands again.

Kole's voice grew louder. "Push, Frisca."

"Shut the fuck up. I'm doing the best I can. If you want harder, come do it yourself." Skyler winced as a strong pain rushed through her.

Brushing a damp strand of hair off her face, her demon softened his expression, his eyes warming. "You're doing great."

Then things happened quickly. She pushed. A baby squalled. Kole gasped.

He accepted something from the healer, a tiny body which he held gently in his palms. Her demon looked nervous as hell with his expression grim. A tear streaked down his face as he followed the healer's instructions.

Once he pulled down the top of Skyler's gown, baring her skin, he placed the tiny being flesh-to-flesh, a breast cushioning its head.

His bundle handed off, he collapsed into a chair. From there, he clutched Skyler's hand. "She's perfect, Frisca. We made a perfect little female."

She glanced down at their babe with platinum-blonde curls. She picked up a tiny hand with perfect fingers, all five with miniature nails. The babe flipped open her eyes. Bright lilac. When the baby squirmed against her, Skyler cradled her soft butt, her legs cycling.

"Oh, Kole, look at her. I hope I won't ruin her. I don't know what to do. She's so small."

"Frisca, if there is one thing I know for certain, it's this. Whatever Skyler Maxwell does, she does well. You made me see you, a female who could tame an animus demon, a female with a heart as big as Scath."

"I did, didn't I? Now we have Kae, a witch-demon mixling who's perfect. A button nose, lilac eyes, and long lashes. I know she'll set the world on fire."

"Is that an animus demon joke?" Kole stroked her hair. "Thank you, Frisca."

"It took both of us."

****

On a mesa in Knife's Edge, Cerberus stared at the valley below, a desolate, flat place interrupted by towering red spires of rock. He cloaked a spell around his form. For today's meeting, he donned a Spriggan's form.

His vampire general joined him, red dust swirling at his feet, his upper lip curled and fangs glistening in the unrelenting sun of the demon region. "Nice disguise, Cerberus."

The ersatz Spriggan dipped his rack of twigs, his cruel smile a slash across his lower jaw. "Don't worry about my appearance. Concern yourself with the rumors. Lawgivers and the Temple justices are abuzz. It seems a human called Dante kidnapped two vampire youths along with a Firebrand, taking them to Earth where he tortured them. Varik, the scion of Viktor, is dead."

"I heard the same scuttlebutt." Lort's laughter pierced the air like a hyena's staccato *hee-hee-hee*. "The same Dante, our human ally, is also dead."

"Yes. The Englishman's betrayal has pushed our schedule earlier than desired, but the shove may be what we needed."

"Will money be a problem?"

Dante's money had been useful, freeing Cerberus's vast wealth to build a garrison, equip it, support an army, and grease the palms of the influential, drawing them to the cause. "Your pay is secure, General Lort."

"I do not worry about myself, but I want to be certain you have funds for the new garrison and our soldiers."

Cerberus fought the urge to toss the insolent general off the mesa. No one should dare question him, but rash actions achieved nothing. Perhaps he would find a new general after he conquered Earth and Scath. One not so arrogant.

With a cold, raised brow and a deep breath to rein in his dark emotions, he smiled at Lort. "Thanks to the drugs distributed by the shifter pack, Arisen Dawn also has a fresh source of income. And I am not without a sizable fortune."

At first, creating the network of distributors was expensive. Now it paid for itself and then some. Drugged soldiers filled the lower ranks of his army. Of course, true believers formed the core and upper echelons. With Earth armies lined up at Scath's portals, fearful and greedy Aeternals would flock to his cause.

Arisen Dawn was Cerberus's baby. At first, they had been loud nationalists. But with seeds of ambition planted here and there, he had shifted their goals. Now the purist group sought to dominate the world.

Cerberus as a Spriggan shook his antlers. "Dante moved too soon, but it was a favor. He distracted the Firebrands while we began to amass an army under their noses. Once we break the warriors, this realm will be ours. Earth will follow."

Of course, to fulfill the prophecy, he needed the Blood Coven. The final step in his march toward destiny required their participation.

But for now, the focus was to gain strength while

the Firebrands crumbled.

Chapter Thirty-Four

Cadmon pushed out of his desk chair at the Ministry of the Shield to greet Alarik.

A loose black robe cloaked the warlock's muscular shoulders as he greeted the warrior ylve. "High Commander."

Cadmon gripped the offered hand. He waved his visitor to a seat. "Rarely do you journey to my territory."

Nodding, Alarik balanced on the edge of his chair, his spine rigid. "Yesterday I spoke to the lawgivers at length. My next step is to warn you. As you know, my ministry employs several covens of mages who monitor and maintain our portals. Watchers. Their names are unknown as are the specifics of their tasks."

"I know of these witches and warlocks." Cadmon shifted in his chair, not so comfortable when he expected bad news.

"To get to the point, the Watchers are experiencing unusual ripples in the portals."

"What does that mean?"

"Not sure. When it happened, they examined the overall structure of the gateways. It is sound. The Watchers are now analyzing each one for anomalies. This effort is time-consuming."

"What have they learned?"

"Nothing. So far, each is perfect, but hundreds of thousands of sites exist around the world."

"Then why the concern?" Cadmon had little patience with magic. He was a man of action. While he respected its use in battle, he knew little about it, trusting it even less.

"Perhaps we are unnecessarily anxious. Still, each mage felt this ripple. When they worry, I listen."

"What could a ripple mean?"

"Nothing. Everything."

Alarik's hesitancy to draw conclusions frustrated Cadmon, who wanted educated guesses. "Let's go with the 'everything' scenario."

"The collapse of the portals is the far-fetched speculation." Alarik sat still, hands in his lap, staring at his fingernails.

Cadmon leaned forward onto his forearms. "A collapse would mean no separate realms. We would be one again? Free movement for Aeternals?"

"And for Darque's creatures. This is, of course, the worst case. No proof exists that a collapse is imminent. The investigated portals are secure. We just have anomalous ripples."

"In the past have portals fallen?"

Alarik paused as if he was thinking.

"Do not think too hard, Director. Either they have or they haven't."

"Yes, long ago. Before my time. Logs say a warlock ruptured a single portal."

"Is this warlock still alive?"

"No, but I reviewed the archives. The record did not report a strange ripple preceding its collapse."

"If a gateway is compromised, can Watchers secure it?"

"Yes."

Before Cadmon could nod, Alarik added to his short answer. "If too many don't fall at once."

The high commander lifted a pen and tapped it on his desk a few times. "What do you want from me?"

"I want the Firebrands alert. If gateways fall, Watchers will close them as quickly as possible. The warriors must prevent humans from crossing onto Scath and Aeternals from traveling to Earth."

"And if all portals fail?"

"What's the saying? Bend over and kiss your ass goodbye."

"I do not kiss my own ass."

As Alarik unfolded his large frame from the chair, Cadmon spoke. "It's my turn to share with you, Director. The commanders are confronting a strange occurrence."

"Which is?"

"Many recruits are appearing at their strongholds. The Phoenix is busy creating a Firebrand army. We wonder how we will train them."

"What do you mean by *many*? I like numbers." Alarik's brows tightened.

"Commander Nace reported twenty-five this week."

Alarik shook his head. "More mysteries. I don't enjoy mysteries."

****

Denim tapped the toe of her boot on the wood porch outside the door. She knew the protocol. Someone was spying on them through the peephole.

When the door opened just a crack, a woman grinned. She slipped the chain off before re-opening it wide.

"Denim. We've been waiting." The young mother, much happier than the last time they had met, balanced the boy on her hip.

"Hi. This is my … um … husband and daughter. Ram and Jonquil, meet Leslie and Jeffie."

The mother's jaw dropped when she spotted Ram. He had that effect on women.

Secure in their relationship, Denim knew he only had eyes for her. Green eyes. Sexy eyes.

Marta came on a run from the kitchen, wiping her

hands on a stained apron. "Denim."

They clasped arms around each other, squeezing in a giant hug.

Backing away, Marta raised brows at the girl. "You must be Jonquil. I've heard many good stories about you." She pinched the girl's chin between a thumb and forefinger, tilting her face from side to side. "Such an *ange*."

"Nice to meet you, mam."

"No, child. I'm Marta to everyone. Or to you, *tante*." She winked when she saw Ram. "You'd look real nice in a Speedo."

Denim laughed as the skin around her satyr's narrowed eyes crinkled. "Private joke. I've pictured him in one also, Marta."

"Come on, folks. I hope you're hungry. I've got cookies for dessert, child." Marta patted Jonquil's back. "We're a noisy bunch. I hope you don't have sensitive hearing."

Ram chuckled. "Marta, I love noise. I love food. And I hope those cookies are for adults, too." He slipped the shelter owner's arm through his and caressed her hand, escorting her into the kitchen where he pulled out a chair for her.

"Laudy, what a gentleman you are."

He took care of Denim and Jonquil after he cautioned the others to wait for him. "None of the ladies sit without my assistance." He winked.

Her satyr was in his glory. After all, he was the only man among so many beautiful females. When he went around the room, seating each woman, they stared at him in wide-eyed adoration. He whispered something special in each ear as he pulled out a chair. They laughed when he kissed the backs of their hands. Most of them had had so little joy in life. Denim worshiped Ram anew for the attention he paid them.

At last he sat down, and the passing of food began. Fried chicken, mashed potatoes, gravy, a gumbo with Andouille sausage and shrimp, seasoned okra, collard greens. Once all the plates were full, loud chatter overflowed the room. Marta blurted out a question. "So, tell me. Since you are married, are more children in the future?"

Denim turned ash white, but Ram didn't miss a beat. "Of course children are in our future. We owe Jonquil brothers or sisters. And you gotta admit, with my brains and Denim's looks, they'll be dynamite."

Before Denim responded, she glanced at Jonquil, whose eyes widened as she mouthed a *please*.

Denim said, "I was thinking of a baseball team. Nine. Maybe a football team. Eleven."

"What?" Ram's throat bobbled while the table laughed.

"Okay. One or two. Right, Jonquil?"

"I'll be a terrific older sister."

The chit-chat resumed. Bowls of food made a second pass.

With everyone occupied, Denim leaned back in the familiar slatted chair and crossed her arms. Jonquil chatted with a younger boy to her left, laughing as he told a knock-knock joke. Ram tilted his head with interest toward a woman who explained how she had come to Safe Haven.

That's when it hit Denim. She had a family. No longer an outsider, she had Jonquil and Ram. And she was so damn proud.

When the satyr glanced her way, his brows arched. She shrugged, mouthed *I love you*, and asked the woman across from her to pass the potatoes.

****

Tyr jacked his boots onto the commander's desk while Thorn sat beside him in the hotter-than-hell seat, the subject of Kole's wrath. The warlock slouched back, flicking imagined lint from his shirt.

Next to the door is a good place to sit. A fast exit for when things go from shit to holy shit for my wolf shifter freron.

"What the fuck did you think you were doing?" A zing of fire followed Kole's loud question.

Defiant, Thorn glared.

"I'm waiting." The commander laced his fingers, probably waiting for them to cool.

"Luka's my brother. It's my pack. I didn't have a choice."

"Son, choices abound in this world. Problem is you made a shitty one."

Thorn shrugged.

"How much did you tell him?" asked Kole.

"I didn't really tell him anything. I asked questions."

"Like what? Don't make me pull this out of your ass." The commander stood to pace the room.

Not a good sign. Up. Back.

"I asked Luka whether the pack was involved with drugs. When he turned furry on me, I shifted to demo who was the better brother. Once I subdued him, my teeth in his neck, he returned to his skin. I told him he was without honor. Our parents would not be proud. I left."

Tyr folded his arms across his chest and coughed a *harrumph.* "Here's the thing." He twisted his body to stare at his *freron.* "By the time Dax and I got to Karth, the whole pack had moved out. Whereabouts unknown. We would have been to North Shelters sooner, but we were caught in a situation with a female. We didn't get on the road again until after Ram's rescue. You fucked up our job, buddy."

"He's my brother."

"So ya said. I told you about Karth because I trusted you. It was a heads-up, not a call to shout out a warning which gave them time to run." Tyr's boots thudded on the floor as he swung them off the desk.

"It was not my intent."

Tyr shrugged. "Yeah. Well, best laid plans and the shit which goes with them."

Thorn shot out of his seat and blocked Kole's back and forth.

Not a wise move.

"Plant your ass back in the chair, shifter. I'm not done with you."

"I'm through. I can't undo what's been done. The ball's in your court. Do what you need to do."

Kole bodied Thorn into the wall. Even though the shifter was strong, he was no match for an angry animus demon. "Son, you picked the wrong time to get on my bad side. Shit's coming at us from all sides. We've got the human female found by Tyr and Dax in the med center. Her injuries are such the healers have her in an induced coma. We don't know her name or story. We've got Arisen Dawn, drugs, humans, and a fucking prophecy staring us down. Maybe I can't stop all the fucking crap we're facing, but I sure as hell can do something about you. You're suspended until I decide you're not. Get the hell out of my sight. When I'm ready to see your ugly-ass self again, I'll give you a buzz. In the meantime, you're on vacation."

When he removed his forearm from Thorn's chest, Kole shoved him toward the door.

Once the shifter exited, Tyr said, "That went well. Now what?"

"Now you and Dax play hide-and-seek with Luka's pack."

"Terrific, except I can't find the cold-hearted vampire bastard."

"Not answering his calls again?"

"Not at the present, but he's probably following some lead. Or…"

"Or what?"

"Or humping some O blud whore till his dick falls off."

****

Dax was trailing two demons and a warlock. A source had come through for him again. Spending his free time in an O blud den paid off in information as well as extracurricular exercise.

He flattened himself against a thick tree trunk in the North Shelters Clawtooth Range, giving his prey time to disappear from view.

He and Tyr had already split when he popped into his favorite blud parlor. After he sucked on the neck of and pounded his cock into a particularly luscious, tasty nymph, a *psst* interrupted his enjoyment of his entertainment's aftereffects. His snitch crooked a finger, calling him over. The male had intel on the location of three drug dealers. Dax, almost regretting his buzz, double-timed it to the shifter region, where he caught up with the miscreants.

Still savoring the drug-laden blood coating his mouth, he shook off thoughts of the female donor as he stepped from behind the tree to continue tracking his prey. When he rounded the top of the rise, he pulled his brows into a furrow.

Since the greenery was thin, he had a clear view down the mountain. He spotted them chatting with some male in a sports car with its top down. The guy looked familiar, but Dax couldn't place him.

The car drove off and his prey hightailed it. Dax shadowflashed down one hillside and up the other. When he paused, his keen vampire hearing picked out the rustling of leaves. He whipped his head around to see a demon slip behind a large boulder. The lumbering behemoth was likely the cause of the racket. Demons were not known for stealth.

When he spotted a warlock crouching behind a bush, he realized they had turned the tables on him. His cover was blown. So much for being a ghost on the ass of the drug dealers.

Fuck.

The predator was the prey. Dax charged ahead, bobbing and weaving to stay out of the path of the warlock. No telling what spells the mage could cast. It was time to out-maneuver the bad guys. With every heavy, strained thigh absorbing his boots pounding into the dirt, he regretted his vices. His hand went out to touch the ground and keep him from going ass over heels as he rounded a bend. Brushing off his near encounter with humiliation, he resolved to train more often with the Firebrands and to stop frequenting O blud dens.

Too ambitious.

Maybe cut down on how many times he sucked neck.

Doable.

****

Ram barreled into Kole's office, waving a thumb behind him. "What's with all the new faces training in the gym? Must be twenty or thirty."

He froze. The conference room was full. Rein, Sabine, Nico, Jezzi, Galena, Brak, Kat, Tyr, Chay. Logan had even escaped from his precious computers. Denim. Despite an hour in bed with her this morning, she still made his heart stutter. The two recruits were here as well. The demon and the sucker. What were their names? Sig and Bade.

"We've been waiting, satyr. You're looking good." Kole stopped tapping his fingers on the table.

"Aren't I, though?" He thumped his once-flayed chest. "Hey. I came as soon as I got the message. Where are Dax and Thorn?"

He yanked out a chair next to Denim, trailing his hand along the inside of her thigh with clear male possessiveness flashing in his translucent eyes. He couldn't help it.

When she smacked his arm, heads pivoted their way, followed by smothered chuckles.

"Doll, save the rough play for when we're alone. What will our *frerons* think?"

Kole pounded out sparks which landed on the papers in front of him. "Cut the bullshit and let's get down to business. Dax is wherever the hell he goes when we can't find him. Thorn won't be here."

Not a good sign. What the hell had the shifter done now? Dax was no surprise. He'd show up when he did.

"To answer your first question, Ramirez, those new mugs are all recruits, fresh-faced and untrained." Kole dropped the bomb on his audience.

"More recruits?" Everyone voiced surprise at the same time. Except Bade and Sig. They didn't know enough to be surprised.

"A shitload of them is arriving. We've got more than the ones in the gym. We can't hold them all at one time. Not only that, but Jarek and Nace are reporting the same story. It's a damn crisis."

"We're busting at the seams." Rein slouched into his chair, resting an arm over the back. "We haven't used the dormitory for years, except for emergency stay-overs. Now, two and three newbies are bunking on the floor in a room. The stronghold is filling fast. Brae and I have a suite, Chay and Margo, you and Skyler, Nico, Denim. Are you moving in, satyr?"

"Already done, Rein Man."

"How about you, Sabine? You spend all your time here," asked Rein.

Nico answered for the nymph Firebrand. "She's already a resident. We're living in sin. I want to make an honest woman of her, but she keeps saying *soon*."

"Awe, throw the poor dog a bone, Sabine." Chay jostled her shoulder. "He's a big enough asshole without you stringing him along."

Sabine cocked her chin, smirking at the ylve. "Stay out of our biz. We have plans."

"Glad to hear it." Kole inclined his head toward Nico. "You better be good to her."

"Hey. Is nobody concerned about me? She's wicked strong. I have bruises." Nico pointed to a bluish mark on his neck. "An elbow followed by a jab during a sparring session." He started to raise his shirt.

Heads shook. Nobody bought his sad line, and nobody wanted to see his chest. Maybe Sabine did.

Kole raised a hand for quiet. "Anyway, Margo's quick-timed the rehab on our building. Descendants and mates will continue to occupy the upper floors. The current remodels are complete, but we'll add more apartments to the third floor, if necessary. The gathering room, kitchen, dining areas, library, and game room on the main floor are for all Firebrands. Even those off-site. Chay's mate king-sized everything, and workers rushed to finish it."

"Nice." Brak waved an upright thumb at the ylve Firebrand. "I'm all for your mate's improves."

"The level below is nearly done. My office will move downstairs. Larger and better training facilities are underway. A new armory. Margo beefed up the lower-level barracks at Indigo's suggestion. Since Alarik opened the way for guns on Firebrand properties only, she added an indoor shooting range. For now. Who knows what the future holds. Outdoor drills and war games will take place behind the stronghold on the field."

"Okay. We're expanding. Which still doesn't explain so many recruits." Ram pushed his chair away from the table, cocking an ankle on his opposite knee.

"No. It doesn't. I wish to hell I knew why new warriors are flooding the stronghold. They're eager but short on skills. Some of them look too young to shave, but they all have the brand. The Phoenix called them."

Sig waved a hand in the air.

"Spit it out, recruit."

"Is this a hint something big is coming, Commander?"

"Yeah. And it's about as subtle as a downpour of elephants. I'm afraid it's going to be war unlike any we've seen. Bigger than the Ylve Revolt. Bigger than the Berserker Raids. Bigger than the Demon Insurrection and the War of the Coalition. Cerberus is hovering over us like a shadow. Earth knows we exist thanks to Dante's military guys who escaped in the chopper. Drugs are running rampant, and Arisen Dawn is rearing its ugly head. Now we have more warriors than we can handle. Rein?"

"Yeah?" He swiped his free hand over his military-cut hair, his other still settled on the chair back.

"You've just become formal management. You'll oversee all recruit training. Shut the fuck up. No backtalk. No posturing. Just do it. Choose an assistant.

And before you go all asshole on me. Yes, you still fight. You can kill as many bad guys as you want."

Rein's lids lowered and he blew out a breath. "Got it, Commander. I don't want a fucking title, though. Ram, you're my assistant. Lucky you."

The satyr nodded while Denim poked his shoulder.

"Nico and Sabine, dig deeper on Arisen Dawn. Who's organizing them? Who's funding? Identify leaders. Where the fuck are they? Tyr, you and Dax, if you can find the vamp, stay on the drug thing for now. If you four bump into each other, confab. We know Arisen Dawn and the drug biz are up each other's asses. See how far. Another thing, warlock. Get over to the med center at the Ministry of Well Being to see about the female you saved. She's still in a coma, but get whatever intel you can from the healers."

The silver bar through Tyr's brow glinted in the overhead light. "Why me?"

When Kole shot a frown and a small stream of fire in his direction, the warlock shrugged.

"Galena, you'll oversee the rotation schedule for any standard ops. Consult with Rein and Ram. We need warriors in the field and warriors teaching combat. A recruit on assignment will always pair with a veteran, but I have an itchy feeling which says the rookies will score action faster than usual. Got me?"

"What about us?" The newbie vamp Firebrand raised his hand to speak again, excitement in every wave of his arm.

Kole's eyes rolled. "This isn't school. Just ask a fucking question if you have one, Sig. You are with Chay. Bade, stay tight with Jezzi. Both of you have shit for brains and swordsmanship, but if you hang with your mentors, you might live through the year."

When the demon recruit winked at the panther shifter, she arched a brow. "Down boy. Or I'll slit your throat myself."

Chairs scratched along the floor. Bad news didn't stop the wisecracking among Firebrands as they filed out of Kole's office.

The End

T.M. SMITH

EVERNIGHT PUBLISHING ®

www.evernightpublishing.com